Shiver

KAREN ROBARDS

Shiver

HODDER &
STOUGHTON

First published in the USA in 2012 by Gallery Books
A division of Simon & Schuster, Inc.
First published in Great Britain in 2013 by Hodder & Stoughton
An Hachette UK company

1

A CIP catalogue record for this title is available from the British Library

Hardback ISBN 978 1 444 76714 8
Trade Paperback ISBN 978 1 444 76715 5
Ebook ISBN 978 1 444 76716 2

Typeset in Stempel Garamond LT Std

Printed and bound by CPI Group (UK) Ltd, Croydon CR0 4YY

Hodder & Stoughton policy is to use papers that are natural, renewable and recyclable
products and made from wood grown in sustainable forests. The logging and
manufacturing processes are expected to conform to the environmental regulations of
the country of origin.

Hodder & Stoughton Ltd
338 Euston Road
London NW1 3BH

www.hodder.co.uk

Christopher, this book is dedicated to you, in honor of your graduation (with honors!) from Washington University in St. Louis. So proud! And Jack, to you, too—you got your driver's license! And Peter, also to you—because you're still alive and rolling on, which sometimes is the biggest victory of all. And finally, Doug, to you, just for putting up with us all.

ACKNOWLEDGMENTS

I want to thank my absolutely wonderful editor, Lauren McKenna, as well as Louise Burke and the entire staff of Gallery and Pocket Books for their unflagging support. I appreciate it. You guys are the best!

CHAPTER ONE

"Mom, I'm scared." Tyler's voice was scarcely louder than a whisper. Curled up in his bed with one arm wrapped around his favorite stuffed bear and the other tucked beneath his head, he was a small, thin boy who hardly made a dent in the covers. His black hair was still damp from the bath she had made him take just before getting into bed and smelled, just faintly, of baby shampoo. The expression in his blue eyes proclaimed his absolute conviction that she could keep him safe from all harm. Samantha Jones looked down at her four-year-old son and felt a pang in the region of her heart. She was a twenty-three-year-old single mother with a precarious job situation, very little money, and absolutely no experience raising kids, and she was all he had.

Probably she wasn't going to get mother of the year anytime soon, but she was doing her best.

"Close your eyes and go to sleep, and I'll be home before you wake up," she promised. Like Tyler, she was slim and fine-boned, with unruly black hair—hers reached the middle of her

back—and blue eyes. She sat beside him on his twin bed in the
pool of lamplight cast by the room's only illumination, the
small red lamp on the nightstand. Her back rested against a pillow tucked against the headboard and her knees were bent to
prop up the book she'd just finished reading to him. Dressed
in jeans and a well-washed blue uniform shirt, all she needed
to do was pull on her boots and she would be out the door and
on her way to work, which was where she was going just as
soon as she finished her nightly ritual of putting Tyler to bed.
"Mrs. Menifee is here."

The sound of the TV in the living room confirmed it. Cindy
Menifee, a fifty-something widow who lived alone in the duplex next door, had a key and let herself in as needed. The first
thing she always did was turn on the TV. Mrs. Menifee worked
days as a bookkeeper for a tire store. Like everyone else Sam
knew, she lived from paycheck to paycheck and was glad, for the
little Sam could pay her, to stay with Tyler at night while Sam
worked, saying that since she was right next door anyway it was
almost like getting paid to stay home.

"I know." Tyler's voice was even smaller. His skin was fair,
like hers, but unlike her he had freckles scattered across the
bridge of his nose. His eyes beseeched her. "Couldn't you stay
home this once?"

Sam's stomach tightened. She knew that feeling guilty because she had to go to work to earn money to support them
was a waste of time, but Tyler actually was a little extra needy
tonight. He'd had a bad day at preschool: his friend Josh had in-

vited two other boys from their class to a sleepover, but had left Tyler out. To make him feel better, she'd rented a movie he'd been dying to see, and he and she had spent the evening eating popcorn and watching it, which was why he was still awake. Almost she hesitated. Almost she gave into the impulse to say, *just this once,* and stay with him. But she *had* to work, or they didn't eat or have a roof over their heads or anything else. She had tried to arrange things so that she and Tyler spent as much time together as possible. During the mornings, while he was in preschool, she took classes, with the eventual goal of becoming an emergency medical technician. As an EMT, she would make enough to one day maybe be able to buy a small house, and pay for things like a bicycle and braces. At night, when he was sleeping, she went out and repossessed cars. She was tired and stressed out a lot, which she tried her best not to let Tyler see, but they were making it.

"Big Red's waiting out front. He'd be sad if I didn't come out." Big Red was Tyler's name for the (big red) tow truck she drove. Sliding off the bed, putting the book down on the nightstand, Sam kept her tone light.

"Did you use the monster spray?" Tyler's lower lip quivered. Sam felt another of those mommy-guilt heart tugs. Tyler had been having nightmares lately, nightmares that the pediatrician said were perfectly normal and part of a developmental phase and yada yada. Still, they worried her terribly. She'd come up with the idea of filling a plastic spray bottle with water and telling Tyler it was a potion to keep bad dreams away. He loved the idea of it, called it monster spray, had her spray it under his bed every night before he went to sleep—and continued to have nightmares anyway.

Sam couldn't help thinking that if he had an older, more experienced mother, if he lived in a house in the suburbs and had a dad who was actually a part of his life and all the good things he should have, he wouldn't have nightmares.

"Tyler, do you want me to sit in here with you while you go to sleep? I can sing to you," Mrs. Menifee said from the doorway. Mrs. Menifee knew the drill: Sam was supposed to be at A+ Collateral Recovery by 11:00 p.m. to receive her assignments for the night. It was twenty minutes until eleven now. She had to go.

"Okay," Tyler said.

"Thanks." Sam smiled at Mrs. Menifee with real gratitude as the older woman pulled the red rocking chair that Sam had carefully painted to match the lamp and the headboard up beside the bed and sank down in it. Mrs. Menifee's tightly curled hair might be a little too red and she might wear a little too much makeup and her blouses might be a little too tight and low cut over her ample bosom in hopes of attracting husband number three, but she was kindhearted and good to Tyler and absolutely reliable. In the year since Sam and Tyler had moved into the duplex next door to her, they'd all three developed a firm friendship in which Sam did things like water her plants and feed her cat when she was away visiting her grown daughter in Chicago, and Mrs. Menifee watched Tyler.

"See you in the morning." Still keeping it light, Sam headed for the door.

"We'll be fine," Mrs. Menifee said comfortably.

Pausing, Sam took one last look at her son. He *was* perfectly fine, cozy in his own bed in his own room, with Mrs. Menifee rocking beside him.

His eyes were wide open and tracking her. "I love you, Mom."

Her heart gave another of those mommy-pangs. "I love you, too, baby."

As she left the duplex to go to work, Mrs. Menifee's slightly off-key voice singing "Camptown Races" followed her.

❄

About fifteen seconds before the first bullet hit him, Daniel Panterro accepted the fact that he was probably going to die. Given the fact that he was bound hand and foot, stuffed into a car trunk, and just conscious enough that he knew something bad was going down, there wasn't a whole lot he could do about it. Except bitterly regret the circumstances that had gotten him into the mess in the first place.

"You really think we wouldn't find you, asshole?" Army Veith was the name of the guy pointing the pistol at his head. Real average looking. Average height, average weight, not old, not young, nothing to make anyone remember him. No way for anyone to guess that he was a killer for hire. One of the best. Currently in the employ of the Zeta cartel. Veith had just arrived on the scene, which was how Danny knew his life could now be measured in seconds. Everything that had come before had been courtesy of his thugs. "Where's the money?"

Danny's mouth was still dry from the gag that had just been ripped out of it so he could talk. He tried to swallow, but came up with so little saliva that it was hardly worth it. He had no idea what money Veith was talking about, but he sure as hell was not going to let Veith know it.

"Sock drawer," Danny croaked. He might be done for, but he'd be damned if he was going to cringe. He tried not to think of his mother, a sixty-six-year-old widow who doted on him, her youngest child and only son. His death would devastate her. It would leave his three sisters reeling. He would never play basketball or video games with his nephews again.

Please God let—

Veith shot him. Just like that.

In the thigh. At the last minute Veith had shifted his aim. The *pfft* of the discharge—Veith's gun sported a silencer—registered in Danny's brain at approximately the same instant the bullet tore through him.

Danny screamed. It hurt like a motherfucker. His thigh felt like a flaming splinter had blasted through it. He could feel the instant engorging of his flesh, the hot upwelling of blood. Had the bullet hit an artery? Broken a bone? Sweat poured over him in a wave. He almost vomited. His body wanted to roll and kick and contort in protest, but between the way he was tied and the fact that he was a six-foot-two, 190-pound guy crammed into a car trunk, the opportunity for movement was limited. Cursing, he tried to block out the pain, tried to force his poor battered brain to work, to think of some way out of this.

Unfortunately, his brain was coming up with zilch.

"Next one goes through your elbow." Veith's eyes were as cold and merciless as the black waters of the Mississippi River that ran behind the warehouse. The river where, unless Danny was mistaken, his corpse was shortly going to end up. "I'm gonna ask again: where's the money?"

Shit. Danny realized that he was panting like a dog. He could feel blood gushing from his leg, soaking his jeans, and knew that blood loss was going to be a problem if he lived longer than the next few minutes. Which, face it, meant it probably wasn't going to be a problem at all. A black wave of anger hit him: somebody had fucked up big time. But this wasn't the moment to get pissed about it. This was probably the moment to be making peace with his maker, but he'd rather try to come up with some way to survive. Forget cringing. Now that he'd gotten a real taste of what was getting ready to come his way, he would have begged if he'd thought it would do any good. Despite his efforts to block the pain, it threatened to overwhelm his senses. Jesus, when he'd signed on for this gig he had accepted the possibility that he might die—it came with the territory—but getting himself blasted to bits before they killed him was worse than anything he had foreseen.

Damn Crittenden anyway. Where was he, where were they all, while this shit was going down? The key here was that he wasn't actually supposed to die.

Veith's gun hand moved, almost imperceptibly. Danny's heart lurched. He thought of his mother having to identify his mutilated body, pushed the image out of his head.

"Santos has it," he groaned. It was a lie, but if lying worked to buy him some time, he was ready, willing, and able to lie like a two-dollar whore.

Veith didn't fire.

"Santos?" Veith repeated. Except for one dim lightbulb swinging from a wire high overhead, the warehouse was dark. If you didn't count Danny, Veith, two other thugs, and the BMW Danny was crammed into the trunk of, it was also deserted. *The better for torturing and killing you in, my dear.* Given Danny's present position, reading Veith's expression was nearly impossible. But he could hear the sudden interest in his voice.

Veith thought there might be a possibility that he was telling the truth. Danny automatically filed that information away to be passed on to Crittenden later before he remembered that he most likely was not going to be passing on anything.

Because he was going to be dead.

Jesus, Mary, and Joseph, he didn't want to die. He was thirty-two years old. Had a big, boisterous extended family. A hot girlfriend. A good (although dangerous, see present situation) job. Tickets to the NBA championship game in two weeks. Lots of things in the works.

"You have five seconds to tell me everything you know."

Veith was taking careful aim at his right elbow. The one that was uppermost. If a bullet tore through his elbow at that angle, the pain would make the blazing agony in his leg feel like a mosquito bite. To say nothing of the fact that it would shatter the joint and he would probably never regain the full use of his arm. Not that he was going to need it where it looked like he was going anyway, but still.

Shit.

"One. Two. Three. F—"

It was the thought of more pain that pulled his foggy thought processes together enough to allow him to try to improvise.

As a new wave of sweat enveloped him, he broke in on Veith. "Like I said, Santos—"

"They're coming. They know where we are." Thug number one—Danny hadn't gotten a good enough look at either of them to be able to identify them—came running, his feet thudding on what sounded like a concrete floor. From where? Danny didn't know, although he presumed a lookout was being kept.

Theoretically, he was too valuable to the feds who'd been holding him for them to just abandon him. Veith would expect a search-and-rescue team to be coming on strong.

So did Danny, for entirely different reasons.

Veith swore under his breath. To Danny's immense relief, he lowered the pistol.

"We'll finish this later, Marco," Veith told him.

Yeah, Marco, as in Rick Marco, because Veith had no idea who he really was. Which was the only reason Danny was still alive.

Then Veith stepped back, and the trunk lid slammed down.

A moment later, the car was peeling rubber out of there. Danny lay in the trunk, blind as a mole in the pitch dark, woozy with pain, fighting to find enough oxygen to keep him conscious in the superheated, carbon-monoxide-tainted air.

He was still trying to process exactly what had happened. No, *how* it had happened: the assault on the safe house where as Marco he'd been under twenty-four-hour guard, the lightning-fast slaughter of the U.S. Marshals assigned to protect him, his own kidnapping and brutal interrogation.

They're coming. Danny held onto the promise implicit in that gasped warning like a drowning man to a lifeline. "They" had to refer to the feds. He was an undercover FBI agent, for God's sake. His fellow federal agents would not just leave him to die.

❄

Two a.m. in gorgeous downtown East St. Louis, which was an oxymoron if she'd ever heard one, Sam reflected glumly. A Friday night turned into the wee hours of a Saturday morning. She was still pretty enough that guys were always hitting on her. She should have been out dancing, partying, or at least seeing a movie and getting a pizza. Something.

She sighed. *Get real. If you weren't doing this, you'd be working the third shift at Walmart. Or Waffle House. Or somewhere equally shitty.*

Instead she was driving Big Red, a junky hook-and-chain tow truck, down a pothole-heavy street lined with bars and tattoo parlors and seedy restaurants and liquor stores. Getting double vision from looking at too much neon. Ignoring the streetwalkers and drug pushers on the corners. Ignoring the bands of looking-for-trouble punks, too. If they wanted trouble, she had a Smith & Wesson revolver on the passenger seat beside her. And a tire iron tucked beneath her seat. Much as she hated to admit it, these were her people. These mean streets were her mean streets. She could handle herself.

Didn't mean she had to like it.

Her cell phone rang. Her best friend, Kendra Wilson.

"What?" Sam said into it.

"I'm just about to leave work." Kendra cashiered weekends at the local Publix grocery store. They'd been besties since kindergarten. When the shit had hit the fan in Sam's life some five and a half years ago now, Kendra had been one of the few people Sam had been able to count on. "You need anything?"

"Could you get me some pancake mix?" Sam answered. "And syrup. Tyler likes pancakes on Saturday morning, and I'm out."

"Some five and a half years ago" meaning when she'd found out she was pregnant with Tyler. Fresh out of high school, working as a waitress at Red Lobster while she tried to figure out what she wanted to do with her life, she had been a wild, heedless eighteen-year-old who had just wanted to have fun when the pee-stick had turned pink. Now she was a struggling single mother, and "fun" had given way to "survive." Which was why she was driving around in a tow truck in the middle of a starry June night. Her "uncle"—actually a geriatric former boyfriend of her great-aunt's who had been kind enough, after Tyler's birth, to give her a job in the office of his small towing company that had allowed her to keep the baby with her—had died the previous year, leaving her Big Red, along with his working relationship with A+ Collateral Recovery. Most nights, especially since the economy had tanked, A+ would give her a list of vehicles to be repossessed, and she would go out on the hunt. She was paid a bounty for every collateral recovery (that's what the contract called it; in reality it was a repo) she completed. She wasn't getting rich, she wasn't even getting middle class, but she was keeping a roof over her and Tyler's heads and food on the table, and that was what counted. And lately business was picking up: last week, she'd towed in ten vehicles. At seventy dollars per, minus expenses, she'd cleared five hundred dollars, which was more than she could make doing anything else except stripping, which she wasn't yet desperate enough to do. Of course, almost the entire amount had gone for rent, but at least she'd been able to pay rent, even if it was a week late. Out of the check she was expecting tomorrow, she would have to pay utilities and Tyler's preschool, plus Mrs. Menifee and the usual expenses associated with the truck, and then add a little to her tuition-for-her-upcoming-fall-class account. Which would leave her just about enough for a week's worth of groceries, if she was careful.

"Tyler's lucky it's Friday." By that, Kendra meant she had gotten her paycheck tonight. Like the rest of them, Kendra was always broke by the end of the financial week, which for her ended on Fridays. Which was why she had offered to pick up groceries for Sam. Sam's week ended on Saturday nights, when A+ Collateral ponied up.

"I'll pay you back Sunday," Sam said.

"I know," Kendra answered. "Will you be done soon?"

"Should be. I'm on the trail of this BMW. When I find it, that's it for the night."

"Nice car." Kendra's voice perked up. "Maybe the owner will be around. If he owns a BMW, he could be your ticket."

"If his BMW is being repossessed, I doubt it," Sam retorted. "Anyway, I don't need that kind of ticket. Tyler and I are doing just fine."

"Yeah, I heard it before." Kendra was determined to get her fixed up, and Sam was just as determined to resist. Tyler was a wonderful gift, but his father—not so much. In fact, as soon as he'd found out Sam was pregnant he'd cut and run. Sam had seen him exactly twice since. He'd contributed zero dollars to Tyler's support, and since he didn't have a steady job there was nothing Sam could do about it. They were the same age, and he was still running around free as the wind, while she—she had grown up. And in the process pretty much sworn off men for life.

"Got to go," Sam said as the locater affixed to the dashboard beeped, and disconnected. The beep meant she was getting close. Fortunately, the car she was after was only two years old and fancy enough to have its own built-in GPS, with its own built-in special signal. Sam's equipment wasn't exactly state of the art, but it was up to date enough to lock onto the signal once she was within a few blocks of her quarry.

Left on First, another left on Hennessey. Right down by the river. The night was black and breezy, and the mighty Mississippi gleamed like an oil slick under the light of the pale full moon. Across the river in St. Louis proper, she could see the twinkling lights of the big paddleboats that were the city's floating casinos. The bridges, the Arch, the tall buildings that made up the St. Louis skyline—all were glowing with light and, from this distance, beautiful.

Across the river in Illinois, where Sam lived, East St. Louis was like that other St. Louis's really ugly stepsister.

"There you are," Sam murmured with satisfaction as her beeper started going off insistently. The car she was looking for was parked at the end of Fortnum, just up from the warehouse district. She spotted the big black Beemer with a satisfied smile. A distant glow from the security lighting on the warehouses was all the light there was. On a nearby corner, the only streetlamp for a couple of blocks wasn't working. From the look of it, it had been beaten into submission long ago. There were other cars on the street, most of them junkers, none parked too close to her objective. The buildings across the street were brick tenements, condemned and slated for destruction as part of the city's effort to combat blight. Started before the economy tanked, it probably had seemed like a good idea at the time. But besides moving the tenants out and boarding up the windows, nothing more had been done. And now the buildings were reoccupied, by the local gangs and drug dealers, free of charge. A lot of activity going on over there tonight. Probably something she wanted to keep her eye on, in case the Beemer's owner was across the street making a buy.

People, especially men, had a tendency to object if they caught her repoing their cars. Which was why she worked in the middle of the night, and at least part of the reason she kept the gun and tire iron handy.

Maneuvering the truck to within about nine feet of the

Beemer's front bumper, Sam lowered the winch, shoved the gun into the waistband of her jeans and pulled her work shirt down over it, and got out, casting a quick glance inside the Beemer just to make sure that it was as empty as she'd thought at first glance: it was. All black leather, clean and expensive, with no personal belongings in view. *Good.* Personal belongings were a bitch: people were always claiming they'd been stolen.

A gust of warm summer wind sent a tendril of her hair skittering across her mouth. Impatiently Sam pulled it free, tucked it behind her ear. The mass of her hair she'd confined in a low ponytail to keep it out of the way, but it was thick and wavy with a mind of its own, and strands inevitably worked loose. So close by the river, the air smelled a little like dead fish, with a hint of something acrid—probably burning meth or crack. The chug of her truck engine was loud, and so was the clank of the big metal chain as she got it into position. The racket always made her a little nervous—no covering up that sound—and given the activity across the way it could conceivably attract attention.

Keeping an eagle eye cocked for trouble, Sam got to work. Her truck was a piece of crap, but she'd used it long enough that she knew its quirks inside and out, and could work fast. Grabbing the heavy chain and yanking in order to extend it fully, she hooked it to the BMW, secured the safety straps, and pushed the lever that would haul the BMW up on its back tires.

That done, she was just checking the straps one last time before getting back into the truck when she noticed that the Beemer's trunk had popped open. The trunk's interior light hadn't come on, but the lid was up and rocking. Frowning, casting a cautious look at the boarded-up houses where things were really starting to hop, she walked around behind the Beemer to shut the trunk before taking off for the drop yard.

She was within a foot of the rear bumper, her hand already up in the air reaching for the trunk lid, when she saw that there was a man, bloody and bound and looking like he'd been beaten to within an inch of his life, in the trunk.

Black hair, cut short; thirtyish, maybe; tall (from the way he was curled in there like a paper clip); solid-looking shoulders and chest; muscular arms pulled tightly behind his back beneath a short-sleeved T-shirt; narrow hips and long legs in—black, wet, shiny?—jeans.

Black-wet-shiny equaled . . . blood?

All that registered in a stunned instant. As she stared down in shock at the man he groaned.

Sam felt a cold shiver of fear run down her spine.

CHAPTER TWO

Danny figured he'd probably been inhaling fresh air for maybe a couple of breaths before the fact with its concordant implications registered. He had been drifting in and out of consciousness, and it was getting harder and harder to resurface every time he went under. The blood pouring out of his leg was probably largely responsible, but trussed up like he was there wasn't a whole hell of a lot he could do about it. He needed a tourniquet, or at least a pressure bandage, neither one of which he could do a damned thing about.

The good news was, it was starting to seem more and more likely that he would bleed to death before Veith got back to him.

At least, that was the good news before the fresh air intrigued him enough to bring him to the surface one more time, and he forced his eyes to open long enough to behold a truly startling sight: a girl was staring down at him.

Pretty girl, early twenties, delicate nose and jaw, tendrils of long black hair blowing in the wind. Baseball cap pulled down low over her eyes, which were narrowing even as he met them. Grim cast to a wide, luscious mouth.

His brain was admittedly a little scrambled, but in no way was he hallucinatory: she was definitely there, silhouetted against the starry night sky, one hand on the open trunk lid. She stood maybe five-seven depending on the shoes she wore—he couldn't see much lower than her waist—and she was wearing a short-sleeved blue shirt with a name badge on it sort of like a service station attendant would wear. She was pale and very slim, and she seemed as surprised to see him as he was to see her.

Only a whole lot less happy about it.

"Help," he croaked.

Her brows snapped together.

"I'll call the cops." She started to turn like she was going to leave.

"Wait! No!" Jesus, it was hard to think coherently, much less talk. But he knew this: if she went running off, he'd be willing to bet dollars to doughnuts he would never see daylight again. "You've got to—"

But he never got to finish what he was going to say.

"What the—" The hastily broken off exclamation from somewhere behind her, uttered in a harsh male voice, was the only head's-up either one of them got. Even as Danny opened his mouth to warn her, she whirled in response. Too late: a pistol butt slammed hard into her temple. Danny saw the flash of it as the moonlight caught the metal. The resultant *thunk* made him sick. The girl dropped like a rock. The burly outline of

Thug One took her place, staying visible just long enough for Danny to identify him before he disappeared from view, stooping down in the wake of the girl. Sergio Torres, a Zeta enforcer and Veith minion. Thirties, short with no neck, dark hair and skin, got his jollies hurting people. The fact that the girl had absolutely nothing to do with any of this wouldn't weigh on him in the least. The thought of yelling for help while the opportunity existed occurred, only to be discarded for two reasons: one, he was fairly certain, if Torres was cold-cocking a girl, that there was no one nearby; and two, he was absolutely certain it would earn him a clout over the head, if nothing worse. Danny was just cursing himself and God and the universe in general for his absolute inability to do anything to help her, or to take advantage of this split-second opportunity to shout for help, make a break for it, something, when Torres straightened with the girl in his arms—

—and dumped her into the trunk behind him. Just threw her in like she was a load of garbage. Limp as a rag doll, slumped against his back, she was warm, solid, not particularly heavy, but took up all the extra space there was. The weight of her landing against his hands, bound behind him at the wrists by a pair of plastic zip ties, was excruciating. They'd quit hurting a while back, and now Danny knew that it was because they'd gone numb.

They were numb no longer, and he grimaced as he cautiously moved his injured fingers. At least one of them felt like it was broken.

That was when Danny realized that he was in a weird kind

of semifetal position, all scrunched up against the lip on the open end of the trunk. And the reason for that was that the front of the car seemed to have been raised up in the air while he was unconscious. Whatever, the shift had scooted him forward and left a small amount of space behind him. Which the girl's body now filled.

"See you again soon, Marco," Torres said.

The trunk lid slammed shut. Once more Danny found himself trapped in cavelike darkness.

Shit. He'd missed his chance.

To do what? He'd already nixed yelling. Jumping from the trunk and running for it likewise wasn't going to happen, not bound as he was, and not injured as he was. Hell, even if he wasn't hobbled hand and foot he wasn't even sure he could walk. Talking them into letting him go wasn't going to happen, either.

So just what exactly did he think he should have been able to do?

Good question. Answer: something. Because the alternative was lie there and wait to die.

"Why the hell didn't you just shoot her?" Thug Two demanded. Muffled as they were by the closed trunk lid and the sound of the girl's breathing and his own pulse hammering in his ears, the words were still audible. Danny heard them, but didn't recognize the voice.

"Out here on the street?" That was Torres replying. "Anybody could be watching."

"I don't see nobody."

"Doesn't mean they don't see . . ."

Danny lost the rest of it as they apparently moved away from the trunk. He lay there in the stifling darkness, feeling like there wasn't enough air in there to permit him to draw a good breath, woozy as all get out, hurting all over, although the pain in his thigh was the worst by far. The carpet covering the floor of the trunk was scratchy against his cheek and the bare skin of his arm. The metal floor beneath was hard as granite.

Jesus Christ, where had the girl come from? Whoever she was, they were going to kill her, too. Nothing else they could do now that they'd thrown her in the trunk with him.

The fact that she was an innocent, a civilian, with nothing to do with any of this wouldn't even slow them down. Although Danny had never had up-close-and-personal contact with Veith before, Veith was well known to the FBI. He was as ruthless a killer as any hit man the Bureau had ever tracked, and the fact that he was now working for the Zetas would make him an even higher-priority target, providing Danny lived long enough to tell anyone about it. The Zetas themselves were the most notoriously brutal of Mexico's drug cartels. Just a couple of weeks before, a video had surfaced of them beheading six members of one of their rival gangs, the Gulf cartel. The fact that one of those killed was an undercover DEA agent named Carlos Ramirez was known only to a very limited circle within law enforcement. But it had been that murder that had allowed the newly busted Rick Marco to make his sweetheart deal with the government he had betrayed. It had also created the job opening that called for Danny, who in height and weight and coloring bore enough of a general resemblance to Marco to be tapped to take his place, to pretend to be Marco to draw the Zetas' fire while the real Marco was whisked off to a secure location to spill the beans about everything he knew.

A loud grinding sound from outside the car refocused Danny's attention in a hurry. It was accompanied by a jolt: by whatever weird means they were moving, they were under way again now. It felt like the car was being towed, which would at least account for the sensation of the car having been hoisted onto its back wheels.

Clearly he'd been out of it for long enough to have missed something.

Something connected with the girl.

Time to make a move, or pack it in.

"Hey," he said into the airless darkness. "Hey, girl, can you hear me?"

She lay heavy and inert against his back, increasing the discomfort in his cramping arms and injured hands, her weight pressing him inexorably forward. He could hear her breathing, so at least there was no doubt that she was alive. Remembering the sound of the blow that had struck her down, he figured she might be out for a while. Delicate bones, slender build—a fragile flower, if looks meant anything. Decorative, maybe, but he doubted that she was the type to bounce back fast.

Right now, he needed fast.

Danny cursed under his breath. With him in the shape he was in, she was the only hope either of them had.

"Miss," he tried again, more politely in case that struck a

chord, his tone urgent but not so loud that it would penetrate beyond the confines of the trunk. "Miss, can you hear me? You've got to wake up."

Nothing. Danny tried jostling her, but regretted it almost as soon as he hunched up his back and pushed against her. There wasn't any room, and moving hurt like a bitch.

He did it again anyway.

"Goddamn it, woman, if you don't wake up we're both going to die."

She groaned. Danny could feel her stiffen against his back. Hope stirred inside him. Was she moving? Had she heard him? It was hard to tell. The car swayed and creaked. The little space they were in tilted and rocked. The impression he got was that the vehicles were turning a corner. At any minute Torres and company might stop and then Veith would show up and then . . .

Bang, bang. You're dead.

"Miss, can you hear me?" Tension vibrated in Danny's voice. Keeping himself conscious and focused required increasing effort. He wasn't going to last much longer, he feared. And if he fainted, they were done for. "Miss?"

She sucked in air, stirred a little. Something—a change in her breathing, in the atmosphere around them—made him think she was conscious.

"Miss?" He felt like a fool calling her that. "What's your name?"

For a moment he thought he'd been wrong: she wasn't conscious after all.

Then a wobbly voice muttered, "Sam."

Danny felt a rush of relief.

"Okay, Sam, this is really important." Keeping his cool under extreme conditions had saved his life before. It didn't seem likely that it was going to make much difference now, but he wasn't ready to give up and die yet, either. "I need you to focus here. We've only got a few minutes before they kill us."

Again with the fluttery breath. "What—happened?" She sounded groggy, confused, but at least she was awake and talking.

He didn't have time for lengthy explanations. "You ran across some bad guys, got hit in the head and thrown into a car trunk. This car trunk, with me. When we stop moving, the bad guys are going to open the trunk and kill you. And me, too, but probably you first, because they don't need you for anything."

"Who . . . ?" she began, still sounding out of it, but he cut her off ruthlessly.

"Doesn't matter. There's no time. Did you hear what I said about them killing you?"

He thought she nodded. Then, her voice scarcely more than a reedy breath, she said, "We're in the trunk of the BMW, aren't we? The one I was getting ready to tow away."

"You're a tow truck driver?" There you go: the information he'd been missing.

"Yes."

"That's good to know. Now listen. My hands are fastened behind my back with a zip tie. I need you to get me loose. Root around back there, see if you can come up with something sharp. *Anything.* Use it to cut the tie."

He could hear her breathing, feel her shifting around a little. She didn't reply.

"Sam? Hello? Did you hear me?" His voice was tense. It was all he could do not to yell. Hell, the situation was dire.

"I heard you."

"Okay." His patience was stretching thin. "Could you please try?"

"How do I know you won't, like, turn around and attack me if I cut you free?" she asked, sounding like her marbles were coming together at last. Unfortunately, they were coalescing into a configuration that wasn't helpful. "Maybe you're a bad guy, too."

Any dithering on her part was as maddening as it was terrifying. He felt like he was in the final minutes of a basketball game, his team ten points behind with the shot clock running down.

"Who's in the fucking trunk with you?" he countered. Just staying conscious was requiring increasing amounts of effort. Arguing he didn't need. "I think that puts us on the same side, don't you?"

Danny got the impression that she was turning the situation over in her mind. The car swayed and bounced and seemed to pick up speed. Was it rumbling through an intersection? Yes, he decided.

"Sam, look, we don't have much time," he said. "They're taking us somewhere remote where they can shoot us in private. Before they get us there, it would be really helpful if you could *find something you can use to cut my hands loose. Please.*"

He heard her take another deep breath, felt her tense, as if she was gathering herself.

"Okay, fine," she said.

"You can trust me, I promise. We both want the same thing, to get out of this alive." The trunk felt hotter and more airless than ever. It was dark as the grave and cramped as a womb. Besides the faint odors of exhaust and oil and sweat, the raw meat smell of fresh blood was inescapable. Of course, she probably wouldn't recognize the smell, or know what it meant. When she started moving, really moving, rooting around, he let out a relieved breath. He thought, hoped, prayed that she was doing as he'd told her: hunting for something with which to cut him free.

She was the only chance they had.

"How many of them are there?" She was breathing too fast, and her voice sounded a little thin. He deduced from that that she was smart enough to be scared, but at least her thinking seemed to be clear.

"When the trunk opens? Should be two. Maybe three." He could feel the unmistakably female shape of her pressed close against his back. Under other circumstances, he might almost have enjoyed it, but what it meant now was that there wasn't much room for either of them to maneuver.

"With guns?" It wasn't really a question.

"Yes." He felt the cool touch of her hands on his forearms, sliding down to his bound wrists. Then she found the place where his wrists crossed, where the zip ties were practically slicing through his skin, and seemed to want to explore that, too. What was she doing, checking out the restraints? Mary Mother of God, they were running out of time.

"It's a plastic zip tie," he explained again. It was too dark for her to see anything. Like him, she was effectively blind. "Two of them, one on top of the other. You can't break them. You need something to cut them with."

He felt her breasts pressing into his back, felt her knees digging into him. A soft sweet scent—shampoo?—cut through the stale air. All potent reminders that she was a woman. Who would die soon if he couldn't find a way to save her.

If he let it, the thought would make him crazy.

"Hurry," he said.

"Hold still." Her fingers on his wrists tightened into a real grip. Then she bore down. Pain rocketed up his arms.

Ow. But he didn't say it out loud. He didn't want to do anything that might spook her.

"You're going to have to cut the ties," he repeated through clenched teeth. Something sharp stabbed into his left wrist— a blade, the business end of a blade—surprising him so much that he let out a small yelp.

"Sorry," she said. But it didn't matter, because between the pressure and the prick of the pointed blade and the subsequent sawing sensation he was beginning to see some light.

"You found something to cut with." Impossible as it seemed, she'd done it, and incredibly quickly, too.

"I carry a pocket knife."

The rush of thankfulness that he experienced was devout in its intensity. "There you go. That's my girl."

"Hold still."

Trying to gather his strength in preparation for what was to come, Danny did his best to keep his arms rigid while he took stock of the rest of his body. The pain was bad, so he tried to block it out. He was conscious of his heart thumping. His pulse pounded in his ears. He was swallowing air through his mouth now, drawing in what little there was in greedy gulps, trying to keep his head clear. Thanks to her, it looked like they might actually have a shot at making a stand. But even if she was able to cut him free in time, he was still going to need a miracle to get them both out of this alive. His ears were acutely attuned to the various sounds outside the trunk. They were still rolling, but that wouldn't last forever. When the vehicle came to a stop—

She said, "You want to tell me who you are and why you're in a car trunk?" Sawing away, she caught him in the wrist with the blade again. He needed to be free too badly to make so much as a sound.

"I'm the unluckiest son of a bitch in the country?" Danny tried, feeling the sudden release of a portion of the pressure around his wrists like a gift from on high. Then he remembered the state he was in, and didn't know whether to laugh or howl. Unarmed, weak from blood loss, beat to pieces, with a bullet through his thigh and a possibly broken finger and countless other injuries he hadn't even begun to try to catalog, he was going to be a hell of a warrior, for sure.

But he was going to give it his best shot. Aside from really, truly not wanting to die tonight, now he had this girl to protect.

"Is that supposed to be an answer?" Voice edgy, she was already sawing through the second zip tie. She stopped sawing as she spoke. He could almost feel her frowning at him.

Jesus, this wasn't the moment for attitude. The close, airless confines of the trunk were zapping what little strength he had remaining to him. The thought of what was waiting beyond it scared him to the bone.

"Keep cutting that tie. If you want to have a chance of living through this, I need to be free to move before they open that trunk again."

"Do you have a name? Or not?" But at least she comprehended enough of the desperateness of the situation to start sawing away again.

"You don't need a name. All you need to know is that I'm the guy who's going to keep you alive, all right?" He thought about that for a second. "At least, if you hurry and I can."

The smallest of pauses. "Oh, wow, now I feel all safe."

The sarcasm was absolutely deserved, and might even have made him smile under less harrowing conditions. As reassurance, he had to admit that his probably too truthful promise left something to be desired. But at least she was still working that knife against the tie.

"So can you tell me *why* you're in this trunk?" she asked.

He'd give her this much: she didn't give up. At the moment, he wasn't sure if that was a good thing or a bad one.

"You don't want to know," Danny said. "Believe me. The less you know, the safer you are."

She snorted. "Like anything you tell me is going to make a difference now?"

Okay, so she was smart enough to realize that she was in deep shit however this played out.

"All you need to remember is that helping me is helping yourself," he said. "We're on the same team."

She made a skeptical sound. "And I'm just supposed to take your word for that?"

"You got any alternative?"

The second tie broke, which happy circumstance he thought distracted her from answering. God almighty, his hands were free! Relief was accompanied by lightning bolts of pain shooting up his arms, into his shoulders, then firing back down into his hands, as the position into which they had been forced abruptly eased. Gritting his teeth against a groan, Danny brought his arms around in front of him, moving slowly, gingerly shaking his hands out, flexing his fingers as best he could.

The beating he'd endured before they'd pistol-whipped him senseless had done some damage to his hands, that was for sure. How much, he didn't have time to assess.

"Give me the knife." He thrust his hand behind him to receive it, ignoring the searing pain that attacked him as he moved.

"Why?" Sudden suspicion laced her voice.

Was it his imagination, or was the car slowing down? The swaying was definitely less pronounced.

"Why do you think? Oh, are you worried I'm going to turn around and attack you with it? I'm not, okay? I've got two more ties around my ankles. You can't reach them. *So give me the knife.*"

The sound she made defied interpretation, but she pressed the knife—one of those small, Swiss-army-type pocket knives with a million gizmos attached, from the feel of it—into his palm. There wasn't much room, but difficult as it was he managed to stretch down enough to start hacking away at the ties binding his ankles. The blade was small, the movements required to cut through the hard plastic ties accompanied by a thousand different versions of pain. Through it all, he was supremely conscious of a fresh upsurge of blood oozing from his thigh.

Got to stop the bleeding. That was the next item on his survive-the-night list.

"How sure are you that they're going to kill us?" The girl's voice was breathier than before. Probably because she now had enough of a handle on the situation to be really, truly frightened. His initial instinct was to reassure her, to tell her that everything was going to be all right. Under the circumstances, though, his initial instinct was shit. Truth was what she needed to hear.

"One hundred percent. I'd be dead already if they hadn't gotten interrupted." The question was, who, exactly, had interrupted them: Crittenden and the cavalry, or more of the contingent of hapless U.S. Marshals out of whose custody he'd been snatched, or someone else hunting Marco? Or even a new player whose moves he wasn't yet trying to follow around the board?

Answer: impossible to know. As Danny assessed the truth of that, he sliced through the first tie, and was on to the second. It *wasn't* his imagination: the car was definitely slowing down.

The sudden crunch of gravel under the tires acted on him like a warning siren: wherever they were going now, it was somewhere off the public roads. Which meant they might very well be nearing Veith's killing ground of choice. Because of course Veith was on his way, planning to rendezvous with Torres and finish the job.

Under those conditions, the sudden turn onto gravel could not be good.

He would be a fool to assume anything other than that they were approaching their destination.

"Hear that gravel? I think we're just about to get where we've been going."

"We're probably in the scrap yard," she said.

"Scrap yard?"

"For old cars and things. They recycle scrap metal. It's not too far from where I found you. It's all gravel."

That made sense. A scrap yard in the middle of the night sounded like Veith's kind of place. He knew it was probably a waste of time, but still he tried to identify any source of possible help.

"An attendant on duty? Anything around, like a bar or an open-all-night convenience store or something?" Someplace she could head for when she bolted.

"No." The tempo of her breathing had slowed down, like

she was deliberately calming herself. He succeeded in cutting through the second tie: hallelujah, his feet were free.

As soon as he moved his cramped legs, pain shot through his body like a thousand flaming arrows. He felt the hot slide of more blood leaving the hole in his thigh. Who was he kidding? He was going to fight off Veith and his thugs with a pocket knife? In the shape he was in? Hell, he was surprised he wasn't already unconscious from blood loss. Chalk it up to adrenaline, he thought. Forcing himself to concentrate, he moved on to item two on his survive-the-night list and started tugging his belt from its loops.

"What are you doing?" she asked, clearly having felt the change in his movements. There was definitely fear in her voice now: it was sharper, more tightly wound. Well, he thought as he pulled his belt free, if she wasn't scared she would have to be brain-dead.

"I've got a bullet hole in my leg. I'm going to use my belt to put a tourniquet on it."

"They shot you." It wasn't a question. "That's where all the blood came from."

"Yeah."

"What, is this like a hit on you or something? Who *are* they?"

"Again, you're better off not knowing."

A long, harsh grinding sound from outside, from somewhere toward the front of the car, made Sam inhale sharply.

"That noise you're hearing? That's the brakes on the tow

truck," she told him, even as the car lurched and rocked in a way that was different from before. "We're stopping."

Queasy and light-headed, sucking in the too-hot, oxygen-deprived air like they weren't making it anymore, knife tucked carefully away into his T-shirt pocket so there was no danger of him losing it in the dark, Danny was already wrapping his belt around his thigh and pulling it tight. God, that hurt. It made a rough but effective tourniquet, and if he left it in place longer than about the next fifteen minutes he would probably be in danger of losing his leg.

Which, unfortunately, seemed like the least of his problems at the moment.

"As soon as that trunk lid opens, I want you to be ready to go. Jump and run. Just run away into the dark as fast and as far as you can. For your life, you hear?" he told her.

"I hear." The tempo of her breathing had slowed down, as if she were deliberately calming herself. "Oh, God. I'm scared."

"In a situation like this, fear's a good thing. Keeps you sharp." He reached around, caught her hand. It felt slender and fine-boned and, surprisingly considering the temperature in the trunk, cold as ice. Or maybe not so surprising: he could feel a slight tremor in her fingers that underlined just how truly afraid she was. Her hand clung to his, clutching it, telling him that she needed comforting in the worst way. Pulling her hand around in front of him, he surrendered to the impulse of the moment and lifted it to his mouth, kissed the knuckles. He felt her slight movement and took it for surprise, but again she didn't try to pull away.

"We got this," he told her. He was still holding her hand, and she was holding his hand back even more tightly. Maybe it was a lie, but right now he felt she needed to hear it. To stand even the smallest chance of escaping, she was going to need confidence and courage. "We're going to make it. Just do what I tell you, and you should be fine."

"I will." Her voice had steadied. "What about you?"

"You let me worry about me."

The car stopped its forward motion. Then the rocking stopped. They weren't moving at all any longer. His body tightened as his heartbeat speeded up. Behind him, Sam caught her breath and quickly withdrew her hand from his. She must have realized what the fact that they had stopped meant, too. He felt her tense, and then her weight no longer pressed into his back as she edged away from him, scooting as best she could back toward the rear of the trunk. While he could still feel the warmth of her touching him in places, she seemed to have put as much distance between them as possible, as if she thought maybe they might overlook her or something when the trunk opened. Which he didn't have a problem with: at least it gave him some room to maneuver. As long as she remembered to jump.

"Here's the deal." He fished the knife—the pathetically small and way-less-than-lethal knife—out of his pocket. Ironically, now that he had cut off the blood flow to most of his leg it hurt worse than ever. Enough to where not thinking about it required real effort; fortunately, he had distractions. "I'm going to go after whoever opens the trunk as soon as it happens. They think I'm still tied up, so they won't be expecting that. You take advantage of their distraction, and jump out of the trunk. You'll probably only have a few seconds, so run like hell the minute you hit the ground."

"Shh." She breathed the warning.

That was when he heard it at last: the slight crunch of footsteps on gravel.

They were coming.

Danny tensed. He took a deep breath, centered himself, and felt his pulse rate slow way down: battle mode. At least now, unbound, he had a chance, however slim it might be. He braced the foot of his uninjured leg against a protuberance at the side of the trunk, the better to help him spring out, and got a good grip on the knife. His hand-to-hand combat skills were top-notch, but the sad truth was that, virtually weaponless, it was hard to defend against one gun, let alone two. Uninjured, he might have stood a fighting chance, but as it was . . .

The footsteps stopped. Danny's every sense went on red alert. From the sounds, he knew that there were still only two of them, even knew where they were. Both stood behind the car, one in the center, one to the left.

Torres and Thug Two, he presumed. If Veith was there, or anyone else, they'd arrived earlier. He would have heard another vehicle crunching over the gravel.

"Heads up," he whispered.

Just as Danny realized that he couldn't hear her breathing any longer, a metallic click sent the hair on the back of his neck into bristle mode. It also gave him a split second's warning:

someone had hit the trunk release button on the BMW's key ring.

This is it.

His gut clenched. His muscles bunched. Adrenaline shot through his veins like a speedball rush.

The trunk rose at a measured, majestic pace that reflected the luxury brand of the car rather than the urgency of the situation. In the space of about a heartbeat, as fresh air wafted in and a swath of starry night sky was revealed, Danny registered that they were outside rather than in a building, that the balmy summer's night now smelled of garbage and the river, that Torres and Thug Two were approximately where he had pictured them, and, as the moonlight turned its snub-nosed black barrel to silver, that at least one gun was pointed right at his face.

Game on.

Gathering himself, he prepared to spring. The distinctive sound of a weapon being cocked behind him—behind him!—caused his eyes to widen. It was the only warning he got.

CHAPTER THREE

As the Beemer's trunk lid rose, Sam's heart jackhammered—until it didn't. Her pulse accelerated to the point where it was all she could hear—until suddenly it slowed way down.

By the time she inhaled her first lungful of fresh air, beheld the first sliver of starry sky, heard the sudden, unmuffled onslaught of night sounds, every bit of fear she was experiencing had vanished, swept away in a flood of icy resolve.

She wasn't dying tonight. No way, no how.

If she died, Tyler had no one.

That was all the motivation Sam needed. Whatever it took, she was going to survive for her boy. When the lid rose high enough to reveal two men silhouetted against the night sky, she had her own gun out and ready, down close to her chest, pointing out. One of the men was aiming a gun into the trunk: with moonlight glinting on its barrel, she saw it as plainly as if it were high noon outside. Lying awkwardly on her side, she angled her weapon more accurately, aiming up through the small space she had managed to create between her body and the muscular back of the man wedged into the trunk with her. The Smith & Wesson was heavy and warm from her body heat. Her palms were sweaty, which made its metal grip slippery, which made her tighten her hold on it. During the heartbeat it took her to reconfirm the deadly reality of the mess she was in—oh, yeah, it was bad—her stomach cramped. She ignored it, just like she was ignoring the painful throbbing in her head where one of these bozos had clobbered her, just like she was ignoring the fear that would have swamped her if she'd let it. If this was a fight for her life—and Tyler's—then hell, yeah, she was going to fight. Gritting her teeth, she targeted just above the gleaming black barrel of the bastard's gun. It was taking careful aim—at her, not her companion. Like he'd said, they were clearly going to kill her first. Tamping down hard on a rising wave of terror that turned her blood to ice and made her pulse race and her heart pound, she fired with grim determination, pulling the trigger multiple times, shooting at both dark shadows, blasting away for her life—and Tyler's—in big explosions of sound.

"Holy shit!" the man in the trunk with her yelped, his arms flying up to shield his head, as her targets screamed, reeled away, then dropped from sight with heavy, crunching thuds. Clambering up onto her knees, looking wildly around for any possible new threat, Sam ignored her companion as he rolled onto his back to stare up at her. He said something else to her that didn't register. Everything—the bang of the gunshots, the sulfuric smell of the recently fired gun, the screams and sounds of bodies dropping, and the terrible reality of the deadly violence that had suddenly forced its way into her life—had such a nightmarish quality to it that she was having a hard time processing that *this is real*.

Don't think. Just get out of here.

Ears ringing from the noise of the gunshots, mind surprisingly detached in the midst of her body's knee-jerk panic, she sprang out of that trunk like a gazelle—or a mother whose kid was in danger, which was what she was.

The men she'd shot were down, dark shapes sprawled on the silvery gravel near the back of the car, she saw as her feet hit the ground. One of them writhed and moaned. The other lay still. For a second, as the gun hung heavy in her hand, she stared at them. The one looked dead; the other clearly wasn't, but neither seemed capable of posing any kind of a threat. Heart pounding, breathing way too fast, she forced herself to look away from them and take stock of her surroundings. She was outside, close enough to the river so that she could catch a glimpse of its rolling waters, standing in the middle of a shadow-filled open space. The moon and stars gleaming down from the black sky high above, the distant glow from the city of St. Louis across the river, and her truck's white beams pointing like twin light sabers away from her made it plenty bright enough to see what was going down, even if darkness obscured a lot of the details. As she had suspected, they were in the scrap yard, a football-field-size cemetery for junk cars and trucks and discarded metal of all types, in which she personally had scrounged numerous times looking for parts for various vehicles, including the truck. Piles of would-be scrap were stacked up everywhere like mini-mountains, some reaching as much as twenty feet high. Two long, low warehouses formed a wall between the piles of scrap and the street. A ten-foot-high chain-link fence designed (unsuccessfully) to keep scroungers out surrounded the entire property. Making an instantaneous visual sweep of the area, Sam concluded that there was no one else around.

Except, of course, for the man who had clambered out of the trunk in her wake. Catching his laborious movement toward her out of the corner of her eye, she turned in his direction, of two minds about whether or not she ought to just go ahead and shoot him, too, and be done with it. Her lips compressed. It was obvious that he was badly injured. His right leg dragged. His shoulders hunched. His face looked like somebody had used it for a punching bag.

As she hesitated—cold-blooded murder wasn't really her thing, although she guessed she could change if she had to—a dozen conflicting thoughts whirled through her mind. He hadn't thrown her into the trunk; he had been imprisoned with her. He had tried to reassure her. He had held her hand, kissed it even. The feel of his lips against her skin had provoked a wayward tingle. On the other hand, *he had been in the trunk in the first place.* Her gut might tell her that he was a good guy, but good guys usually didn't end up in trunks. Anyway, when it came to men, her gut wasn't worth shit. She was still wavering between pulling the trigger and not when he reached her side.

"Give me that." The pistol was snatched from her hand

before she realized what he meant to do. So, choice made: she should have shot him. Only too damned late to do anything about it.

"*Hey.* That's mine." She grabbed at her gun to no avail.

The man who'd been in the trunk with her—her ally? Yeah, no, to hell with that, that kind of thinking was dangerous—gave her a reproving look before limping away toward the men she'd shot.

"Jesus, you could've told me you had a gun," he flung over his shoulder at her.

"I could've." Except he would have taken it from her, and she had needed it to protect herself: trusting him to that extent had never even been something she had considered. For an instant she watched him: for all the Hunchback of Notre Dame lurch he had going on, she could see that he was indeed tall and athletically built. Handsome? Hard to tell, but she was going with probably yes. Along with his bloody jeans, he was wearing a gray T-shirt that showed off the kind of muscles that would have made Kendra, for one, drool, and well-worn sneakers. End dangling from the belt he had pulled tight around his right thigh. Clearly injured in ways other than the gunshot he'd told her about. Weakened as he plainly was, he was still big and muscular enough to lead her to conclude that trying to physically fight him for her gun would be a gamble. Even with him injured and limping, trying to wrest the gun away from him was likely to end poorly for her. Whatever he'd done to get himself beaten up, shot, and thrown into a car trunk to die, it couldn't have been anything good. Odds were that he was as much a bad guy as the thugs who had hit her over the head and thrown her into the trunk with him. She could very well wind up getting shot, or being taken captive again, or something equally horrific, by him, and anyway the fight itself would take up valuable time. Let him keep the gun, she decided: all she really wanted was to get away in one piece. Survival was her goal, and to hell with everything else. Taking advantage of his concentration on the men on the ground, mindful that an unwary crunch from the gravel underfoot could swing his attention back in her direction at any second, she snuck toward the cab of her truck. The engine was idling, which meant that all she had to do was hop in and take off. Generally, the scrap yard was kept locked. When she'd come hunting for parts, unless someone else was paying, she had scaled the fence. But to get the truck out—with a quick look around, she located the gate. It was open. *Yay.*

Bang. A shot exploded behind her, making her jump, galvanizing her into breaking into a run. Whoa, who had fired that? Was it aimed at her? Sam didn't know, but she wasn't waiting around to find out. A snapped glance over her shoulder found her trunk companion standing over the man who'd been writhing and moaning a moment before. The guy now lay silent and motionless in the gravel, while her new pal held her gun in such a way that she had little doubt it was he who had just fired. Could anybody say, kill shot? An icy shiver raced down her spine. *She* might not be into cold-blooded murder, but this guy clearly had no such qualms. Was he killing all witnesses? God in heaven, was she next? *Go,* her every instinct screamed, and Sam went like the wind. When she reached the truck's door, she was stymied briefly because the damned thing, as it had a tendency to do, was stuck. Finally succeeding in wrenching it open, she jumped into the high cab, yanked the door shut, and locked it. *Bang!* Another shot rang out. Impossible to see what was happening; the truck was facing in the opposite direction. She was betting on another kill shot. Was her buddy coming for her now? Sam's mouth went dry and her heart slammed in her chest as she grabbed the stubborn old gearshift and wrenched it into drive, then put the pedal to the metal. The engine roared: no hiding what she was up to now. Its inner workings always balky and slow, Big Red didn't move.

"*Come on!*" she screamed at it out loud, banging her palms against the steering wheel. As if in answer, the transmission finally engaged with a jolt. The truck shot forward.

"*Go!*" she encouraged it.

Unfortunately, the only way out that she knew of required a U-turn.

So jittery with fear by this time that she was practically bouncing up and down in the seat, Sam executed the tight half-doughnut with a grinding of gears and a shower of gravel. The headlights cut a crazy arc through the darkness, the towing assemblage clanked in noisy protest, and the Beemer fishtailed wildly behind as she goosed the accelerator. The truck, finally fully responsive, charged toward freedom. Her cell phone bounced out of the little plastic tray beneath the cassette player and landed in the passenger foot well. For a moment she looked after it with dismay—calling 911 was high on her list of priorities. But stopping and diving after it wasn't happening: getting out of there was Job One. The open gate—escape!—waited directly in front of her, perhaps half a football field away. To her left, the long, low warehouses on the other side of the piles of scrap blocked her view of the street. Just ahead and to her right, the two men she had shot, both motionless now, curled like black commas in the gravel.

"Hey!" From out of nowhere the man who'd been in the trunk with her jumped directly into the truck's path. He stood facing her, her gun held down by his side as, bent and grimacing, he waved at her, signaling her to stop.

Like that was going to happen.

"Move!" she yelled at him through the windshield. She doubted that he could hear her. Certainly he didn't get out of the way. Clutching the steering wheel hard with both hands, she stomped the accelerator with everything she had. She wasn't stopping, not for anything. He might have given her a tingle when he kissed her hand, but she didn't care. He had a choice: move or be road kill. The truck surged, engine gunning, wheels spitting out sprays of gravel, as it bore down on him like a bull charging a matador.

"Get out of the way!" she screamed again, making exaggerated shooing motions with one arm. If what they were playing was chicken, she knew who was going to win. She just hoped he wasn't too stupid to . . .

"Fuck!" At what was almost the last minute, he leaped to the side. The headlights picked up the startled, angry expression on his face.

"Good call," she yelled at him. A triumphant smile just

touched Sam's mouth as the truck plowed over the place where he had been standing seconds before. The resultant flutter of relief that she wasn't going to have to run over him to escape did not mean that she really wouldn't have run him down. It just meant that she was glad she hadn't had to. She was just starting to put him out of her mind when a thump against the passenger-side door ripped her gaze from the now-clear path to the open gate in front of her and redirected it toward the sound.

"Stop!" It was a roar. A battered face glared at her through the passenger-side window. With one eye swollen almost shut and bruises on the forehead and a cheekbone and a bloody, lumpen-looking nose, it was downright scary. It was also unhappily way too familiar. Scrabbling at the door handle—the door was locked, thank God!—then banging on the rolled-up passenger window with *her* gun, Quasimodo was hanging onto the too-damned-sturdy struts of the oversize side-view mirror for dear life.

Oh, no.

"Goddamnit, let me in!"

"In your dreams!" Keeping one wary eye on him, she jerked the steering wheel back and forth in a desperate effort to dislodge him. It didn't work: at the end of every maneuver, he was still there. Sending sprays of gravel everywhere, zigzagging wildly, Big Red kept on barreling toward the street. Only one side of the big double gates was open, which meant the space the truck momentarily would be shooting through was narrow. Narrow enough to knock him off?

Please, God.

"Lean over and open the door!" He banged on the window with her gun again. He banged so hard she was afraid he might break it. Then she remembered that the window had been broken the previous year by an irate debtor whose car was in the process of being towed away, and replaced by heavy safety glass. Which, she had been assured at the time by the guy installing it, was practically unbreakable.

"No! Get off my truck!" She jerked the wheel sharply to the left, then to the right. Yelling curses, swinging precariously back and forth, he nevertheless managed to hang on. Hoping to attract attention—attract *help*—she hit the horn. The resultant air-horn-quality blast split the night. She winced. So did he.

"Are you brain-dead? Quit blowing the fucking horn!" he roared, swinging toward the door again and grabbing for the handle.

"Get off my truck!"

"Open the damned door!"

"No way in hell! Get off!"

The only way she was knocking him off for sure was if she took out the side mirror, too, was Sam's lightning conclusion as she glanced from him to the gate the truck was quickly closing in on. Even then it wasn't a done deal unless she wanted to risk trying to scrape up the entire side of the truck, which she hesitated to do. Number one, she needed her truck to make a living, and didn't have the money to fix any damage that might result. Number two, if she miscalculated, she could end up having a wreck, getting the truck hung up on the gate, and thwarting her own escape. Mashing the horn again—"For fuck's sake, stop doing that!" he screamed through the window at her—she jerked the wheel back and forth in quick succession, fighting to make him lose his grip. It didn't work. He didn't even flap around as much. From his sudden relative stability she surmised that he had found a way to wedge his feet more securely onto the running board, where they were obviously perched. His expression, she thought as she cast another poisonous glance at him, had turned purposeful. She frowned. Just as it had been, one arm was hooked around the mirror strut while the other hand— Sam's heart leaped as she watched it jerk upward, watched him aim the gun inside the cab. Sweet merciful God, was he going to shoot her?

Her blood ran cold.

"No!" she screamed, cringing even as she whipped the wheel hard to the left and then to the right. The tires spun. Gravel flew everywhere. Her cell phone skittered uselessly over the hard plastic mat lining the foot well, tantalizingly close but impossible to reach. Quasimodo teetered backward with the motion of the truck, then swung forward again, then reaimed the gun . . .

When it blasted, blowing out the passenger window and showering the seat and rear windshield and tiny backseat of the truck with BB-size chunks of safety glass, Sam shrieked and ducked and almost drove into one of the mountains of scrap. Only at the last possible minute did she see where the truck was headed and correct course with another sharp jerk of the wheel.

"Jesus!" he yelled, windmilling wildly as the maneuver threw him off balance again. Only his arm hooked around the strut kept him from being flung off. Warm night air gushed in.

Without the barrier of glass between them he suddenly seemed way too close, much closer than before. She thought, hoped, prayed he might lose his grip on the strut—or at least the gun. "*Stop*, you crazy . . . !"

"No fucking way!" Sam screamed back. The words had no sooner left her mouth than Quasimodo launched himself right in through the window he'd blown out. Cursing a blue streak, he torpedoed through the opening.

CHAPTER FOUR

"Get out! Get out of my truck!"

"Like hell," Quasimodo growled.

Driving one-handed, Sam leaned over and shoved his broad back as hard as she could. When that didn't work—might as well have shoved at a fallen tree—she pounded at his head and shoulders with her fist in an effort to force him back out of the window.

"Ouch! Shit! Goddamnit, stop that!"

"Get out! Get out of here!"

The tire iron was out of her reach beneath the seat; her phone bounced near the passenger door; he had her knife and gun. Knowing that she had left herself basically defenseless made her nuts. They battled, her to push him out and him to slide the rest of the way inside, as Big Red zoomed through the gate. It careened with squealing tires out onto the street, which besides the scrap yard was home to an abandoned factory and a number of other now closed and mostly derelict commercial buildings. The street was dark as pitch and deserted except for a man, al-

most certainly drunk, staggering down the shoulder in the direction of the river, where Sam knew the homeless congregated
to sleep on the bank on warm summer nights. Caught in the
headlights, face a study in horrified astonishment, he leaped for
the fence surrounding the factory across the street as the truck
hurtled in his direction. At the last moment Sam corrected
course with a frantic yank of the wheel. An old car parked on
the shoulder barely missed being flattened. Then the truck was
back on the street, bouncing on its tires, barreling toward an
intersection that would take them someplace more populated.
It veered drunkenly as Quasimodo tried to heave himself the
rest of the way inside while Sam, driving one-handed, fought to
keep him out.

He won.

Shit.

"Both hands on the wheel!" he roared as he used brute
strength to defeat her frantic efforts to expel him, then surged
into a sitting position on the passenger side of the bench seat.
Facing her, he was off balance, but still solidly there. Sam's lips
tightened as she saw that her gun was now aimed at her.

Would he shoot her? He hadn't yet. She didn't think he
would, although being wrong was always a possibility. But
whether he would or not, he was still inside her truck, with no
way to get him out.

Shit again. Her clenched fist, primed to deliver more blows,
lowered. Then the truck jolted over a pothole and she automatically gripped the wheel with both hands.

"Keep 'em there."

Like she'd done it because *he* had told her to. She shot him a filthy look. He was panting, sweating, glaring at her as he leaned back against the passenger door. Flexing the fingers of his left hand—the ring finger was swollen and seemingly immobile—he grimaced. In such close quarters he seemed bigger than she had thought. He was broad shouldered and muscular, bad-ass-looking enough to be intimidating, if she had been the type of person to ever let herself be intimidated, which she emphatically was not. His black hair was just long enough to be ruffled by the wind blasting in through the destroyed window. About a day's worth of black stubble darkened his chin.

"What the hell is wrong with you?" he growled.

Sam clamped both hands tighter around the wheel as a means of controlling her impulses, which urged launching another all-out attack on him. Knowing that anything of the sort would be stupid to the point of suicidal, she cast him a furious look instead.

"Get out of my truck!"

"Yeah. No."

She was so wired, so upset and scared and angry, that the fact that he could shoot her at will didn't seem to be registering with her like it should. She was in mortal danger: the gun he was pointing at her was proof positive of that. But she wasn't as terrified as she should have been, and she blamed the adrenaline that had to be flooding her system by now for that.

Or maybe it was the lingering memory of the gentle way he'd kissed her hand.

"That's my gun," she snapped. "You had no right to take it."

"You ever hear of 'might makes right'? Yeow!" It was a near-shout as, focused on him, she let the truck wander off onto the shoulder where it barely missed sideswiping a utility pole. She corrected course with a last-minute jerk of the wheel that had the weathered pole zipping past millimeters away from the mirror—on his side. "Watch where you're going. And slow the hell down!"

All righty, then. The briefest of grim smiles curved her mouth as she stood on the brake. The usual grinding sound the worn brake shoes made when they were called into service was amplified into a grating shriek as the truck convulsed before jerking to a dead stop. As she had intended, he was thrown violently forward. The bad news was, he managed to catch himself with a hand on the dashboard before he banged his head or any other significant body part. And he never lost his grip on her gun.

Damn it.

"What the fuck?" He looked pissed. "You did that on purpose."

"Ya think?"

"Why?"

"Why do you think? I want you *out*." Clutching the wheel so hard the rigid plastic hurt her hands, she screamed it at him. "Out, out, out!"

"Give it up, baby doll. It's not happening." His tone was brutal. Her gun suddenly looked way more threatening as he pointed it at her again, this time with what seemed to be real purpose. "Drive! Now!"

"You wish." Sam grabbed for the door handle, prepared to leap from the truck. As her foot slid off the brake, Big Red started to roll. Lunging toward her, surprisingly fast despite the injuries that were obviously causing him both pain and mobility issues, Quasimodo caught her wrist. His fingers snapped closed around her delicate bones like he meant business; she knew instantly that she wasn't going to be breaking that grip anytime soon. Then the mouth of her gun suddenly jammed into her ribs, and she cried out.

And froze. And glared at him.

"Hit the brake." His voice was hard with menace. The look he gave her sent a shiver down her spine as she sulkily complied. Suddenly she did feel a little afraid of him, and she didn't like the feeling. The sensation of the gun pressing into her flesh made her heart speed up. "Let's get this straight: you're not getting rid of me, and you're not going anywhere without me. For which you should be prepared to kiss my ass. At this point, I'm all that's standing between you and a bullet in the brain. So if you want to live through this, *drive.*"

Sam took a breath. His battered face was misshapen enough to make his expression impossible to determine, but his jaw was definitely set. His swollen right eye was an unblinking black slit. His uninjured left eye wasn't much wider as they both bored into hers. She was almost positive he wouldn't shoot her, much less at point-blank range like this, but, she decided with one more furious look at him, it was a chance she couldn't afford to take.

For Tyler's sake.

"Now!" he barked when she still hesitated, weighing her chances. "Unless you'd rather sit here and wait for more of the group who just tried to kill us to show up. Because I guarantee you, they're on their way as we speak."

That thought was way more terrifying than he was. Sam's stomach clenched like a fist. Lifting her foot from the brake, she stepped on the gas instead. The truck rattled as it got under way again. Behind them, the Beemer lurched and swayed into motion like a dragging, too-heavy kite's tail.

"Not too fast," he said as, with his warning about more killers being on the way lighting up her brain, she stepped hard on the gas and the truck obediently gathered speed. "Nice and easy, like you've actually got a brain in your head."

"Screw you." She flung him a killing glare. But she eased off on the accelerator, although her every instinct urged her to stomp it. "By the way, it'd be a lot easier to drive 'nice and easy' if you let go of my wrist."

To her surprise he did, and eased back onto his side of the seat. The gun moved with him, withdrawing from her ribs. She could see it once more. He gripped it firmly; it remained pointed right at her, a deterrent to impulsive actions. Thinking furiously, Sam curled her fingers around the wheel and stared almost sightlessly out through the windshield. Trying once more to leap from the truck and run occurred to her, but the last attempt hadn't gone so well and she doubted that exiting any faster was going to be possible: getting the balky door open just couldn't reliably be done in an instant. Maybe a half mile up ahead was the junction with Story Avenue. If she followed Story along to St. Clair, the route would take her past bars and strip clubs where there would be people, i.e., witnesses, which should make him even less likely to shoot her if she jumped. It was also where, she calculated, she had a fairly good chance of encountering a cop. If she had to drive right into the side of a fuzz-mobile to get out of this, that's just what she was going to do.

Only there was the small matter of the two men she had just shot. It had absolutely been self-defense, but what would it take to convince the cops of that? In East St. Louis, the residents universally mistrusted police. The police, in nice reciprocation, equally universally mistrusted the residents. In the "us" versus "them" world in which she had grown up, the cops were "them."

They probably weren't going to believe her. And even if somebody ultimately did, how long would it take to convince the powers that be to release her from jail, where she was sure to be taken as soon as the first cop got the first whiff about there being two dead bodies involved?

If she was taken into custody, even for a short while, what would happen to Tyler? Kendra would take care of him, as would Mrs. Menifee, but . . .

Sam felt the tiny muscle beneath her left eye start to twitch. An annoying barometer of her emotional state, it was something that happened when she was under extreme stress. Automatically pressing a cool forefinger against the jumping spot, she cast her captor a look of supreme loathing.

"I don't want any part of this," she said. "Whatever's going on, it's got nothing to do with me."

"It does now."

That was so horrible to contemplate that, staring at him, Sam drove off the road again.

"Watch out!" His one good eye widened with almost comical alarm even as the vibration of the tires rolling onto the shoulder jerked her attention forward. It was just in time to allow her to avoid driving straight into a drainage ditch. She yanked the wheel, and with a couple of bounces they were on the pavement once more. "The last thing we need is for you to wreck us. The goal is for us to get away from here, remember?" He sounded like he was speaking through his teeth. "Although probably the gunshots and squealing tires back there screwed the whole 'let's try to sneak away quietly' thing. To say nothing of the fucking air horn."

"You can have the truck, okay?" Sliding him a sideways glance, Sam wet her dry lips. They were nearing the intersection with Story, which was a little far from her duplex, although the distance didn't constitute anything resembling a problem under the circumstances. She could hitchhike. She could walk. Whatever it took. "Just let me go and take it. I won't report it stolen, I swear."

"With my leg like it is, I can't drive." He said it flatly, as though that was the end of the discussion. The words rang in Sam's head like the tolling of some terrible bell. If he couldn't drive, he wasn't going to let her go. He needed her. God help her.

The atmosphere inside the truck was suddenly thick with tension. As the hard truth sank in, Sam stared up ahead without really seeing anything.

"What part of 'we're on the same side' did you fail to understand back there?" His voice was lower and grittier, and, glancing at him, Sam got the impression that he was in considerable pain. She had a happy thought: *maybe he'll pass out.*

Then what?

I'll push him out of the truck and drive like hell.

Call that plan B. What she needed was a plan A. Something that was actually likely to work.

Maybe she could reason with him.

She took a deep breath. "Look, whatever you're involved in, I don't want anything to do with it. I'll drop you off anywhere you say, okay? Just tell me where."

A beat passed. "Fair enough."

Did that constitute a deal? Sam couldn't be sure, and realized she wouldn't trust it even if she thought it did. He had given in way too easily: it didn't take genius to suspect that he was stringing her along, trying to keep her cooperative while he got what he wanted out of her. His breathing was sounding a little ragged; out of the corner of her eye, Sam watched as he gingerly touched the far side of his thigh just below the constricting belt and winced. She couldn't see the wound itself—it was on his outer thigh—but she surmised it was bad. His face hardened as he glanced up and caught her looking at him.

"First thing we need to do is lose the BMW. It's got a GPS in it, and believe me, as soon as they realize what's happened they'll be tracking us by it. What's involved in unhooking it? Can you do it from inside the truck?"

He didn't *sound* like he was about to lose consciousness.

Damn. Sam shook her head even as the thought of being tracked by GPS made her heart beat faster.

"I have to get out to work the winch."

He gave her a long look. "You're going to run away from me the first chance you get, aren't you?"

The answer was so obvious that she didn't know why she even bothered to lie. "No."

"Maybe I better explain that those guys you shot back there are just a small part of the crew who'll be looking for us as soon as they realize that I—we—escaped. They're ruthless, vicious killers, and they're going to keep coming after us, you understand?"

Just the idea that a gang of ruthless, vicious killers might be coming after her made Sam nauseous.

"Us?" Sam shook her head. "Oh, no. Uh-uh. There's no 'us' in this. There's you. They're coming after you. Not me."

"I hate to burst your bubble, baby doll, but they're coming after you, too." His voice was grim.

Sam felt cold sweat popping out around her hairline. "Not if you let me go."

"It's too late for that. Even if I didn't need you to drive, you'd only wind up getting yourself killed."

A single traffic light suspended on a drooping wire marked the Y-shaped intersection. It was red although they were the only vehicle within sight on either road. Even though they were still a couple of blocks away, Sam started applying the brakes, and they in turn started to groan in protest. She paid no attention as she considered her next best step. Story ran east. East was the direction she meant to take. East led to people, possible escape opportunities, the heart of East St. Louis, and eventually, home and Tyler. North-south, following the path of the river, was the other choice. South led to a whole lot of nothing, while north eventually provided access to the Poplar Street Bridge, which carried three interstates across the Mississippi into St. Louis itself and beyond.

As the intersection grew closer, she applied more force and the brakes groaned louder. Sam took a deep breath and looked at him. "I've got a kid, okay? A four-year-old boy. Whatever you're into, I can't be a part of it. I'm a single mother, and I'm all he has."

He looked at her for a moment without saying anything. His eyes narrowed. His lips tightened. "I'm sorry to hear that." Sam was just starting to think that maybe her words had made a difference when he added, "I hate to break this to you, but that doesn't change a thing. You think the people who are chasing us are going to cut you any slack because you've got a kid? Nice dream world you're living in."

"If you let me go—" Desperation laced her words.

"We'll talk about it," he interrupted. "Later. Once you get me to where I want to go." He paused, glanced away, looked back at her. "So, where's your kid?"

CHAPTER FIVE

The question jolted Sam. No way was she telling him *that*.

"What's it to you?" The look she shot him crackled with suspicion.

"They can't find you, they might very well go after him. It's the way these bastards work."

Sam's chest tightened with horror, rendering any answer impossible for the moment. Her stomach plunged straight to her toes. As they reached the intersection, she smashed the protesting brakes into the floor, grinding them down until the truck came to a full stop.

"They'd go after a little kid?" She found she could talk again, barely, as the truck, swinging wide, got under way once more. The idea that Tyler might be in danger flooded her system with icy waves of panic. It was an effort to try to think clearly, but she did her best. And what she came up with was, rush home, grab Tyler, and run.

Only she had to ditch Quasimodo first.

"They take him, they get leverage. They kill him, it instills fear."

"Kill him?" Heart thudding, Sam had to consciously order herself to take a breath. "He's *four*. What kind of monsters are they?"

"You said it: monsters." He hadn't objected to her left turn, but now he pointed right. "Pull into that alley." He indicated a shadowy path that snaked between a broken-down service station and a closed Italian restaurant to disappear into the darkness beyond. "We'll cut the BMW loose there." He threw her a sharp look. "And if you're thinking of cutting and running, just keep in mind that if you do, when they find the BMW—and they will—they'll find this wrecker still attached to it. They'll use it to track you down."

Sam felt her stomach tighten. Finding her wouldn't be hard: the license plate was registered to her. To say nothing of the fact that the name of the business—Sam's Towing Service—along with her cell phone number was painted in big, glow-in-the-dark white letters along both sides of the truck.

What could she say? It had seemed like a good idea at the time. Now, just thinking about how big those letters were and how easy they were to read in the dark made her want to give her clueless previous self a swift kick in the butt.

"Yeah, that's right, your name's on it." It was like he could read her mind. "And a phone number that I bet is yours is on there, too. Great big. Hard to miss."

"Both those men back there are dead," she said in a constricted voice as she followed his directions and pulled into the alley. "They were the only ones who saw me. There may be an army of killers after *you,* but they're not after me. Once I get the BMW unhooked, they won't even know I exist."

"That's one of the reasons I finished them off. I was trying to make sure you'd be safe."

Her expression must have been doubtful, because he continued, "It's the truth. And look at the thanks I got: you tried to run off and leave me. No, you tried to run over me. Not nice."

Sam shot him a look. "Sorry if I didn't quite get that you were trying to help me out back there by killing two men."

"You shot them first, baby doll."

"I had no choice! You were right, they were going to kill me! And you." She shot him a furious look. "I saved your ass. And look at the thanks I got: you're kidnapping me!"

The slight quirk at the corner of his lips almost could have been the beginnings of a smile. It vanished as quickly as it appeared.

"What can I say? Shit happens."

"*Shit happens?*" Her voice quivered with indignation. "We're talking about my life here. And my son's life. Those two men are dead. They can't identify me. You've got to let me go."

"Can't." He shook his head. "Now that I've had time to consider it, I don't think those two jerk-offs being dead is going to be enough to get you off the hook. I grant you that they're looking for me, but what do you think the odds are that somebody didn't see you hooking your truck up to the BMW to tow it away? Then there are always surveillance cameras. Google Earth, even. They'll be moving heaven and earth to find me, and the smart money says they're going to stumble across you in the course of the hunt. I wouldn't want to bet against it."

Sam went cold with fear as she remembered the partying going on across the street from where she had picked up the Beemer. As noisy as Big Red was, it was more likely than not that somebody had noticed what she was doing. And Google Earth—there was no escaping Google Earth.

She almost wailed, "I didn't see anything. I don't know anything."

"Yeah, well. These guys aren't the type to take a chance on that. They're big believers in scorched earth. Pull in here. This should work."

They were behind the service station now, approaching an empty lot that already held the chassis of an eighties-era Impala riding on cement blocks where its wheels had once been. He indicated the lot with a gesture. It was dark, shadowy, strewn with trash. A gravel parking area just off the alley at the front of the lot was overgrown with weeds. Scrub bushes grew tall against a broken-down privacy fence at the rear. A single-story building that Sam took to be a garage shielded the near side of the lot from view, while what appeared to be a metal storage shed squatted on the other side. The backs of various three- and four-story brick buildings crowded together across the alley. All the structures were dark and seemingly deserted, forming a wall of dense black rectangles that looked like uneven teeth getting ready to take a chomp out of the star-sprinkled charcoal of the sky.

"Turn off the lights," he directed, and she did. The night

swallowed them. Sam immediately felt safer: at least no one chasing them down Story would be able to look over and see where they were.

Of course, the bad guys didn't need to see them to find them, she reminded herself grimly. They had the Beemer's GPS.

Wincing a little as Big Red rumbled noisily into the lot, she steered it around in a circle so it was facing forward again, haunted by the fear that they might need to make a quick exit. Knowing that at that exact moment a gang of killers might very well be tracking the Beemer's every movement alarmed her to the point where the only thing she wanted to do was get away from it. Braking, praying the resultant sounds weren't as loud as they seemed to her, she couldn't slam the gearshift into park and get out of the door fast enough.

"Hang on." Quasimodo grabbed her wrist again even as she wrestled with the damned uncooperative door latch.

"What?" Yanking against his hold in a futile attempt to free her wrist, she glared at him. If he were weakening, his grip showed no sign of it. His fingers were warm and strong. Except for a slight sheen of sweat on his forehead and maybe an increased degree of tightness around his mouth, he looked no different than when she had first set eyes on him. "Let go of me. Let's get this done."

"Just one thing first." Without releasing her, he reached over the back of the seat into the rear compartment.

"What?" Jiggling with nervous impatience, Sam watched as he grabbed the jumper cables she always kept on a pair of hooks above the shelflike rear seat and hauled them into the front. His damaged finger stayed stiffly erect while the rest of his hand curved around the cord. It was now the approximate girth of a hot dog in marked contrast to the rest of his long, tapering fingers, and just looking at it told her it had to hurt. *Not my problem.* "What do you want with those? According to you, we're running out of time."

"We are."

"So?" She yanked at her wrist again, still without results.

"I'm not taking any chances." He thrust the jumper cables at her. They were twenty feet long, maybe an inch in circumference, black, with the flexibility of a bungee cord and a pair of colorful clamps dangling from both ends. "Tie the cord around your waist."

"What?"

"Do it."

She understood then: he was afraid she was going to run away. Well, she was, first chance she got, but that didn't stop her from feeling a rush of indignation.

"Now," he ordered.

Her lips compressed. Arguing was a waste of time, she concluded. Taking the cable, wrapping one end around her waist, Sam cast him a fulminating look. "You can trust me to dump the BMW, you know."

"Funny thing is, I actually believe that. But can I trust you after, is the question."

When Sam didn't reply—if he knew she was lying, what was the point?—he made a gesture with her gun at the cord she had looped around her waist.

"Tie it. In a knot."

She did.

"Once more." He indicated the knot. Sulkily, Sam made another loop. The knot wasn't anything she couldn't untie, but it would take a moment, and that would give him time to stop her. She knew it, and he knew it, which was why the look she gave him when she was done was venomous.

"Satisfied?"

"For now. Out my side." Hanging onto the other end of the cable, he opened the passenger-side door—not without having to put some force into it, because it tended to stick, too—and slid to the ground. Since the truck had been modified to carry out its mission of carting off repossessed vehicles as unobtrusively as possible, the cab's interior light had long since been disabled. Except for random night sounds, the empty lot stayed as dark and silent as a graveyard. Following him out, she was encouraged to see that he was bent almost double and leaning heavily against the side of the truck. She could hear the harsh rasp of his breathing. He was growing weaker, she thought hopefully. Maybe the prospect of him passing out wasn't quite as much a case of wishful thinking as she had supposed.

"Cut the car loose," he ordered as he saw her looking at him.

She didn't need him to tell her. In this one matter they were in perfect accord. The idea that the bad guys might be homing in on the Beemer's GPS and even at this moment might be closing in on them made her blood run cold.

The motor operating the winch had never sounded so loud. Sam winced as she switched it on and it roared to life, but there was no help for it. There was no other way to put the car down. If anybody hunting them got within earshot, it was all over. The darkness, the deserted lot, the late hour, wouldn't help one iota in the face of that nerve-jangling noise. Might as well beam a giant spotlight in the sky flashing *"we're here, we're here, we're here"* and have done. By the time the Beemer's front wheels touched the ground, Sam was so antsy she was ready to jump out of her skin. Her heart pounded like a piston in her chest. She was breathing way too fast. Casting anxious glances all around, she ran to disconnect the sling even as the car was still settling onto its tires.

"Come *on*." Like a dog coming up short on the end of a too-restrictive leash, she gave an impatient tug to the cord tethering her to him as she moved faster than Quasimodo could keep pace. Unfastening the sling was the work of only a few moments, but she was sweating by the time she was done. At any second she expected to see cars screeching into the alley after them. Waiting impatiently as the winch and sling swung back into place, she shifted from foot to foot while her eyes darted everywhere. Her captor betrayed no similar signs of anxiety. He leaned against the truck's rear fender just a few feet from where she guided the winch back into position. His head was lowered, his shoulders slumped, and the foot of his wounded leg barely touched the ground. The gun was no longer aimed at her, but rather pointed down. His hold on the cable that served as her leash seemed slack. Was he still watching her? She couldn't be sure: the shadows obscuring his face were too dense.

As she shut the motor down and secured the winch and sling, she kept a covert eye on him. What was the likelihood that she could give the cable a hard jerk and successfully wrench the other end away from him? How was he holding it? She couldn't quite see, but it was in his left hand, and she remembered that injured finger. How secure could his grip be? If she tried and succeeded, then maybe she could jump inside the truck and drive away. Or even just run for it. She was, she calculated, maybe seven miles from her duplex. On foot, it would take her . . .

"Let's go." He straightened and tightened his hold on the cable even as she did the math. She wondered if something in her body language had given her away.

Whatever, she had lost the chance. He now stood straighter, seeming fully alert. And he was definitely watching her. In response to his gesture, she walked around to the passenger door and opened it. A tiny glow deep in the recesses of the foot well caught her attention: her phone. Her eyes widened. Her heart lurched. His injuries made him slow, and he hadn't quite caught up with her yet; she had still been contemplating the possibility of jumping inside and trying to slam and lock the door in his face when she had spotted her phone. Instead she used those few precious seconds to snatch up her phone, then slid it into the front pocket of her jeans as she clambered up into the truck and slid across into the driver's seat.

First chance she got she was calling 911. Whether they believed she'd acted in self-defense or not, she would way rather deal with the police than with whatever murderous criminals were on Quasimodo's trail. At least with the police she wouldn't have to worry about Tyler's safety.

Although if they put her in jail, what would happen to him? And if Quasimodo was telling the truth and not just exaggerating to scare her, and someone went after Tyler, how would she be able to protect him if she was locked up in a cell?

Worrying the matter like a dog with a bone, she automatically started to untie the knot in the cord around her waist.

"Leave that alone, and get us the hell out of here." Quasimodo sounded short of breath as he hitched himself onto the seat beside her and closed the door. The other end of the jumper cable was not only held in his left hand, she saw; it was also wrapped around his left arm, which meant that just jerking the cord out of his grip and running wouldn't have worked even if she had tried it. He wasn't taking any chances on losing her, it seemed, and his forethought earned him a spurt of grudging admiration. The gun he had thrust into the waistband of his jeans. The butt protruded; he would be able to grab it easily. His wounded leg angled stiffly down into the foot well, so that he had to turn sideways in the seat to accommodate it. He wasn't looking at her, but rather out through the passenger-side window. It was hard to be sure, but she thought his expression was grim. Sam followed his gaze, then stiffened, her attention riveted by the intermittent bursts of light that he, too, must be watching. The headlights of a car speeding down Story, just glimpsed between the buildings lining the street. Identifying the light bursts made her breath catch.

The car was moving way too fast to be anything but bad news, and it was coming from the direction of the scrap yard. Of course, there were lots of reasons cars might be speeding through East St. Louis, and a number of places in that general direction that the car could have been coming from besides the scrap yard, but still she caught her lower lip between her teeth and wrenched the truck into gear.

"Go left." There was tension in his voice.

Since left was away from Story, she was down with that. Even as she complied, Sam saw a second set of headlights racing behind the first.

Her hands tightened on the wheel. It was tempting to floor it, but trying to speed away over the alley's pitted asphalt would, she feared, make way too much noise. At the best of times the truck was an unpredictable collection of rattles and groans. At full speed, over rough terrain like the broken pavement of the alley, it could get loud enough to wake the dead. All it took was one person looking out one window to see what was up. Just in case no one from the tenements had noticed her truck preparing to tow away the Beemer earlier, she didn't want to draw anyone's attention to the name and number on the side of the truck now.

"Do you think that's them?" She glanced fearfully back over her shoulder as she spoke. The first vehicle was nearing the gas station. If it were following the Beemer's GPS signal, it would turn into the alley in the next few seconds.

"Don't know." He shifted so he could look out the rear window as she drove as fast as she dared toward the end of the alley.

The truck trundled over the ruts, making way more noise than Sam would have liked even at the relatively sober speed she was keeping it to. With the window blown out, she could hear every clank and rattle. "But I'd rather not find out."

"Me neither." Nearing the end of the alley, Sam braked just enough to make the turn safely. Remembering the brake lights, which were intact, she winced at the sudden mental picture she had of them glowing brilliant orange through the darkness. The alley was straight; anyone turning in would be able to see the twin red lights shining at its far end. As the truck slowed with its usual painful screech, she glanced fearfully into the rearview mirror. As far as she could see, there were no head-lights turning into the alley, which didn't mean that it couldn't happen at any second.

"Not that way." He shook his head as she eased up on the brake and started to pull the wheel around so they were headed toward town. "Go north."

Her eyes widened. "There's nothing that way."

"The expressway on-ramp is that way."

The expressway on-ramp. Where was he planning to make her drive him? Her already frayed nerves stretched tighter. She couldn't just disappear.

"Home's the other way. I need to go home. Like I said, I have a little boy." There was a note of genuine desperation in her voice.

CHAPTER SIX

"You really want to take this home with you?" Quasimodo must have read the instant negative in her face, because he gave a jerk of his head toward the north and once again said, "That way."

Sam's lips tightened, but she turned the way he wanted. What choice did she have? Leading trouble right back to Tyler was the very last thing she wanted to do. He would be asleep right now in his bed in their duplex, with Mrs. Menifee stretched out on the couch, probably sleeping, too. *Take me home safe to him.* She wasn't a praying person, because in her experience praying was pretty much a waste of time, but for Tyler's sake she sent the plea winging skyward as she cast another glance at the rearview mirror: still nothing. But the truck had no sooner made the turn and started to chug away down the street than she caught a glimpse of headlights pulling into what she thought, from the headlights' position, must be the other end of the alley the truck had just exited. She sucked in air. Her heart skipped a beat.

"Look," she breathed, but he was already looking. From his

expression she knew he was harboring the same suspicion she was. "Do you think it's them?"

"No way to be sure."

But his tone told her that he thought it was likely.

Her stomach tied itself into a knot. "That was quick."

"Yeah, well, they want me real bad."

Her chest tightened.

"Why?" The question was almost a wail. It emerged of its own volition even as she glanced fearfully back at the lights.

"Let's just say I pissed some people off."

Sam's lips tightened as she shot him a scathing glance, but she knew that was all the explanation she was going to get. She didn't really want to know the answer anyway. Like he had said earlier, the less she knew, the safer she probably was. One thing she had learned in the course of growing up in East St. Louis was that too much curiosity could get you killed. Mind your own business, do your own thing, look the other way: those were words to live by. Anyway, she didn't care what Quasimodo had done. All she wanted was to get away from him, grab her son, and run somewhere safe where she could hide until it was all clear and things got back to normal. To think that earlier she was pretty much hating her life. Would she ever complain about it again? Knowing herself, Sam gave a wry inner grimace. Probably, but only after this night was a distant memory. Because at least in her regular life she and Tyler were together, and she wasn't afraid they were going to die. Panic dampened her palms and dried her throat as she thought of her son: whatever it took, she had to get back to him. Fighting off the urge to scream or launch herself on her captor or do something else totally unproductive, she looked toward the headlights again. Had the car stopped? She couldn't tell for sure. It would have stopped if whoever was driving had been looking for the Beemer and found it.

"You got any more bullets for this gun?" He had pulled the revolver out of his waistband and was checking the cylinder.

The question rattled her. "No." A building blocked her view of the alley. No way to tell what was up with the headlights now.

"Too bad." Snapping the cylinder back into place, he thrust it back into his waistband.

Sam's heart stuttered. "What, are you planning a shootout?"

"I like to know where I stand."

Her eyes fastened on him. She realized that until now she must have been in some kind of shock that had dulled her responses. Fear suddenly felt as sharp and painful as a stomach full of glass shards. She was cold all over, and breathless.

Her mouth was so dry she had to swallow before she could speak. "Let me go. Please."

He met her gaze. Her eyes blazed with intensity, she knew. For a moment, as their gazes met, she thought—maybe. Then he gave a single negative shake of his head.

"Like I said, it's too late for that."

"Bullshit." Casting another scared glance toward the alley, she saw another building instead. It was one of a long row lining the block. Her pulse thundered in her ears. The look she shot him was hunted. "You could absolutely let me go if you wanted to, and we both know it."

"We've been over this before: I can't drive. Anyway, even if I could let you go, I wouldn't. You'd just get yourself killed."

Try as she might, she could see nothing more of what was happening around the Beemer, so she ignored her pounding heart to concentrate on putting as much distance between them and it as she could. The street was largely deserted so late at night, but signs that people were near abounded. Cars were parked all along the curb. A man emerged from one of them and hurried inside a building even as the wrecker trundled past. A couple of lights in upstairs windows made Sam think that they were apartments in which people might be still awake. Knowing that potential help was so close was tantalizing, but she knew, too, that there was no way to take advantage of it. Closing her mind to the impossible, she stepped harder on the accelerator. Seeing what the headlights in the alley were up to was now impossible; escaping while the escaping was good was something she could still do.

"Suppose you let me worry about me," she said.

"Suppose you keep your eyes on the road."

Sam swallowed the retort that immediately sprang to her tongue. Antagonizing him wouldn't be helpful, so the best thing she could do was keep a lid on it for now. Be reasonable, let him think she was going to do exactly what he said, watch for her opportunity and take it. That was the plan.

"So where are we going?" The truck rattled and banged as it picked up speed. As Sam glanced in the rearview mirror again, anxiety formed a cold knot in her chest. Her pulse skittered and jumped. Two vehicles were on the road behind them. Had either of them pulled out of the alley while she was watching the road? There was no way to be sure.

"Somewhere else." His voice was dry. "Uh, probably be a good idea to turn on the headlights."

"Oh. Right." Sam had forgotten they were off. Another way to attract unwanted attention: drive through the increasingly dark streets without lights. That she had forgotten was a good indication of how rattled she was, she thought as she pulled the knob that turned them on. Immediately the bright beams slashed through the night. Instead of feeling safer, Sam felt like she now had a glowing neon target on her bumper.

If they were spotted, the situation was not likely to end well. In any chase, the wrecker was not going to win. And if it came to a shootout—Sam shuddered.

I can't get killed. I have to get back to Tyler. Stress quickened her breathing.

"Remember, they're not looking for your wrecker. Yet."

His words were so spot on that it was almost as if he had read her mind. Casting him a careful look, Sam let out the breath she hadn't until that moment realized she was holding.

"I don't want any part of this."

"So you've said. Sorry, I'm fresh out of magic wands that I can wave to make this whole thing go away. Truth is, you're in it and you're stuck."

"I don't have to be," she said. "You could get me out of this real quick by letting me go."

"Give it up, baby doll." His voice sounded grim. "It's not happening. So why don't you just concentrate on driving?"

Sam didn't say anything for a moment. Various scenarios that might afford her a chance to escape chased themselves through her head.

"Soon we're going to need to get some gas," she said.

He leaned over to look at the gauge. It was down to about an eighth of a tank. Her words weren't a complete ploy: the wrecker drank gas. An eighth of a tank wouldn't get them far.

"We're good for now."

So much for that. Well, she hadn't really expected it to work. She needed to find a way to call the cops and turn the whole thing over to them. The phone was practically burning a hole in her pocket, her secret ace in the hole. There was no way to use it with him sitting right beside her, though. She would have to wait.

The question was, *should* she call 911?

Or maybe just Kendra for a ride home?

Oh, God, then Kendra would be involved. Putting her friend in danger was the last thing she wanted to do. After endangering Tyler, that is.

"Look at it this way," Quasimodo said. "The good news is, you're still alive."

Once again she had the unnerving feeling that he knew what she was thinking. Which, of course, was impossible. She cast him a hostile look. "Just so you know, that sucks."

"What? Being alive?"

"The fact that that's the good news."

The sound he made almost could have been an aborted laugh. Certainly his grim expression relaxed for a moment. Casting another anxious glance in the rearview mirror, Sam was in no mood even to smile.

"You wouldn't have any water in here, would you?" he asked after a minute.

Her response was short. "No."

But the idea that he possibly wanted water because he was weakening gave her hope.

The next couple of blocks took them past rows of run-down buildings punctuated by towering signs advertising everything from Wild Turkey whiskey to Larry Flynt's Hustler Club, which was one of a number of strip bars lining the express-way into St. Louis. Then the populated area thinned out until there was nothing much left except miles of broken concrete and tunnel-like underpasses. The road stretched away into a moonlit darkness filled with rusting railroad trestles and weed-filled empty lots and the occasional derelict building as it wound through what was essentially wasteland toward the distant pinpoint of light created by the giant streetlights that marked the expressway on-ramp. Other vehicles were few and far between, but each time she saw a pair of headlights Sam's heart jumped. A motorcycle roared up behind and then zoomed around them, making her tense up as lightning visions of a lone assassin firing through the window as he passed filled her head. An ancient minivan, trundling along behind them for a mile or so, practically gave her palpitations. A late-model, dark-colored Lexus popping out of a side street to purr in their wake made her breath catch. The longer it stayed behind them the more nervous she grew. Was it . . . ?

She was just opening her mouth to draw it to Quasimodo's attention when the Lexus veered off down a side street.

"You have a first-aid kit in this thing?" They were the first words he'd spoken in several minutes, and she was so focused on what the Lexus was doing that they made her jump. Immediately she pulled her eyes from the rearview mirror to look at him.

He'd slid down so that his head rested against the seat back. His face was turned toward her; swollen and battered from the beginning, it was now totally covered with a fine sheen of sweat. His hair fluttered in the warm, river-scented air that rushed in through the broken window. His lips were parted as if he were having to work to inhale enough oxygen. His one good eye was ringed with shadows, and there was a tautness around the edges of his mouth that spoke of pain.

In short, he looked in much worse shape than he had when they'd gotten back into the truck after unloading the Beemer. To her disgust, Sam discovered that her first reaction was to feel worried about him.

"In the glove compartment," she replied before she thought. Then she gave herself a mental kick. Helping him was not something that was in her best interest to do. Getting away from him was what she needed to concentrate on. But once the words were out of her mouth, there was no taking them back. He nodded and sat up, which seemed to require a great deal more effort than his previous movements. Leaning forward, he opened the glove compartment—not without some difficulty, because like everything else in the truck the catch was old and temperamental—and pulled out the red plastic box with the white cross on it that had been a staple of the glove compartment forever. It had been put there by the wrecker's original owner, her uncle-by-affection Wilfred Purvis, who had been better to her than most of her own kin until he had died, and whom she still missed. She had only glanced inside it once when she'd needed a Band-Aid, so she had very little real knowledge of what was in there. Leaning back again as if the effort had drained him, Quasimodo opened it, rifled through the contents, and then looked up, frowning at the road ahead. They were running parallel to the river; Sam could occasionally see the water's black gleam in the distance. Closer at hand, a concrete drainage ditch flanked by scruffy trees ran along the edge of the flat fields of the floodplain. What few structures they passed were old, empty, and largely commercial in nature. No signs of human habitation to be seen.

"Pull over behind that building," he directed after a moment, pointing.

"That building" was a three-bay cinder-block garage. The doors were closed, the chain-link fence that had once surrounded it was broken down to the point where more of it was missing than standing, and its nearest neighbor was a burned-out structure that might once have been a house.

Sam was immediately suspicious. "Why?"

"Just do it."

Sam gave him a long, mistrustful look, then reluctantly did

as he said, easing the truck off the road and onto what was left of the pavement before bumping through the grass as she drove around the building.

When she was parked behind the garage, with the engine and lights turned off at his direction, he took a deep, shuddering breath. He was obviously in pain, obviously having trouble staying focused. His eyes were overbright in the moonlight as he looked at her. Once again Sam had to battle back the impulse to worry about him.

"Take off your shirt," he said.

CHAPTER SEVEN

"What?" She looked startled. Alarmed, even. Her widening eyes fastened on him like she was Little Red Riding Hood and he was the Big Bad Wolf.

Well, maybe for her, tonight, he was. But not in the way that was clearly worrying her.

She was definitely pretty enough to make him sit up and take notice under other circumstances. But right at the moment, injured as he was and with Veith and half the Zeta cartel and God knew who else hot on his trail, sex was the last thing on his mind.

The pain in his leg was bad. The sad thing was, Danny knew that it was about to get about a thousand times worse. But he was already past the fifteen-minute limit he'd allotted himself on the tourniquet. Much longer, and he risked doing serious damage to his leg, if not losing it altogether. And now that it was starting to look like he had a real shot at making it out of this alive, he was going to do his best to keep all his body parts attached and functional. On the theory that later they might come in handy.

The girl—Sam—was looking at him like he'd just grown horns.

Oh, right. He'd told her to take off her shirt. The couple of seconds it had taken him to remember why she was giving him that look worried him. His thought processes were starting to go fuzzy, he realized, which was never a good sign. He blinked and scowled, trying to keep sharp. It was hard when his leg burned like somebody had shoved a hot poker through it, and he was feeling more light-headed with every passing second.

"I need something to cover this wound," he explained, because her expression made it clear that thoughts of having her bones imminently jumped were dancing through her head. Which, with him in his current condition, was laughable just on the face of it. He must be doing a better job than he'd thought of pretending that he wasn't on the verge of total collapse if that was what was worrying her. "I'd use mine, but it's too damned dirty."

Relief shone from her eyes. Her face was easy to read, her expressions transparent, her thoughts visible in the curve of her lips, the quirk of her eyebrows, and, of course, her wide blue eyes. Jesus, she was pretty. And young. Too damned young to be caught up in something that could easily get her killed, but there was nothing he could do about that: through no fault of his, or hers, she was well and truly in this thing with him now. Anyway, the impression she gave of vulnerability lost something when he remembered that she'd just coolly shot Torres and Thug Two with the Smith & Wesson revolver she'd been packing. *That* he had not seen coming. Briefly it occurred to him to wonder what a girl, let alone one who looked like her, was doing carrying a gun, but speculating on extraneous things took brain power that he didn't have to spare just then, and anyway he had other fish to fry. Like trying to survive.

"Do it." When she continued to look at him without making a move, he frowned at her. Her lips tightened, and her whole expression turned way less than friendly, but to his surprise she didn't argue. Instead she unbuttoned the loose blue cotton shirt she wore, pulled it free of the cord he'd made her tie around her waist, and handed it over, all without a word. Beneath that boxy uniform shirt, she was wearing a snug white tank that, he saw as she stripped the uniform shirt off, clung to her slim, supple shape like a second skin; he'd caught glimpses of it in the V of her neckline earlier. For such a slim girl, she had nice breasts, not too big, but firm and round as Florida oranges, which it was almost a relief to realize he still was functional enough to notice. Still, he had expected at least some discussion on the subject of taking off her shirt. So far in their acquaintance, she'd argued about everything. But not now.

Again, he didn't have time to worry about the whys and wherefores. In all kinds of hair-raising ways, he was running out of time.

And options.

"What I'm going to do is loosen this tourniquet on my leg." Even though she hadn't asked, Danny spelled it out for her as he folded her shirt into a rectangular pad. The shirt was cotton, soft from what he guessed were repeated washings, hopefully absorbent, certainly cleaner than anything he was wearing.

He kept talking because, like planning his next moves, talking helped him stay focused. "Then I'm going to pull my jeans down. I've got on boxers, so don't freak out. When the wound is exposed, I want you to put this over the hole and apply direct pressure to it. That means press down hard with both hands. When I tell you. Be prepared for blood. A lot of it."

Her eyes narrowed as she glanced at his leg. He followed her gaze: the area around the belt was black with blood and looked—and felt—so swollen that his jeans could have been sausage casing. He got sick to his stomach every time he looked at it. So unless it was absolutely necessary, he just didn't. Only now, it was necessary.

"You really think taking off that tourniquet is a good idea?" She glanced up at him. Her expression was uneasy.

"It is if I don't want to lose my leg. Which I don't." He handed her the folded shirt, then picked up the roll of gauze that had been in the first-aid kit. Along with an Ace bandage, a tube of antibiotic ointment, some surgical tape, and a small pair of scissors, all also from the first-aid kit, that was all he had to work with. He placed each item carefully on the dashboard, within easy reach of his outstretched hand. Once the tourniquet came off, he was going to have to work fast. The darkness was an issue—moonlight only went so far—but he could see well enough to bandage the hole in his leg, and turning on an interior light would make them too visible. Finally, he pulled the pistol out of his waistband and tucked it down into the pocket on the door beside him, which put it out of her reach but kept it close enough where he could grab it if he needed it. When everything was ready, he unbuttoned his jeans and slid his zipper down, the better to get his pants out of the way fast when the tourniquet came off. Then he looked at her.

"Scoot on over here."

"What happens if you bleed out?"

Trepidation showed in every line of her face, but she scooted obediently, sliding toward him until her knee just touched his good leg. Given the angle at which he was situated on the seat, that was as close to him as she was going to get without putting herself through some major contortions. But she was near enough to do what he needed her to do: apply pressure to the wound while he bandaged it up.

"Then I guess you get lucky." Reluctantly, he slid his fingers along the narrow leather strap constricting his leg to where the fastened belt buckle strained to hold it tight above his lacerated flesh. There was no exit wound, at least none that his probing fingers had been able to discover, which meant that the bullet was still in his leg, but digging for it wasn't going to happen under these conditions. He didn't see any way that what he was getting ready to do could be anything but bad, but he equally didn't see any real alternative. The tourniquet had to come off. The wound had to be bandaged. He looked at her bent head. She was intently watching his fingers as they got reacquainted with the cool silver of his belt buckle. "Or not. Just so we're clear, me dying does not get you off the hook. They'll still come after you. And without me around to protect you, you've got about as much chance of surviving as a mosquito in a zapper."

"Protect me?" Her eyes snapped up to meet his. Indignation

sparkled in them. "Since when are you 'protecting' me? You said we were on the same side in the trunk, and then you kidnapped me at gunpoint. You 'protecting me' isn't what's happening here."

She had him there. At least, he could definitely see things from her point of view. "It wasn't my fault you got thrown in that trunk. And, believe it or not, I'm trying to keep you alive."

Her lips curled scornfully. "Get real, why don't you? The person you're trying to keep alive here is you."

"Okay, so I'm trying to keep both of us alive. Same thing."

"No, it definitely is not."

"I'm not going to argue about it. You're just going to have to trust me on this."

The sound she made was rife with derision. But she didn't argue anymore; instead, her gaze shifted to his leg.

"I think you ought to let me take you to a hospital." She was eyeing his leg as if she wanted no part of what was getting ready to happen. Well, fair enough. He didn't want any part of it, either, but they both had to deal.

"I do that, and I'm a dead man. You're dead, too. They know I've been shot, and believe me, they're hoping to capitalize on it. I've got no doubt that they're already keeping watch on all the hospitals in the area. We show up at one, they'll grab us both. Like that." He snapped his fingers.

Her eyes flicked up to meet his. "*Who* are *they*?" was the question he read burning in them, but this time she didn't even bother to ask it. Smart girl, she was learning.

"You bleed to death trying to treat yourself, and you're just as dead." Her voice was flat.

"Do your part, and I won't bleed to death. And maybe we'll both get out of this fiasco alive. Ready?"

She looked alarmed. "No."

"Too bad. Here goes." Taking hold of the dangling end of the belt, bracing himself for what he was about to do, Danny nevertheless succumbed to the smallest of grim smiles as he got a good grip on the buckle that was digging into his flesh. She looked so apprehensive that he couldn't help it. Her eyes were big, her mouth was tight, and she was gripping the pad—white-knuckling the edges of it, actually—in both hands.

"Probably you should know that I'm not a fan of lots of blood," she said, unexpectedly meeting his eyes.

"Me neither. Especially when the blood's mine." Gritting his teeth, he eased the leather free of the buckle, then groaned as the belt loosened, blood flowed in a warm gush, and a wave of agony rolled down his leg. Not pain, mind you. Pain he had been prepared for. But this was something different, like a chainsaw chewing up his leg from the inside out. Gritting his teeth, he lifted his rear off the seat and shoved his jeans down his legs, moving fast before the pain had a chance to overwhelm him. To his surprise, she helped him, gripping the waistband and yanking hard. The feel of the bloody fabric of his jeans releasing its hold on the wound was a revelation, and not in a good way.

"Ah, shit," he breathed as the world receded and he had one final second of clarity in which he knew he was going to faint.

Then he did.

The surprise was that he woke up again. He became aware of something jabbing uncomfortably into the right side of his neck and opened his eyes and turned his head to find out what it was. An outdated, knob-style car door lock, he discovered, was gouging him right in the tender flesh just below his jawbone because his head had been slumped against it. The reason his head had been slumped against it was—it took a second, but then he had it—that he'd passed out. The top of his head protruded through the open window. He realized that when, still slightly disoriented, he glanced up and saw the dense black of the night sky punctuated by stars. The chirping of insects and the rustle of the tall grass surrounding the truck he was sitting in filled his ears. He was . . . where? Then something in his brain clicked on, and the events of the preceding four hours fast-forwarded through his mind in what was basically the highlight reel from hell.

He should be dead already. But he wasn't, not because of the overwhelming might of the various government agencies charged with keeping him safe, not because of his own smarts and physical prowess, but because he'd gotten lucky.

Well, lucky worked. So far.

And he was lucky again, he thought as he shifted position so that he was more or less sitting up back inside the cab, that the window he'd landed on had been made of safety glass and had exploded into nothing when he'd shot it, or he would have been in danger of cutting his throat on the remaining jagged shards when he had keeled over.

"Don't move." A sharp voice caused him to glance down in surprise. A girl—*the* girl: Sam, he identified her almost instantly; yeah, he knew who she was, he wasn't as out of it as all that—crouched in the foot well beside him. She was close, close enough so that he could smell the same faint floral scent he'd caught a whiff of in the trunk earlier, close enough so that his hand brushed the soft cotton covering one warm, firm breast when he moved. He shifted his hand away, of course, but not before registering the unexpected sexiness of the sensation. She'd lost the baseball cap long since, and long, wavy strands of inky hair that had worked loose from her ponytail were tucked behind her ears. Turned slightly sideways as she leaned in over his still-teeth-clenchingly-painful thigh, she filled the space where his legs would have rested under normal circumstances. At the moment, though, he was sprawled in a semireclining position along the cracked vinyl seat with both of his legs from the knees down hanging off into the driver's foot well. His feet were hobbled together by his jeans, which from the feel of things were down around his ankles. After he'd fainted, she'd clearly pulled them well out of her way and gone to work on his wound on her own. So his dignity was in tatters; at least he was alive.

"I passed out." Stating the obvious, he was chagrined to realize that his voice was thin.

"Yes, you did."

Danny took a second to absorb the fierce expression on the pale oval face that she turned up to him, and to appreciate the slender flexibility that allowed her to curl so efficiently into the foot well. Then his gaze moved on to her hands. Even while she frowned at him, she kept a firm hold on the end of the Ace bandage she had apparently just finished wrapping around his injured thigh. She was, he saw, in the process of securing it with small metal clips.

"How's the bleeding?" he asked, his eyes on her. It was dark, but moonlight flooded the truck and her slim fingers moving against the bulky bandage were easy enough to see.

"It was bad. I got it stopped. Lucky for you." There was that word again; he supposed that if he survived this he ought to get it tattooed over his heart. She was no longer looking at him. Instead, she was working the clips into the bandage with deft efficiency. The pertinent leg of his bloodstained blue boxers had been shoved up as high as it would go, presumably to get it out of her way. His bare thigh above and below the bandage was caked with blood. A lot more blood than he remembered seeing when he'd pulled his jeans down, because of course the act of removing his jeans had wiped most of the old blood away.

"So, what happened?"

She shot another quick glance up at him. "You blacked out. You bled like a stuck pig. I saved your life. Again. You owe me. Big time."

If he'd had any strength at all, her truculence would have made him smile. "Duly noted."

Jesus, he felt like shit. The absolute agony in his leg had subsided, but it still throbbed and ached and burned like napalm bubbling through his veins. Even his foot was getting into the act: the only way he could describe the sensation was pins and needles to the nth degree. That was good, probably, because it meant his circulation had been restored, but it hurt like a mother. He had a feeling that, best-case scenario, he wasn't going to be walking anywhere that required more than a few limping steps anytime soon. In addition, he was woozy, with an overall sense of physical weakness that warned him that another fainting spell wasn't out of the question. He couldn't afford to faint again. For whatever reason, she had stayed put the first time, and helped him. He couldn't count on her not booking it if there was a second. And the death squad on his trail was good. He might have lost them temporarily, but if one thing was absolutely certain it was that they hadn't given up. They were going to keep coming until they were stopped, or he was dead. He should try to find a phone and call Crittenden—no, wait, he couldn't. Rick Marco didn't know Crittenden. That was what the fuzzy-headedness was doing to him: putting him in danger of forgetting that he was Marco, and the guiding principle behind this run for his life had to be, what would Marco do?

Shit.

"You okay?" She was frowning at him. Probably he'd gone a little glassy-eyed there, remembering that he had to play this thing out like Marco.

He focused on her again. For whatever reason, that made him feel more on his game. Probably because her life depended on what he did next, too.

"Relatively. How'd you control the bleeding?"

"Pressure point." She shot him a glinting look. Remembering how rucked up the leg of his boxers was, he got the picture:

she'd stuck her hand in his crotch to apply the necessary pressure, which he appreciated, both for the unexpectedly sexy image it conjured up and for the fact that it had worked. "Followed by direct pressure to the wound. After that, I packed the wound with gauze and antibiotic ointment, put my shirt on top of that, and wrapped the whole thing up with more gauze, and tape, and this. Be glad I've taken some EMT classes." She carefully smoothed the bandage. "I think as long as you don't go moving around too much, you won't bleed to death." Her hands were busy, and she wasn't looking at him any longer. Instead, she was gathering up her supplies. "There's no way to be sure, though."

"You've taken EMT classes?" Talking kept him in the moment, which was a good thing. He felt light-headed and queasy, probably from blood loss.

"Yes." She grimaced. "Three, actually. If I keep going at the rate I'm going, I might even manage to get licensed by the time I'm, like, fifty or so."

"So how does that work if you don't like blood?"

She shrugged. "I don't like a lot of things. But without a college degree, there are only so many jobs I can get that pay enough to give my kid a decent life. Being an EMT is one of them. So I suck it up about the blood."

"What about this tow-truck thing you have going on?"

"It works for now. But I only have the one truck, and it's old. When it finally breaks down for good, where am I going to get the money to buy another?"

"What about your kid's father?"

This time the look she shot him was wary.

"What's it to you?"

"Nothing. Just seems hard that you should have to provide for a kid on your own."

"Life's a bitch, or haven't you heard?"

He studied her averted face as she crammed the last of the remaining supplies back into the box, then restored it to the glove compartment. She could have let him bleed to death, but she hadn't. Well, he meant to repay her by keeping her alive.

"You want to help me get my pants back on again, we'll be good to go." Having his jeans down around his ankles was almost as bad as having his legs tied in terms of what it did to his mobility. Plus, it was embarrassing. But he had a bad feeling that he might not be capable of the effort required to do it all by himself. What he needed was some time to recover his strength. Unfortunately, time was something he didn't have to spare.

Her lips compressed, but she reached for his jeans and started pulling them back up over his calves. The feel of her cool hands brushing against his bare skin triggered another one of those instant, instinctive moments of awareness of her as a woman, which was, fortunately or unfortunately, depending on how he looked at it, a little muted by the circumstances. When he could reach the waistband without shifting around too much, he grabbed hold.

"I got this," he said, even though his head swam alarmingly as he moved. Jesus, he felt weak.

"Don't be an idiot." Ignoring his directive, she helped him get his jeans up, which was a good thing. In the end, he wasn't sure he could have managed on his own.

"Ah." Despite his efforts at stiff-upper-lipping it, the sound emerged as he sank back onto the seat less gently than he'd intended and the wound got jostled. She shot him a look, but didn't say anything. Instead, while he fastened and zipped up his jeans, she began to extricate herself from the foot well, moving carefully so as not to jar his injured leg. Her snug white tank was liberally covered with dark streaks now, he saw, and it didn't require much of a mental stretch to figure out that they'd been made by his blood.

"Thank you," he said, meaning it.

"It's only a temporary fix. You still need to get to a hospital," she warned, slithering around him until she was once again sitting behind the wheel. Clearly drained, she slumped against the door, letting her head rest back against her intact window as she looked at him warily. Moonlight played over her face. She was exquisitely pretty: her skin was creamy smooth, her cheekbones were high, her jawline determined but delicate. Her lips were full and soft looking. Her nose was small and straight. Her eyes—by moonlight they were a deep, clear blue—were thickly lashed and faintly slanted. Now that she was minus the shape-concealing uniform shirt, he was able to see that her shoulders were slender but well formed, her arms firm and sleek, and her breasts—well, suffice it to say that even under current conditions he was definitely a fan. The cable cord was still tied around her waist, which was slender and shapely; apparently she had been too consumed with patching him up to take the time to untie it. He undoubtedly would have been feeling guilty about now for forcing her to tie herself to him if what he had told her hadn't been 100 percent accurate: she was in too deep to get out. Without him, she was a dead woman walking, unlikely to live out the next few hours, collateral damage as Veith et al came after him full bore.

"So why'd you do it?" he asked, as he finished inventorying long, slim legs in blue jeans over sturdy black hiking boots and his gaze returned to her face.

"What?"

"Stay. Bandage me up."

"I couldn't just let you bleed to death." Her tone was testy. It didn't take a genius to infer that she was having second thoughts about the wisdom of what she'd just done. Using her teeth to tear open a small foil packet that she'd produced from somewhere, she pulled from it a pair of wet wipes, unfolded them, and proceeded to wipe her face and arms then scrub at her hands. "I'll drive you to wherever you're going—as long as it's fairly close—but then I'm out of this. I have to get home to my son."

Something in her tone told him that she thought the tide of power had turned in her favor. Danny frowned. Arguing with her at this point seemed counterproductive, however, since she had professed willingness to drive at his direction; his best bet was to wait until she was no longer willing and revisit the discussion then, when hopefully his head was a little clearer. He was just coming to that conclusion when an alarming possibility occurred to him. Thrusting a discreet hand down into the door pocket at his side confirmed what he already suspected: she'd taken the gun.

He withdrew his hand slowly. She watched him. From the expression on her face, she knew what was up.

"We're both better off if I have the gun." His tone was even, reasonable.

She snorted. "I don't think so."

"How about if I give you my word I'm not going to shoot you?"

"How about if I give you *my* word I'm not going to shoot *you*?" She paused. "Unless you deserve it."

"Professional killers are hot on our tail. I need to be able to shoot them."

"If they find us, *I'll* shoot them."

"No offense, baby doll, but—"

"Just so we're clear, I'm not your 'baby doll,'" she broke in. She was busy untying the cord around her waist as she spoke. Concluding that since she hadn't bolted while he was unconscious she probably wasn't going to anytime soon, he merely watched as she undid the knot and, with a hard look at him, gathered up the jumper cable and dropped it into the back, where it landed with a clatter on the floor. "And you're not getting my gun back, so you might as well give up trying. Where do you want me to drive you? If I were you I'd make up my mind fast, before I decide my best bet is straight to the nearest police station."

"The police can't protect you. Even if they threw you in jail you wouldn't be safe. These people can get to you anywhere."

"So you say. I just have your word for that."

They exchanged measuring looks.

"Let's get out of here. Head for the expressway." With that, he tacitly conceded that he wasn't going to be wrestling her for possession of the gun anytime soon. Staying on the move was vital if he wanted to keep them one step ahead of Veith. His original intention had been to head across the river into St. Louis. The breached safe house, as well as the other nearby house where Crittenden's group was based, was located over there, in the Riverview neighborhood. But then he remembered that Marco would know nothing of the second house, or hovering FBI agents. All Marco would know was that the U.S. Marshals guarding him hadn't been able to keep him safe, that Veith and the cartel had found him, that he'd escaped by the skin of his teeth, and that he was running for his life.

So what would Marco, badly wounded and panicking, aware that it was just a matter of time until Veith or somebody else equally lethal caught up with him, do?

If he were smart, he'd turn himself back over to the marshals. First of all, he needed medical attention. The patch-up job on his leg wasn't a long-term fix by any means, and if the way he felt was any indication, he needed to get it, as well as his other injuries, seen to pronto. Plus there was the girl, whom his version of Marco was determined to keep safe, which in his present condition he wasn't going to be able to do on his own. All things considered, and tonight's fuck-up notwithstanding, the marshals were probably Marco's best bet for staying alive. And the thing about a fuck-up was, it looked bad on the records of everyone involved. The marshal's office would be pissed, embarrassed, reeling from the black eye. They would pull out all the stops to make sure Marco was safe under their protection. Nobody would be getting through their defenses a second time.

Danny caught himself: he was thinking like an FBI agent again. He had to be careful about that. Nobody, outside his contact and supervisor, Crittenden, and Crittenden's small, elite group, knew that he wasn't Marco, or what his mission really was.

If at all possible, until this operation was over, he needed to keep the deception in place. He wasn't going to die as Marco if he could help it, but as long as he considered that he had at least a decent chance at staying alive he was going to play this out like Marco would.

"So why don't you give me that phone in your pocket?" He held his hand out for it. Watching her slight start and widening eyes flash a look in his direction as he revealed his knowledge of what she undoubtedly considered her guilty secret would have been amusing if he hadn't felt so bad, so light-headed and nauseous and like he was growing weaker by the second. As it was, he just wanted to get them both somewhere safe as quick as he could. Before, as he feared was going to happen soon, he was no longer able to function. "There's a call I need to make."

CHAPTER EIGHT

"You know a place called Miss Kitty's?" Quasimodo covered the mouthpiece of her phone—a cheap, folding silver Nokia, a poor substitute for the piece of technology she had long coveted, which was an iPhone—to glance at her.

"Yes." It was all Sam could do to keep to keep from sounding as out of sorts as she felt. She couldn't believe she had just tamely handed over her phone to him. Just because he'd told her that he needed to call someone who would come and pick him up didn't mean she had to do what he asked. She had the gun; she could have held it on him while she used the phone herself to call 911. Of course, she wasn't going to shoot him, probably, and he knew that, so holding the gun on him wasn't going to act as much of a deterrent. Still, giving him her phone might well have been a step too far. If it came to that, what was she still doing driving this guy around? She'd had the perfect opportunity back there to escape, and she hadn't taken it. He had blacked out; instead of pushing him out of the truck, or even leaping from the truck and running away herself if she was afraid he'd revive before she could get his door open, what had she done? Stayed put and used her training to save his sorry-ass life. Why? At least that had a simple explanation she could latch onto: she was pretty sure that he would have bled to death if she hadn't.

Given that she wasn't feeling bad at all about the two men she'd just shot, why letting this one die had felt different was something she was still trying to work out.

Maybe because of that kiss on her hand. Maybe because she was secretly kind of attracted to him. Maybe because stupidity where men were concerned was her fatal flaw. Who knew?

Examining her own motives had never been something she wasted much time on, but this particular Gordian knot was beginning to unravel in her mind. If she hadn't shot those two men, they would have killed her. She knew it as surely as she knew her own name, and not just because Quasimodo had told her that that was their intent. She had felt it in some deep, instinctive place as soon as the trunk had opened and she'd seen that gun pointing her way.

Quasimodo hadn't harmed her, had never tried to kill her, and in fact had seemed intent on making sure she didn't die.

There was the real difference, not the physical attraction thing, not that any of it really mattered now that the thing was done. What mattered was that, for whatever reason, here she was, listening to him talk on her phone, chauffeuring him around when what she needed to be doing was racing home, grabbing Tyler, and taking off for parts unknown on a long, enforced vacation that she didn't want and couldn't afford.

It was like she and Quasimodo had bonded or something. The thought made her scowl.

"I'll be there. And, hey, Sanders—don't fuck this up." He disconnected, clicked her phone shut, and looked at her. By this time he basically had one good eye: the other was swollen almost shut. His nose was looking more misshapen than ever, too, sort of like a potato stuck in the middle of his face. If in real life he was good-looking, and she suspected he was, right now you couldn't tell it. In other words, it sure wasn't his good looks that had kept her from abandoning him. Maybe she should just chalk it up to her own soft heart.

Yeah, right. She didn't have a soft heart. She'd never been able to afford one.

"They're going to meet us in the parking lot of Miss Kitty's." The words had a forced quality that made her think he was having to work to get them out. He was growing weaker, she could tell, and she would be glad to pass him off to Sanders, whoever he was, and get him off her hands as soon as possible. The good news was, Quasimodo wasn't actually her problem. The not-so-good news was, she had plenty of problems of her own, although the scariest of them were absolutely his fault. "They're heading there now. How far away are we?"

"Maybe ten minutes." Miss Kitty's was a strip club on the other side of town, where it was one in a string of similar establishments. The clubs were the best-paying employers around, hands down, and a lot of young, attractive women in the area worked at them, including a couple of her friends.

"Good." He closed his eyes. Sam felt a niggling of alarm.

"Don't you dare pass out on me again."

A corner of his mouth quirked up in what she was beginning to realize passed for his smile. His eyes opened, and he looked at her.

"You almost sound like you're worried about me."

Sam snorted. "I'm worried about *me.* You passing out complicates my life."

"Just get me to Miss Kitty's." His eyes closed again.

"So what's going to happen when we get to Miss Kitty's?" she asked uneasily. Keep him talking, and he'd be less likely to lose consciousness, she figured. As the truck rattled and bounced over the uneven pavement of the neglected road, the dark closed in around them. Except for the slashing headlights, moonlight was the only illumination. It washed down over the silver towers of an electric power station, over rusting train trestles, over a jumble of abandoned railway cars locked away behind a fence. No other vehicles were anywhere in sight; no people, either. Hitting the gas hard in an effort to speed them on to their destination, Sam started feeling more and more uneasy at the prospect of encountering whomever he was planning to meet.

"Bottom line is, we'll be safe," he said.

"Ye-ah." Probably the drawn-out way she said it was the giveaway to how little she believed in that. Whatever, he opened his eyes again and turned his head to look at her. "Pardon me if I'm have a little trouble accepting that a bunch of criminals can keep anybody safe."

He drew in a long, audible breath. She got the impression

that he was fighting off an onslaught of—something. Pain? Dizziness? She didn't know. "They're U.S. Marshals, okay? You don't have to worry."

Sam gripped the wheel tighter, not sure if this was good news or not. All in all, she was going to go with the "not." "Want to tell me why U.S. Marshals are coming to meet you in Miss Kitty's parking lot?"

"Us. They're coming to meet us. They'll protect you, too."

"Uh-huh." She wasn't a natural dissembler; there was no hiding the skepticism in her tone. The thing was, she couldn't even be sure that anything he was telling her was the truth. And even if it was true, whatever this thing she had fallen into was, she didn't want any part of it. All she wanted to do was go home. And get Tyler. And get out of town. Maybe even flee the country. Only she couldn't afford to. Doing a quick mental review of her bank account, Sam despaired. Until she got paid, she couldn't even afford an entire tank of gas.

"You have to trust me," he said.

"Trust you? I don't know anything about you. Except that for some reason, which you won't tell me, you wound up beaten to a pulp, shot, and stuffed into a car trunk. With a posse of killers on your trail."

"My name's Marco, all right? Rick Marco." The glassiness taking over his eyes scared her. He was talking slowly and carefully, as if forming each word involved a tremendous effort. "I'm kind of in the witness protection program. Some bad people found out where I was, and tonight they came after me. That's what you and your tow truck interrupted. If it wasn't for you, I'd probably be dead now. I'm going to get the marshals to take you into protection, too. And your kid, if you want."

"If I *want*?" She looked at him like he was speaking a foreign language. "You don't have kids, do you?"

"No," he said.

"First thing you need to understand is that whatever goes down, my son and I are a package deal. We're together. And I won't have him put in danger." Her pulse raced as she drove under one final overpass and the bright lights of the expressway exchange popped up in front of her. Suddenly gas stations, car lots, and fast food restaurants crowded in everywhere she looked. Miss Kitty's was close now. There wasn't much traffic; it was too late at night. But there was some. Enough to be comforting—and to make her nervous.

For all she knew the vehicles were full of would-be murderers—or U.S. Marshals. Or both.

"Hmm," he murmured.

"What did you do to get put in the witness protection program, anyway?" Earlier, he'd refused to tell her anything. To keep her safe, he'd claimed. The fact that he was talking now alarmed her. What had happened to the whole *if I tell you I'll have to kill you* thing he'd had going on?

The thought that he considered that she was now so caught up in what was happening that it didn't make any difference what she knew was too terrifying to contemplate.

The truck had already sped past the little cluster of light and commerce surrounding the expressway entrance when it occurred to her that it was taking him a long time to reply. Glancing his way, she felt her stomach drop. His eyes were shut again. As bruised as it was, it was hard to be sure, but she thought his face had gone slack.

Her heart thumped.

"Hey." God in heaven, she was so rattled she'd forgotten his name, which he had just told her maybe three minutes before. As the truck rolled past the giant Repent and Turn to Jesus sign that a church group had erected beside the cluster of nudie clubs she was coming up on, she racked her brain. "Marco?"

That was it. She was sure of it. But he didn't respond. Didn't move. Didn't so much as flicker an eyelash.

He'd blacked out again.

"Marco! Rick!"

Nothing.

What to do? Stop the truck and attempt to revive him? Hurry on to their destination? Dump him? Okay, that last was out, she couldn't just stop, open the door, and let him fall from the truck in the condition he was in, but Sam was still torn between the other two when Miss Kitty's loomed up on her left. A giant neon sign flashed the words *Miss Kitty's* above an image of a woman wearing kitty-cat ears and a long feline tail. When the lights outlining it glowed green, she was wearing a pink bikini. When they glowed pink, she was naked. The long, low white brick building below the sign was situated in the middle of a black asphalt parking lot. Its size would have done justice to a shopping mall. Although it was nearly 4:00 a.m., there were still maybe two dozen cars parked close to the building. No one was in sight, but Sam circled the parking lot warily, staying to the shadows, keeping to its perimeter.

Get the hell out of here.

Every instinct she possessed screamed it. Driving around the back of the parking lot, Sam tried to look in every direction at once. If anyone was there to meet her companion, she couldn't tell it.

"Marco." Reaching over, she tried shoving his shoulder. No response: he was out of it, eyes closed, dead weight.

Shit.

Her nerves were going haywire. She was breathing too fast, sweating, looking everywhere, seeing nothing pertinent.

She shoved him again. "Damn it, Marco—"

Her voice broke off as she spotted a pair of cars turning into the parking lot, one after the other, moving very fast. Big, dark cars: both Tauruses, she thought, or Saturns, which looked almost the same. Her pulse went into overdrive. Her heart thumped in her chest.

"Oh, God, it's them, isn't it?" She jostled her companion again, with the same result as before. "Marco! You've got to wake up."

The cars made a beeline toward her. Sam didn't recall Marco telling Sanders that he would be in a red wrecker, but somehow the cars seemed to know it anyway. Then she got it: the truck was the only other vehicle in the parking lot that was moving, and the only other one with its lights on. They had spotted her as easily as she had spotted them. Fighting back panic, driving slowly, and hugging the far edge of the parking lot as she conducted a furious internal debate about what best to do, Sam clutched the wheel so hard her fingers hurt as she watched the cars racing toward her. Should she stop, or say to hell with it and try to make a run for it?

She only had his word that they were U.S. Marshals, after all. Maybe he was wrong. Maybe he was lying. And even if he were right and telling the truth, did she want to get messed up with U.S. Marshals anyway? What would they do with her—and Tyler? What if they tried to whisk her away without her son? Being in their custody meant being under their control.

Panic tightened her throat, formed a knot in her chest, and quickened her breathing before she managed to tamp it down again. It wasn't like she had a whole lot of options at this point. There was only one way out of the parking lot, and the oncoming cars were between her and it. The realization sent Sam's stomach plummeting.

"*Damn it, Marco, wake up!*" This time, when she shoved his shoulder, it was violently.

"Mm." He made a sound just as the cars got close enough so that she could see that there were two people in each of them, but by then she was too distracted to even glance at him. The cars were no longer traveling in a straight line with one following the other, but parallel with enough space between them to bookend the truck, to box it in. Looking at the four headlights closing in fast, Sam felt like a fist was tightening around her windpipe. Cold prickles raced over her skin. Marshals or not, they were absolutely zeroing in on the truck, and in just a minute or so this thing would be a done deal. She would be at their mercy, to do with as they would. The knowledge was terrifying.

She still hadn't hit the brakes.

Stopping felt like surrender, like ceding control, like putting her fate in the hands of whoever was in those cars. Not stopping let her retain the option of smashing the accelerator to the floor and speeding away.

Or at least it gave her the illusion of retaining the option.

"Marco! They're here." She shoved him. The shove, or the urgency in her tone, must have finally penetrated, because he opened his eyes a slit.

"What?" He sounded groggy.

"Your friends are here," she said, impressed by the steadiness of her own voice as she looked from him to the cars that were now only a few dozen yards away. She had slowed to a near crawl instinctively, probably because somewhere deep inside she knew that fleeing wasn't going to work out. And the reason it wasn't going to work out was that Big Red couldn't outrun those cars. It wasn't possible, although she faced the truth reluctantly. But stopping and just letting whatever happened next happen seemed about as smart as playing Russian roulette.

Marco hitched himself up a little in the seat, and she knew from the direction of his gaze that he was looking at the oncoming cars.

"Stop. Park." His words had a bitten-off quality. Like he was having trouble mustering the strength to speak at all.

"I don't know if . . ." *this is such a good idea,* she was going to say, but her words trailed off as nerves closed her throat. Then she came to the reluctant conclusion that there was nothing else to do *but* stop. If cooperation was her only option, best to act like she was cooperating willingly. Moving like her leg weighed a thousand pounds, she put her foot on the brakes and pressed down.

Screech. Even the brakes seemed to scream that she was making a mistake.

"It's going to be okay. Trust me." He sounded more alert now as Big Red shivered and lurched in apparent protest. For a second, as the truck finally shook to a stop, her eyes held his. *Did* she trust him? The answer was, maybe she did. At least, she trusted him not to kill her. Even to keep her safe if he could. But that left huge, gaping holes that allowed for lots of bad things to happen. Those holes scared her. Her eyes were wrenched from him to the cars as they slammed to a halt mere feet from both the front and back bumpers. Just like that, any semblance of choice had been taken out of her hands: the truck was well and truly blocked in. Game over. Nothing to do. Even as Sam registered that and felt fresh panic surge through her veins, two clean-cut men in dark suits leaped from each of the cars and converged on the truck.

They were armed.

Her stomach cramped.

"You never . . ." Sam began, shooting Marco an accusing look, but she didn't finish because two of the men appeared at Marco's window just then, looming up behind him, drawing his attention as well as hers.

"Get out," one of them ordered him. The tone, the attitude:

cop to crook. It was eye-opening. She'd known it, of course, but still Sam felt a suffocating rush of dismay. *So what's the big surprise?* she asked herself fiercely. He'd been in custody; they were treating him like he was a criminal. And that would be because he *was* a criminal. Somehow that nugget of truth hadn't really crystallized in her brain before.

So are they going to treat me like I'm a criminal, too? Sam thought of the two men she'd shot and felt a spurt of panic. *Do they know? Will that make a difference? Oh, God, am I making a huge mistake here?*

A tap on her window brought her gaze swinging around. The other two men in suits stood just outside her window frowning in at her. Both looked like they could have been marshals, but then, she wasn't about to rely on that. Books and covers, she knew the drill. One sure thing was that both carried pistols, which meant they both were to be treated warily. The man closest to her pecked on her window again with an imperious forefinger. Like he expected her to just reach right down and open the door for him.

"Talk about your fuck-ups," Marco said to the men on his side, drawing her gaze again. His tone confirmed what she already knew: he had issues with them.

"Tell me about it." One of the marshals, if that's who these guys really were, reached through the broken window to pull up the lock on Marco's door. He was stocky and blunt featured, with dark brown hair cut military style. "Won't happen again, though."

Marco replied, "Once was plenty," and the two men exchanged less-than-friendly looks.

I'm getting a really bad feeling here.

"I don't like this," Sam said and Marco looked around at her.
Their eyes met. Stupid to feel like he was somebody she could
count on now, when fear and indecision were running rampant
inside her. When she didn't know anything about him, really.
When he was the one who'd been in the custody of U.S. Marshals, who'd been nearly murdered by criminals, and who was
being taken back into custody now.

"Stay cool," he told her as his door was jerked open. "Just do
what they—" He broke off as the men reached in to grab him.
Yelping "Hey, watch the leg!" Marco was hauled ungently out
of the truck.

Sam's stomach twisted into a pretzel.

"Open the door, please." The tapping on her window
morphed into an aggressive knocking accompanied by the impatient jiggling of her door handle. Sam's head whipped around
to check it out: the first guy, who she now registered had a
blond buzz cut and a pugnacious expression, was trying to get
in her door. Just beyond his shoulder, the other guy, tall and
thin and bald as a billiard ball, glared in at her. With her peripheral vision, she watched Marco on the ground, his arms draped
around the shoulders of the two men who'd pulled him out of
the truck, being hustled away in a fireman's carry toward the
car blocking the truck in from the front.

"You! Open up," Blondie boomed. His tone made it clear: he

was in charge. Sam's heart thumped. The underlying message was: she had no choice but to do what he told her.

No. But she didn't say it out loud.

They'll take me into custody, too. What's going to happen to Tyler?

"I'll go around to the other side," the second guy said.

Blondie nodded, and the other guy started walking toward the front of the truck. Watching him, Sam's breathing suspended. Her heart thumped like it was trying to beat its way out of her chest.

To hell with this.

That thought sprang fully formed into her consciousness, stiffening her spine, sending warm darts of courage to penetrate the cold fear that held her in thrall. Sam made up her mind just like that: she wasn't giving herself over to these guys, U.S. Marshals or not. She was going to take care of herself, and her son, in her own way.

I've got to get out of here.

How?

The solution came to her in the blink of an eye. Big Red might not be able to outrun the cars. But there was another way . . .

Grabbing for the seat belt, she yanked it around herself and clicked it into place.

"Hey." Blondie rapped the window, scowling through the glass at her. The other guy was almost even with the front of the truck. "You're just making this hard on yourself."

It was now or never.

Her hands still clutched the wheel. She still stood on the brake.

Taking a deep breath, Sam moved her foot, slamming it down hard on the gas. The engine roared. There was a moment's lag time; jaw tight with determination, she stared straight ahead, concentrating on her target. With her peripheral vision she saw Blondie's eyes widen. Baldie's head whipped around. Then the transmission caught, and the truck hurtled forward. Slow and cumbersome, it was also big and heavy as hell. Big and heavy enough to do what she needed it to do. The men half carrying Marco to their car—it was parked maybe two yards away from her front bumper—leaped out of the way in the nick of time, nearly dropping Marco on his butt in the process. Even as she registered their wide-eyed, slack-jawed expressions, Sam closed her eyes. She just had time to brace herself before the truck slammed into the side of the sedan.

Boom! The sound of the crash was as loud as an explosion. Flung violently forward, she was grabbed by the seat belt—the truck was too old for air bags—and held fast before she could hit anything damaging. Her eyes popped open. The Taurus flew sideways, the shiny black metal crumpled like a squashed Coke can with both front and rear doors caved in.

Yes! Sam yanked the gearshift into reverse even as she reoriented herself in the seat. Then, looking over her shoulder at her second target, she stomped the gas again. Outside, the men, Marco included, yelled threats and curses. Sam didn't even try to understand the specifics of what they were saying. Three of the suits started running toward her, shouting and raising their guns like they would open fire, while the fourth one stayed where he was, supporting Marco. Sam registered all this in a split second as her head whipped around to watch where she was going through the rear windshield. She held on tight to the wheel as the truck shot backward, slamming into the car behind. *Boom!* Metal crumpled. The car bounced up on its two passenger-side wheels. Sam watched wide-eyed as the sedan tilted onto its side before rolling over onto its hood. As a bonus, the door Marco had left open on the truck had slammed shut on its own.

The noise from the men watching jerked her gaze forward again.

Three of them were running toward her, closing fast. Behind them, Marco, his arm still around the fourth guy's shoulders, shouted something Sam was too agitated to understand. Her attention was all on Blondie, who was aiming his gun right at her.

Sam's heart leaped. She ducked. Then she put the pedal to the metal and kept on going, staying in reverse as she skirted the overturned car and zoomed away. If Blondie or any of the others fired, there was no bang and no bullets hit the truck. Almost sure that neither of the cars she was leaving behind was up to mounting anything approaching a high-speed chase, she felt a rising tide of excitement as she realized that she was on the brink of actually getting away.

The sounds of the crash were still ringing in her ears as she shifted into drive and peeled rubber out of the parking lot.

CHAPTER NINE

Sanders drove. Danny, in the backseat, center, with his injured leg stretched out through the gap between the front bucket seats, a bulky, grim-faced marshal on either side of him, was doing his best to stay in the game for as long as he could. Light-headed as all hell, sick and dry-mouthed, he wasn't about to slide gently into the beckoning oblivion of unconsciousness if he could help it. There were too many loose ends left to be tied up. Like retrieving Sam. Which Sanders was flat-out refusing to even attempt.

In reply to Danny's demand to know where they were going, Sanders said, "Scott Airfield. Until we figure out what the hell went wrong tonight, I'm not taking any chances."

With Supervisory Deputy Marshal Bruce Sanders, everything was strictly by the book, which, Danny was discovering, wasn't necessarily a good thing. Thirty-something, dark brown hair with a military cut, six feet tall with the stocky build of a former football player and the arrogant features of a first-rate asshole, Sanders tonight wore the hunted look of a man who feared that he was hovering on the brink of having his career go down the toilet. An operation that he was in charge of had just blown up in his face, costing the lives of two of his men. Any more risk he was not prepared to take.

"I gave 'em a heads-up that we were on the way in," Groves, who was wedged in to Danny's right, told Sanders. The heads-up had been over secure radio: Danny knew that because he'd seen Groves, who had a blond buzz cut above a baby face, talking into it, although, since he'd been busy arguing with Sanders at the time, he hadn't been paying attention to what was being said. Groves still held the radio.

"Which we are," Sanders emphasized.

So frustrated that he would have jumped out of the car and gone after Sam on his own if it had been possible, Danny all but leaned forward to smack Sanders in the back of the head. "We're not going anywhere without—"

A blare of music interrupted: "Here's my number, so call me, maybe?"

Coming out of nowhere as it did, the bubbly song was so unexpected that all five men in the car, including Danny, froze. The incongruously lighthearted tune repeated itself one more time before Danny realized that what they were hearing was a ring tone.

"Is that a fucking *cell phone*?" Sanders demanded with outrage. "Didn't I say *no phones*? Didn't I *say*?"

That must have been before he joined them, Danny reflected. They were in the black Taurus that *hadn't* just been flipped on its hood. Damaged but still drivable despite Sam's mind-

blowing assault on it, it had just pulled out of Miss Kitty's parking lot and was racing for the expressway. With his mobility
severely limited by his leg and other injuries, his authority nonexistent because in the eyes of these jokers he was a protected
witness cum prisoner, and any chance he had of breaking free
and going to Sam's rescue himself further hampered by being
the only unarmed one of the lot, all Danny had to work with
was words. He might be having an inner meltdown over Sam's
safety—Veith and his surviving thugs would almost certainly
come across her in the course of their search for him, and if they
found her it was a foregone conclusion that they would torture
and kill her in an attempt to wring his whereabouts out of her—
but rushing to her rescue on his own was impossible in his current state. He had to persuade Sanders that saving her life was
worth the effort, and so far Sanders wasn't persuaded.

"... call me, maybe?"

"Is that *you*?" Sanders glared at him through the rearview
mirror. On either side of him, Groves and O'Brien were staring
at him, too. Even Abramowitz, who was riding shotgun, had
turned around to look.

That's when Danny made the connection: it had to be Sam's
phone, which he had pocketed after calling Sanders, bebopping
away.

"Oopsy," Danny said. Wincing at the pain involved in moving, Danny pulled the phone out of his pocket. O'Brien and
Groves frowned at it.

"You want me to confiscate it, boss?" Groves sounded just a
hair too eager. His shoulder jostled Danny's. On Danny's other

side, O'Brien tensed like he was just waiting for the word. Both of them radiated aggression. The three of them were crammed into the backseat together because Sam's escape had left the other car totaled. A clean-up crew was already on its way to deal with the mess they'd left behind, but Sanders, afraid of being overtaken by another Zeta assassination squad before he could get the government's star witness—that would be him, Danny, or rather, Rick Marco—to safety, had refused to wait. Having been swiftly bundled into the car as Sam had hightailed it out of the parking lot, Danny had been demanding that they go after her ever since while his rescuers had alternated between affixing blame for the night's series of debacles anywhere it would stick and flat-out refusing to do what he was telling them to do. Their mandate was to ensure his safety and no one else's, Sanders told him, and that, as Danny knew from his own experience with orders from on high, was a hard nut to crack.

"Touch this phone and I'll break your faces," Danny said, meaning it. "Keep your mouths shut, all of you. I'm answering this." He frowned at the incoming number in the glowing little box on the phone's case. The name on the caller ID—Cindy Menifee—meant nothing to him. The fact that whoever was on the other end was calling Sam at this hour did. It seemed like a pretty safe assumption that the caller had to know her well. He briefly considered the possibilities: maybe this person could get a message to her for him, warning her again about what she was facing, reminding her how thin was the thread by which her life now hung, telling her someplace she could meet up with him. Or maybe it was Sam herself, realizing that he had her phone, borrowing a phone to call him. Maybe she had figured out what a mistake she had just made, or . . . something.

Okay, his thinking was admittedly a little bit fuzzy. The wonder was that he was still thinking at all. He was dizzy and in pain, and if ever the adrenaline coursing through his system wore off he figured he would crash like a freight train with no brakes. But right now he had to do what he could to save the girl who had saved him, because he owed her and because she was an innocent bystander who didn't deserve to be caught up in this. Also, because he liked her. Plus she was a woman, and pretty, and—well, he wasn't prepared to let her get herself killed if he could help it, that was all. First he was going to answer her phone and then he was going to wing it, depending on who was on the other end and what they said, figuring out the best way to use the contact as he went along.

"Anyone finds us through that phone and I'll kill you myself before the Zetas can do the job," Sanders threatened as Danny flipped the phone open. Making his thumb and forefinger into a pseudo gun, Sanders glanced around to point it at Danny. "Like this: *boom,* shot to the head."

Danny ignored him.

"Mm-hmm," Danny said into the phone, his voice a little higher pitched than normal. He didn't want to give away immediately that it wasn't Sam who was answering, just in case whoever it was had no interest in talking to him or anyone who wasn't Sam.

"Mom?" The voice on the other end was soft and quavery, kind of. A kid's voice. Jesus, it had to be Sam's kid. Whispering.

Danny sat up straighter, and to hell with the pain. "Mom, where are you? Some men are here."

Danny racked his brain. It was a piss-poor time for it to be shrouded in layers of fog, but there was nothing to do but . . .

"Mom?" The kid's voice was even smaller. And definitely scared. "They broke in the kitchen door. They're in there with Mrs. Menifee. They're hurting her. What should I do?"

Danny's blood ran cold.

"Tyler." The kid's name popped into his head just like that. It was like he could hear Sam's voice saying it. "Shh. You want to be real quiet. Don't let them see or hear you."

"Who are you? Where's Mom?"

"I'm a friend of your mom's, okay? She isn't here right now." He hoped, no, he prayed, that she wasn't there, either. But he knew as well as he knew the sun would rise in the morning that she'd been heading home for her kid. Had she made it? Was she there, too, somewhere?

The possibility scared the bejesus out of him.

There was a sniffle. The sound made Danny's stomach twist.

"Are you Carl?" the kid asked.

"Shh," Danny warned again. He had no idea who Carl was, but he wasn't going to claim to be him. The name *Rick* stuck in his throat. Anyway, to give him that much information would be to put the kid in more danger than he was in already. He sure as hell couldn't tell the truth, either. "I'm Trey." A nickname bestowed on him at Texas A&M, where he had been the sixth man on the Aggies basketball team whose specialty had been three-point shots.

"Are you a stranger?" The kid sounded wary. Danny supposed Sam had drummed the "stranger danger" bit into his head. Danny was familiar with it from his own nephews. Important information, but definitely not helpful now.

"No. I'm a friend of your mom's, remember?"

"I don't know if . . ."

A woman's scream in the background interrupted, sending the hair on Danny's nape shooting upright. His heart leaped. *Sam?* was his immediate, gut-wrenching reaction. But he didn't say it. Not to her kid. Anyway, it couldn't be her, or the kid would be having a cow. It had to be that Mrs. Menifee the kid had been talking about.

"No! Please, *please,* I don't . . ." The woman's voice was shrill with terror. The rest of her plea degenerated into unintelligible syllables. Listening, Danny gritted his teeth, consumed with his own helplessness. He knew what was happening. They were trying to force his—or maybe Sam's—whereabouts out of her.

"They're hitting Mrs. Menifee," the kid whispered, his stranger-danger problem clearly having been overridden by events. "With their fists. They shouldn't do that." He sounded angry now as well as scared. "Mrs. Menifee is nice." Danny found that his hand was clenched so hard around the phone that he had to consciously ease his grip or risk breaking the plastic. "I need my mom to come home. I need her right now."

That was the last thing any of them needed, but Danny

didn't tell the kid that even as he prayed that Sam stayed far, far away.

"Don't let them see you," Danny warned.

The kid didn't answer.

"Tyler—"

"Mrs. Menifee's crying." It was the merest breath of sound. "They're tying her up in a chair now. One of them's got a big knife."

Telling the kid to hang up and call 911 sprang to the tip of his tongue, only to be instantly dismissed. For the kid's sake, he absolutely needed to keep the phone connection going. He said, "Whatever you do, don't hit the end-call button. You hear?"

"Uh-huh." The kid's barely there voice had a catch in it. Danny thought he might be holding back a sob.

"We're coming to get you, Tyler. Where are you? Do you know the address?"

"It's 237 C-Clark Street." Danny could hear a kind of slithering noise that he couldn't identify.

He asked, "Tyler, what are you doing?"

"Hiding under the bed."

"Good plan." Danny's pulse hammered. The kid was obviously frightened out of his gourd. Danny could almost feel the icy pulse of his terror through the phone. He was only four years old. For how long would he be able to keep quiet and out of sight? "Okay, 237 Clark Street. I got it. Hold on. Stay real quiet."

Danny covered the mouthpiece and looked at Groves, who was frowning as he listened in. Danny could no longer hear the woman in the background, which wasn't a good thing for many reasons.

"Groves. Get on the fucking radio and tell whoever's on the other end to call 911," Danny said. "Tell them to send the cops to 237 Clark Street. Do it right now." The harsh growl of his voice was a testament to how much the idea of a little boy falling into the hands of the Zetas terrified him.

"What the fuck?" Through the rearview mirror, Sanders looked at Danny like he'd just grown a second head.

"The woman in the truck. This is her kid on the phone. The Zetas are there where the kid is, looking for me. Trying to torture information out of another woman. The kid's there, too, scared out of his mind." At the expression on Groves's face, Danny barked at him, "Goddamnit, man, do it." He would have snatched the radio out of Groves's hand and done it himself except he had a damaged finger on one hand and Sam's phone in the other, quite apart from the fact that in his present condition he was almost certain to lose the fight that such an action would start. Just managing not to shout, he looked at Sanders again. "We need to head for 237 Clark Street. Fast."

Sanders said, "Hey, Marco? Guess what? You don't give the orders here."

"So give the fucking orders."

Sanders's face tightened. He glanced into the rearview mirror. "Groves. Tell Morrison to call 911. You got the address?" Groves nodded. "And tell 'em to haul ass."

"Okay, 237 Clark," Groves repeated, pressing a button on the radio. "I'm on it."

"Trey. Are you still there?" Tyler whispered.

Danny uncovered the mouthpiece. "Yeah, Tyler, I'm still here. We're on our way. How many men are there?"

"Two. Or maybe three. I can't tell."

"Okay. Just stay cool."

While he had been talking, Danny had been eyeing their progress on the portable GPS that was stuck to the dashboard by some sort of suction device. He covered the mouthpiece again. "Abramowitz, type in 237 Clark Street. Let's see where it is."

Abramowitz, who was tall, thin, bald as an egg, and currently extremely nervous looking, hesitated, glancing at Sanders, who to Danny's relief gave a curt nod of permission. Even as Abramowitz started to key in the address, another agonized *"Please..."* followed by unintelligible syllables and a soul-shattering scream shivered through the phone. When the scream was abruptly cut off, Danny realized that he was sweating. They'd gagged her, he figured. That was how they operated: give the victim a chance to spill the information they wanted, then if the victim wasn't forthcoming gag and torture her some more before removing the gag and giving her another chance to talk. They'd never been known to leave a torture victim alive, either. How long did Cindy Menifee have? How long before she gave up the kid? Answer to both: the way the cartel worked, not long.

"They put something in her mouth," Tyler said. "They're hurting her."

"Wait a minute." Danny uncovered the mouthpiece. "How are you seeing all this? I thought you were under the bed."

"I got out to look."

Jesus Christ, the kid was scaring the life out of him. "You get back under the bed, right now, and stay out of sight," he ordered, using the tone he would have used to an errant nephew. At the thought that if the kid was somewhere where he could see what was going down, he could also be seen, Danny felt his heart rate hit turbocharge. Covering the mouthpiece, he said urgently to Sanders, "We're going to need more than street cops on this. Get somebody else on another radio, call somebody higher up the food chain. Get SWAT over there, maybe even the FBI. ASAP."

"We don't have another radio. Anyway, 911's the best I can do." Sanders's shrug brought a string of curses to the tip of Danny's tongue. He swallowed them as counterproductive. "Can't let anyone know we're involved here. Too much at stake."

"Trey, are you almost here?" Tyler's frightened question riveted Danny's attention again before he could do more than shoot Sanders a lethal look. On the GPS, the route calculator snaked an arrow south, then east. "They cut Mrs. Menifee's arm. With their knife. There's blood everywhere. Tears are coming down her face."

Tyler sounded like he might have tears coming down his face, too. Danny's gut clenched.

"Are you back under the bed?" he asked fiercely.

A few soft footsteps followed by a slithering sound gave him his answer.

"I am now."

"*Stay there.*" Beside him, Groves was telling whoever was on the other end of the radio to call 911. God in heaven, glaciers moved faster than these guys.

"We'll be there real soon," he said to Tyler, trying to sound as calm and steady as he didn't feel. "We're coming just as fast as we can." Covering up the mouthpiece again, he looked at Sanders. "We're going to 237 Clark. *Now.*"

"No can do," Sanders replied. They were nearing the expressway interchange. Danny could tell that by the giant streetlights that he could see clustered together maybe a block to the west. Once they were on that, there was no turning back: they would be on a one-way ride over the mighty Mississippi. "Not our mission. You know that."

Danny shot him a look that promised death as soon as he could deliver it. "You listen to me, you son of a bitch. I told her everything. The woman in the truck. Veith and the Zetas get their hands on her, she'll sing like a bird, I guarantee it. Where the safe houses are. Who I'm fingering. The whole deal."

Beside him, Groves was still talking to whoever was on the radio, patiently walking them through the situation. According to the arrow on the GPS, the Taurus was only about five miles from 237 Clark.

Sanders's expression turned ugly. "You're lying."

"You want to take the chance? That I didn't tell her *something*? Hell, man, they're torturing a woman as we speak. Somebody doesn't stop them, they're going to kill a four-year-old kid. While we drive away, listening on the *goddamned phone.*" By the end, it was a barely muted roar. He pointed at the GPS. "We're five miles away. *Go.*"

"Trey?"

Danny took a deep breath and uncovered the mouthpiece. "I'm here, Tyler. We're coming to get you. Sit tight." He slid his palm over the mouthpiece again. Fear for the kid—and his mother—made him so antsy he could feel nerves jumping under his skin. Under other conditions, he would have shot the asshole driving if he'd had to and commandeered the car. "She heard me talking to you on the phone, Sanders. She knows your name. She was sitting right beside me when I called you. Think about it: you know it's true."

"Fuck." Sanders's face reddened as anger infused it. The look he sent Danny was as murderous as Danny felt. At that moment they reached the next intersection, where the GPS arrow pointed left. Looking like he was ready to explode, Sanders cut the wheel sharply and went left on what felt like two wheels.

Thank you, God.

"I'm scared," Tyler whispered.

Danny knew the feeling; he was scared, too. "I know you are. Nothing bad's going to happen to you, I promise. We'll be there real soon." Cold sweat slid down his spine as he prayed he could deliver on that promise.

"This is a mistake," Sanders said. "I fucking know it."

"They're going to kill a kid," Danny shot back, his palm over the mouthpiece again.

All of a sudden Mrs. Menifee screamed like an animal being slaughtered. Even through the phone, the sound was so loud and shrill and full of pain and terror that it filled the car. When the scream cut off, abruptly like it was deliberately stopped, Danny found that he was holding his breath.

"You hear that?" he asked Sanders fiercely. Even as the other man's jaw set, Danny heard Tyler whimpering. *Please God let them not find the kid.* He didn't have to see it to know that whatever had just gone down had been real bad. Uncovering the mouthpiece, Danny spoke as calmly as possible into the phone. "Tyler. You need to stay real quiet, remember? Is there any way you can get out of the house without them seeing you? You'd have to be real sure they couldn't see you before you tried it, though."

"Locals are on their way," Groves announced.

"Then we can damned well leave them to it," Sanders growled.

Danny put his palm over the mouthpiece again. "You do that, you abandon this kid and his mother, and the government will never get another word out of me, I promise you. I won't say a fucking syllable, you understand that?" He cut a look at Groves. "Get back on the radio and tell whoever that this is a potential hostage situation and they're going to need SWAT. Then tell them to contact the FBI."

"Boss?" Groves looked at Sanders.

"Do it," Sanders snapped.

"I think Mrs. Menifee might be dead," Tyler said.

Briefly Danny closed his eyes. "Don't think about that. Remember what I asked you? Can you get out of the house without them seeing you?"

"When I go to the door of my bedroom, I can see them."

Tyler's voice was barely audible now, the faintest of whispers. "That means they can see me, right? I have to go out of my bedroom, and run down the hall, and get out the front door."

"Don't try it." Just picturing it made Danny's skin crawl. "You're under the bed again, right?" A sound from Tyler confirmed it. "That's a good place to hide. You just stay put, then. We're coming to get you. We're almost there." According to the GPS, they were a little over four miles away and closing fast. The dark streets were almost deserted. Although Danny realized that he was automatically listening for them, no sirens could be heard dashing to the rescue. Beside him, Groves was once again on the damned radio. Shoving a shoulder into him, he mouthed, "Hurry the fuck up."

Groves glared at him, then said into the radio, "Yeah, it's going down right now. Tell 'em to hurry up."

"There's blood all over the kitchen floor. They cut Mrs. Menifee real bad. She wasn't moving." Tyler's voice caught on a sob.

"Don't think about it. Try to think about something else instead," Danny instructed, sick at the thought of what the boy had seen, what he *would* see if they didn't get there in time. Or worse than see. The fact that Tyler was a four-year-old kid wouldn't even slow Veith and company down. Danny thought about his own nephews, attempted a distraction. "I bet you like the Avengers, right?"

"I want my mom," Tyler whimpered, undistracted. Hell, no surprise in that. Danny heard him take a long, shaky breath. Then Tyler added, "What happens if they find *me*?"

Danny's throat went tight. "They're not going to find you. Just stay where you are and be as quiet as you can."

"Mom's here." The relief in Tyler's voice was palpable.

"*What?*" Something that felt like a giant fist grabbed Danny's heart and squeezed.

"She's here. I know she is. I can hear Big Red. That's the truck she drives. It makes a lot of noise. She's probably parking it out in front like she always does."

"Jesus, Mary, and Joseph." Exhaling the words, Danny felt like his insides had just been flash frozen. Then a second, terrifying thought hit him. Would the kid pop out and go running to her? "Tyler, you stay where you are, you hear? *Tyler?*"

But the kid wasn't there anymore, or if he was, he wasn't answering.

CHAPTER TEN

Sam's heart rate hit about a thousand miles a minute as she pulled up across the street from her duplex. Terrified of attracting any notice at all, she winced at the loud groan of the brakes. The fear that she was being followed—chased— had had her stealing terrified glances through the rearview mirror the whole way home. So far, nothing. At least, nothing that she could spot. She'd practically broken land speed records getting there, helped by the fact that traffic was so light as to be almost nonexistent. The moment it stopped, Sam slammed the transmission into park, grabbed the keys and her gun, and leaped from the truck. Ignoring the engine's last shuddering gasps, she sprinted across the dark street, trying to look in a dozen directions at once. No streetlamps around here, and no friendly night-owl neighbor types walking a dog, either. The residents had long since learned that their health was best pre- served by staying off the streets in the small hours of the night. Nothing but a cat on the sidewalk, and it took off running as soon as it saw her coming. The yard was about the size of a postage stamp, with grass that had gone crispy from the heat and one bedraggled pine tree that was slowly turning brown from the bottom up. Like the rest of the yards on the block, which was an eclectic collection of aging shotgun-style single-family homes and duplexes, this one was enclosed by a saggy chain-link fence. Thrusting her gun into the front waistband of her jeans, yanking her shirt down over it so that Tyler wouldn't see and ask awkward questions, Sam struggled with the latch on the gate, which was rusty and difficult to work, then flew up the walk toward the front door. The duplex itself was one story, pale blue frame, with two deep blue doors, one on either side of the covered front porch. She and Tyler lived in the unit on the left, which had two small bedrooms, plus a bath, kitchen, and living room. Although by now it was well past 4:00 a.m., some lights were still on inside her unit: she could see the pale glow through the drawn curtains. Mrs. Menifee was almost always asleep on the couch by the time Sam got in. But since she never would admit that she fell asleep, the TV was always left on, along with a fair number of lights.

A white plastic grocery bag waited on the weathered wood porch by the front door. *Kendra.* She'd come through with the pancake mix and syrup. Sam's chest felt tight as she scooped it up. Where would she be in the morning, when it came time to make Tyler breakfast?

Short answer: not here.

We'll head into St. Louis, then keep going toward Branson, or maybe Kansas City, she planned frantically as she thrust her key into the front door lock. *Make it Kansas City, because it's got more people, which means we'll be harder to find. God, how far can we get on a little over a tank of gas?*

I should ask Mrs. Menifee if I can borrow some money. But she knew already that she wasn't going to do it. Asking to borrow money would take time; Mrs. Menifee would want an explanation. The last thing Sam could tell her was the truth and coming up with a plausible lie was, she feared, beyond her at the moment. Anyway, time was what she didn't have. As it was, she was going to have to practically push Mrs. Menifee out the door. Usually the two of them had a nice chat, but Sam had a gut feeling that now every second counted. She needed to get Tyler, and get gone.

When the lock clicked open, it was all she could do to restrain herself from bursting through the front door. Instead she walked in very calmly, closing the door behind her, glancing around the living room. The room was small, the furniture early Goodwill, but it was clean and comfortable and that was all she asked of it. As she had expected, the TV was on, a lamp burned beside the couch, and the throw that she kept on the back of the couch was flung across the coffee table. Mrs. Menifee had obviously been taking her usual nap in her usual place. Just at that moment, however, she was nowhere in sight.

Maybe she's in the bathroom, Sam thought, frowning as she glanced toward the back of the duplex, where the light was on in the kitchen, which was straight ahead at the end of the short hallway. But the bathroom door was open, and the light was off.

"Mrs. Menifee?" Dropping the groceries onto the coffee table, she headed for the kitchen. It was the only place the other woman could be. Ordinarily Sam would have been careful not to wake Tyler, who should be curled up in his bed sound asleep, but since she was going to be bundling him out to the truck in the next few minutes anyway, being quiet as a mouse wasn't anything she needed to worry about. Her bedroom was closest to the living room, Tyler's was next to the kitchen, and the bathroom was in between. Like the bathroom, the bedroom doors were open and the rooms themselves were dark. For the briefest of seconds she pictured Tyler curled up in his cozy bed in the room she had painstakingly decorated with images of dragons and wizards and lightning bolts that she had cut out of a children's magazine then enlarged with a copying machine so he could be surrounded by his favorite characters. Then her heart contracted as she realized that Tyler wouldn't be sleeping in his room again for a while.

How long until it would be safe to come back? She didn't know. She didn't know anything, except that she needed to run.

"I'm home," she called as, hearing nothing from Mrs. Menifee, she plunged into the shadowy hall, heading for the kitchen.

Do not forget Ted. Sam was just reminding herself about the small brown Beanie Baby teddy bear that Tyler absolutely loved and couldn't go to sleep without when something—a sound, a shadow, a feeling—slowed her steps just about the time she found herself opposite the bathroom door.

Whatever it was, she couldn't put her finger on it. It felt like—a kind of heaviness in the air. A hush. A sense of expectancy. Sam registered all those things at the same moment as it occurred to her to wonder why Mrs. Menifee wasn't answering, or bustling through the kitchen door to meet her, or something of the sort. The duplex was small. Mrs. Menifee had to have heard her . . .

Something's wrong.

Her body knew it before she did. The tiny hairs on the back of her neck prickled to life. Her stomach tensed. A shiver slid over her skin. Nearly opposite Tyler's bedroom door by then, she could see almost a third of the kitchen. The familiar white cabinets, white counters, lemon-yellow walls . . .

A deep red rivulet snaked slowly across the kitchen's white linoleum floor. Sam frowned at it for a second before what she was seeing registered.

Blood!

Sam stopped dead, her breathing suspended, her gaze riveted on the creeping thread of scarlet.

Tyler.

Oh, God, had something happened to her baby? Had the men Marco warned her about already found their way here? That was the fear that catapulted her forward into a run, that made her snatch her gun from her waistband, that wrung a strangulated sound from her throat. A split second later, Sam saw to her horror that the rivulet led to a widening scarlet pool that led to a plump arm trailing limply from one of her kitchen chairs. Alongside the chair's slender aluminum leg hung a motionless hand with long, deep pink fingernails awash in blood, a limp palm streaked in scarlet—wait, there were only four fingernails. *She could only see four fingernails.* The truth burst upon her in an explosion of horror: the tip of the index finger had been severed at the knuckle. The mutilated joint was running red. Her heart gave a great leap in her chest. Her pulse shot through the roof. Her stomach clenched. *Mrs. Menifee . . .*

She didn't need to see more than that small sliver of the gruesome scene to know that something terrifying awaited her just steps away.

A cold hand grabbed hers even as she started backpedaling only a foot or so before she reached the white linoleum, scaring her so badly that she jumped and squeaked and almost fell. Her shoulder crashed into the wall as she whirled to confront whoever it was.

"*Mom!*" Tyler tugged frantically at her hand. His voice was a terrified whisper. His face utterly white, his eyes big as quarters, he had an expression on his face that struck fear into her heart. He looked like he had just seen every horrible monster that haunted his bad dreams come to life. "Don't go in there! There are bad men! Quick! We have to hide!"

"Tyler!" Because he was alive and apparently unharmed, his name emerged in a rush of thanksgiving. It was all Sam got a chance to say before a man stepped into her peripheral vision, blocking her view of Mrs. Menifee, planting himself just inside the kitchen doorway. For the briefest of moments she got the impression that he was looking beyond her, down the hallway toward the front door. He balanced on the balls of his feet in a way that told her he was prepared to move fast if he needed to. Medium height, medium build. Medium brown hair, cut like a businessman, short and neat. A pale, round face with ordinary features. Maybe forty, forty-five. Nondescript clothes. Nondescript man.

Except for the gun in his hand, which he used to make a beckoning gesture toward her. *Dear God, no.* Sam's breathing suspended. Her stomach plummeted down past her toes.

A satisfied smirk curled his lips. "Samantha Jones? Where's Marco?"

Sam's heart convulsed. If she ran he'd shoot her. If she stayed—he'd have Tyler, too.

"Run, Tyler!" Sam shrieked, shoving her son back behind her, knowing that she had no chance of surviving this but going for it anyway, because if she could slow down what was getting ready to happen long enough to give Tyler a chance to escape that was the best she could hope for, and what she was going to do. Jerking up her gun, whirling to face the intruder, she opened fire—*bang, bang, bang, bang, bang* in huge, earsplitting explosions that clearly caught the intruder by surprise, that tore up her cabinets and shattered her counters and filled the air with a sulfurous smell, that didn't cause Mrs. Menifee's poor bloody fingers to so much as twitch. To her astonishment the man didn't fire back, didn't shoot her dead where she stood, but jumped back out of sight into the kitchen, yelling, "What the fuck?" or maybe that was somebody else, because a different voice roared, "Get the bitch!"

That's when it hit her: they didn't want her dead, not yet, not until she told them where Marco was. So she turned to follow Tyler, turned to take a chance, to run—and saw that instead of bolting toward the front door, Tyler had fled into his bedroom.

Out of the corner of her eye she caught the flash of his bare legs, the light green of his Incredible Hulk short pajamas, disappearing into the dark.

"Tyler!"

Behind her, the man popped into view again, filling the space just inside the kitchen, his gun up and aimed at her.

"No!"

Dizzy with fear, Sam leaped headlong after her son just as a bullet smacked into the wall inches away from where her left leg had been. No bang—a silencer. They might not want her dead—yet—but this guy had no qualms about shooting her. And there was nothing they wanted from Tyler. The knowledge galvanized her.

These had to be professional hit men. Hadn't Marco warned her?

"Mom! Mom! Are you shot?"

Tyler slammed the door behind her as she hit the floor hard on her hands and knees, hanging onto the gun for dear life. Until then, she hadn't even realized that she'd been screaming like a woman faced with imminent death—which it was terrifying to realize was exactly what she was. The hardwood was unforgiving. The jolt of her landing cut off her scream and shot through her wrists and knees. But she was so frightened that she barely even registered the impact. With the door closed, only moonlight filtering through the thin curtains kept the room from being pitch black. On the shelf above Tyler's bed, a favorite stuffed snake glowed faintly yellow through the dark.

"No. *Lock the door.*" Still clutching the gun, she scrambled to her feet. Tyler did as she told him, his hands looking tiny and pale through the shadows as he snapped the tarnished brass dead bolt into place. But even though the door was big and heavy and old, she didn't trust the lock to hold for longer than a minute or two. A grown man would be able to kick his way in easily, or they could shoot out the lock.

Even as the thought occurred, Sam's heart leaped into her throat and she shrieked, "Tyler! Get away from the door!"

He did, darting toward the far wall.

She was already spinning away toward the rocking chair beside the bed, the one in which she'd left Mrs. Menifee, in which she had spent many an hour soothing Tyler when he was a baby, an old friend. Purchased at a yard sale and lovingly repainted, it had a wood slat back and a cane seat, and it was sturdy and just the right size and absolutely better than nothing. Picking it up—it was heavy—and practically lunging with it the eight or so feet needed to reach the door, she strong-armed the chair beneath the knob, wedging it tight, bracing the door as best she could. It wouldn't hold up to a full-scale assault, but at least now, she hoped, the door wouldn't spring open under a single hard kick.

A bullet drilled the door. Clearly aimed at the lock, which it just missed, it plowed into the floor near Sam's feet. She screamed, an instinctive reaction that tore its way out of her throat and that she quickly swallowed for Tyler's sake. Tyler gave a high-pitched cry that ripped at her heart and threw himself toward her. Catching him, throwing an arm around him, she took him with her as she bolted toward the room's solitary window. Escape, was what she was thinking. They had to get out of that room if they were to have any chance of surviving.

"Are they gonna get in?" Eyes huge with fear, Tyler clung to her even as Sam, struck by an epiphany, whirled back to face the door.

"No," she promised grimly. Clapping Tyler's head to her side and covering his exposed ear with her free hand, she pointed the gun at the wall in the approximate vicinity of where she calculated the shooter might have been standing in the hall beyond it, gritted her teeth, and pulled the trigger.

The enormous *bang* bounced off Sam's eardrums. The bullet tore through the plaster, leaving a pale pockmark on the navy blue wall. The resultant shouts from the men outside told her that it had gotten through and that they had taken notice, which was what she wanted, even if she hadn't hit one of them. Anything to hold them off.

"They killed Mrs. Menifee." Tyler was trembling.

"They're not going to kill us," she promised, thrusting the gun back down into her waistband, and hoped with every fiber of her being that it wasn't a lie.

Turning, whipping the curtains open, she found herself looking out at a scraggly honeysuckle bush, the blank side wall of a neighboring garage, and the narrow strip of grass between residences, all shrouded in the deep charcoal of night.

"Cover your ears," she warned as she went to work on the window lock. Tyler did, and she screamed at the top of her lungs, "Help! We need help! Call 911!" toward the glass, hoping that it would penetrate far enough for a neighbor to hear, knowing even as she did it that it was probably a waste of breath, because even if someone did hear the people around there had been programmed by many long years of casual neighborhood violence not to get involved and above all, not to involve the cops. Gunshots, screams, shouts for help—they weren't so unusual that anybody would stick his neck out unless she got very, very lucky.

"Trey's coming," Tyler told her, his eyes big dark pools in his small face. She could feel shivers racking the warm little body pressed against her. "I called him. He's on the way."

That made no sense, but Sam didn't have time to worry about it. "Okay."

"Can you get it open?"

"Yeah." As she wrestled the recalcitrant lock the final few millimeters needed to free the bottom half of the window, she tried to sound calm. Which was a joke: her kid wasn't an idiot, he knew she was scared witless, knew that they could die, but still the mom in her tried to protect him from the full magnitude of her fear.

"I tried. I couldn't open it."

"I'm bigger."

With half her senses focused behind her, on what was going on outside the bedroom door—she could hear nothing, which made her so nervous she wanted to puke—she grabbed the handles at the bottom of the sash with both hands and yanked.

The window didn't budge.

"Hurry, Mom," Tyler said breathlessly.

"Get her out of there," she heard one of the men order as she strained without success to pull the window up. From the direction of his voice, he was in the hall, near the kitchen. But closer than before?

If there was a reply, she didn't hear it.

Sam thought about snapping off another shot in their direction, but she really didn't want to ignite a firefight that the other side was sure to win and that would endanger Tyler. Anyway, gunfighting was not her thing; before tonight she had only ever fired a gun at a practice range or in the air as a warning. Besides, she only had—a quick check confirmed it—two bullets left.

Her stomach twisted into a pretzel.

That was not enough. Not near enough to save them.

"Pull harder," Tyler urged, and Sam did, planting her feet, putting every bit of strength she had into dragging open that window. It didn't work.

"I'm pulling as hard as I can." Her voice was thin and breathless. Probably she shouldn't have admitted it, not to Tyler, but the admission just came out.

"We don't want to hurt the kid," another man yelled, the words clearly intended for her ears. He sounded closer, nearer the door. "Come out now, and we'll let him go. You make us come in and get you, and things could go real wrong in that regard."

"Mom." Tyler tightened his grip on her.

Sam's heart pounded so hard that it felt like it was trying to beat its way out of her chest. Her pulse thundered in her ears. Whatever it took, she was not letting them get their hands on

Tyler. Swallowing the panic that rose like bilge in the back of her throat, she shook her head reassuringly at him.

"You come anywhere near us and I'll blow you to hell," she yelled back. They couldn't know she only had two bullets left. *I don't care how bad they are, they have to be wary of a gun.* She figured that the knowledge that she had it was the only thing keeping them from storming the door.

"Will you really shoot them if they come?" Tyler whispered. He was holding tightly to her, hampering her movements more than a little as she tried rocking the window, shoving hard against the frame, jiggling the sash this way and that, but there was no way she was pushing him away.

"Yes," she said, and this time she wasn't lying. If they came anywhere near Tyler, she absolutely would. Although, and she hated to even let the grim truth into her consciousness, it still might not be enough to save him.

Another bullet plowed through the door. Silent and deadly, it buried itself in the wall maybe a foot away from the window with a sound like a hand slapping flesh. She and Tyler both froze, staring at the pale pockmark where the bullet had hit with widening eyes, before Sam roused herself and gave a desperate, do-or-die heave to the handles. Nothing; she came to the terrifying conclusion that the window was painted shut.

"Are we trapped, Mom?" Tyler sounded on the verge of tears.

"No way." She gave Tyler a fierce, one-armed hug while she frantically assessed the window. She was so frightened that she could hardly stand still. Sweat poured over her body in a wave. She could not—"Tyler?"

He had broken away from her. "I have to get something."

From the corner of her eye she saw him slide partway under his bed and emerge with—of course—Ted. The sliver of her attention that had gone with him returned to rejoin the rest in focusing on the window.

Could she break it? Even if she broke the glass, the wood would still be intact. Maybe . . .

"Mom, here." Tyler was back, holding trusty Ted by the paw, thrusting something—a glance down discovered a cell phone, to which she reacted with a quick, hopeful thrill—into her hand. "I called Trey. You can call somebody."

Trey again. Even as she drew a blank once more on the name—superhero? imaginary friend? playmate she couldn't place?—she gave Tyler a *you did good* look and started punching in 911.

Pheww. Pheww. The peculiar hissing sounds were immediately followed by a pair of sharp smacks as two objects hit the baseboard opposite the door at maybe an inch above floor level. An awful chill of premonition slid down her spine. Casting a startled glance around, Sam heard another breathy *pheww* and watched a shiny sphere the size of a paintball blast beneath the door to slam with a smack into the baseboard maybe a yard away, where it burst. A shimmery aerosol was released into the air, expanding outward in a growing cloud. Two other similar clouds stretched toward each other, the products, she concluded with a thrill of horror, of the other two smacking sounds. Sam didn't have to smell the acrid odor, to feel the first burning tingles in her nostrils, to realize what was happening: they were shooting pepper balls under the door.

To drive her and Tyler out.

"Come to Papa, bitch," one of them yelled gloatingly from just beyond the door.

Sam's blood ran cold.

CHAPTER ELEVEN

"Mom, what is it?" Tyler started rubbing at his eyes.

"Close your eyes! Don't touch your face!"

"It burns!"

It did, like airborne acid feathering across her skin, searing the inside of her nose, making her eyes water, making them sting . . .

"Hold your breath, baby!"

Coughing, gasping, Sam jammed the phone into her pocket, yanked out her gun, pointed it at the window, and shot the glass and the center of the wood strips, aiming right for the spot where the strips crossed: *bang, bang.* She used her last bullets, then kicked out the shards and decimated wooden supports with a desperate strength. Snatching up Tyler, whose eyes were shut and whose face was all puckered up like it got when he got ready to jump off the side of the pool in the summer, which she knew meant that he was holding his breath, she lifted him through the hole she had made into the blessedly fresh night air.

"Watch the glass," she warned in an urgent undertone as

moonlight glinted off the debris from the window that was scattered beneath the honeysuckle bush. Even in this moment of extremis, she took care to set him down in a clear spot.

"Mom!" As his feet touched the ground his eyes popped open and he clung to her.

"*Run, Tyler.*" She pulled free of his grip. "*Go.* Head for the truck. I'm coming."

With one last look at her he turned, shoved his way through the honeysuckle branches, and took off, heading toward the street. The fence was in the way. God, would he have time to get through the gate before the monsters in the house figured out that their prey was getting away? His little bare feet flashed pale through the darkness; his pajamas gave off the faintest of neon glows. Something small and dark bobbed at his side. In the split second that it took Sam to recognize Ted, paw still clutched tightly in Tyler's hand, she already had one foot braced on the windowsill. Eyes burning and watering so badly that things kept going in and out of focus, feeling like her skin was blistering everywhere that it was exposed, Sam took a split second to pulverize the shards that still clung to the sill and then scrambled out the window, taking in greedy gulps of the honeysuckle-scented air even before she hit the ground. Somewhere in the distance she heard a siren; closer at hand, the brittle snap of glass breaking under her boots and the rustling of the bush she'd landed in were overridden by the sound of her pulse thundering in her ears. Careful not to rub at her burning eyes—no stranger to pepper spray, she knew that would only make the effects worse—she cast a quick, involuntary glance behind her, through the shattered window toward the bedroom door. Her vision shimmered and shifted, due to both the watery veil of stinging tears that obscured it and the menacing vapors that filled the room, but she could see the rocking chair, which was still in place, and the door, which was still shut. Wonder of wonders, they weren't trying to break into the room. Maybe the knowledge that they had just filled it with pepper spray was keeping them at bay. Maybe they thought the two shots she had just fired at the window had been aimed at them. Or maybe— horrifying thought—they were already racing for the front door, to catch her and Tyler in the enclosed yard . . .

Terror formed a hard, cold knot in Sam's chest as she, too, plunged through the honeysuckle and bolted for the street.

Bam! Bam! The unmistakable sound of splintering wood behind her made her heart lurch. It sent panic shooting along her nerve endings, gave fresh wings to her feet.

"Party time, bitch." The words, which unmistakably came from inside the room she had just left, had an oddly muffled, slurred quality.

"I don't see her! Or the boy!" It was a different voice, filled with consternation, speaking a heartbeat later. It had the same odd muffled quality as the first.

"She's got to be here. They've got to be here! Search! Check the—"

"They went out the window! Look! There she goes!"

A quick, fear-filled glance over her shoulder showed Sam a man in a dark hoodie leaning out Tyler's shattered bedroom window staring after her. If the moonlight hadn't gleamed off the gun he was holding, she wasn't even sure she would have spotted him through the darkness and the overarching honeysuckle. But it did, and she did, and her breath caught and her heart slammed against her chest wall and her stomach did a back flip. Only, his face was weird—eyes like a bug, dark and featureless lower down.

For a shocked instant that felt like a moment out of time, she went shivery with horror. What kind of men were these?

Then she realized: goggles and a bandanna. He was wearing that, or something similar, plus the hood pulled over his head and who knew what else to protect himself from the pepper spray. They both—all—however many of them there were, however many were in that room—must be swaddled in protective gear. That accounted for the distortion of their voices, for the fact that they had dared to enter the room so soon.

If the murderous asswipes turned and ran for the front door this minute, this second, they would be barely behind her as she raced for the gate, Sam calculated. If they just wanted her dead, they could shoot her—and Tyler—from the porch. It was a footrace now, and not one that she was sure she could win. Heart jackhammering, with all need for subterfuge past, Sam ran for her life, letting loose a scream that split the night as she tore around the corner of the house—

—just in time to see Tyler being lifted over the fence by a man on its other side. In the split second that it took her mind to process what she was seeing, blinking through the darkness

and the burning curtain of welling tears that kept her from seeing anything clearly, she tried to ascertain what was what. She
registered that the man who had grabbed Tyler was wearing a
suit, that another man in a suit was racing toward him, and that
a black car with its doors open and engine running idled at the
curb, double-parked, while Big Red sat waiting directly behind
it, across the street.

Two more men stood behind the idling car, barely more than
shadowy outlines at first glance, two-handing pistols that were
braced on the car's hood and aimed at her house. Sam didn't
care about them, just like she no longer cared about the men
who at any second now should be bursting out her front door.

Every last molecule in her body was focused on saving her son.

"Tyler!" she shrieked, her feet seeming to turn heavy as lead
as she tried for every bit of speed she could summon to reach
her boy in time. But it was too late, the man in the suit was
handing Tyler off to someone in the car, her kid was disappearing inside . . .

"Mom!" he cried, twisting to look back at her, Ted clutched
to his chest, a small hand reaching out for her.

"Tyler!" Feeling as if her heart would explode, Sam screamed
his name again. It was useless. Her son was already out of sight,
thrust into the car. If it drove away now . . . but the first man in
the suit, instead of disappearing into the car, too, as the other
man did with Tyler, ran back to drag the gate open for her.

"*Move it*, Ms. Jones." Sam's vision was so blurry that she
was seeing shapes rather than details, but she was sure she
didn't know him. Whoever he was, though, he knew her—or at

least her name. Tonight, in this waking nightmare that she was trapped in, it seemed that everybody did. It was horrifying, terrifying, because it meant that these men who were snatching her kid were doing it because of Marco, but then she'd known that from the first instant she'd spotted Tyler being lifted over the fence. Anyway, it didn't matter now: whatever the cost, she was going after her child.

Darting past the suit guy at the gate, she yelled, "Give me back my son!" at him, and was surprised at the sound of her own voice: instead of being loud and demanding, it was hoarse and croaky. Her tongue and the tissues of her mouth felt bone dry. A hideous taste—she was guessing it was from the pepper spray—clung to the back of her throat. Swallowing didn't help.

Reaching the car, she leaned down to look inside—both passenger-side doors were still open—and found herself being half lifted, half shoved into the backseat.

"*No!*"

Her empty, useless gun was snatched away from her. Hands grabbed and held her, trapping her inside the car, constraining her arms, her legs. She fought like a demon to get away.

"Let me go!"

"Mom!"

Tyler's voice was drowned out as a cacophony of shouting voices filled the car. They made no sense to her in her panic. Amid the pitched battle she'd been plunged into, both doors slammed shut and the car took off, peeling rubber away from the curb. Through the tinted windows, she saw that her neighbors were not quite as deaf or indifferent as she had thought: a light flicked on in the house next door; across the street, a man holding a baseball bat stepped out onto his porch, looking in the direction of her house. At the far the end of the block, as the car bearing her and Tyler away raced toward the opposite corner then took it on what felt like two wheels, she caught the merest glimpse of the brilliant red and blue flashing lights of a police cruiser lighting up the night as it zoomed onto her street.

She wanted to scream at it, *Where were you thirty seconds ago?* But that would have been a waste of breath.

"Tyler!" Her desperate gaze locked onto her son. They were holding his head out the window now, doing something to him. She couldn't tell exactly what, but they seemed to be pouring something in his face, something that splattered in a stream down the side of the car. He squirmed like a fish on a hook, his hands restrained by a dark-jacketed arm clamping his arms to his side, his head jerking as little pained cries emerged from his throat: "Ah, ah, ah!"

"Let go of me!" Throwing elbows and kicking, Sam got away from the arms imprisoning her and practically swam across the backseat—three men were crammed into it shoulder to shoulder—as she fought to reach him. "Tyler!"

"Watch the leg!" The voice, the words, scratched the surface of her panic, but she was so frightened for her son that they didn't really register.

"Lady! Calm the hell down!" Hands tried to pin her again, then as she sank her teeth into the nearest stuffed suit sleeve just as quickly let her go. "Ow! Damn it! She bit me!"

"Let me *go*!"

"Sam, stop!" It was a roar, uttered as arms once again locked around hers, clamping them to her body.

"Tyler!" The man who was holding him pulled him back inside the window. Blinking furiously in an effort to clear her vision, struggling for all she was worth, she strained to get to him, to see if he'd been hurt.

"Mom, I'm okay!" Her son was rubbing vigorously at his eyes with something—something white. A rag? "You let my mom go!" He directed a fierce frown at the men holding her.

"We're going to. Just as soon as—"

"Get your hands off me!" Pinned but undaunted, Sam twisted and bucked ferociously in an effort to get loose, then, having freed a leg, slammed a knee into the nearest rib cage.

"Ow! Damn it! Sam, stop fighting, it's me!"

"*Mom!* You let her go!"

Blurry as her vision still was, Sam saw that Tyler's hair dripped liquid and his face was shiny wet, but otherwise he did indeed seem okay. The worst of her panic began to subside. Now sitting in the lap of the man who'd held him out the window, Tyler shook his head like a wet dog, splattering drops everywhere, including a few that felt cool and soothing as they hit her face. The good news was, he didn't seem to be hurt or even particularly afraid. As Sam realized that, the terrified haze that had held her in thrall slowly started to dissipate. Calming down enough to realize that fighting was a waste of effort, because there was going to be no escaping the car even if she did get free of the men holding her, she felt her heart, which had been beating a thousand miles a minute, settle into mere pounding, and she managed to catch her breath. At the same time she began to take in her surroundings, and saw that the entire driver's side of the car was dented inward and the guy holding Tyler looked vaguely familiar.

"Sam, damn it, I've got you! Look at me."

That's when she recognized the voice: Marco. Blinking wildly, she managed to clear her distorted vision enough to make sure. It was him, all right, wedged in the middle of the three men in the backseat. She had scrambled across him un-knowing. Now, in her quest to reach Tyler, she was practically lying across his lap. His arms imprisoned hers, and he was hold-ing her clamped against his chest. She realized that he was tak-ing care to keep her elevated, and off his wounded leg. For the first time since she'd been thrown into the car she went com-pletely still, blinking up at him.

Marco frowned down at her. Their eyes met, and the fight went out of her like air escaping from a balloon. Going limp with relief, she sagged in his hold. Truth was, she didn't think she had ever been so glad to see anyone in her life.

She felt suddenly, ridiculously (because after all, what did she really know about Marco, or any of them, except what Marco had told her?) safe. But then, safe was probably a compara-tive thing. As in, compared to what she and Tyler had just es-caped.

And Mrs. Menifee hadn't.

The words practically tripped over each other as she rushed to get them out.

"Our neighbor. She was baby-sitting Tyler. She's back there in the house, with those men you warned me about. They were waiting for me when I got home. Mrs. Menifee's hurt or . . ." Her voice trailed off. She did not want to complete the horrible thought while Tyler was within earshot. The thing was, she strongly suspected Mrs. Menifee might be dead. Even knowing what she knew for sure about what had been done to Mrs. Menifee made her heartsick.

"I already told Trey about Mrs. Menifee. I told him I think they killed her." Tyler sounded both sad and surprisingly matter-of-fact.

"Trey?" Sam blinked hard at her son, trying to bring him into focus. Discovering that she was almost too spent to move, Sam moved anyway, saying, "Let me go" to Marco and the man still holding her legs, easing into a sitting position carefully, mindful of Marco's wound. She was blinking away, resisting the urge to rub at her eyes only because she knew that rubbing them would just make them feel worse. There wasn't any room, so she ended up perched on Marco's good thigh, leaning back against the solid warmth of his chest with his arm heavy around her waist, squinting in an effort to see properly. His expression was difficult to read. Her head leaned against his shoulder, making the angle odd, and anyway she couldn't really focus still. From the way his leg shifted beneath her she thought that it wasn't the most comfortable situation for him. But there really wasn't anywhere else for her to go. Uncomfortable or not, he didn't shove her off him and she wasn't about to move onto anyone else's lap of her own accord. Better the devil you knew, and all that.

"I'm Trey," Marco told her, as Tyler scooted close and Sam wrapped a protective arm around him. He felt thin and frail— bird bones. In that, he was like her. Clutching Ted, her son snuggled against her side. "It's a nickname."

Sam ignored the questions that were dying to be asked in favor of the more crucial matter. "We"—oh, God, she didn't want any part of this, but she had to get help for Mrs. Menifee; terror for the other woman kept her heart pounding and knotted her stomach—"have to go back. Somebody has to help her. She was hurt. Bleeding. And those men were still in my house. They still had her."

She hoped her tone conveyed everything else that she didn't want to say where Tyler could hear: that Mrs. Menifee had been tortured. That if they hadn't murdered her by the time she and Tyler had escaped, she felt that they almost certainly would have done so once they saw that their primary prey was gone. But there was always a chance that Mrs. Menifee was still alive, still suffering, still being tortured for information, and while there was that chance they had to go back and do what they could to save her.

"No can do." Sounding clearly indifferent to Mrs. Menifee's fate, the driver made no effort to so much as slow the speeding car down. Bright lights flashing into the car's interior, along with a glimpse of tall metal light poles and clustered service stations and fast food places, told Sam that they had reached the expressway interchange, and then they were zooming up the on-ramp onto I-64. Sam thought the driver was looking at her through the rearview mirror, but she couldn't be sure. "You're damned lucky we came after you."

Sam stiffened, and Marco's arm tightened around her waist. Tyler lifted his head, and for his sake she forced herself to moderate her tone. "You can't just leave her!"

"Sure we can," the driver said. "And we're going to."

"You're U.S. Marshals! You have to help her." Then Sam had a thought. "You *are* U.S. Marshals, right?"

The men around her all nodded. Marco gave her a look as though to say, *oh ye of little faith.*

"Yeah, we are. And we have a job to do." The driver's tone said the discussion was over. "That job is getting him"—he jerked his head in Marco's direction—"and now you and your son, out of harm's way. Which is what we're doing."

"But Mrs. Menifee—"

"The local cops are on the scene," Marco told her quietly. "They were pulling up as we were leaving. They'll handle it. There's nothing else we can do."

"I saw a police car, Mom," Tyler said. "The police will help Mrs. Menifee. Won't they?"

The uncertainty of his voice as he said that last made Sam's throat tighten. He'd been through so much tonight—way too much for anybody, much less a four-year-old, to have to endure. She gave him a reassuring hug. Thank God they hadn't found Tyler! Just thinking about it made her sick.

"Yes," she told him. "They will. Of course they will."

"You can thank us for that. We called 911," the guy whose

lap Tyler was still partly sitting on told her. He sounded a little defensive. "The local yokels will play mop-up. They'll find your friend, get her to a hospital."

"Best we can do," the driver said.

Outside the window, Sam saw metal struts flashing past. Beyond them curved the starry night sky. Below slid the denser black that was the river. They were on the bridge, one of a number of vehicles streaming into St. Louis. The giant, imposing curve of the Arch that was the symbol of the city glowed silver just ahead. Sam reluctantly understood that there was no going back. What happened to Mrs. Menifee now was beyond her control.

She felt terrible for her kindly neighbor, shaken and sad and guilty, and deeply, deeply sorry that such a horror had befallen her because of Mrs. Menifee's connection to her. But however reluctantly, she understood, too, that there was nothing more that she could do.

I'm lucky to still have Tyler. We're lucky to be alive.

"Before you got in the car, Tyler told us some of what happened. He said that the bas—"—Marco broke off, cast a glance in Tyler's direction, and corrected himself—"*bad* guys in your house hit you both with some kind of chemical spray."

Sam nodded. The effects of the pepper spray were wearing off—thank God she'd gotten only a small dose, and Tyler, she was almost certain, had gotten even less—but still her eyes teared and her vision was blurry and her eyes and skin stung. She had to keep blinking rapidly just to keep everyone in focus.

"We locked ourselves in Tyler's bedroom. They shot pepper balls under the door." Sam swallowed, or rather, tried to swallow, remembering. Her mouth was still Sahara dry, and what little saliva she had tasted bitter. She made a face, shuddering.

"Here." Marco passed her a half-full bottle of water that he got from the guy holding Tyler, plus a box of Kleenex. "Wipe out your eyes. Wipe your face and any exposed skin."

"Mom shot them," Tyler said as Sam accepted the items, then immediately took a swig from the water bottle. The wetness was heaven to her parched mouth, but the taste as the water went down made her think of Brussels sprouts mixed with battery acid. She grimaced and shuddered again. "She had her gun. She said she was going to shoot them some more if they tried to get into my room."

"You shot them?" Marco asked the question, although all the men looked at her with widening eyes. Sam nodded as she grabbed a handful of tissues from the box, wet them, and started applying them to her eyes. Oh, the relief!

"I shot *at* them. I don't think I hit any of them. I wish I had, though, believe me. Speaking of, I'd like my gun back."

A few *yeah, right* looks, a couple of negative headshakes, and one definitive *no* from the driver were her answer. Sam thought about arguing, decided it was a waste of time, and remembered that she was out of bullets anyway. Then a thought occurred, and she quit wiping her eyes long enough to frown up at Marco. "How did you find us? How did you find my house? I never told you where I lived. In fact, I was really careful not to."

"I said my address." Tyler sounded proud of himself. She'd spent days teaching him his address and phone number just the month before.

"When the—bad men—first broke into your house, Tyler called your cell phone looking for you. I have your phone, remember? He told me everything that was happening as it happened," Marco answered the look she gave him. "And he gave us your address."

"I told you I talked to Trey, Mom. I told you he was coming," Tyler said.

"I remember." She managed a smile for Tyler, along with another quick hug. "You did good, baby. I'm proud of you. You saved us."

"Are the bad men gone forever?" Tyler asked. His voice was suddenly very small.

"I hope so," the driver said grimly. But something about his tone told Sam that he wasn't convinced. Then she realized: the looks she'd thought he'd been giving her through the rearview mirror? They hadn't been directed at her at all. They'd been aimed behind her, as if he were watching for a following car. In fact, the marshals on either side of Marco had been casting quick glances behind them all along. The guy in the front passenger seat had been keeping a lookout through his side-view mirror.

"Yes, they are," she told Tyler in a firm tone that dared any of the men to contradict her. But even as she said it, her eyes met Marco's, and what she saw in them made a chill run down her spine.

They said as clearly as words could have done that the men who were hunting Marco weren't going to stop until he and, Sam very much feared, now her and Tyler, too, were dead.

She hated to pose the question in front of Tyler, because she hated to plant so much as another sliver of worry in his mind. But she had to know.

"So what happens now?" she asked.

CHAPTER TWELVE

"They stay with me," Danny told Sanders fiercely, referring to Sam and Tyler. He looked at Sam, who was
seated in one of a line of folding chairs placed against
the cinder-block wall of a small, dimly lit office off the National
Guard hangar at Scott Airfield. Drooping and pale, she looked
indescribably weary, along with a number of way less relevant
things, like far too young to be anybody's mom and absurdly
pretty, given what she had been through and the circumstances.
She had an arm around her kid, who was curled up against her
side, clutching his teddy bear and sound asleep. "*Sam.* You
make sure you two stay with me. Don't let them railroad you
and Tyler into going anyplace without me. Do you hear?"

"I hear."

The last glimpse he got of her was of her frowning after him
as he was rolled away. It was getting on toward 5:00 a.m., and
besides being scared to death and traumatized, she had to be
dead tired, but she was still hanging in there and he knew that
her continued vigilance was for the sake of her boy. A pair of

army medics, having loaded Danny onto a gurney, were hustling him away to emergency surgery in a hastily rigged operating room, where he would be put out briefly while they patched up his leg and other injuries. He didn't have much choice but to let it happen, but the catalog of things that could go wrong while he was out of commission was so long that he was worried sick. Over the week and a half before tonight's debacle that he as Marco had been in Sanders's supposed custody, Danny had learned something of how the other man worked: he was the master of high-handed decisions reached in the spirit of getting the job he was assigned to do done. He was perfectly capable of deciding that Sam and her kid were not his problem, and in fact were a detriment to doing what he had been ordered to do. He was, in short, perfectly capable of shipping them off somewhere while he, Danny, lay unconscious, then shrugging his shoulders about it after the fact.

Bottom line was, nobody official much cared about the fate of Samantha Jones and her son. Their involvement was accidental, and their rescue was, in Sanders's case at least, grudging. They had nothing other than basic descriptions of their attackers—which they had already provided to the marshals, during the latter part of the car ride to the airfield, confirming that Veith at least had been on the premises—to contribute to the case. With no vested interest in keeping them safe, no one, in any agency, would be going out of his or her way to do so. As long as Sam and Tyler had no knowledge of where "Marco" was being taken next, it wouldn't even officially matter to anyone in the game if Veith or some other whack team sent by the Zetas should find them. Which, unless mother and son were provided with first-rate assistance, the Zetas' guys eventually would do. As far as the government was concerned, Sam and Tyler were unneeded and expendable, which placed them in extreme danger.

Unless they were with him. The protection surrounding him had its flaws, not the least of which was that he had to be at least a little bit traceable to keep the Zetas on his trail rather than that of the real Rick Marco, but it was reasonably solid protection, the earlier debacle notwithstanding. But the thing was, as long as Sam and Tyler were with him, *he* could protect them. Which he had just made it his own personal mission to do. Of course, it would help if he were operating at something near full capacity, but he was hoping that would happen soon. The good news was, he tended to heal fast.

"You understand me?" he said to Sanders as the gurney was pushed through a pair of double doors into the small clinic where the surgery was going to happen. The antiseptic smell hit him in the face first. Then a glance in the direction that he was headed found a number of gowned and gloved medical professionals looking at him expectantly as he was rolled into view. *Damn, this is going to hurt.* But other, more urgent matters pushed the thought out of his mind. Danny frowned up at Sanders, who had already made it clear that he wasn't about to leave his charge's side. "They're not with me when I wake up, I don't say a word to anybody about anything."

"You get your kicks trying to blackmail the government?"

Sanders growled in reply. But Danny was reasonably sure his point had been made. If it hadn't been, it was too late to do anything about it. They were already at his side, shoving a needle into his arm. As something cold shot into his veins, he grimaced . . .

When he woke up, he was groggy and dry-mouthed and feeling way too good for it to be due to anything but a particularly felicitous combination of IV drugs. For a moment he floated, not thinking about anything in particular except that not being in pain was something to savor. Then reality started to intrude—his leg had hurt like a mother and there'd been an operation on it. He was still lying flat on his back, still on a gurney, but now he was strapped to the damned thing, across the chest and, he thought, the hips, which worried him, although probably less than it would have done if he hadn't been high as a kite on whatever narcotic elixir they had him on. He was in a small, narrow room with a curved ceiling. A half-full IV bag hung on a pole beside him with clear plastic tubing that allowed a golden liquid to drip down into his arm. It was cold, and he was covered by a white blanket to the armpits. His hands and arms, he was glad to discover, were free, and further groping exploration found that the buckles securing the straps were within reach, which meant that he could free himself if he had to, although probably not with any degree of speed. What light there was came out of weird little circular openings on either side of the ceiling. There was a sound, a deep, throbbing sound that made the room vibrate—a generator of some sort? An engine?

Then a figure stirred in the shadows at the far end of the room, separating itself from the wall. As Danny craned his neck to see better, whoever it was came walking toward him.

Danny tensed. He was feeling way too mellow to go on full-body alert, which would have alarmed him except that he was feeling way too mellow to feel particularly alarmed. He would have swung into a sitting position, except the straps securing him to the gurney wouldn't allow it.

Oh, yeah, the straps. Why the hell was he strapped down?

He felt for the buckle around his chest. But his hands were slow and his fingers were clumsy, and the hard truth was that freeing himself quickly just wasn't going to happen.

In worrisome evidence of how slow his thought processes currently were, yelling for help had just crossed his mind when the figure came close enough for him to identify it.

"Crittenden." He said his boss's name out loud. He should have felt relief, but he didn't.

"You left a hell of a mess for us to clean up, Panterro. Five goddamn bodies." A solid two hundred pounds at six foot one, with short, graying, dark hair, sharp features, and a perpetual deep tan, forty-eight-year-old FBI Special Agent in Charge Timothy Crittenden looked less than happy. He also looked the part of the National Guard officer whose uniform he was currently wearing. National Guard officer? Uniform? He even had an ID badge affixed to his chest. Danny blinked, turning that over in his currently slow-as-a-paddleboat mind. It didn't compute. Then he realized: Crittenden was undercover. Of course he was. Just like Danny himself was undercover, as federal-agent-on-the-take-turned-federal-stoolie-who-was-marked-for-death Rick Marco, also known as the Dirtbag for short. Nobody, including U.S. Marshal Bruce Sanders and his band of clowns, currently charged with his protection, could be allowed to know that the "Marco" they were guarding was not the real one, or that he had any connection whatsoever to the FBI. On the heels of that *aha* moment of remembrance, a frightening thought—if Crittenden could infiltrate Sanders's security arrangements then Veith and the Zetas probably could, too—caused Danny so little internal agitation that once again he had to chalk it up to the drugs.

"I only killed two of them," Danny protested. An urgent piece of information he needed to impart to Crittenden surfaced. "And, by the way, Army Veith is working for the Zetas now. He's the one who came after me."

"Veith, huh?" Crittenden's lips pursed in a soundless whistle. "They must really want you—ah, Marco—dead. Well, maybe we can end up taking him out as part of this operation, too."

"A happy thought."

Crittenden frowned at him. "So what the hell happened back there?"

"You tell me." The whole thing was slowly unspooling itself in Danny's mind. The assault on the safe house. The dead marshals. His own near-death experience. Sam. And Tyler. Anger, mild but measurably there, which given the apparent strength of the drugs he was on told him something, bubbled up inside him. "Where the fuck were you guys?"

"We couldn't get to you in time." Crittenden didn't sound

particularly apologetic. More like he had been late to an administrative meeting. An *unimportant* administrative meeting. "Hoffman and Lutts had eyes and ears on the place, but the thing about remote monitoring is it's remote. By the time we got to the scene, you were gone."

"I could've been killed." Ordinarily he wouldn't have bitched about it—the possibility of death was part of the job description in deep undercover ops like this one—but his internal censor was doing backstrokes in the sea of feeling-no-pain meds. "I *would've* been killed, if it hadn't been for this girl."

Crittenden gave a curt nod. "Samantha Jones. Age twenty-three. Single mother to Tyler, age four. Owner-operator of Sam's Towing, which consists of one wrecker and a contract with A+ Collateral Recovery. High school grad, a few college classes, now studying to be an EMT. Product of the foster care system. One arrest at the age of nineteen for shoplifting. Baby formula. No other record."

Danny gave Crittenden a long look as that information fit itself in with what he already knew about Sam. The shoplifting-baby-formula thing did a slow spin around his mind, but couldn't find a place to settle. Reason? It bothered him. In what kind of financial straits did a young mother have to be to shoplift baby formula? "You did a background check on her."

"Hell, yeah, I did. What if she was a plant?"

"She's no plant."

"And you know that because—oh, that's right, she's a real hottie."

"Nothing to do with that. She saved my life. If she hadn't shown up to tow away the car Veith had thrown me into the trunk of, this conversation wouldn't be happening because I'd be dead now. I owe her. I mean to make sure nothing happens to her or her son, you got that?"

Crittenden held up both hands in a gesture of innocence. "You say that like I've got a problem with that. I don't." His expression turned wry. "Beautiful young woman, though, I have to say. You always were the luckiest son of a bitch I ever met."

Danny fixed Crittenden with a look. He went for hard and purposeful but he wasn't exactly sure how that worked out, because he was feeling about as intimidating as a marshmallow. But still, he meant what he said. "Nobody's cutting her loose. She and her kid stay with me, get protection just like I do. Or you can take this assignment and stick it up your ass."

"No need to get testy." Crittenden's tone was reproving. "Actually, adding them to the mix works surprisingly well for us. Since they know about the girl, and they've already shown a willingness to go after her, it just lays down a heavier trail for the hunters to go sniffing for. Keeping them busy until Marco fingers every mule, supplier, and dirty agent he's worked with is the name of the game."

"So make sure it happens."

"I will. You have my word."

"Unless something goes wrong, huh?" The recent debacle being a case in point.

"Now that's just cynical. The girl will be protected, okay?"

A memory made Danny squint hard at his boss as it unfolded

at a maddeningly slow pace in his too-sluggish-to-survive mind. "Veith asked me where the money was. Right before he blew my leg to shit. When it looked like he was getting ready to do the same thing to my arm, I told him Santos had it. He seemed willing to believe me."

Crittenden's gaze sharpened. "What money?"

"Don't know. But Veith seemed to think there was some. From how bad he wanted to know where it was, I'm guessing it's a substantial amount."

"He didn't say—" Crittenden looked up sharply. A sound from outside the room penetrated Danny's consciousness a split second later, like his senses were on tape delay or something. Someone was coming. Maybe several someones.

"I need a weapon." Danny's tone was urgent. It was clear that his one-on-one with Crittenden was getting ready to be history.

Crittenden glanced down at him. "I'll see you get one. Not here. Later."

A metallic clunk, followed by the opening of a narrow door at the far end of the room, refocused Danny's attention in a hurry. He hadn't noticed the door before, probably because until that moment it had seemed to be part of the mysteriously curved wall. It rose up toward the outside like a lifting wing, letting in a burst of fresh warm air and a glimpse of what appeared to be dawn's early light. The slice of sky he could see was pale gray touched with pink. Blinking lights on a tower threw red flashes against the metal roof of a long, low building with giant garage doors: a hangar. That's when it hit him: he was inside an airplane. A small plane outfitted with maybe six seats, up toward the front, which he could only see if he lifted up his head. He and the stretcher were in the small cargo area in the back. A curtain separated the two areas, but it was only partially drawn. The plane was probably designed for patient transport, which would account for facilities to accommodate and secure a gurney.

"I'll be in touch." That was how Crittenden left it as he started walking toward the door. Danny didn't have a chance to reply.

"All squared away in back," Crittenden said to the scrubs-clad medic who stepped through the door just as he reached it. The medic didn't even seem surprised to see him. He just nodded and walked toward Danny as Crittenden exited the plane.

"Glad to see you're awake." When he was near the end of the gurney, the medic apparently saw Danny looking at him. "Sorry to leave you, but I had to take an emergency call. Hennessey get you all bolted down?"

Danny assumed that Hennessey was Crittenden, and by all bolted down, the medic was referring to the stretcher.

"Good to go." Danny gave the medic a thumb's-up. The guy checked his IV, which, Danny saw to his regret, was getting down to about a quarter full. Then Danny's attention was grabbed by the arrival of Sam, who stepped through the door with Tyler in her arms. The kid wasn't all that big, but he was big enough so that his feet dangled down almost to Sam's knees. She was a slender girl, and he looked way too heavy for her, but she was managing. His head was on Sam's shoulder, and it was obvious from his posture that he was sound asleep. Entering the small cabin, Sam seemed hesitant, but as she cast a swift look around the plane's interior and saw him he thought she relaxed just a little. He knew how she felt: he was relieved to see her and the kid, too. Until that moment, he hadn't realized just how worried he had been that she might not appear. Not that he didn't trust Sanders, or Crittenden—okay, truth was that he *didn't* trust them. Not either of them, not fully, not where Sam was concerned. Because they were both the same kind of by-the-book, the-mission's-the-thing operatives. If either of them thought having Sam and Tyler on board interfered with the job they had been entrusted with, then they would be looking to lose Sam and Tyler as fast as possible, with very little concern about how it impacted Sam and her son.

But here Sam was, her face pale and drawn with exhaustion, her hair having been reconfined into a haphazard ponytail that hung down her back in an unruly black mass, her white tank top and jeans stained with his blood, and still, as Crittenden had pointed out, looking hot. He gave her a brief wave, to which she responded with narrowed eyes and a grimace. Not exactly heartwarming, but at least she and the kid were there. Behind them came Sanders, with Groves, Abramowitz, and O'Brien. They looked tired, too, but Danny didn't care. A guy in a uniform brought up the rear, closing the door behind them. The pilot, or pilots, must have already been in the cockpit, because as soon as the door shut the engines started to rev. Everybody—everybody except him—sat down and strapped in. The medic pulled down a jump seat from the wall near Danny's head and strapped into that. Seconds later the plane was moving down the

runway, gathering speed. Then it took off, rising gracefully in a
steep ascension that would have sent him rolling if the stretcher
hadn't been fastened properly to the floor, which led Danny to
conclude with grudging admiration that Crittenden was a man
of unsuspected talents. Moments later, they were winging their
way to God knew where.

Nobody came to talk to him, and the movement coupled
with the droning of the engines was soporific. Danny didn't
even realize that he had fallen asleep again until he woke up.
The plane was just touching down, bouncing along the runway,
jarring him into wakefulness. By the time it taxied to a stop, he
was definitely aware that his leg was still far from 100 percent.
His other injuries were making themselves felt, too. Oh, not in
any way that was too acutely painful, but insistently enough so
that he didn't have to look at the IV bag to realize that whatever
wonder drug they'd been pumping into him had run out.

Shit.

A quick glance confirmed that Sam—and presumably Tyler,
although he couldn't see the kid—was still with him. That freed
his mind enough to consciously not think about the pain.

By the time they'd transferred out of the plane into a waiting
Chevy Suburban, tan instead of black as if to foil the suspicions
of any observers that the ride might belong to federal agents,
Danny had given up on the whole not-thinking-about-the-pain
thing as a lost cause. He felt like he'd been run over by a Mack
truck. One that had backed up an extra time over his leg. It was
still early morning, not quite 9:00 a.m. according to the clock in
the SUV's dashboard, but the sun was bright in a near cloudless

blue sky and the day gave promise of being a hot one. Mountains in the distance rose with cool purple majesty that contrasted with the flat, arid land through which they were driving. From various landmarks, Danny was pretty sure they were in Nevada, heading north. The only thing Sanders and his little band of unmerry men had said about their ultimate destination was that they were driving, not flying, the rest of the way in because planes were easy to track, while cars were less so. Not that their destination really mattered; the operative principle was to hide, and where was immaterial.

Before getting him up and into a wheelchair, which was waiting for him upon landing along with a pair of crutches for later, when he was ready to forsake the wheelchair, and then leaving him to Sanders and company's tender mercies, the medic had handed Danny a plastic bag full of medicine bottles with instructions for what he was to take, and when. The instructions had gone in one ear and out the other—taking pain meds was something that, since he needed his wits about him, he felt that it was probably better that he not do—but now that they were zooming along the expressway, traveling at a steady seven miles over the speed limit to stay with the flow of traffic without getting pulled over and keeping to the middle lane and doing everything else possible to blend with the other vehicles on the road, his leg was hurting worse than it had when he'd first been shot. Giving up—with four armed marshals for protection exactly how sharp did he need to be?—he fished out a bottle, checked the label just to make sure, popped the childproof lock, shook a couple of Lortab into his hand, and swallowed them without water. Then, just to be on the safe side, he swallowed two more.

And choked. And coughed. And choked some more.

"Here." Tyler, who'd woken up when they'd landed, offered Danny the battered orange juice box that Sam had procured from somewhere and that he'd been sipping on since they'd gotten into the SUV.

Ordinarily, he wouldn't have taken the kid's OJ. For one thing, the box had a picture of SpongeBob SquarePants on it, which made him think it was some kind of kid concoction that he wasn't going to like. For another thing, it had kid germs all over it. For a third, the kid was kind of pasty and big-eyed and looked like he needed the OJ way more than Danny did. But the pills were stuck in his throat and he really, really needed the pills.

His leg felt like something was trying to chew it off.

"Thanks." Accepting the juice box, he pulled out the straw and squirted some liquid into his mouth straight out of the little hole. Swallowing the stuff—it wasn't half bad—then restoring the straw to its rightful place and handing the juice box back to Tyler, he encountered a grim look from Sam.

"He offered," Danny replied to that look defensively.

He was in the very back seat, with his leg stretched out straight in front of him. Bandaged and splinted, it rested on a cooler that had been placed between the bucket seats one row up. He couldn't see exactly how his leg was trussed, because while he had been unconscious his clothes had disappeared, to be replaced by a set of baggy blue scrubs, but the whole thing felt way too tight. The bucket seats on either side of the cooler were occupied by Groves and O'Brien. Sam and Tyler, who like him had been relegated to the very back, bench seat—him, because of his need to stretch out his leg, and them, because of their relatively small size, and because they were the only other occupants of the vehicle who felt like getting that friendly with him—sat on either side of him, Tyler to his left and Sam to his right. In front, Sanders was driving and Abramowitz was once again riding shotgun. All of them looked like the morning after the night before. Danny guessed that he and Tyler were the only ones who'd gotten any appreciable sleep on the plane.

"Tyler needs breakfast," Sam said, first to him and then, leaning forward and repeating it more loudly, to the other occupants of the vehicle at large, in a tone that told Danny that she wasn't in the sunniest of humors. "We need to stop soon."

"We're not stopping until we get where we're going," Sanders replied. "Another few hours."

"I got a Snickers in my pocket the kid can have," Groves volunteered, looking around at them.

"Thank you, but it's probably better if he doesn't eat candy for breakfast. Or in the car. It might make him sick."

"Ri-i-ight. Don't want that," Groves replied, and wasn't alone in shooting Tyler a wary look.

"It's okay, Mom," Tyler intervened. "I'm not hungry."

"What's in the cooler?" Danny asked, hoping the answer was food, knowing that getting Sanders to stop before he felt safe in doing so was the closest thing to a lost cause there was. If the kid needed breakfast, the cooler was his best hope.

Sam's eyes narrowed at him. "G-U-N-S," she spelled, clearly not wanting Tyler to know the answer. "I already checked."

"Guns," Tyler repeated happily, perking up a little. "Can I see them?"

"No," Sam said, looking so cross that Danny had to smile.

The sharp look she sent him in response wiped the smile from Danny's face.

"Good job teaching him to spell," Danny offered hastily. Sam didn't look appeased.

"So where *are* we going?" Sam's arms folded over her chest as she settled back against the seat. "Mr. Sanders, I'm talking to you."

The vibes she was giving off were pure cranky. A couple of tendrils of sooty hair curled around her face, and Danny guessed that they were coming loose again because her ponytail, which she'd scraped back from her face and resecured once more before they'd left the plane, was already giving up the ghost. The ponytail, plus the fact that she was wearing no makeup—she'd washed her face in the plane's restroom; he knew because she had emerged while still drying it with a paper towel—should have detracted from her prettiness. It didn't. What it did was make her look like she was about fifteen years old. Unless, of course, he checked out her body, which he was happy to discover was absolutely 100 percent adult. Since he was taller and she was wearing a clingy, low-cut tank top and was sitting right beside him, the round firmness of her breasts, along with the shadowy cleavage between them, was difficult to miss every time he glanced her way, especially since the

Lortab was interfering with his internal control panel to what he suspected was a significant degree. Getting his mind off of the creamy curves that were just a sideways slide of his eyeballs away required discipline, which apparently he didn't have a whole lot of at the moment. But Danny summoned enough willpower to look straight ahead, out through the windshield at the vehicles rushing by on either side, then kept his mind out of the tank top by focusing on Sam's chutzpah in continuing to harangue Sanders, which was really quite considerable when he thought about the fact that the other man was a fortyish federal agent of the domineering type and Sam was—well, unintimidating was probably the best way to put it. Danny could have told her that asking the other man where they were going was a waste of time, but he was busy working on enjoying the effects of the Lortab without doing anything too stupid, like getting caught looking down her shirt.

"Somewhere," Sanders answered repressively.

"This is crap." Sam's eyes snapped. They had dark shadows beneath them, from lack of sleep Danny was sure, but, seen by daylight, they looked even bluer than he had thought they were the previous night. Lapis lazuli, maybe, or sapphire. Her lashes were long and thick and unmistakably girly, and as inky black as her hair. Her eyebrows, black, too, and delicately arched, almost met above her nose as she scowled at Sanders. Her mouth, for all her irritation, which was causing it to tighten, was full and naturally pink and temptingly soft looking. Just like the upper slopes of her breasts, barely visible above the curve of her top, looked temptingly sof—

Hold it. No. Not going there.

"What, exactly, is crap?" Sanders countered.

"This whole freaking mess. From beginning to end." Her eyes lifted, and collided with Danny's. "When do we get to go home?"

There really wasn't any truthful answer to that, so Danny gave her a semiapologetic grimace.

"Soon as possible?" he tried.

"More crap."

"Best answer you're going to get," Sanders put in. Unwisely, in Danny's opinion, but at least it got Sam's attention off him.

The Lortab was really kicking in, he realized just then. Jerking his eyes up from where they had landed during their latest accidental downward slide, Danny focused on something, anything else—her eyes—instead. They now blazed at Sanders— thank Jesus—who, with his back turned, was oblivious. Danny was only glad that her ire was directed toward Sanders and not at him. From the way the other men subtly adjusted their positions so that none of them was looking in Sam's direction any longer, Danny got the feeling that he was not the only one glad not to be in the line of fire.

"I want to know where you're taking us." Sam's tone was even sharper than before. "I have a right to know."

Through the rearview mirror Danny saw Sanders's eyes narrow, and surmised a reply was in the offing that would piss its target royally off.

"We're in Nevada," he intervened, before Sanders could respond with something that would just make life more difficult for all of them. "Going north." Glancing toward the mountains in the distance, making a quick calculation, he added, "I'm guessing we're heading toward Idaho."

Sanders's through-the-mirror frown told him that he was correct.

"Where in Idaho?" Those big blue eyes turned on Danny. They were not filled with sweetness and light. Damn, he should have stayed out of it.

"Don't know," he had to admit. She glared at him.

"Where in Idaho?" Sam addressed the back of Sanders's head.

Sanders threw the reply over his shoulder. "That's on a need-to-know basis."

"So I need to know."

"I was told to keep our destination a secret until we get there," Sanders said grimly. "And that's what I mean to do. It's for your safety, Ms. Jones. All of our safety."

Watching Sam's lips tighten—and, as an adjunct, her chest swell—Danny forced his eyes forward again even as he braced himself for a blast of indignation.

"Are the bad men still looking for us?" Tyler piped up, his voice sounding small and strained. He sidled a little closer to Danny's side as he spoke, prompting Danny to glance down at him. On Danny's other side, Sam made an inarticulate but pained sound. Her eyes had darkened and she was giving Tyler a worried look.

Before she could say anything else, or Sanders could come out with something that might be even more kid-fear-inducing, Danny said lightly to Tyler: "Your mom scared all the bad men off. Think about it: would *you* go anywhere near her if you thought she had a gun?"

That made Tyler chuckle. He shook his head. "No."

"Me neither." Danny grinned at him.

"We're fine, baby. You don't have to worry." Sam's voice had lost its edge as she sought to soothe her son.

"I know, Mom. We're safe now that we're with Trey."

From Sam's expression, Danny could tell she didn't exactly buy into that. He also knew she wasn't going to argue. Then Danny felt a small hand sliding into the crook of his elbow. Glancing down, he saw that Tyler was hugging his arm. Apparently feeling Danny's gaze on him, the kid looked up and smiled at him. He had black-lashed blue eyes that were exactly like his mom's—except Tyler's shone with trust. In him. Bandaged finger or no, Danny shifted so that his arm was draped around the kid's shoulders. Tyler snuggled closer against his side.

The small action touched something deep inside Danny that he hadn't even known was there.

Whatever happens, I'm keeping this kid—and his mother—safe.

Sam gave him a look that he found impossible to read. He was pretty sure that it didn't translate into *thanks for being nice to my son*, however.

He smiled at her. She scowled at him.

For a while they rode in silence except for the hum of the pavement beneath the wheels. The sun rose, and the day got hotter. Danny knew, because even inside the SUV it was starting to get warm. At least, it was getting warm in the backseat, where the air-conditioning apparently didn't altogether reach. With both Tyler and Sam leaning against him, drowsing, Danny felt himself starting to sweat. Plus, his leg was starting to hurt, which meant the Lortab must be wearing off. Now was the time to pop a couple more pills—before the pain set in again for real—but he hated to reach for the plastic bag in which they were tucked away in the seat back pocket in front of Sam because he didn't want to wake up either Sam or Tyler.

He set himself to endure.

The marshals were talking quietly among themselves. Danny couldn't really hear what they were saying, and he didn't much care. He watched out the window as the flat plains turned into wooded hills and thunderheads rolled in to obscure the mountains to the west. An eighteen-wheeler roared past, shaking the SUV. Beside him, Tyler gave what sounded like a little burp.

At the sound, Sam woke up instantly, straightening away from him like he'd suddenly turned red hot. She stretched a little, glared at Danny in passing—maybe she was pissed because she'd been leaning against his shoulder as she slept? Otherwise, he didn't have a clue what that was about—then looked anxiously at Tyler.

Tyler was awake, too, ducking out from under Danny's protective arm, rubbing his hands over his face.

Taking advantage of the moment, Danny leaned forward to grab the plastic bag of pills.

"Mom," Tyler said in the tiniest voice Danny had yet heard from him. "I think I'm going to be sick."

Sick? As in, upchuck?

After one frozen-in-place instant, during which Tyler made a terrifying gagging sound, Danny had his answer: yep.

Galvanized, desperately thankful that the Lortab had worn off enough for his reflexes to be halfway close to normal, Danny dumped his pills from the plastic bag into his lap. Even as Sam leaned across him, crying, "You need to pull this car over *right now*," to the unsuspecting chumps up front, Danny took one look at Tyler, snapped the plastic bag open, and held it by its handles in front of the kid's pale and perspiring face.

Just in time for the kid to fill it up.

CHAPTER THIRTEEN

It had been, hands down, the worst twenty-four-hour period
of Sam's life. Mrs. Menifee was definitely dead: that information had been relayed to Sanders right before they had
boarded the plane. Sanders had passed it on to the other marshals, who had passed it on to Sam, and she felt by turns heart-
broken, horrified, grieving, and guilty. So far she hadn't told
Tyler. She wasn't sure that she would, certainly not if he didn't
ask. She and Tyler had nearly been killed, too, and were still, she
feared, marked for death, so she was in a constant state of low-
grade fear. Plus they'd been ripped away from their home and
everything they knew, and she had no idea when they would be
going home again. In other words, her life been run off the rails
straight into the twilight zone, and she didn't see any way that it
was going to improve anytime soon.

Head pounding, so tired that just putting one foot in front of
the other was an effort, Sam walked out of the unfamiliar bedroom in which she had just told her son what felt like a million
bedtime stories—usually she read to him, but here they had no

books—until he had fallen asleep. What she saw as she stepped into the darkened hall stopped her in her tracks. In the bathroom opposite, wrapped in a white toweling robe, Marco stood balanced on one foot, leaning precariously against the sink, the aluminum crutches he'd switched to upon reaching this house leaning against the sink next to him, his head tilted back and his hand at his mouth as he swallowed. The small brown plastic pill bottle clutched in his other hand told the story: he was downing more pain meds.

Her brows snapped together.

Crabby didn't even begin to describe how out of sorts she was feeling. It was after 11:00 p.m. mountain time, which meant that it was after midnight back home in East St. Louis. Except for the catnap she'd grabbed in the SUV earlier—annoying to remember that she'd wound up snoozing against Marco's shoulder—she'd had no sleep for about thirty-six hours. Lunch had been McDonald's, procured on the fly via a drive-through after Tyler, poor baby, had done what she had feared and succumbed to motion sickness. It happened sometimes, usually when his stomach was empty. She should have insisted that they stop for food, but she hadn't. She had still been running scared, damn it, and Tyler had been the one to pay the price, which wasn't going to happen again if she could help it. Supper had been pizza, picked up on their way through the small town of Pocatello, Idaho. That's where they were currently holed up, in a three-bedroom town house in a quiet middle-class neighborhood near the Portneuf River. Upstairs, which was where she, Tyler, and Marco presently were, there were two full bathrooms—one connected to the master bedroom—along with the three bedrooms. She had the master, Tyler had the bedroom next to hers, and Marco had the third, on the opposite side of the hall. Downstairs, there was a half bath, plus a great room with a huge fireplace, a kitchen with an eating area, a den, and a screened porch. O'Brien was at that moment standing guard—or, rather, watching TV—in the great room. Having apparently drawn the night's short straw, Groves was stationed in the SUV, parked strategically in the driveway next door, keeping watch through its tinted windows. Sanders and Abramowitz, meanwhile, were in the town house that belonged to the driveway, one assigned to watch the security cameras that monitored all entrances to the town house where she, Tyler, and Marco were holed up, and the other presumably getting some sleep.

These security arrangements had been explained to Marco when they had first arrived at the town house, while she had listened in. None of the men had bothered to explain anything to her. At the time, with Tyler plopped down beside her on the couch, nibbling on a slice of pizza while watching TV and apparently paying no attention to what was going on around them while she knew perfectly well that he was actually absorbing everything like a little sponge with ears, she hadn't asked any questions, not wanting to let on to Tyler how worried she was about the situation they were in.

Which didn't mean, then and now, that she wasn't bursting with them.

How long would they be there? She had no idea. What were they supposed to do now that they were there? She had no idea about that, either. What was happening at home? Same answer. She had no idea about anything, and anxiety about it was driving her around the bend. The icing on her particular cake was that she had a splitting headache: the blow she'd taken to the head before she was dumped into the Beemer's trunk was definitely making itself felt. Or maybe it was a tension headache, because she definitely was experiencing tension. Whatever, she was feeling decidedly subpar. Plus she wouldn't be surprised if Tyler woke up with screaming nightmares.

Actually, given all that he had just been through, she would be surprised if he *didn't* wake up with screaming nightmares.

And the cause of all her problems was standing right in front of her, in a robe, barefoot, with a deep vee of tanned and muscular bare chest exposed, giving not the smallest indication that he was concerned with anything except downing way too many pills.

"You're not supposed to take more than eight of those pills in twenty-four hours, you know," she snapped, pausing just outside the bathroom door to glare at him because she just couldn't help herself. Not that she'd been keeping track, but this was the fourth time she'd watched him gulp down pain pills, and every time she'd counted he'd swallowed at least four pills at a time. She was too tired to do the math, but that brought the count to way over eight pills in way less than twenty-four hours. That she knew of. And who knew how many she'd missed? "What, are you a druggie along with everything else?"

Groves and O'Brien had taken what had seemed like a great deal of pleasure in filling her in on exactly what "everything else" was while Marco had been having his leg operated on. Learning that he was a corrupt federal agent—"used to be one of us" was how Groves had put it—who had turned against his own side and secretly collaborated with the drug traffickers he had supposedly been targeting as part of an ongoing investigation wasn't a total surprise, because he was fit and smart and she could totally picture him as a former federal agent and clearly he'd been in the custody of U.S. Marshals for a reason. But the knowledge bothered her, much as she hated to admit it. Until then, she'd almost felt like he was someone she could trust. Now she knew better. He was someone *nobody* could trust, and she meant to keep that in the forefront of her mind.

"I'm not a druggie. My leg hurts." His tone was mild as he set the pill bottle down. Cupping his hand, he took a couple of gulps of water from the sink, shut the faucet off, and turned to eye her appraisingly. Either the bathroom was smaller than she'd thought when she'd helped Tyler take a bath in there earlier, or Marco was bigger than she'd thought. Either way, he seemed to take up a lot of space. The top of his head was almost even with the top of the big mirror that ran along most of the left wall, and his shoulders were broad enough that they seemed to fill most of the space between the tub and the sink. "Anyway, how do you know how many pills I'm supposed to take?"

"Because unlike you, I was listening when the doctor told you." Her answer was tart.

"Ah." With his hip braced against the sink cabinet, Marco looked her up and down, his expression way too alert for the kind of day he'd had. His hair was wet and shiny black in consequence, and slicked back from his face. His nose was still swollen, one eye was still black, purpling bruises marred his forehead and left cheekbone and the left side of his jaw, and a small cut was visible at the corner of his mouth. But he'd been applying ice to his face off and on for much of the day, and in consequence looked much better. Handsome, even, just as she had suspected. From the dampness of his hair, his bare feet and calves, and his apparent lack of clothing apart from the robe, she surmised that he had just gotten out of the shower. Since she had recently showered and was wearing a white toweling robe herself, over too-large white granny panties and a man's white T-shirt—the furnished house had come complete with a small selection of brand-new, still-with-the-price-tags-on clothing in the dresser drawers, which had been presented to them as theirs to use as they saw fit as part of their temporary new identities as a married couple, Greg and Laura James, and their son Tyler— she couldn't fault him for that. But she could—and did—fault him for everything else. The whole damned mess, in fact.

"Tyler get to sleep?" he asked.

She didn't want to talk about Tyler with him. "Yes."

She started to move away.

"Hang on, I need to ask you something. Okay, so I was kind of out of it when the medic was explaining about my medication. I've got the pain pills and the antibiotic pills pretty much down, I think. But what am I supposed to do with the lube tube?"

"Lube tube?" Sam had hesitated and glanced around at him when he'd started talking, but she had been just about to shut him down with the astringent observation that his meds were his problem and then once more head off for bed when that semirevolting description caught her attention.

"This." Glancing down, he picked up what looked like a family size toothpaste tube and held it up for her viewing pleasure (or not). It was black and yellow, with a screw-off lid. "You have any idea what I'm supposed to do with this?"

It was quite possible that she didn't want to know, but curiosity won out: Sam stepped closer, onto the beige tiled floor—everything in the house seemed to be beige or brown or some other muted earth tone—the better to see the tube. The bathroom was still steamy warm and fragrant from his shower, and a small degree of condensation still clung to the edge of the big mirror behind the sink. The shower curtain was still inside the combination tub/shower, which was beaded with water droplets. Stopping just inside the doorway, she peered at the writing on the tube: Bactroban ointment.

"It's an antibiotic ointment. Tomorrow—that would be twenty-four hours after they removed the bullet from your leg—you're supposed to change the bandages and apply it to the wound. Liberally. Then bandage it up again. Repeat once a day." She couldn't help it: she glanced down at his damaged leg, currently not visible because of the sheltering robe, which reached just past his knees. On her, what seemed to be the identical robe went clear down to her ankles, and was big enough to wrap around her twice. Probably, she thought, they were one size fits all, which served as a pretty good indication of just how large he was. "And you're supposed to keep the bandages clean and *dry*."

"I am keeping them clean and dry. See?" Before Sam realized what he meant to do, he twitched the edges of his robe apart to give her a look at his thigh. For a hideous moment she feared he might be flashing her. Then she saw the barely visible pale blue hem of what she assumed was a pair of boxers, and felt a little spurt of relief. A black plastic garbage bag swathed his leg from just below the boxers to the top of his knee. While she watched, he pulled the bag off so she could see what looked like acres of white gauze wrapped around and around his thigh beneath. "Not even damp."

"Oh, yay." The marked lack of enthusiasm with which she said it made him smile. It was, Sam realized, the first time she had seen him really smile, and it was a revelation. *Cute guy.* The words popped into her head of their own volition, and she immediately realized that was how she would have described him to Kendra. It didn't please her. At the look she gave him the smile broadened into a grin that was slightly lopsided, possibly due to his cut lip. It revealed strong white teeth and crinkles around the corners of his eyes, which, she was just now observing, were a deep, coffee brown. It was a teasing grin, and it made him look younger than she had thought. It was also sexy as hell.

That thought made her scowl again. *Sexy* was the last word she wanted rattling around inside her head when it came to Marco. Almost as annoyed at herself now as she was at him, she started to turn away. She was so tired she was drooping with it, and the only cure for that was sleep. Sleep, too, would probably cure her headache. And what was that saying about everything looking better in the morning? She could only hope. Catching a glimpse of herself in the mirror, she saw that she was as pale as chalk, with shadows beneath her eyes. Even her mouth looked pale. She had washed and towel dried her hair—if there was a blow-dryer around she hadn't found it—and tucked it behind her ears before going in to put Tyler to bed. Nearly dry now, it hung to the middle of her back in an unruly tangle of midnight black curls.

She was something else that would hopefully look better in the morning. Or at least when she located a blow-dryer and had time to tame her hair.

"Good night," she added over her shoulder.

Marco stopped her exit by coming out with a hasty, "Uh, by the way, since you were listening so well, did you happen to hear anything about how long until I'm good to go again? Because if anybody said anything about that, I totally missed it."

Turning back around, Sam shot him a scathing look. "You totally missed a lot, didn't you? Probably because you've been high as a kite all day."

"I am not high. I'm on pain meds. And that would be because I'm in pain. At least, when I'm not on the meds." That grin flashed at her again. When she narrowed her eyes at him, he added hastily, "So did you hear anything about how long it's supposed to take for me to be able to walk without crutches again, or not?"

"Nope." He was reaching for his crutches, and against her

better judgment she helped him out by handing over the one that was farthest from him. "Although he did say that you were supposed to change your bandages and put ointment on the wound every day for a week."

"Ah." Marco looked pleased. "A week, then."

"But, see, I think you're also supposed to stay off the leg for a week. As in, use the wheelchair they gave you. The crutches were for after that."

He shrugged. "I don't like being pushed around in wheelchairs. And they're hell climbing stairs."

Watching him fit the crutches under his arms, impressed by the muscles that she could see flexing in his chest and arms and then feeling annoyed at herself, first for looking and then for being impressed, she frowned at him. "Since we're talking about how long things are supposed to take, do you have any idea how long it'll be before Tyler and I can go home again?"

Again with the shrug. Accompanied by a quick, assessing glance at her. That she read as meaning, *You don't want to know. And I don't want to be the one to tell you.* Then as her frown darkened he got busy hopping around trying to get his crutches situated. On purpose, she had no doubt.

That lack of a direct reply made her angry. She folded her arms over her chest and fixed him with a simmering look.

"Because we can't just disappear, you know. Not for long. People will be worried about us." Sam thought about Kendra, and her other friends, and her great-aunt Marla, former girlfriend of her aforementioned "uncle" Wilfred, whom she didn't see a whole lot of but whom she did see from time to time and who would miss her eventually, and Tyler's father, whom she saw even less often than she saw Marla but who at some point would surely realize that his son was nowhere to be found, and the people at A+ Collateral Recovery, and . . . "People probably are already worried about us." She thought about Kendra again. "If they know about Mrs. Menifee, they'll be going out of their minds."

Marco had both crutches firmly under his armpits now, and was standing on his good leg. "You gave your phone to Sanders, didn't you?"

Sam nodded.

"Then he'll have passed it on to the cleanup crew, and the people you call most often, or who call you most often, will have gotten a text from you saying something like you were called away on a family emergency. It was probably sent even before we got on the plane this morning."

"Nobody who knows us is going to believe that!" Sam thought about her great-aunt, who was ninety-two and lived in a nursing home in Wentzville. Kendra might actually believe the emergency concerned Marla, who had been kind of sickly lately. If Kendra didn't hear from Sam and Tyler in a few days, though, she would almost certainly call Marla, or rather the nursing home where Marla was living, to be told that no, it didn't, then start calling around to their various friends, to check out other possibilities. If Kendra then found no trace of them, what would she do? Call the police? Maybe, but calling the police wasn't something that people in East St. Louis did. File a missing persons report? Maybe again, but . . . Sam frowned as one really good reason why nobody would believe she'd just been called away on a family emergency hit her. "Nobody's for sure going to believe it when they find out that poor Mrs. Menifee was *murdered in my house.*"

"Maybe they'll think that's the real reason you left. That you were involved in something bad that went wrong. Maybe you found the body and were scared and ran away. Or maybe you committed the crime and fled."

"Nobody's going to think I killed Mrs. Menifee." Sam's eyes widened as she made some unwelcome mental connections. "Oh, my God, that's not what the police think, is it?"

"She was killed in your house, and when the police got there you were nowhere to be found."

Sam must have looked horrified, because his grin flashed at her again. That's when she knew she was being teased.

"This isn't funny," she said crossly.

"The look on your face is, just a little bit. Uh, didn't you say you fired some shots in your house? I bet the police will be able to trace those bullets back to your gun."

Sam had an electrifying thought. "What about those two men I shot? Will they be able to connect the bullets they recover from my house to them?" Visions of being charged with murder—maybe three murders if they included Mrs. Menifee—made her stomach knot.

He shook his head. "I doubt the cops will ever know anything about those guys. They're probably making the acquaintance of the Mississippi River catfish about now."

"Oh, my God." Sam didn't know what her face looked like, but it must have been expressive, because he laughed.

"Anyway, since Sanders took your gun, it's long gone. No ballistics to compare."

"That's a good thing." If she sounded slightly doubtful, it was because that was how she felt.

"Yeah." His eyes still danced. Then, in response to something he saw in her face—probably stark fear—his expression turned serious. "The cleanup crew—the agents on the ground—they're pros. They'll see to it that there's some sort of cover story about what happened to Mrs. Menifee that most likely won't involve you as the murderer, and that includes where you and Tyler went, and they'll wrap it up in a big bow that will make it easy for the local cops to buy. They'll pacify whoever needs pacifying, and they'll make sure nobody goes all Nancy Grace looking for you. Believe me, you won't even make the papers."

Sam was aghast. "They can do that?"

"Oh, yeah."

She looked at him with disbelief. "Who *are* you guys?"

The grin came and went. "Your tax dollars at work, baby doll."

Remembering that he was no longer entitled to be paid by those tax dollars, Sam didn't say anything for a moment. When she did, her voice was softer, troubled.

"Mrs. Menifee—I saw her. Tied to one of my kitchen chairs. It looked like—" Sam took a deep breath. "It looked like they tortured her. There was blood everywhere. I'm pretty sure they"—she hesitated because it was hard to even get the words out—"cut off the tip of one of her fingers." She fixed him with an accusing gaze. "Because they were looking for you."

He wasn't smiling any longer. His eyes held hers. "I'm sorry they did that to her. I'm sorry you had to see it. I'm sorry any of you got involved."

Sam's throat felt tight. "She had nothing to do with any of this. She was just baby-sitting Tyler."

"I know. These guys—they have no respect for human life. They'll kill anyone who gets in their way."

"They would have done something horrible to Tyler if they'd found him." It wasn't a question; she knew it for an absolute fact. Even thinking about what could have happened made Sam feel cold all over. "They would have killed him. And me. They *will*, if they find us."

His expression acknowledged the truth of that. "Which is why you and Tyler are staying with me."

Sam made a scoffing sound. "Like being at ground zero is going to keep us safe? *You're* the one they're really looking for."

"Ground zero or not, you're safer with me than you would be anywhere else."

"So you say. I'm not so sure."

"You got some alternative you want to share with me, I'm all ears."

He had her there. There was no alternative that she could come up with. Kendra, Marla, a host of people might be willing to take her and Tyler in and even help them hide, but after seeing what had been done to Mrs. Menifee, Sam wouldn't inflict such a danger on her worst enemy, much less people she cared about. She thought about just taking Tyler and running and hiding on her own, but immediately dismissed it. First, not being a professional fugitive, she didn't have a great deal of confidence in her ability to disappear without a trace, and second, she had no money to run away on. Being broke, as she had discovered a long time ago, tended to severely limit your options.

The sense of being trapped was suffocating.

He was watching her. "You got nothing, am I right?"

Reluctantly Sam shook her head. Still, there was no way she and Tyler could just drop off the radar so easily. He had preschool, and play dates, and she—she had classes. And work. And bills. As the inescapable realities of life started crawling out of the hole where terror had buried them, her eyes widened.

"I have a class on Monday. I guess I can miss it, but . . . I can't miss more than three or I don't pass the course. Plus my electricity bill is due on Monday. I mean, really due. I got a shut-off notice. If I don't pay by then, they'll turn the electricity off. And I have to pay Tyler's preschool Monday, too, or he'll lose his place. And . . ." As Sam thought about all the things she had coming up, she felt her chest tighten. If she didn't go to class, she would flunk. If she didn't go to work, they didn't have any money. And if she wasn't home, she couldn't work. "I have a check waiting for me at A+ right now. I need to pick it up. Oh, my God, I'll lose my contract with them. If I'm not there to repossess the cars they need to have repossessed, they'll just give the work to someone else." Probably Bobby Thompson at Thompson's Towing, or Al Fisher at Downtown Towing, or—

there were so many. At the idea that she could lose her liveli-
hood, Sam felt growing panic. She had worked too hard to find
a way to scratch out a living for herself and Tyler just to let it go
like this. "I left the wrecker on the street across from the duplex.
You can only park there on weekends. If I'm not there to move
it by early Monday morning, they'll tow it. Then I'll have to
pay who knows how much to get it out. I can't afford it. I have
to go home."

He was looking at her steadily. "You know you can't, right?"

"I have to. We'll lose everything." Sam's stomach was in the
process of turning inside out.

He frowned. "Make a list of what has to be paid. I'm sure
some kind of arrangements can be made."

"Some kind of arrangements can be made? What about my
class? And who's going to go out every night and haul cars in
for me? Who's going to keep my business going?" Sam's fists
clenched, and she turned away abruptly. "And then there's
Mrs. Menifee. She was never anything but kind to Tyler and me,
and she's *dead*. She's dead, and Tyler and I almost died, and now
our lives are going to be ruined. And it's all because of *you*."

"Sam." He was following her into the hall when the edge of
his crutch caught on the threshold, where tile met thick beige
carpet. "Look out!"

Sam turned in time to see him stagger. Just as quick as that
he lost his balance and started to fall. Instinctively she surged
toward him, tried to grab him, to steady him, only to have him
crash into her and send her reeling into the wall.

God, the guy was big.

"Umph." The sound was forced out of her as he smacked into her. With the wall hard against her back, she felt like a bug being squashed.

"Ow! Damn it!" The exclamation came from him as, in trying to regain his footing, he apparently accidentally put weight on his injured leg. He pitched sideways. The crutches went tumbling. Clutching at her shoulders, he tried to save himself. Locking her arms around his waist, Sam did her best to hold him up, but he was too heavy, and was off-balance to boot. There was nothing she could do. They performed a kind of staggering dance that ended badly: together they tumbled to the floor. Sam landed flat on her back, with him partly beside and partly on top of her. For a stunned moment she lay unmoving, fighting to catch her breath, as a stream of muttered curses passed over her head. His fall had loosened his robe so that what was pinning her to the floor was a lot of near naked man. He was heavy as a sack of cement, and she pushed at him in a vain attempt to shift his weight. With his robe askew, her hands encountered smooth, damp skin over sinewy muscles; she was pushing just above his hipbones, on the sides of his taut waist, without making any appreciable difference at all to their respective positions. She could feel the expansion and contraction of his rib cage as he breathed. Unwillingly inhaling the scent of soap and man, she felt the prickly warmth of hair-roughened bare skin brushing her cheek, along with the solid length of his uninjured leg lying against hers. A lightning sideways glance told her that it was his chest that her cheek was touching. Tan like the rest of him, his chest was wide and muscular, with a wedge of black hair in the center. The unmistakably masculine look and feel of it—of him—bothered her in a way she refused to even try to define. Jerking her face clear of skin-to-skin contact, she shifted as best she could, managing to scoot upward an inch or so, winding up at approximate eye level with his square chin and his grimacing mouth. One of his hard-muscled arms rested beneath her head. The other curved across her shoulders. His injured leg lay across her thighs. His entire body was tense, with pain, she thought. Uncomfortable with the closeness of the contact, she would have shot to her feet if it had been at all possible, but it wasn't. There was no way she was getting up until he moved. Shifting her gaze higher with some reluctance, she met his eyes. They were a little glazed, unfocused even. She wasn't even sure that he knew whom he was looking at.

Which suited her fine.

"Are you okay?" she asked, although from his expression it wasn't hard to guess that the answer was no. The fall had undoubtedly jarred the wound. She only hoped that it hadn't done more than that, like make it start bleeding again or something. Luckily the carpet was thick plush, and his leg had landed on her rather than anything less yielding.

"I'll live." His voice was tight, but at least he was answering.

She took a steadying breath. If having him wrapped around her like this was making her feel ill at ease, she sure wasn't going to let him know it. "See why you should have stayed in the wheelchair?"

"Staying in a wheelchair doesn't work for me." She could feel the tension slowly easing out of his muscles. Out of the corner of her eye she watched him carefully flexing his hand, and re-membered that his leg was just the worst of his injuries, and not the extent of them by a long shot.

"Why not?"

"I need to get back up to speed. ASAP."

"That's really not going to happen if you keep falling all over the place."

"The end of one of my crutches got caught on the carpet. Pure accident."

"You're trying to do too much too soon." Good God, she sounded like she could have been scolding Tyler, if he were do-ing something of which she disapproved. The smallest upward quirk of Marco's lips told her that he recognized the tone, too.

"I'm a little older than four, you know."

"You could have fooled me." She squirmed discreetly, just to see if there was any possible way she could get out from under him. There wasn't. But she needed to. The warmth of his body, the feel of so much nearly naked masculinity wrapped around her, was doing funny things to her insides. "Do you want to try to get up now?"

Their faces were only inches apart, so close that she could smell the faint minty aroma of the toothpaste he had apparently just used. He needed a shave: probably two days' worth of stub-ble darkened his jaw. Glancing up in an effort to avoid looking at his mouth, which was actually really very nicely shaped, she met his eyes instead. He was regarding her almost meditatively.

"Yeah," he said, without making the slightest move to do so. "Did I hurt you?"

"No." She looked at him more closely. His eyes were more black than brown now, and she realized that it was because his pupils were dilated. Of course, there was a reason that he had stumbled, a reason he had knocked them both down, and a reason he wasn't moving faster to get up. As that reason became crystal clear to her, she gave him a disgusted look. "You're really flying now, aren't you?"

"Flying?" He frowned, then as comprehension dawned gave a negative shake of his head. "Nope. Not flying. Thing is, you're not high if you really need the pain meds you're on. And right now, I need them." He inhaled, seemingly more deeply than before, and his lids lowered a little. From beneath a fringe of stubby black lashes his eyes held hers. There was something in the look he was giving her . . . "You know what? You smell like strawberries."

Before she could even begin to formulate a reply to that, he lifted his head, shifted a little, and kissed her.

CHAPTER FOURTEEN

I t had been way too long since a man had kissed her. That
was the problem, Sam told herself fiercely as his mouth
molded to hers like the two were separate parts of the same
whole, like they were meant to fit together. That explained why
she didn't jerk away at the first touch of his lips on hers, why
she wasn't trying to shove him off her, why she wasn't saying no. That explained why her body clenched and her heart
speeded up and her pulse went haywire.

Why she wasn't even thinking *no*.

Why she was letting him kiss her.

Why she was lying there with her hands splayed flat against
his bare chest and her head nestled on his robe-cushioned arm
and her lips parting to let him in.

Why her eyes were closing.

Why she was kissing him back.

It explained everything. The intensity of her response. The
electricity that arced between them.

The heat. Oh, God, the heat.

He was kissing her with a raw hunger that made her burn deep inside. That made her go all soft with pleasure, and arch up against him and slide her hands up over the hard warm muscles of his chest until her arms were wrapping around his neck.

His lips were firm and dry, and he knew what to do with them—and what he was doing dazzled her. His tongue was hot and wet and tasted faintly of mint. He was bigger than she was, stronger than she was, all muscles and sinews and hair-roughened flesh, unmistakably, overwhelmingly male—and she loved that he was. His arms were hard around her, pulling her closer. Only the thin cotton of the shirt she was wearing separated her breasts from the unyielding wall of his chest. The silky nylon of her granny panties slid against the smooth cotton of his boxers.

He was aroused.

So. Was. She.

She couldn't believe it, but it was true. So aroused she was burning with it. Melting with it.

Just from a kiss. It was because it had been too long, because she had been caught off guard, because he was a really, really good kisser, she told herself feverishly. But none of those things explained the intensity of her reaction entirely. The only thing to do was put it down to chemistry.

He slanted his mouth across hers, licking into it and sending ripples of fire shooting through her. Her heart pounded. Her pulse raced. Her body pressed against his. The hot sweet throbbing that he was awakening in her was the most erotic thing she had ever felt in her life.

Never in her wildest dreams would she have thought that he, of all the men in all the world, could excite her like this.

She made a small, involuntary sound deep in her throat. He raised his head briefly, and she thought he looked down at her. She could have stopped it then, could have opened her eyes and turned her head away, could have said *let me go.*

She did none of those things. Instead she lifted her mouth toward his, blindly seeking his kiss. When his lips touched hers again, she responded instantly, tightening her arms around his neck, sliding her tongue into his mouth.

He kissed her like he couldn't get enough of her mouth, and she kissed him back just as hungrily. Who would have thought the taste of mint could turn her on so? But coupled with the hot wet slide of his tongue against hers, it set her on fire. Pressing closer still, she rocked against him and felt the delicious thrill of desire shoot clear down to her toes. He was rigid with wanting her, hard and ready, radiating heat.

The thought *this feels so good* revolved in her steam-fogged mind as her breasts tightened and her nipples contracted into greedy little nubs that pressed against his chest and her body moved sensuously against the hard bulge that was right there, right at the apex of her thighs, positioned in a way that was just too tempting, that was impossible to ignore. Moving against him like this was the sexiest thing she had done in forever. Forget sex, she had been telling herself for ages; who needs it? It just leads to trouble. But now she remembered vividly what sex was all about, and the real and very solid reminder made her breathless, made her tremble, made her go all liquid inside.

"I want—" Oh, God, she was breathing the words into his mouth. At least she had the good sense to break off before she added *you*.

But she did want him. So much she was dizzy with it.

"Sam," he murmured against her lips.

It was hearing her name that did it, that almost broke through the blaze of passion, the wildfire of desire. For a moment her lids fluttered up, as one tiny, cold-eyed part of her brain tried to tell her that this—*he*—was not what she wanted at all.

Too late. Lost cause.

Her mind might know better, but her body did not. She was so turned on that she was stupid with it. She might even recognize that she was being stupid, but the kicker was that she just didn't care.

His mouth left hers to trail hot, wet kisses along her jaw and down the side of her neck.

"You're beautiful," he whispered. "So sexy. So sweet."

Take off my clothes. She retained just enough presence of mind not to say it out loud. But she rocked against him and kissed him back with abandon when his mouth returned to find hers, and didn't do one thing to stop him when his hand slid inside her robe and cupped her breast through the thin T-shirt.

What she did do was arch up into that hand. It was big and warm and knowing, and having it caressing her breast was just what she wanted, she discovered. When his thumb slid over her nipple, her bones liquefied.

He was just repeating the exercise when she was jerked back

to reality by a muffled cry. It shot straight to her heart, piercing the urgency that had her in its grip, causing her to pull her mouth free of that mind-blowing kiss and open her eyes and shove against his chest in a silent demand to be released. The sight of his big, tanned hand wrapped around her breast sent shockwaves through her system. It branded itself forever on her mind.

The cry came again.

"Tyler!" she said.

Marco let her go, and, tightening her robe, she scrambled to her feet even as her son let loose with a full-blown scream.

"*Christ.*" Marco's reaction followed Sam down the dimly lit hall as she raced to Tyler's side, along with a vivid mental image of him lying there looking after her as he sprawled on the carpet. His open robe revealed enough so that she knew exactly how wide and muscular his chest was, and how the wedge of black hair in the middle of it tapered down to a fine line as it disappeared into his boxers. She knew that his navel was an innie, and that it was positioned smack in the middle of a set of six-pack abs. She knew that he had the narrow hips of an athlete, and that he absolutely rocked the plain blue boxers that were all that kept him decent. She knew that the thigh that wasn't bandaged was long and powerful, his knees were well shaped, his calves taut with muscle. She knew that his skin was tan everywhere that she could see, and that apart from his recent injuries he seemed healthy as a horse.

Marco was balanced on one knee, grabbing for his crutches and doing his best to get to his feet as she reached the open

bedroom doorway. Behind him, she heard Groves yelling something as he came bounding up the stairs. Then Tyler screamed
again, a long, high-pitched scream that, even though she should
have been used to it, still had the power to make the hair on the
back of her neck stand up. The bedroom was dark, but not so
dark she couldn't see Tyler instantly. Racing across the carpet
toward him, Sam felt her heart slamming in her chest. Her son
sat bolt upright in the middle of the unfamiliar double bed, his
small body rigid, his arms straight down at his sides, his eyes
tightly closed even as his mouth opened to blast out another of
those spine-chilling screams. In that instant she forgot all about
Marco, and about those blistering kisses. She forgot all about
the terrible situation they were in. She forgot about everything
in the world except Tyler. Her entire focus was on her son.

"*Tyler.*" She scrambled onto the bed, scuttling toward him
as fast as she could. The skirt of her robe got caught under her
knees, impeding her progress. Impatiently she jerked it out
of her way. Just before she reached him his eyes opened. The
fear and bewilderment on his face turned to instant relief as he
saw her.

"*Mom.*" He held out his arms to her. Reaching him, she en-
folded him in a warm embrace. Wrapping his arms around her,
he clung to her. She could feel him trembling. "You forgot to use
the monster spray."

This one had been bad. But then, was it any wonder?

"I know. I'm sorry. I'll get some tomorrow."

"There were monsters. They were trying to eat me."

"It's okay, baby, I'm here," she crooned into his hair, rocking him back and forth, her knees folded beneath her, her hair spilling over them both.

"I couldn't run. My feet wouldn't move." Tyler burrowed closer against her.

"You know it was just a bad dream. It wasn't real."

Marco appeared in the doorway, with Groves showing up a split second later just behind him. Both of them were staring in at her and Tyler. Neither said a word.

"I want to go home." There was a quaver in Tyler's voice.

"I do, too. We will, soon."

She couldn't see the men's expressions because what light there was came from the bathroom in which she had discovered Marco, and was at their backs. But remembering how clearly she had been able to see Tyler from that same position, she knew that they had an equally good view of her. She frowned at them: the moment should have been a private one. Even with Marco leaning on his crutches again, he was slightly taller than Groves. His shoulders were wide enough to almost fill the doorway. His robe was closed and securely tied around his waist now. With Tyler safe in her arms, Sam found that the memory of what had just transpired between them came flooding back; all of it, the heat, the hunger, every tiny detail, flashed into her mind with fresh, vivid intensity.

She forced it out again instantly.

"What happened? Did he hurt himself?" Marco's voice was low, and she realized that he was doing his best not to make a big deal, not to up the ante on the situation, not to further upset Tyler.

She shook her head.

"He has nightmares." Her response was equally quiet. Her arms were around her son. Her cheek rested on his hair.

Marco said nothing for a moment. Then he spoke over his shoulder to Groves, too quietly for Sam to make out the words. The two of them moved away, Groves first with Marco turning to follow, out of the doorway, out of her sight. She could hear them talking as they walked down the hall, but she couldn't understand what they were saying, and she didn't particularly care. She gave Marco points for having the sensitivity to leave her and Tyler alone, and then she pushed everything else out of her mind and concentrated on Tyler.

He told her all about his nightmare. By the time he was finished, he was once again lying down, his head nestled on his pillow, although her arm was beneath his head now, too. Curled up beside him, Sam made appropriate comments and gave him the comfort of her presence and waited for him to fall asleep.

The thing was, she was really, really sleepy, too.

She would just, for the teeniest tiniest second, rest her eyes . . .

CHAPTER FIFTEEN

Okay, it was official: he had a major case of the hots for the woman he had charged himself with protecting. Danny had stopped at the top of the stairs, both because there wasn't anywhere besides the second floor of this nondescript town house cum safe house that he wanted to be under the circumstances and because negotiating the stairs while on crutches was tricky at best. Watching Groves head down, Danny recognized the fact that he'd made a major mistake. Too late: not a damned thing he could do about it.

He'd kissed the girl.

"Hey, Marco, I'd keep what I just said in mind, if I were you." Groves threw that, along with an ugly look, up at him as he reached the bottom of the stairs. It was the tail end of the conversation they'd been having. Danny had said something like, *we need to give them some space, you can head on back downstairs,* to which Groves had replied along the lines of, *I'm just doing my job here,* whereupon Danny had said, no irony intended, that he appreciated that, which Groves had taken poorly and possibly as sarcasm and in reply growled that if it was up to him he, Groves, wouldn't be laying his life on the line for a damned traitor who deserved to be spending the rest of his life in jail. Or worse.

Danny had barely stopped himself from saying amen to that. The thing was, though, Marco wouldn't. So he'd said *screw you* instead. Thus provoking Groves's less-than-friendly reply.

What made it difficult, Danny reflected as he headed back down the hall, was that he could actually appreciate where Groves was coming from. Rick Marco had besmirched the honor of all federal agents everywhere, committed crimes as heinous as those of any of the drug kingpins they were chasing, gotten a bunch of agents and civilians killed, and then, when he was caught, cut a deal and started singing like the yellow canary he was.

Marco deserved every bit of Groves's antipathy.

But that made the relationship tricky for Danny while he was being Marco.

He couldn't wait for the damned gig to be over. For many reasons. One of which, of course, was that it would be a nice change not to have to worry anymore about being tortured and killed, at least until the next death-defying assignment came along. Which it would. See, he was a troubleshooter. The Bureau had a team of them, under-the-radar players who were sent in on the most dangerous undercover assignments as needed. For security reasons, none of them knew the identities of the others. Crittenden was their boss. Crittenden knew them all. Except for Crittenden's superiors, who Danny expected but did not know for sure were kept in the loop, and the tight little cadre of agents who were Crittenden's support staff, Crittenden was also the only one who knew the details of their assignments.

It helped that Danny was armed again; Crittenden had delivered on the gun. When they had arrived at the town house last night, and he had gotten a good look at the crutches that had been provided for him as they were unloaded, Danny had almost been surprised. Almost, because not much Crittenden managed to pull off surprised him anymore. But this, a piece of masking tape stuck to the underside of the shoulder support of the left crutch with the number 342 scrawled on it, had done the trick—342 was Crittenden's top-secret extension at Quantico. Only his team knew it. Seeing the tape with the number on it had been like seeing Crittenden's signature. It had told Danny that there was something up with the crutch. After he'd insisted on switching out the wheelchair for the crutches and then hauled his ass up the stairs on them—an exercise in pain, danger, and frustration that he didn't relish repeating any more than he had to—he had hobbled into his bedroom, locked the door, and proceeded to take them apart.

A 9mm model 26 Glock, known in the business as a pocket Glock because of its small size, was concealed inside the left crutch, cleverly inserted into the triangle that fit beneath his armpit. The long shaft that stretched from the triangle to the floor was hollow, and contained two ten-round magazines. In the same place in the right crutch, he'd found a cell phone. Generic, disposable, untraceable. Just to be on the safe side, he'd taken the battery out.

Hot damn, he'd thought at the time, he was in business again. After careful consideration, Danny had decided to leave both phone and gun concealed in the crutches. Otherwise, Sanders and company might well spot them. And take them: as a fed turned criminal turned protected federal witness, Rick Marco was allowed neither a personal cell phone nor weapons. Then after they took them, they would start asking questions. Like, how the hell had he gotten them?

Since Danny couldn't tell the truth, the whole thing just got awkward from that point.

Even if he had to disassemble a crutch if the shit started hitting the fan again, it was a lot better than being unarmed, as he had been the last time the cartel had found him. An optimist might believe that there wouldn't be a second time, but Danny considered himself a realist.

And realistically, the whole point was for the Zetas to be chasing him rather than the real Marco. The exercise got kind of pointless if there was no trail. And if there was a trail, the team the Zetas had in place would sooner or later pick up on it. Because Marco knew where all the bodies were buried, and they were desperate to silence him before he could point them all out.

Dangerous situations were what he excelled at, the latest fiasco notwithstanding, and Danny wouldn't even have been much more than glumly resigned to the prospect of being found again if he'd just had himself to worry about. But now there were Sam and Tyler.

They added a whole new layer of concern to the situation.

The kid was a kid. By virtue of that fact alone, Danny wasn't about to let him get hurt or killed. Whether he liked him—which he did—or not didn't matter.

And Sam—well, he wasn't about to let her get hurt or killed, either.

For a whole host of reasons, including the fact that she was a girl, and an innocent bystander, and he owed her, and . . .

Face facts, she was getting under his skin.

He should never have kissed her.

Danny would have cursed himself for letting it happen, except that was an absolute exercise in futility. Bottom line: learn from your mistakes, don't do it again.

Ordinarily he wouldn't have done it the first time, no matter how hot Sam was or how attracted he was to her. He was on the job, working undercover, and he was professional enough to maintain a certain degree of detachment from an unsuspecting civilian who had accidentally gotten caught up in the investigation and was now, as a result, under his protection.

He blamed the damned painkillers. They made him just loopy enough so that his inner self-control system was shot to hell.

The solution was easy enough, even if he cringed when he thought about it: no more pain pills for him. When the pain came back, as it was going to do, and pretty shortly, too, he was just going to have to hurt till he healed. Dangerous as the situation was, he needed a clear head anyway. Along with no distractions: as in, lay off the girl.

She was beautiful, sexy, just his type with her lovely face, long black hair, and big blue eyes. He liked the attitude she gave him, admired her guts. Add to that, her lips were soft, her mouth hot, her body killer. Plus, she'd been surprising him from the beginning, when he'd looked up from his prison in the car trunk to see her frowning down at him. She'd kept surprising him at every turn since. The biggest surprise of all might have been the way she had caught fire when he'd kissed her. He definitely hadn't seen that coming. In his experience, beautiful girls—the latest woman he'd been seeing (read sleeping with) in the weeks between assignments being a case in point—tended to be lacking in the passion department. Not Sam. She had caught fire as quickly as he had. Impossible to miss the fact that she had been vibrating with eagerness to get naked and get it on with him.

Hot and horny: when it came to women, it was his favorite combination. How could he resist taking what she was obviously ready, willing, and able to give?

Libido-squashing answer: because he had to.

Her life, her kid's life, and his own life were on the line here. For all their sakes, sex couldn't be allowed to enter into the equation at all.

No matter how much he wished things were otherwise.

Without really even meaning to wind up there, Danny found himself standing at the doorway to Tyler's bedroom again. Behind him, the bathroom light was still on; it provided enough illumination for him to easily see the pair on the bed.

They were curled up facing each other, both black heads nestled close on the same pillow. Clutching a small teddy bear close to his chest, Tyler looked small and frail under the protection of Sam's arm, which was draped over him. Sam looked—well, the only word he could come up with was delectable. Her hair fanned out over the white sheets like a banner, and her features, seen in profile, were strong yet delicate and were echoed in miniature by her son's. She was wrapped in the thick white robe, which precluded him from seeing any real detail of the curves that had made him burn earlier. But the robe parted just below the belt that she had cinched tight around her waist as she'd run away down the hall, high enough so that he could see a silky white triangle of cloth curving between her legs. He realized that what he was seeing was a little bit of the underwear he'd felt sliding against his shorts earlier, and his body responded with an instant surge of heat. He assumed that the panties, like the boxers he was wearing, had come with the town house, and seriously doubted that they were the kind of underwear she would choose if she had been choosing. Whatever their origin, just a glimpse of those thin white panties was enough to turn him on. To add to the problem, below that triangle of white her bare legs were on full display. They were long and lithe, and looked very tan against the white sheets. Her thighs were slender, her calves well shaped. Her feet were long and narrow.

He had no trouble at all imagining her legs wrapped around his waist.

Do not go there. But it was too late. The instant, involuntary mental picture had already made his heartbeat quicken. His body hardened faster than quick-set cement. With the best will in the world for it not to happen, his mind instantly shot back to those hot kisses. To the soft roundness and hard little nipple that was her breast.

Damn it to hell, anyway.

Cursing himself under his breath, Danny abruptly turned away. Clumping along the hall to his own room, he did his best to replace the image of Sam in that bed with anything and everything else he could call to mind, anything that he thought—hoped—might drive her out of his head. But the image of her lying there sleeping, that silky triangle of white promising all kinds of luscious secrets yet to be revealed, her sexy bare legs just about begging to be wrapped around him, was, he discovered, impossible to override.

When he slept, finally, his dreams were so erotic as to be embarrassing when he woke up and semiremembered them. By then, it was morning. And not early, either. He could tell that by the quality of the light that was filtering in through the curtains that covered the single window. One result of dreaming about rather than actually having an orgy of hot sex with his pretty companion in hiding was that he felt grouchy as all hell. And really, really horny. Plus his head ached. Practically every bone and muscle in his body hurt. And to top it off, as he had expected, his leg felt like a thousand angry wasps were going to town on it with red-hot stingers.

What could he say? Another day in the life.

Moving gingerly, he barely managed to suppress a groan. Even the slight weight of the covers lying across the bandage now felt unbearable. He tossed them aside.

Bring on the Lortab. Quick.

No. Not going there. From here on out, it was cold turkey all the way.

Cursing silently, grimacing, Danny tried to go all Zen and practice mental control and block out the pain.

Didn't work.

Gritting his teeth, hitching himself into a sitting position, getting ready to carefully swing his legs off the bed preparatory to standing up, Danny glanced around in search of his crutches. In the process of doing so, he discovered that he was the object of what appeared to be fascinated attention by a pair of big blue eyes.

Fortunately, or unfortunately, depending on how he looked at it, they didn't belong to Sam.

It was Tyler who stood in the open doorway watching him.

CHAPTER SIXTEEN

"Pancakes," Sam called out to Tyler in as cheery a tone as she could muster, scooping up the last of the golden brown disks from the skillet where they had been sizzling and sliding them onto a plate with the others. The unmistakable smell of breakfast—pancakes, plus bacon and coffee—filled the air. It made her stomach growl, and she realized that despite the circumstances she was actually very hungry. Like the rest of the house, the kitchen was clean, completely furnished and well equipped down to the dish towels, decorated in earth tones, with a big sliding glass door at the far end that was only partially veiled by sand-colored vertical blinds. Having already filled another plate with a dozen crispy strips of bacon, she picked up both plates and turned around to set them on the table. That's when she discovered Marco. He leaned on his crutches just inside the kitchen doorway watching her. Her stomach instantly tightened, and her heart quickened its beat.

Oh, no. After a lifetime's worth of making bad choices where men were concerned, was she really still this stupid?

He was clad in loose gray sweatpants and another of the house-favorite ubiquitous white T-shirts, plus his own sneakers. She was wearing one of those white T-shirts herself, along with a pair of too-big black gym shorts that she'd found among other garments folded in the drawers of the dresser in the master bedroom. The shorts hung past her knees, and the only way she was keeping them up was by the drawstring, which she had cinched supertight around her waist; since her boots were the only shoes she had, she wore them as well. With no makeup—whoever had stocked the town house apparently hadn't thought of that—and her hair twisted into a loose knot on the top of her head, she was not feeling particularly attractive, which didn't make her any happier to see Marco standing there.

"Hey, Mom." Tyler stood right in front of Marco, and it didn't require much imagination to guess where he'd run off to when he had disappeared from the kitchen as she had started pouring the pancake batter into the skillet. What was it they said about hindsight? She would have stopped him if she had realized. The more distance she kept between herself and Tyler and Marco, the better. She couldn't have felt much warier of a snake—unless, she thought with an inner grimace, she was sexually attracted to the snake, too. "It smells good."

Tyler wore another of the white T-shirts. Adult size, it was as big on him as a dress and completely hid his short pajama pants, which he had on beneath. As he'd brought no shoes, he was barefoot. Clothing, or rather her and Tyler's lack of it, was an issue that Sam knew she was going to have to address with somebody, but that was added to the discussion-to-be-had-later list and consigned to after breakfast.

Right at the moment, she had Marco to deal with. Even stooped over the crutches as he was, he was physically impos- ing, tall and wide shouldered, with muscular arms, big hands curled around the handles, and an athlete's body complete with long, strong legs, the foot of one of which was barely touch- ing the floor. His black hair was unruly and he badly needed a shave. Her eyes collided with his, and to her dismay instant electricity blazed between them. As the memory of their last, charged encounter sizzled in the air like a heat shimmer—his hand on her breast being the crowning moment—Sam felt a wave of embarrassment. Luckily, she wasn't prone to blushing, or she probably would have turned the color of a ripe tomato. As it was, biting down on her lower lip was the only outward sign of discomfiture she gave, and as soon as she realized she was doing it she stopped.

"I told Trey breakfast was almost ready." Tyler glanced over his shoulder at Marco as he spoke. "He's hungry just like us."

"Only if there's enough." The smile Marco gave her made her heart skip a beat. As a result, her brows snapped together in a quick frown. God, had she really kissed him like that last night? What had she been thinking?

Obvious answer: thinking was *not* what she had been doing.

"He wants to try your pancakes. I told him you make the best pancakes ever."

"Thank you, sir." Getting a grip, Sam managed a smile for her son. Tyler's answering smile as he headed toward the table was so sunny that Sam didn't have the heart to do or say anything that would dim it. He had been through enough trauma over the last thirty-six hours or so to last several lifetimes. Keeping things as normal and unterrifying as possible had to be a top priority for her now. At least, for as long as she could manage it. But whatever the day, or the coming days, might bring, there was nothing she could do to change any of it at the moment, so she tried to push from her mind the gnawing fear that had been threatening to consume her ever since she had woken up and realized where she and Tyler were.

"There's plenty," she told Marco. Okay, so maybe her tone was a little short. Acute anxiety coupled with an attraction to a man she absolutely should not be feeling attracted to tended to make her cross, she was discovering. When Tyler glanced at her, looking faintly curious, she tried to compensate for her tone with a brief and very insincere-feeling smile, manufactured entirely for Tyler's benefit, which she directed at Marco.

He did not smile back. Instead he stayed where he was, studying her just a little too intently. She had almost no doubt that he was recalling those kisses, too, probably way more graphically than she was, and the knowledge rattled her.

"Come on, Trey." Tyler pulled out one of the four wooden chairs that were arranged two by two on the long sides of the rectangular, farmhouse-style table, plopped himself down in the chair next to it, and patted the seat of the one he had pulled out invitingly. "It's getting cold."

With a wry inner grimace, Sam recognized the words she regularly used on Tyler to get him to leave whatever game had him enthralled and come to the table. Marco's gaze flicked from Tyler to the dishes Sam was holding. Until that moment she hadn't realized that she had been frozen in place with a steaming plate of food in each hand. Reluctantly acknowledging that there was no way out of feeding Marco breakfast that wouldn't involve upsetting Tyler, or making plain to Marco just how unsettling she now found having him around, she moved toward the table and set the pancakes and bacon down on it. Then she forked a couple of pancakes onto Tyler's plate, and added several strips of bacon. Tyler reached for the syrup with enthusiasm.

"Fix Trey's plate," Tyler said. It wasn't such an unusual request. If Kendra or another friend stopped by when she was cooking, Sam automatically put food on a plate for them at the same time as she served herself and Tyler. But fixing Marco a plate *felt* different.

Lips firming just a little, Sam put two pancakes and some bacon on the plate she had set out for herself, and slid the plate to the spot beside Tyler.

"The food's getting cold," she said over her shoulder to Marco as she turned toward the refrigerator to get out the carton of milk so she could fill Tyler's glass. Unlike the clothing that had come with the town house, the food she'd found in the refrigerator and pantry when she had checked was varied and for the most part actually stuff that Tyler would eat. He loved pancakes, for example, and since he'd been cheated out of his Saturday morning ritual, when she'd gotten up that morning and found that the supplies included pancake mix and bacon she had decided to fix his favorites. The familiar ritual of making breakfast had brought thoughts of Kendra and poor Mrs. Menifee and home and everything that had been left behind rushing into her head, but she had deliberately forced them out again. Worrying about what she could do nothing to change didn't help anyone. It certainly didn't make the present situation easier.

"It looks great." Marco was easing himself down into the chair beside Tyler when she returned with the carton of milk. His crutches were propped against the wall within easy reach. He cast a quick, assessing glance up at her as she filled Tyler's glass, and she noticed a kind of shadow at the backs of his eyes that made her wonder if he were in pain. Having slid her glass over in front of him when she'd repositioned her plate, she automatically proceeded to fill the glass that was now his with milk, too.

"Thank you," he said politely. Something in his expression as he flicked another look up at her immediately brought on a vision of him telling her, *I'm a little older than four, you know.* A lightning memory of everything that had taken place between them after that exchange rolled through her mind like the most unwanted highlight reel ever, and was just as quickly pushed away.

You are not going to fall for this guy.

"You're welcome." Her tone was maybe a little less than friendly. She set the milk carton down on the table with a definite *plop.* "Eat."

"I'm stealing your breakfast, aren't I?" The look he gave her was impossible to read.

"No." She nodded at the plates in the center of the table. There were still several pancakes and a few strips of bacon remaining. She'd made extra, just in case Tyler was super hungry, or she had wanted more than her usual one pancake, or—well, just because she could. Usually she had to be careful about the amount she cooked to stretch out the number of meals she could get out of the ingredients. Since Tyler's birth, being thrifty had become like her religion. It had been nice to make a little more than they maybe needed. "Like I said, there's plenty. Don't kid yourself: if there wasn't, no way would you catch me giving you my breakfast."

That made him smile. Because she found it sexy, and charming, and it made her want to smile back, his smile earned him another quick frown.

"Don't you like Trey, Mom?" Tyler asked through a bite of pancakes, looking from her to Marco with a flicker of trouble in his eyes. For about the millionth time, Sam was reminded of the truth of the saying that little pitchers had big ears and vowed to watch what she said and how she said it around him, especially now. Keeping things calm and unterrifying for Tyler had to be the name of the game for her at the moment. If she had an issue with Marco, it was something to be dealt with between the two of them when Tyler wasn't around.

"Sure she likes me." The wickedly teasing look Marco sent her made her long to dump the glass of milk she had just poured for him over his head. "Don't you, Sam?"

What could she say? "Of course I do," she said to Tyler. Sitting down at the table and eating breakfast with Marco and her son was not something she wanted to do under the circumstances, but there didn't seem to be any way around it.

"So sit down and eat." Marco nodded at the other side of the table.

Every instinct she possessed warned, *bad move.*

How breakfast might be rescued from turning into a cozy, pseudofamily meal with just about the last man she wanted to encourage either herself or Tyler to think of in that way burst upon her then in what felt like a brilliant flash of insight. Acting on it, Sam said, "I'll be right back," and walked out of the kitchen in search of whatever marshal was on the premises. She found him almost at once. Clean-shaven but grim-faced, wearing what looked like the same clothes he'd had on since she had first set eyes on him, Sanders sat reading the newspaper in one of two rust-colored recliners on either side of a tan leather couch in the great room. The seating arrangement faced a big stone fireplace with a flat-screen TV mounted on the wall above it. Coupled with the usual tables and lamps, a few pictures on the white-painted walls, and more of the beige carpeting on the floor, the furniture was both comfortable and practical. To her left, Sam could see the front door, solid wood, painted white, hopefully equipped with something on the order of a triple dead bolt. It opened into a tiled entryway that was separated by a half wall from the great room. Directly opposite the door were the stairs that led to the second floor. Despite the brightness of the day outside, the heavy, brown burlap-looking curtains in the great room were closed over the two smaller front windows and a large window that, Sam thought, must look out over the backyard. The lamps plus track lighting overhead provided ample illumination, but Sam preferred natural daylight, and under other circumstances she would have swept open the curtains as soon as she could. The reason that the curtains were drawn on this gorgeous, sunny day hit her almost as soon as she pictured herself opening them: no one was supposed to be able to see in. Why? Because they were in hiding from a pack of vicious killers who at that very moment were doing everything they could to hunt them down.

At the reminder of the very real and immediate nature of the danger she and Tyler were in, Sam felt a chill run down her spine. Why it had taken the closed curtains to drive it home she couldn't have said, but they did and her stomach knotted even as she transferred her attention from the curtains to the marshal whose job it was to keep them safe.

Sanders hadn't even looked up as she entered, nor did he acknowledge her presence in any way now, although she was looking at him from only a few feet away. Sam knew that she and Tyler were unimportant to the marshals—Marco was the reason for all the protection—but at least the others were reasonably friendly. Sanders didn't even bother to be minimally polite.

Yeah, well, she loved him, too.

"I made pancakes," she said, striving to sound at least slightly more enthusiastic about the prospect of him eating them than she was feeling. "There are plenty, if you want some."

Glancing up at her at last, he shook his head. "I've eaten." There was no smile on his face. He barely even seemed to see her, and Sam was reminded once again that in terms of importance she and Tyler were barely a blip on his radar screen.

After that, there wasn't anything to do but return to the kitchen, defeated. So that's what Sam did, casting a disgruntled look at the table where her son and the criminal who'd burst into their lives and blown them to smithereens sat chatting and eating her pancakes like neither of them had a care in the world. Which in Tyler's case she was glad of, but when it came to Marco—not so much. Crossing to the counter, fulminating silently over the unfairness of life in general and the absolute unbelievable ongoing crappiness of her life in particular, she poured herself a cup of coffee, snagged a clean plate and some silverware, and finally gave up and sat down at the table across from them.

Only to find Marco glancing at her coffee with such longing that, mentally heaping scorn on her own inner marshmallow, she immediately got up again and poured him a cup.

"Sugar? Cream?" she asked over her shoulder from the kitchen counter. Her tone was maybe a little short again, because she was still disgusted at herself for noticing, much less caring, that he obviously wanted coffee. And noticing and caring, too, that it was hard for him to maneuver easily with the crutches, and that carrying a cup of coffee while on crutches would be pretty nearly impossible, which meant that if she didn't bring it he probably wouldn't get any.

What she told herself was, she needed coffee too much in the morning herself to deny it to a fellow human being. If the truth was maybe something a little different, well, she wasn't going there.

"Black is fine."

When she returned to the table, setting the coffee down in front of him before sliding back into her seat, Marco mouthed, "Thank you," and smiled at her again even as, beside him, Tyler chatted away. When Marco turned his attention back to Tyler, listening to her son describing the various misadventures of a friend's puppy with every appearance of real interest, Sam's eyes narrowed on them. The last thing in the world she needed Marco to be was nice.

So maybe he couldn't help the fact that she'd found him in a car trunk and been thrown in on top of him. If he hadn't been what he was, none of this would be happening. Which made the whole terrifying mess still all his fault. And made him a dangerous man, in more ways than one.

"Why are you frowning at Trey like that, Mom? I thought you said you liked him." Looking her way suddenly, Tyler caught her off guard.

Over his coffee cup, "Trey's" eyes met hers and twinkled.

"I'm tired, okay?" Sam said, putting her own coffee cup down and reaching for a strip of bacon. "Eat your pancakes."

Tyler obediently took a huge bite. "How did you two meet, anyway?"

Mumbled around a mouthful of pancakes, it was such an obvious question that Sam, crunching into the bacon, didn't know why it surprised her. The hopeful interest in the look Tyler sent from her to Marco and back told the tale. It confirmed for Sam the direction her son's thoughts were taking: just as she had been afraid would happen, in his head he was pairing them off. It was a problem that caused her increasing worry. The older he got, the more he seemed to miss having a father figure in his life. If he even saw her talking to someone remotely suitable, he started matchmaking. Which was one more reason she rarely dated anymore, and almost never brought the men she did occasionally go out with anywhere near Tyler. Unfortunately, under the circumstances keeping him away from Marco was going to be difficult. So was staying away from Marco herself.

"Don't talk with your mouth full," she told him repressively, putting down the half-eaten strip of bacon, while Marco—so helpful!—forked a pancake onto her plate and pushed the syrup in her direction as he answered Tyler.

"I was in trouble, and she saved me. I owe her, big time."

Tyler's eyes widened. "She saved you? Like a superhero?"

"No," Sam answered crossly, while Marco nodded and replied, "Just exactly like a superhero. A superhero who showed up in a wrecker."

Tyler chortled. "Wrecker-Woman! That's you, Mom. You could be in, like, the Avengers. We could get you a costume."

He was so obviously finding the idea funny that Sam forced a smile even as she shook her head at him. "Forget it, buddy. And finish your breakfast. I don't want to be in the Avengers. And I really don't want a costume."

"Think how tight those superhero costumes are." Marco paused in the process of lifting a heaping forkful of pancakes to his mouth to shoot another twinkling look at her. "All that spandex. You could really rock one if you wanted to be Wrecker-Woman."

"You don't think she's too skinny?" Tyler asked Marco with a touch of anxiety.

Marco shook his head. "I don't think she's too skinny at all."

Sam couldn't help it; she felt a spreading rush of warmth. Despite Tyler's presence, she shot Marco a dark look. He grinned at her. It was such a purely masculine grin, so damned engaging, that it blasted through a few of the barriers she was trying to erect between them and reminded her of just exactly why she had kissed him the way she had. In pure self-defense, she frowned fiercely back at him.

"So what kind of trouble were you in?" Tyler asked him. Sam could have told Marco: Tyler never forgot anything you said. Once you mentioned it, if it interested him, sooner or later you would be called upon to explain it.

"Those bad guys the other night?" Sam cringed a little as Marco so matter-of-factly brought up what she felt it would be better not to remind her son of. "They were after me first."

"And Mom saved you from them?" Tyler looked at her with dawning pride. "She saved me, too."

"Then I'd say we both owe her, wouldn't you?"

"Yeah." Glancing at her, Tyler nodded, and then his attention was once again all on Marco. "Did you see her gun? She shot out the window in my bedroom with it so we could escape."

Tyler's tone when he mentioned the gun was way too enthusiastic for Sam's liking.

"I did indeed see her gun."

The look Sam shot Marco forbade him to so much as think about mentioning what he had seen her do with it.

"Guns are dangerous," she told Tyler firmly, reinforcing a theme she had repeated to him so often that she was starting to feel like a recording. But as a woman living alone with her young son in a bad part of town, she'd felt that it was necessary to have a gun where she could get to it in case of emergency. At home, she kept the weapon locked up, and warned Tyler repeatedly against ever touching it. When she worked nights in the truck, she took it with her. "I used ours because I had to. But you know better than to ever pick one up."

It wasn't a question.

"I know, I know. You've told me like a zillion times." He made an impatient face at her. Then he looked at Marco again. "But she saved me and her with it."

"She saved me with it, too." Marco's eyes met hers. He wasn't smiling now. They were serious and dark with something she couldn't quite identify. Whatever it was, it made her heart start to beat a little faster. Hastily she looked away.

Tyler said, "And then you came and saved us both."

"I did."

"You won't let them get us again, will you?" Tyler asked, so earnestly that Sam felt a knot start to form in her chest.

He is *afraid.* Then she thought, *Of course he is. He's four, not stupid.*

"No. I won't let them get you again." Marco was promising something that Sam was pretty sure he had no power to deliver on, but she was glad he was promising it anyway. Tyler clearly took the promise as gospel, looked relieved, and started scarfing down pancakes and milk.

"You fell asleep fast last night," Marco said to Sam under the cover of Tyler's renewed attack on his breakfast. It was such an innocent-sounding observation on the surface, and so loaded with subtext given what had happened between them, that it was all Sam could do not to choke on the coffee she was in the act of swallowing.

"I always fall asleep fast," she replied, just as soon as she succeeded in getting the hot liquid all the way down. And was proud of how cool and unbothered she sounded.

"I was worried that"—here the tiniest of pauses caused her to read all kinds of meaning into the inscrutable expression in those coffee-brown eyes—"you might have trouble sleeping. Considering everything."

Yeah, like how hot he'd made her. "I didn't," she assured him.

His eyes slid over her face, lingering just a second too long on her lips. To her chagrin, Sam felt the urge to wet them. Her pulse started to pick up the pace.

I love the way he kisses. The thought sprang full blown into her mind. Horrified at herself, she dismissed it instantly. But even instantly wasn't quick enough to stop her from feeling a quick rush of desire.

"So what should we do today?" Tyler piped up, directing the question at Sam. She almost jumped. She was glad of the interruption, of the chance to redirect her thoughts before they could

travel any further down the road they seemed hell-bent on taking. Tyler's question was one that they always asked each other
on weekend mornings, and it helped her to get her bearings.
The very normalcy of it underlined the absolute abnormality of
the situation. Pushing away the last of her breakfast (pancakes
and bacon were Tyler's favorites, not hers; she actually preferred
something like half a peanut butter sandwich, peanut butter
having been a staple food for breakfast, lunch, and dinner when
she was growing up), Sam looked at her son and found herself at
a loss for words. She had no idea what rules governed this new
existence they had been thrown into: was going to a park, or a
swimming pool, or for something as ordinary as a walk, even an
option?

"You can help me clean house," she countered with a playful
smile, because on weekends at home cleaning house was one of
the things they did. Not that Tyler liked being part of what she
called the Jones family cleaning crew. But he did it.

"No way. We're on vacation. Anyway, it's not even our
house," Tyler objected.

Vacation? Sam didn't say it aloud, but her eyes shot to
Marco, because she was pretty sure that there was only one
place the idea that they were on vacation could have come from
and it was from him. He was chomping down on the last of his
bacon when their eyes met and she frowned suspiciously at him.
His reply was a wry half smile, and a shrug.

Translation: guilty.

"It's like a vacation. Kind of," he replied to the look in her
eyes.

Except for the whole everyone-wants-to-kill-us thing. But Sam didn't say it out loud. She gave Marco a narrow-eyed look instead.

"We'll make it a vacation," he promised, sliding a significant look in Tyler's direction.

Given her son's presence, what could she reply to that?

"Sounds good," she said.

"Is it okay if I go check out the backyard, Mom?" Having finished his breakfast, Tyler slid from his seat. From where she was sitting, through the not-quite-completely-drawn blinds, Sam could see several slices of well-cut green lawn and a large, leafy tree. The backyard looked like the perfect place for a four-year-old to play. The whole thing seemed to be surrounded by a six-foot-tall wooden privacy fence, but she had no way of being sure it was safe.

Automatically she looked at Marco for guidance. Tyler did, too. Annoying to realize that they both assumed he was the one with the authority to decide, to tell them yes or no.

"Why don't you check out the rest of the house first?" Marco suggested. "I bet there are all kinds of nooks and crannies you haven't seen."

"Okay," Tyler agreed, and hopped up from his seat. With a quick look at Sam, he picked up his plate and glass and carried them to the sink. She smiled at him: that was something he always did. She gave herself a mental high-five for having raised him well.

"Thank you," she said.

"I'll be back in a minute," he told her, and ran off.

Left alone with Marco, Sam felt every bit of discomfort she'd managed to push out of her mind earlier return in a rush. Desperate to find something to do, something to focus on besides the two of them alone at the table, she started to gather up the plates and silverware, preparatory to standing up and carrying them to the sink.

She was just reaching for the syrup bottle when his hand descended on hers, closing around it, holding it trapped against the smooth wood.

Her eyes shot to his.

"We need to talk," he said.

CHAPTER SEVENTEEN

Talking was *not* what Sam wanted to do. Escaping was more like it. But Marco picked her hand up from the table, holding it in such a way that she doubted she could have pulled free without a determined jerk.

A jerk that would reveal how uncomfortable she was with having him hold her hand.

Even as she hesitated, she very unwillingly registered the size and strength of his hand—way bigger and stronger than hers—and its masculinity, and the warmth of it. She remembered the way he had kissed her knuckles in the trunk. Then he ran his thumb over the silky skin on the back of her hand—shades of that thumb running over her nipple!—and her insides turned to mush.

Sam's heart was beating a mile a minute. She was breathing way too fast. She was so focused on the way his thumb moving against her skin was making her feel that she didn't even realize she was staring at their joined hands until he said, "Sam," and she looked up to meet his eyes.

He was regarding her with a rueful expression that immediately made her brows twitch together.

"What?" Her tone wasn't quite snappish, but almost. The way he was holding her hand, the way he was kind of leaning in toward her, the intensity of his gaze, was throwing her for a loop. A relationship with this guy was the last thing she wanted, or needed, but something about the way they were together kind of felt like they were sliding down the slope of starting a relationship. *Oh, no. Not happening. Reverse course.* She wasn't making any more bad decisions where men were concerned. She had already screwed (and screwed was definitely the operative word) up enough in that department. She wasn't doing it again. No how, no way.

Even if just having him hold her hand like this was making her go all jittery inside.

"About last night," he said. That wasn't a surprise—from the second he'd picked up her hand she'd had a pretty good idea about what the topic of conversation was likely to be. But his expression wasn't jibing with the racing of her pulse, or the buttery warmth that was starting to spread deep inside her. It wasn't saying, *I want to take you to bed.* It was saying—what?

Not anything she was going to like, she was starting to feel pretty sure.

"I'm sorry, okay?" He was playing with her fingers now, which were long and slender but not elegant, not perfectly manicured—actually, not manicured at all—a working woman's hands. "I shouldn't have done what I did. It was a mistake. I blame it on the pain pills. You were right, I was high as a kite."

Talk about your wake-up call. *He* definitely wasn't going all gooey inside. And sure as God made little green apples *she* wasn't going to be going all gooey inside any longer, either. To hell with how he interpreted it; she gave the determined jerk necessary to free her hand from his.

"Let me get this straight: you're saying you only kissed me because you were high?"

"I kissed you because I wanted to. But I wouldn't have done it if I hadn't been loopy from those damned pain pills."

She felt affronted. She felt—okay, face it, a little hurt. It was all she could do not to get up, turn the appropriate part of her anatomy in his direction, say something like *kiss this* as she smacked it, and then stomp away from the table, but she didn't, because above all else she was determined to keep her (outward) cool. The slight edge to her voice that she couldn't quite seem to help notwithstanding. "Good to know. Thank you very much for telling me."

She got the impression that he almost smiled. If he had, the way she was feeling right at that moment, she would have decked him.

"Sam." He reached for her hand again. *Forget that.* Curling her fingers into fists, she crossed her arms over her chest. And did not glare at him, although it cost her a real effort. "Look. You're beautiful. And sweet. And sexy as all hell. I want you. I'd give my right arm to sleep with you, but we're in a danger-ous situation here. I need you to be able to trust me. I don't want sex to get in the way of that."

Affronted didn't even begin to cover how she was feeling.

Try—damned mad. For starters. "Me *trust* you? Probably not going to happen. Me have sex with you? Definitely not going to happen. So it's looking like you strike out on both counts."

His expression turned rueful. "The thing is, I can't afford the distraction."

"You say that like you think us having sex was actually a possibility. It wasn't." She seethed (invisibly, she hoped). "It *isn't*."

If that was humor she saw springing to life in the backs of his eyes, she would—she didn't know what she'd do, but it wouldn't be pretty.

Impossible to tell. But there was a suspicious glint in those dark brown depths that made the glare she finally directed at him feel extra good.

"Don't give me a hard time, okay? I want you so much I've got a hard-on right now, just from sitting at this table looking at you. But I'm trying to do what's best for everybody here."

She made a rude sound. "You know what? I don't want to know about your hard-on. You ever hear, too much information? Anyway, I don't care. You could have a baseball bat in your pants and it wouldn't mean anything to me."

"I'm just trying to explain—"

"Explain *what*?"

"Why I'm backing off here. Why us having sex isn't going to happen."

Sam almost sputtered. "Like I thought it was? Like that was even a possibility? Listen, Mr. Criminal in Federal Custody, you seem to have a pretty skewed idea about how much you appeal to women. Maybe you ought to try getting real."

"Come on, Sam. After the way we were last night, of course you would naturally expect—"

"Naturally expect? I didn't *naturally expect* anything. So last night we made out. So what? No big deal. It was an accident, practically, and it was never going to go any further than that. Believe me." So she was lying, probably; he couldn't know it.

He fixed her with a level look. "Now who needs to get real?"

She bristled. "Meaning?"

"Meaning it was completely obvious where last night was going. If we hadn't gotten interrupted, we would have wound up in bed. I figured today you'd be expecting us to pick up where we left off, and I wanted you to understand why that can't happen."

Sam wouldn't have been surprised to learn that steam was coming out of her ears. "I understand why that can't happen, all right. Because there's no way in hell I'd ever wind up in bed with you. Not last night, not today, not ever."

"We're on the same page then."

Now, that calm statement was infuriating. Sam tried not to let it show.

"Absolutely we're on the same page."

A smile just touched his mouth. "So why are you so mad at me?"

"What makes you think I'm mad at you?"

"Oh, I don't know. Maybe because last night you kissed me like you were dying to crawl into my bed and when I showed up in the kitchen this morning you made big bedroom eyes at me and now here you are spitting fire and yelling at me?"

"I am not spitting fire. And I am not yelling."

"Yes, you are." His voice went very soft. "And just for the record, baby doll, I think it's cute."

Sam saw red. "You know what you can do with that, right?"

"Easy." He actually had the gall to smile outright at her. "All I'm trying to do here is make sure you and Tyler stay safe."

"You keep talking like you're the one who's supposed to do that." Sam was practically speaking through her teeth by now. "News flash: you're the reason we're in danger, remember? Keeping us safe is why there's a U.S. Marshal in the next room."

"Sam—"

Whatever he had been going to say next was lost as Tyler came bouncing back into the room. Marco quit talking. His mouth closed into a firm line. Sam tried to wipe all negative emotion from her face.

Luckily, Tyler seemed happily oblivious to the tension between the adults. His gaze slid past Sam toward the sliding glass doors as he asked, "Mom, can I go outside now?"

Hostilities instantly—and very temporarily, at least on Sam's part—set aside, she found herself instinctively shooting Marco a quick, inquiring look.

"Hang on a minute," Marco said to Tyler. Scooting his chair back, he spoke to Sam. "I don't see why not, but I'll check out the backyard."

"Shouldn't we be getting Sanders—the U.S. Marshal—to do

that?" Okay, so there was still some bite—a lot of bite—in her voice.

If Marco heard, he ignored her, getting to his feet with the combined help of the table and the chair back. From the way he grimaced, Sam was sure he was in pain, and found herself wondering sourly how many pills he was going to have to swallow to control it. Enough to make him "loopy" again? Even thinking about that was infuriating—and, if she was honest, a little humiliating. The idea that while she'd been going up in flames in his arms he had been too bombed out of his mind to know what he was doing made her nuts.

I want you so much I've got a hard-on right now . . .

Arggh. She could still almost hear him saying it.

I'm not going to think about that. I'm not going to think about him. *And I am* not *going to look at the front of his pants. I'm going to be smart for once in my stupid life, and keep sex out of it, just like the rat bastard said.*

"Here, Trey." As Tyler darted into position to hand over Marco's crutches, one at a time, clearly eager to be of help, Sam turned her back on them and crossed to the sliding glass doors to look outside for herself. Pushing the blinds aside, she saw that the backyard, while not overly large, was indeed surrounded by a six-foot-tall solid wood privacy fence, at least as far as she could see. There was a concrete patio complete with lawn chairs and what looked like a grill, with a basketball goal set into the ground at the far end. The grass had been cut recently, and was thick and green. Sunflowers towered in a corner. Best of all, hanging from what proved to be a big, leafy red oak, was a tire swing. *Tyler's going to love that.* Instantly transported, she reached for the handle to open the door.

"Sam. You want to wait for me." Marco's warning was soft and almost casual. Glancing around at him—he was getting the crutches into position under his arms, while Tyler (got in the way) assisted—she understood from his expression that the warning was serious, although he was doing his best not to make Tyler think there was any reason to worry about what might be waiting outside.

Instant visions of snipers on the roof, assassins hiding behind the tree, murderers of all types and stripes and in all possible locations ready to blast the first person who appeared sprang into her head, making her heart lurch, and she quickly sheared away from the door. Beneath the dangling blinds, it was one big panel of glass, after all.

"Shouldn't we *all* wait for Sanders? Having you go outside first seems a little silly, considering everything." Meaning considering that he was the one the killers were really after, although with Tyler listening in she didn't want to be too graphic. She couldn't help uttering the warning, however, and never mind how irate she was feeling toward Marco at the moment. She might not want him to die, but a lesser bad fate, like having him fall flat on his face on the kitchen floor if one of his crutches caught on, say, a table leg, suited her just fine.

"Oh, right." Something about his tone struck her as a little odd, like his mind was having to switch gears to acknowledge that he was the primary target. But then she forgot about that as their eyes collided. Instantly she felt the flash of (oh, so unwanted) attraction between them, and caught herself wondering—damn it!—if there was something wrong with her, that she was consistently drawn to men who turned out to be total losers, Tyler's father and this guy being two obvious cases in point.

Before she had a chance to follow that thought through to its obvious conclusion—something in the nature of, *you're an idiot*—he added, "Cover your ears," to Tyler. As Tyler obeyed without question he bellowed, "Hey, Sanders, you're needed in the kitchen, pronto," before maneuvering out from behind the table, careful and slightly awkward on his crutches.

Tyler's hands dropped away from his ears as he scrambled to pull a chair out of Marco's way. "You yell really loud."

Watching Marco smile down at her boy, Sam felt her chest tighten. Hero worship shone out of Tyler's eyes. Clearly she and Marco were going to have to have another talk, only this time she was going to be the one to spell things out: bottom line was, she didn't want him getting too friendly with Tyler. Because soon, she hoped, Marco would be out of their lives. Really out of their lives, as in, on his way to prison or something. The downside to that was that Tyler would be the one who was left behind, hurt by the ending of the association. If she could prevent it, Sam vowed, that just wasn't going to happen.

Marco's expression as he crossed the kitchen left Sam in no doubt that he was indeed in considerable pain. This time she absolutely refused to feel sorry for him. Instead, despite the nervousness brought on by the idea of possibly exposing herself or

Tyler to the danger that might be lurking outside, she followed Marco and Tyler to the door and looked out over Marco's broad shoulder through the glass.

Everything she could see looked peaceful and serene.

"What's the problem?" Sanders entered the kitchen fast, his footsteps loud on the tile floor, his hand reaching beneath his jacket, which, Sam knew, was where his gun was kept in a shoulder holster. She, Tyler, and Marco all looked sharply around at his appearance.

Sam answered him first. She'd had it with being told what to do, and absolutely refused to find the burly marshal—or any of the men around her, for that matter—intimidating. "Tyler wants to play in the backyard. Before I just let him go, I thought somebody should check it out."

Hand withdrawing from beneath his jacket, Sanders looked at Marco with disgust. "That's what you were yelling about?"

Seeming unbothered by Sanders's barely veiled antagonism, Marco shrugged. "Seemed smarter to check than not. And as the lady pointed out, I'm probably not the one to do it."

"Worried about catching a bullet in the head?" Sanders's tone made it almost a sneer. Sam's mouth tightened as she watched Tyler's eyes widen, watched him cast a quick glance up at Marco. Sensitive Sanders was not. "What does the kid need to go out for, anyway?"

"I don't have to." Looking abashed, Tyler sidlcd a little closer to Marco's side.

"Sure you do." Marco looked down at him. "It's a pretty day. I want to go out, too. No point in us staying locked up in the house." He looked at Sanders. "You can check out the backyard or I will." His voice had hardened just enough to be noticeable. His quick assumption of authority reminded Sam once again that he, too, had been a federal agent before he had betrayed everyone who had believed in him. That, she realized, was the guy she was attracted to. The other part of him—the weasel— well, she didn't know that part. Or maybe she just wasn't very good at recognizing it.

Whatever, for now she and Marco were on the same side.

"You're supposed to be protecting us, aren't you?" Sam's eyes challenged Sanders before he could growl back at Marco, which she could see from his expression he was getting ready to do. So Marco was the bad guy, and Sanders was the good one. Much as it annoyed her to face the truth, she liked Marco more. "So protect already. Make sure the backyard's safe."

Sanders's face tightened as he looked at her. "I wouldn't push it, if I were you, Ms. Jones. Left to me, you wouldn't be here."

As he was already moving toward the door to do as she'd asked, Sam didn't reply. Unlatching it, sliding it open, Sanders stepped outside, looked around, took a quick walk to the left out of sight, and came back.

"Should be fine," he said, stepping back into the kitchen. "Just stay in the yard and don't unlock the gate."

"Yay! Come on, Mom." Skittering around Sanders, Tyler darted out the door, with Sam a few steps behind him. As she slipped past Sanders, who was now closest to the door, Sanders said to Marco, "We're here to keep *you* alive, not baby-sit a damned woman and her kid."

Even as Sam bristled, she heard Marco's reply: "Kid's part of the package now. So's the woman. End of discussion."

"Fuck," Sanders said bitterly. Then the door closed behind Sam, and there was no way to hear more.

A few minutes later, the door opened again and Marco maneuvered through it, then swung across the patio toward her.

After that first quick glance, prompted by the sound of the opening door, Sam didn't look at him, except peripherally, which she couldn't help. But still, by the brightness of unfiltered daylight she saw that the swelling in his face was definitely going down. His nose was almost normal size again. It was going to be straight and high-bridged, a handsomely masculine nose, when it had healed. *Put him out of your mind,* she told herself fiercely, and in the spirit of making sure that happened deliberately concentrated all her attention on her son. Tyler was already climbing onto the tire swing. Despite everything, his obvious enjoyment, coupled with the absolutely beautiful weather, made her feel a tad more cheerful. As in, a little more optimistic that maybe they would actually get out of this alive. Now that she had reminded herself of the danger, though, she darted apprehensive looks around, searching, she supposed, for places a would-be killer might lurk. Close at hand, the second story of the town house next door, the one in which the marshals had set up base, looked into their backyard, and next to that she could see the tops of two more, nearly identical town houses that all seemed to be connected. At the very back of the yard, appearing to be maybe a back alley or another backyard away, the black-shingled roof of what she thought must be a single-story house was just visible. From the apparent absence of any residences on the other side, Sam deduced that the one she and Tyler and Marco were staying in must be the last town house in the row. Since she didn't spot snipers on any of the roofs, or gunmen in the windows, she allowed herself to relax enough to take in the rest of the view. In the distance, a line of purple mountains iced with snow drew her eye. Overhead, the sky was a perfect pale blue. The temperature, which was in the midseventies, felt wonderful after the ninety-plus-degree heat East St. Louis had been enduring. Sam took a deep breath, savoring the fresh-cut-grass scent in the air.

"Listening to Sanders, I get the feeling that if bad stuff starts going down, Tyler and I are on our own," Sam said without looking at him as Marco stopped beside her. She could feel the connection between them, feel the attraction like a physical pull. Folding her arms over her chest, she grimly ignored it.

"No worries." Marco leaned on his crutches, his eyes on her face as she resolutely kept hers fixed on Tyler. Still, she couldn't help seeing the slight smile that curved his mouth. "You've got me."

At that, Sam shot a look at him. Out here in the bright sunlight, it was all too easy to see the tightness around his mouth, and the shadow of pain in his eyes. The pills might be making him too loopy to get a handle on whom he was kissing, but they clearly weren't doing a whole lot to relieve his distress. Not that she cared. Not one bit.

"Like I'm really going to count on that," she scoffed, and stepped off the patio to give Tyler a push on the swing.

CHAPTER EIGHTEEN

Later, after Sam had cleaned up the kitchen and fed herself and Tyler a peanut butter sandwich for lunch—everyone else was on his own, as she said maybe a little too forcefully to Tyler when he suggested that she make Trey one, too—she took Marco's suggestion and presented Sanders with a list of the obligations that she needed to have taken care of in East St. Louis so that she didn't lose everything she owned. While Sanders was looking it over, pursing his lips and frowning, she announced—didn't ask—that she needed to make a quick trip to the Walmart they had driven past on the way in, and added that since she obviously couldn't use a credit card (not that she possessed one that worked, although she didn't tell him *that*), she needed a means of paying for her purchases. Although she hadn't invited Marco to take part in the discussion, he emerged from the den where he'd been holed up in time to hear the last part of what she had to say, and told her (and reminded Sanders) that the marshals had plenty of government-issued cash and could easily fork over the funds she needed. Once Sanders was made to understand that the marshals could either go out and find and purchase the clothes and other personal items she and Tyler needed or she could do it herself, he quit insisting that the trip to Walmart was a nonstarter. Instead, after telling Marco to butt the hell out of the conversation and then, a little later, not to even think about it because he wasn't going with her, which last part at least Marco didn't dispute, Sanders agreed to let her go and deputized Groves to go with her. Sam hated leaving Tyler behind, but as he was barefoot with only his pajamas and a choice of too-big white T-shirts to wear, and was emphatic in saying he didn't want to go anyway, there wasn't much choice.

The urgency of her mission was such that leaving him behind was something she was prepared to do.

"I'll keep an eye on him," Marco told her. It was not the ideal setup, but since she was actually quite sure that he would do as he said and Tyler was perfectly happy in his company, she bowed to necessity. Trying to keep Tyler away from "Trey" was something she was going to have to put off until later.

A little stiffly, she said, "Thank you."

"My pleasure," he replied, and smiled at her. That smile did really unwelcome things to her insides, so she turned away without another word.

Since the house had come equipped with a washer and dryer concealed in a closet off the kitchen (there was no basement), Sam already had laundered the clothes she had arrived wearing. She had feared that her tank top might be permanently stained with Marco's blood, but once washed, it was wearable, and her jeans and underwear were perfectly fine. Confining her hair in

a long braid that hung down her back, she was good to go. Just
another Walmart shopper, ready to blend into the aisles.

"I won't be gone long," she promised Tyler, who was en-
sconced on the couch in the great room watching TV. A quick
glance reassured her that what was on was the Disney Channel,
and she immediately understood why he looked so entranced.
At home, they didn't have cable, because she couldn't afford it.

"Bye." Her son waved her off, clearly unconcerned about
her pending absence. Having eased himself down in the same
chair Sanders had occupied earlier and picked up the newspaper,
Marco regarded her sardonically.

"You can relax. He's still going to be here when you get
back," he said.

Sam was already heading out the door when she realized
that she really wasn't anxious about leaving Tyler at all. As soon
as she figured out why—the reason stood about six-two and
walked on crutches—she frowned ferociously. But it was too
late. She was in the car by then, and there was nobody who mattered to see.

"Sun in your eyes?" Groves asked solicitously, and flipped
down her sun visor for her to block the rays that she hadn't even
noticed. He was driving the Toyota Corolla that had been in the
garage. It was blue, it was a four-door, it was nondescript. In
other words, it was perfect.

"Thanks," Sam said from the passenger seat beside him without explaining that her fierce look had had nothing whatsoever
to do with the blinding summer sun. Banishing the Marco-
induced scowl, she slid a sideways look at Groves. Sanders

might be about as chatty as a wall; she might not feel like having any kind of real conversation with Marco. But Groves was friendly. Groves she liked. Him, she might get to talk, and in this case knowledge just might prove to be a valuable thing. "So where did the car come from?"

Groves shrugged. "It was there with the house."

"Just like this T-shirt"—Sam plucked at the one she was wearing—"and the rest of the clothes we've been wearing were there with the house?"

"Yup."

"Who put them there?"

Groves shrugged again. "The house was set up fully equipped for us to use. What can I tell you?"

Sam felt a chill. If the house was set up for them, then the number of people who potentially knew where they were was larger than she had realized. What was that saying about three people being able to keep a secret if two of them were dead? What about a whole bureaucracy full of people? Suddenly the quiet neighborhood no longer felt so safe. They'd left the street with the town houses behind, and were now driving through a suburb filled with single-family homes. Late-model cars sat in driveways and kids rode their bikes down sidewalks while the adults did things like mow the yard and water the flowers. It was the kind of place that Sam would have given just about anything to be able to raise Tyler in, but even though the houses didn't look especially pricey they were as totally out of reach for someone like her as the moon. Home for her and Tyler had never been so picture perfect, but still it had been home. Sam suddenly longed for the normalcy the neighborhood represented with a fierceness that surprised her. She wanted to be back in her own life, back in her own house, her job, her routine, in the worst way.

Instead of how to pay the bills—her worst pre-Marco worry—she now had to worry about how to keep herself and her son alive. The trade-off totally sucked.

"When we left St. Louis, nobody was supposed to know where we were going," she protested uneasily. "So how could the house be set up in advance?"

"It wasn't set up for you—or rather, Marco—specifically. It's a safe house; the service maintains a bunch of them in various locations across the country. The couple who was supposed to be sent here got diverted somewhere else at the last minute, when our emergency came up."

"Greg and Laura James? And their son, Tyler?" From the first time she'd heard the names, it had seemed beyond odd that her son and their son were both called Tyler.

Groves shook his head. "Those are cover identities. Greg and Laura James are the names that this couple was going into hiding under while they stayed at the house you're in. They didn't have a kid, so there wasn't a cover ID for him, but that's okay: your kid got sandwiched into the deal, and they decided to keep his real first name. It's easier."

"Who decided?"

Groves shrugged. It was clear from his expression that if he knew, he wasn't saying. "The good news is nobody changed the paperwork on the previous couple, so even if there is a mole they won't be able to find you—uh, Marco. At least, not by going through the paperwork."

Sam suddenly had trouble catching her breath. "A mole?"

Groves looked at her. "Somebody found out the address of the house where we had Marco stashed in St. Louis. How? We got to consider a mole. People are looking into it, but in the meantime we did what we could to keep this location off the grid."

Sam could feel her stomach twisting itself into a knot. "If they found him in St. Louis . . ." Her voice trailed off. It occurred to her that Groves had been checking the rear- and side-view mirrors a little too often. Now she knew why: he was keeping an eye out to make sure they weren't being followed.

"Like I said, we're off the grid." Sam was sure his tone was meant to be reassuring.

Because they were pulling into the Walmart parking lot, Sam let the subject drop. But the fear stayed with her, making her tense and jumpy in a way that she hadn't been before.

Persuading Groves to wait for her by the entrance wasn't hard. All she had to do was mention that her first stop was going to be in the ladies' underwear section and the deed was done. Instead, as soon as she was out of Groves's sight she made a beeline for the hunting gear department. What she wanted, what she needed, her most important objective, was to acquire a weapon. Totally relying on the marshals—or Marco—to defend her and Tyler in a pinch was something that she was not prepared to do. After a quick consultation with the clerk behind the counter, she armed herself with a slender can of bear mace (the clerk described it as pepper spray on steroids, able to stop a charging grizzly at a distance of a couple of yards). Supplementing that with a folding knife small enough to fit in her pocket but lethal enough to do some damage if she had to use it, she cast a regretful glance at the gun case as she passed it—the background check, which usually required a minimum of three days to complete, plus the attention that said background check might attract, plus the price of the guns, ruled out trying to buy one—and hurried to make the rest of her purchases.

The Walmart wasn't particularly busy on that Sunday afternoon, but that just made each individual patron stand out more. Sam found herself casting surreptitious looks at her fellow shoppers, just in case one of them might not be a shopper at all, but a Zeta assassin on a mission to kill her. Finding herself worrying about being murdered in the middle of a Walmart was mind-boggling, but it was also a sure symptom of the hideous, horrible turn her life had taken. What made it so hideous and horrible was that her worry wasn't even particularly far-fetched. The only thing improbable about it was that the assassin would attack in the store. He (or they) was far more likely to follow her home and try to kill the whole party there.

By the time she rejoined Groves by the front entrance, she was so on edge that she jumped when a shopping cart clattered. Spotting the security cameras trained on the checkout lanes had made her heart thump: what if the people hunting them somehow gained access to the footage? Or what if there was an informant in the store, or . . .

Stop it, she ordered herself. *All you're doing is making your-*

self crazy. Still, she was relieved to get out of the store. Neither she nor Groves said much on the way back to the town house, but they both did their fair share of checking the mirrors for tails.

"You buy out the store?" Sanders asked when she walked into the kitchen carrying two big plastic bags loaded with the clothing she and Tyler needed, along with a chapter book (*Silver Wings,* a story about a bat) and a ten-pack assortment of Matchbox cars for Tyler (he loved Matchbox cars), a hair dryer (if she had to live with her unrestrained curls for much longer she would be feeling murderous herself), and a few essential cosmetics. Plus her weapons. "What'd you do with Groves?"

Having pulled into the attached garage, the interior door of which opened into the kitchen, Groves had been busy making sure the overhead door was secured when Sam had last seen him, which had been when she had walked into the house.

"Dumped him."

"Be glad I don't believe you." He was seated at the table eating what looked like a bologna sandwich and his eyes—they were small and blue in his blunt-featured face—squinched up suspiciously as they met hers. Like he was wondering if she really had somehow managed to dump Groves. She even thought he might have gotten up to check, except Groves walked into the kitchen just then.

"Any problems?" Sanders asked him.

"No."

Sanders grunted, and went back to eating his sandwich.

Groves opened the refrigerator and started rooting around in it as Sam dumped the change from the money Sanders had given her on the table in front of him. It amounted to five dollar bills and some coins, which he glanced at with a curl of his lips.

"Receipt?" he asked around a mouthful of sandwich.

"In one of the bags." She kept on walking, bags in hand, no big deal, heading for the great room.

"I'll need that," he called after her.

She didn't answer. The truth was that she had deliberately left the receipt behind at the checkout, because she had no intention of letting anyone see it. Putting five plus dollars down in front of Sanders was an action that she had carefully calculated in advance. Instead of not giving him any change, she had given him that small amount as a decoy, so that he wouldn't suspect she had any more. Sanders had given her two hundred dollars for the shopping trip, which Marco had assured her was expense account money. After a lifetime of pinching pennies, one thing she knew how to do was buy a lot with a little. Even after giving Sanders his supposed change, ninety dollars still remained in the back pocket of her jeans. (Since she already had her new knife in the front pocket, she had opted for the back for the cash so as to keep the evidence that she was thinking outside the box as unnoticeable as possible.) Sam felt like the knife and the neatly folded cash made lumps as big as boulders and were practically sending out bursts of light in an effort to be seen through her clothes, but Sanders didn't appear to notice anything amiss. Keeping the money might make her feel like a thief, but under the circumstances she had decided that she had to do what she had to do. If something were to go wrong, if she had to take

Tyler and run, she had no money. A little cash might make all the difference to them in an emergency. Like buying the bear mace and the knife, keeping the amount she had spent at just around half of what she had received had been a kind of insurance policy.

As Sam walked into the great room, the sight that greeted her stopped her in her tracks.

The TV was on. Focused so intently on it that they didn't even hear her enter, Tyler and Marco were side by side on the couch. They were not lounging comfortably, even disregarding Marco's injured leg, which thrust stiffly out in front of him. Instead they were sitting forward as though whatever was on the screen was of vital interest to them. For a moment Sam blinked at the TV, not understanding the images she saw. Cartoonish soldiers—a sparse terrain—the crosshairs of a rifle—gunfire.

"Got him!" Marco exulted as the TV soldier went down and a bright red spot blossomed on his back. "Good job, Tyler!"

"There's another one, Trey!"

"Shoot him!"

Pow! Pow! Boom! Boom! Even as the sound of gunfire filled the room and more soldiers went down, Sam registered the controllers in their hands, saw the game system, and realized that what she was seeing was a video game. A violent, bloody video game that was absolutely unsuitable for a four-year-old.

"What on earth are you *doing*?" Dropping the bags on the floor, she walked over to the couch and stood there glaring—not at both of them, because Tyler, having only ever been exposed to Pokémon video games at his friend Austin's house and educational video games at preschool, could hardly be blamed for this, but at Marco, who certainly could.

"It's *Halo,* Mom!" Tyler threw at her, barely taking the time to glance in her direction. Instantly refocusing on the TV, he bounced up and down in excitement. "Shoot, Trey, shoot!"

But after one look at Sam's face, "Trey" apparently had enough of a sense of self-preservation to know when to call a halt.

"Time we took a break," he said to Tyler, hitting a button that froze the action.

"Mom, you're interrupting the game!" Tyler howled, looking around at her for real now.

"I got you some cars." As a mother, one of Sam's guiding principles had become that distraction works. That's how she had gotten through the terrible twos with her sanity intact, as well as the troublesome threes and almost all of the fearsome fours (Tyler's fifth birthday was in three weeks). Crouching, rummaging through the bags, she came up with the promised package of toys. Like her, Tyler was something of a car buff, and when she stood up with the pack and said, "There's a Mustang Cobra in here, and a Dodge Charger, too," he was off the couch and running over to take it from her. For a moment he just stood there looking raptly at the cars in their little plastic rectangles.

Then he glanced up at her. "Thanks, Mom."

"You're welcome." She smiled at him. It didn't take much to make him happy; he was such a good, sweet-natured kid. Truth was, he deserved better than her, but she was what he'd gotten. "Why don't you take them up to your room"—it felt odd to refer to the room he slept in here the same way she did to his bedroom at home, but she did it—"and get them out?"

"Okay." He looked around at Marco. "You want to come and see?"

"Thanks, but I think I need to talk to your mom for a little bit." No fool, Marco was clearly able to read the signals she was sending. As in, you're toast.

"'Kay." Holding the package of cars so that he could study them through the plastic wrap as he walked, Tyler headed for the stairs.

Fixing Marco with a gimlet gaze, Sam waited until her son was out of sight. For his part, Marco hit the remote, which turned off the TV, then set the remote down on the coffee table beside the controllers. As if he were a guilty kid trying to hide the evidence of his wrongdoing, Sam thought.

"That game is totally unsuitable for a four-year-old. What were you *thinking*?" She said it as soon as she was sure Tyler could no longer overhear.

Marco had relaxed back against the couch cushions and turned sideways a little so that he could look at her without craning his neck. "Come on, Sam. It's *Halo Reach*. One of the best video games from one of the best video game series ever. A classic. I play it with my nephews all the time."

"How old are they?"

He had the grace to look a little abashed. "Eleven. Twelve. Fourteen."

Sam filed away the fact that he had eleven-, twelve-, and

fourteen-year-old nephews for future reference. "That's still too young for a game like that, if you want my opinion, but it's a lot better than four."

"My sisters don't have a problem with their boys playing it. All their friends play it, too. And Tyler likes it."

Sisters? He had sisters? Something else to ponder later. Not that she meant to spend any time thinking about him. Anyway, she had more important fish to fry.

"Of course he likes it. He loves guns, and pretending to shoot things, and playing army, and all that stuff. That doesn't mean it's good for him." Sam's mouth thinned with exasperation. "He'd love having candy for breakfast, too, if I'd let him."

"He was pretty good at it, for such a little kid."

"I don't care! I don't want him playing a violent video game."

Marco held up both hands in mock surrender. "Okay, my bad. I'll disconnect the game console and put it back in the cabinet where I found it."

"Good." She gave him another stern look and bent to pick up her bags.

"Sam."

Straightening with bags in hand, she glanced at him in answer.

"He is a boy, you know. Boys like guns, and shooting things, and violence. It's normal." At the look she gave him, he added hastily, "Just saying."

"Do you have any children?"

"No." Something that looked suspiciously like a twinkle appeared in his eyes. She was still looking closely at it, trying to decide what it meant, when he added, "No wife, either, if that's where you're going with this."

What? "You know that's not where I was going," she said crossly. "Where I was going is, if you don't have children, you don't know anything about them, so I'll thank you to let me raise mine the best way I can."

"Yes, ma'am." He was openly grinning at her now.

Sam turned her back on him and headed for the stairs. Maybe it was her imagination—she didn't think so—but she could almost feel his eyes on her butt. The thought did not please her, but it did make her step quicken. Along with her pulse.

Which also did not please her.

"Sam." She heard him trying to get up, heard the thump of a dropped crutch, heard a curse. "Wait a minute. Ow!"

That *ow* did it. She couldn't help herself. She glanced back at him. He was balancing beside the couch, one crutch beneath his arm, the other flat on the carpet at his feet. The foot of his injured leg barely touched the ground, and he was grimacing with pain.

Her inner worrywart got the best of her.

"What, have those stupid pills quit working or something?" she asked him sharply.

His grimace was overridden by a gleam of amusement in the glance he shot her way as he gave a single negative shake of his head. "I quit taking them. They got me in trouble."

She absolutely refused to go there. "So you're just going to hurt."

"Seemed like the best idea."

Sam realized that she hated the idea that he was in pain, and then hated that she hated it. It occurred to her then that, much as she disliked having to face it, she and Tyler needed him. If, for example, he should have to go to a hospital to get his leg reoperated on, they would be left alone with the marshals. Or not. Because every single one of their guardians had made it clear that their job was to protect Marco, and she and Tyler were nothing more than excess baggage. Sam was pretty sure that she could count on them only as long as Marco was around to insist they protect her and her son.

All the more reason for the insurance policy she'd tried to put in place.

"Did you change the bandage on your leg?" If she sounded irritable, it was because she was feeling irritable. Constantly battling back fear did not have a good effect on her, she was discovering.

"Not yet."

"You'd better do it."

"Everything I need is upstairs, and I'm not going upstairs again until it's time to go to bed. Getting up and down those stairs on crutches is too damned much work."

He bent over, swiping at the crutch on the floor in a failed attempt to pick it up. Lips compressed, Sam watched as he finally snagged it, in two minds about whether or not she should offer to help him with the changing of his bandage. She pictured the location of the wound and the degree of closeness to him that would be required, to say nothing of the hands-on nature of the task, which she had already experienced. Then she remembered last night—and this morning. *No way in hell,* was her deciding thought on the subject as at last he got the crutches situated beneath his armpits. With that she turned and went upstairs without another word, ignoring him as he called after her. Whatever he wanted to say to her, she was in no mood to hear.

By the time 11:00 p.m. rolled around, they'd had no more private conversation, and she was wiped out. She'd done several loads of laundry: Tyler's and her clothes, their bedding (because who knew who'd been sleeping on those sheets before they had arrived), some towels. She had cleaned her room and Tyler's, and dusted and swept and run the vacuum over the entire house. She'd played cars and hide-and-seek, made a garage out of a shoebox, and baked brownies because Tyler loved them and there was a box of mix in the pantry. All the activity served the admirable goal of keeping her busy, which prevented her from worrying too much about more bad things that might be coming their way. But also, under the guise of cleaning in particular, she had contrived to learn where every window and door (possible exits) were located and how they operated, where an extra house key was kept (on a hook inside a cabinet, along with another, nearly identical key, which she thought might be a key to the town house next door), where the car keys were kept (inside the drawer closest to the garage), as well as where the garage door opener was stashed. As Sanders went off guard duty and was replaced by Abramowitz, she'd learned the code to the security system by watching Sanders type it into the keypad beside the door in the kitchen that led to the garage. When they'd grilled hamburgers for dinner, Abramowitz had sat in a lawn chair and kept guard, Marco had done the actual grilling, Sam had formed the patties for him and made a salad, and Tyler, beaming with excitement about grilling out, which was something he had never experienced because they didn't have a grill, had been in charge of opening the buns. While they were outside, with everyone else pretty much occupied, she had taken the opportunity to check out the backyard gate, how it worked, what it opened onto. And she had done all those things just in case. Just in case the bad guys should find them, or just in case she should decide to take Tyler and go it alone. Or—well, just in case.

Having supervised Tyler's bath and then read a chapter in their new book to him, she stayed with him until he fell asleep and then emerged, yawning, into the hall. Except for being barefoot, she was still fully dressed, in the jeans and tank she had been wearing all day, with her hair still in its single fat braid that fell over her shoulder now. What she was looking forward to doing next with an eagerness that bordered on greed was soaking in a hot bath before falling into bed.

That required use of the second bathroom, because the bathroom off the master bedroom only had a shower stall.

Of course Marco would be emerging from that bathroom at precisely the same moment as she stepped out of Tyler's room. Looking big and broad shouldered and way too hot for her peace of mind, he was once again wrapped in the white robe, wearing nothing else that she could see (although hopefully he had boxers on under there somewhere). Just the sight of him (un)dressed like that brought a whole raft of sizzling images to her mind that she kicked out at once.

Scowling at him, she would have passed on by without a word—although it was slightly difficult getting past him when, on crutches, he took up most of the hall—but he reached out and caught her arm, stopping her.

Her eyes snapped up to meet his. He smiled at her. She absolutely distrusted everything about that smile.

"Got a minute?" he asked.

CHAPTER NINETEEN

The correct answer to that question where he was concerned was no. A thousand times no.

What Sam said was a truculent, *"What?"*

"Something I need to know?"

"I don't know what you're talking about." Seriously. She didn't. But she did know that she didn't want to talk to him at all. Especially not now, when he was obviously just out of the shower and half naked and she couldn't keep her heartbeat from quickening or her body from tightening with excitement stoked by absolutely nothing at all except memories and his proximity. Who would have thought that the smell of soap and toothpaste could turn her on so? But it did. At least, when it was associated with him.

When she tried to pull her arm free, he leaned toward her, crowding her back toward the wall. His chest brushed her breasts. His pelvis nudged hers. She could feel the whole long length of him corralling her, trapping her, and knew that he was doing it deliberately. His body heat surrounded her, making her feel hot in turn. Suddenly she was finding it harder to breathe. Stubble that was way past five o'clock shadow darkened his chin; doing a lightning mental recap of the last few days, she was pretty sure he hadn't shaved since she had met him. His eyes were dark and slightly bloodshot, but alert. His hair was damp, and a few tiny drops of water from his shower still beaded his skin.

Sam couldn't help it; her pulse started to race.

"Do you want something?" She kept her cool, kept her chin up, and kept her voice low so as not to wake Tyler as Marco backed her all the rest of the way up against the wall until she was totally pinned in place by his weight.

"Oh, yeah."

Their faces were so close that she could feel his breath feathering her cheek. One crutch slid down the wall to hit the carpet with a soft thud as he let it go. The other stayed upright, propped against the wall beside her, but he was no longer using it. Instead he was favoring his injured leg but standing on his own, preventing her escape by absolutely misusing his superior size and strength. He wrapped a muscular arm around her, snaking it into the space between the wall and the hollow of her back, pulling her hard up against him. Then he *started to grope her butt.* Squirming at the surprise of it, wedging both hands against the solid wall of his chest and shoving, she didn't manage to either extricate herself or budge him by so much as an inch. Injured or not, the man was *strong.*

The bad news was, she discovered that she liked being plastered up against him. And she liked the feel of his hand on her butt. Way too much. Her body tightened deep inside in the most pleasurable way possible. *OMG, I can't let him know.*

"What the hell do you think you're doing?" she growled in pure self-defense. Only after she said it did she realize that she wasn't shoving at him any longer. Instead her hands had fisted in the front of his robe and were gripping the thick toweling for dear life.

"What do *you* think I'm doing?"

Her pulse pounded. Her breathing quickened. Defiantly she threw back her head to glare up at him even while she was acutely, pleasurably aware of how big and strong and masculine his hand felt as it continued its intimate exploration. "It's obvious, isn't it? Copping a feel."

Looking at him had been a mistake. His mouth wasn't that far from hers; its curve was—sexy. Just like the heat in his eyes as they met hers was sexy.

"If I was copping a feel, I'd have my hand *inside* your pants."

That melted her bones. Her knees went wobbly, just like that. All because she could picture it—feel it—as vividly as if he really was delving inside her jeans and panties to caress her bare skin.

Just thinking about it was enough to make her squirm.

"So maybe you're subtle like that." But she said it without conviction. As much as she wanted to think copping a feel was what he was doing, the real answer was, it didn't seem like something the Marco she knew would do. But then, selling out his fellow agents and joining forces with a drug cartel, and then selling them out in turn, didn't seem like something the Marco she knew would do, either. So the conclusion she reached was, she actually didn't know squat about him.

"You really think that?" His voice was low, and a little husky.

"That you're subtle? Probably not. That you're copping a feel? Sure feels like it to me."

"Guess again, baby doll." He splayed his hand wide over her butt and pulled her closer still in a way that left her breathless. Her nipples reacted instantly to the sudden close contact with his chest. At the unexpected jolt of pleasure that resulted, her mouth went dry. She liked the strength in his grip, she realized, liked the sensation of being female to his male. The way he was holding her, she was practically being squashed into the cushiony layer of his robe. She could feel the bulky knot of the belt tied at his waist. Beneath the toweling, she could feel the firm muscles he had everywhere.

"Let go of me!" She squirmed in a halfhearted attempt to get away. "Are you on those stupid pills again?"

"Nope."

Whether his purpose was to cop a feel or not, that was definitely what he was doing. She could feel his hand palming first one cheek and then the other—and her body's instantaneous reaction did not bode well for her determination to leave sex out of the equation where he was concerned. He caressed the rounded curves, slid his fingers along the indentation between them all the way down between her legs, and as she felt him touching her there she was rocked by a flash of desire so strong

it shocked her. Her lips parted as her breathing went all uneven.
She could feel her body softening. She could feel his hard-
ening.

"Then what the *hell*, Marco?" The objection probably would
have been more effective if it hadn't sounded so breathless—and
if she had been trying harder to get away from him. She wasn't
even squirming in protest (or otherwise) any longer, not that
the squirming she had done there for a minute really counted as
an attempt to get him to stop. If he had been anyone else in the
world, if she had meant business, she would have kneed him.
Or, second option, grabbed his injured leg and squeezed. One
thing she had learned over the years was how to take care of
herself. If she had really wanted to get free, she could have made
it happen like *that*.

Instead she was going all buttery inside even as she let—and
face the truth, *let* was the right word—him get all touchy-feely
with her butt.

"Did you really think I wasn't going to notice the brand-new
addition to your ass?" he asked on a note of grim triumph.

That was so unexpected that Sam frowned. Then she realized: he hadn't been feeling her up. He'd been patting her down.
As he spoke, his fingers were digging down deep inside her back
pocket, and he was pulling out her cash.

"Way to prove you're spending way too much time staring
at it!" Indignation stiffened her spine. When his hand came into
view holding the ninety dollars she had stashed away in her
back pocket, then waggled the tightly folded square in front of
her nose, she met his gaze belligerently.

"Want to explain this?" His eyes would have been hard if it hadn't been for the heat at their backs.

He's turned on, too. The realization made her want to start stripping off her clothes. Then she remembered that both of them had resolved to keep sex out of it—for very good reasons—and determinedly focused on the folded bills he was still holding in front of her face instead.

"It's mine. Give it back."

"Yeah. No. You got something hidden in your front pocket, too. I can feel it pressing against me. Are you gonna pull whatever it is out and show it to me, or do you want me to pat you down all over?"

An honest answer to that question, even if given silently, was not in her best interest, so she thrust it out of her mind. Bottom line was, if he patted her down all over, she would probably end up dissolving into a steaming little puddle at his feet. At the very least, she would get even more turned on than she already was, and that would not be good. Or smart.

So she folded.

Giving him a sulky look, she delved into her pocket and produced the knife.

"Happy now?" she asked.

He took the knife, shot a pointed look at her cleavage. "Is that it?"

Just the idea that he might start searching where he was looking made her heart thump. *Forget about it. Not going to happen.* "Yes."

He gave her another hard look. "You give me your word?"

"You can do a strip search if you want." A little bit of aggression, she figured, was the best way to back him off. Because she was able to see, now, that the heat in his eyes wasn't the only sign. That, plus the flush that had risen to stain the tops of his high cheekbones, the heavy-lidded look to his eyes, the barely perceptible quickening of his breathing, were all signals that, as a woman, she knew how to read: he wanted her bad.

If she'd let it, the knowledge would have made her dizzy. But instead she forced it out of her head, and managed to summon a mocking smile for him.

His lips thinned. As she'd been almost positive he wouldn't, he didn't take her up on her offer. Instead, with her cash and knife still in hand, he levered himself off her, reaching for the crutch that still lay against the wall beside her, wedging it into place, bracing himself with it, surprisingly solid on his one good leg. The net result was that there were now a few inches of space between them, for which she tried to tell herself she was glad. She stayed where she was, back against the wall, her hands flattened against the cool plaster.

To keep herself from doing what she really wanted to do and reaching for him.

He looked at her grimly. "The knife I can understand. You want something to protect yourself with. Under the circumstances, fair enough. The money—that's what's got me worried. Especially since I watched you spend the afternoon checking out the doors and windows, locating the car and house keys, and memorizing the code to the security alarm. You're thinking about taking Tyler and striking out on your own, aren't you?"

Sam thought about lying. She certainly hadn't been expecting him of all people to be so observant, but apparently he had missed very little, which told her that he had been watching her closely while he hadn't appeared to be watching her at all. He'd observed enough to lead him to the money and the knife, too. The idea that she had just been the subject of a very thorough if partial pat-down was finally starting to work its way through her brain, and she was thinking that she ought to be at least a little mad at him about it. What complicated the whole thing was remembering how it had made her feel. Sexy enough to make her start to burn all over again at the recollection.

You need to get laid, she told herself firmly. Then, in a hasty corollary, she added, *just not by this guy.*

But it was too late. She had an instant mental vision of the two of them naked and in bed, and practically ground her teeth as her pulse went tremulous and her stomach seemed to quiver. The tiny stress muscle below her eye started to twitch, most annoyingly. Pressing a calming finger to it, she glared at him, and gave up all attempt at pretense.

"So what if I am?"

His eyes narrowed. "That would be the dumbest thing you could possibly do."

She huffed. "Says you. The guy who screwed up his life so badly that he's got an army of assassins combing the country looking for him, and if he doesn't get himself and everybody around him murdered is going to wind up spending the next twenty years or so in jail."

For a moment Marco didn't say anything, just looked at

her. She realized that throwing what he was in his face was her way of asking him to deny it if he could. But what he said was, "Who's been talking to you? Not Sanders, I'm willing to bet. One of the other three."

"What does it matter? It's true, isn't it?" Although she was giving him one last chance, she did not expect him to say no, and he didn't. Instead, he looked at her without saying anything at all for a moment, then slowly inclined his head: *yes.* Okay, well, now she'd had it straight from the horse's mouth. "The point is, I have to judge this for myself."

"I've kept you safe so far, haven't I? You and Tyler. I'll see you through this, I promise."

"Wait a minute. What happened to that whole 'if I can' thing?"

The slight flicker of his eyelashes told her that he remembered his qualified promise when they had first met: *I'll keep you alive. If I can.*

She had no doubt that he was telling the truth: he would do his absolute best. It was the "if" part that was bothering her.

"Have a little faith in me, Sam." He said it very quietly. His eyes had gone dark. His face had changed in some subtle way that she couldn't quite pinpoint, but he looked tough and capable and like somebody she could absolutely rely on in a pinch.

Have a little faith in me. Oh, God, she wanted to. But if she had learned one thing over the years, it was that the only person she could rely on was herself.

"I have to think of Tyler," she said. "He only has me to look out for him."

"I'm thinking of Tyler, too. On your own, you two would be sitting ducks." His eyes raked her, and then when they met hers again they had turned hard. "Look, we can do this one of two ways. I can dog every step you take until the danger's passed, and by that I mean from here on out I sleep on the floor outside your bedroom door, I eat when you eat, I stand outside the bathroom while you're in it—" He broke off to give her a malicious smile. "I see from your expression you're getting my drift—or you can convince me that you're not just going to grab Tyler and bolt because something spooked you and you think it's a good idea."

She glared at him. "You say that like you think I'm not capable of making a sound judgment about what to do. I am, I promise you. What's it to you, anyway?"

"I got you into this. I mean to get you out. And yes, I do think you're capable of making a sound judgment about what to do. I just don't think you completely understand the situation."

"What don't I understand?"

He shrugged. "How ruthless the Zetas are, for one thing."

"So, bottom line, I should just trust your judgment and do what you tell me."

The faintest suggestion of a smile touched his mouth. "There you go. Bingo."

Her lips pursed. She eyed him. "Here's what I don't think *you* understand. Sanders—the marshals—have no interest in protecting Tyler and me. If you were to have to go to the hospital, say, to get your leg treated—"

"Won't happen," he interjected. "It's getting all better. It's sore, but I'll live. A little time, a little ointment, a few Band-Aids, and I'll be good as new."

Sam frowned doubtfully. "Band-Aids?"

"Band-Aids," he repeated, then twitched his robe aside so that she could see his leg. As he'd said, instead of yards of gauze over layers of sterile padding, which was what had adorned his thigh the last time she'd seen it, a single large Band-Aid was plastered over the place where the bullet had gone in. She goggled at it.

"See?"

From practically the hem of his boxers to the top of his knee, his thigh was black and blue. It still looked slightly swollen and definitely painful, but somehow the Band-Aid made it look much less potentially disabling than before.

"It looks better," she admitted.

"I heal fast." He frowned at her. "How about you give me your word that you won't go running off without at least giving me a heads-up first?"

"You'd stop me," she objected.

The flicker in his eyes told her that she'd hit the nail on the head. But he didn't admit it. "Hell, I'd probably go with you. Because I'm assuming that you wouldn't go haring off on your own without good reason, and if you come across a reason good enough to make you think you ought to take Tyler and run, then I should probably be hauling ass out of here, too."

"You are so full of crap."

Again he almost smiled. "Maybe." His eyes held hers. "Come

on, Sam. Are you really going to make me sleep on the floor outside your door tonight?"

"It's tempting." Sam looked at him meditatively. "Okay, I give you my word," she said, and wasn't even sure whether she was lying or not.

His expression was impossible to read. But all he said was, "Good." Then he handed her cash and knife back to her. Just like that.

"Thank you," she said, trying not to sound surprised as she thrust them down into her front pocket.

There was something there in the depths of his eyes as he watched her that made her heart speed up again.

"Don't ever play poker, Sam," he said softly. Then as she frowned at him, trying to work that out, he slid a hand under her chin, leaned forward, and kissed her.

CHAPTER TWENTY

I t had nothing to do with the damned pain pills. Tonight he
was the opposite of high as a kite, and the sexual voltage
between them was still off the charts. That was the unwelcome knowledge that tore like a bullet through Danny's brain at
the first surprised flutter of Sam's lips beneath his. Rampant desire so hot it would have put a flamethrower to shame raised his
temperature by about a thousand degrees as soon as he yielded
to the damned stupid impulse of a moment and kissed her. Then
she made a tiny sound and her lips parted to let him in, and his
gut clenched and he went instantly hard and for a minute there
he wasn't thinking at all.

Her mouth was warm and wet, sweet and seductive. Her
tongue welcomed his with an eagerness that sent his libido into
turbocharge mode. He kissed her hungrily, fiercely, until he felt
the cool silk of her hands start to slide up around his neck.

Then he had a second, just a second, of clarity.

But it was enough.

Opening his eyes, he forced his mind to function, steeled his will.

Catching her arms before they could lock around his neck, he freed his mouth from hers, lifted his head. And found himself looking down at rosy, full lips damp with his kiss, delicate nose, fringes of flirty black lashes lying against pale, smooth cheeks. With sooty tendrils of hair framing the fine-featured oval of her face, she was so beautiful she made his breath stop.

He'd started getting turned on when he had frisked her, which was why he had stopped with the job only half done. Having succumbed to the urge to kiss her just now simply because she'd looked so damned guilty and vulnerable and sweet, he was paying the price: he wanted her so badly he hurt with it.

You fucking idiot.

"Sam."

Her eyes had opened when he had caught her arms. Danny found himself drowning in pools of intense blue. The passion he saw in them made him burn. The promise of hot, intense, mind-blowing sex crackled in the air. It would be so easy, so damned easy, to give her what she so clearly wanted, to reward himself with what he was dying to have, to take her to bed and rock her world and see if he couldn't make his own world a little brighter, too.

For a moment, as they stared at each other, the issue hung in the balance. He was so aroused that despite every resolution he had made to the contrary he wasn't sure he had the iron control that he was going to need to step away.

Then her brows snapped together in a frown.

"Forget about it, Marco." Her voice was a little husky, her breathing a little fast, but the determination in her tone was unmistakable. He felt the quick rise and fall of her breasts against his chest. The warmth of her, the softness of her, the sweet scent of her, all combined to make him burn. She pulled her arms from his hold, took a step back. He let her go.

By calling him Marco, she had opened a tiny little window that allowed a few beams of sanity to reach his brain. The danger hadn't gone away. He still needed to be clearheaded. He still couldn't afford the distraction.

But he wanted her. Jesus, he wanted her.

She said, "I'm not doing this. No way."

Thank the Lord she had the sense to call a halt, because right at that moment he was having trouble getting there. He was practically clenching his teeth to keep from reaching for her again.

She said, "I'm going to bed. Good night."

He said nothing as she turned and left him, padding barefoot down the hall with her head held high. Tall and willowy, her tank top clinging in a way that showed off her narrow rib cage and small waist, her jeans hugging her absolutely world-class ass and long slim legs, with the kind of sway to her walk that would make a eunuch pant, she took his breath away. If he hadn't been in so highly charged a state, and fighting it so doggedly, he would have smiled at the fierceness of her as she walked away from him.

The girl had attitude. Balls. By putting the brakes on something he knew she was as hungry to have happen as he was, she had surprised him once again. Jesus, he was ready to walk over hot coals barefoot to find out what she would be like in bed. Would she be sweet? Or wild?

Imagining the possibilities set him on fire all over again.

But whether she was hot stuff in the sack or not, taking her to bed wasn't on the agenda. Getting her and her kid to safety was what he needed to be focusing on. What he *was* going to focus on.

Just give him a couple of seconds.

Danny stood where he was for another minute or so, willing himself to chill out with only so-so success. Then he turned and headed for his bedroom. Since arriving at the town house, he'd slept with his bedroom door open, the better to keep an eye and an ear on Tyler and Sam. Sam slept with her bedroom door open, too, to listen for Tyler, he knew. And Tyler's bedroom door was left open, probably so Sam could hear him if he cried out in the night.

But a moment ago Sam had shut her bedroom door with a decided snap, which he had taken as another manifestation of *ain't happening* directed at him. And now he was closing his, too. And locking it. And turning on the radio that also served as an alarm clock, the better to keep from being overheard.

His bedroom was the smallest of the three, and simple: white walls, beige carpet, a framed landscape over a double bed. Plain oak headboard, oak nightstand with a lamp and the clock radio, oak chest. Navajo looking bedspread, and in one corner a small brown armchair.

He sat down in the armchair—it was a rocker, he discovered, upholstered in some kind of plush—and started taking apart his right crutch. The handful of Advil he had popped maybe an hour before had taken the edge off his leg, but it still hurt like hell. He was just getting better at ignoring it. His finger, his bruises, and other injuries, they were healing, and he barely noticed them now. They were nothing he hadn't suffered before. His worst problem at the moment was that he was horny as hell and stuck with it, no relief in sight. In fact, he was getting ready to make sure that the woman he was jazzed with lust over to the point where he was having trouble thinking about anything except taking her to bed was whisked away out of his reach.

With the crutch lying dismantled near his feet, he snapped the battery back into the cell phone and turned it on. A second later, it flickered to life. He punched in a number that only a few people knew, and waited.

"Panterro," he identified himself to the man who answered. Using his real name felt risky—when he was undercover he did his best to forget it—but this situation had gone so far off the rails that the rules he usually operated by had flown out the window. Besides, unless the house was bugged, no one was listening. And if Veith or the Zetas knew where the house was, bugging it wouldn't be what they did, so talking freely should be safe.

"Danny." Associate Deputy Director Keith Mayhew didn't sound particularly glad to hear from him. Which Danny could understand. Last time they'd talked, which had been about six months previously, Danny had just completed an undercover operation into a foreign government that provided prostitutes for members of Congress and other high-ranking officials, then videotaped and subsequently blackmailed them. The fallout hadn't been pretty, and the director's office had caught significant flack. Fortunately he and Mayhew went further back than that, all the way back to when Mayhew, as special agent in charge of the Houston office, had hired him straight out of college. "What bad news do you have for me now?"

"None." Danny almost smiled at the resigned tone in the older man's voice. "I'm on assignment. I need a favor."

"So lay it on me."

Danny gave him a quick rundown of the situation. "Bottom line, I got two civilians in the line of fire. I want them out of it."

"What do you expect me to do about it?"

"Send a crew you trust to get them out of here. Take 'em back to Washington or somewhere and protect the hell out of them until I get this over with."

"They're that important to you, hmm?"

Until Mayhew said it, Danny hadn't really thought about it that way. But the truth was, protecting civilians usually happened on a pay grade level way below Mayhew's. What Danny was asking for was a five-star, gold-plated personal favor. He recognized that Mayhew wouldn't forget it, that he'd be throwing it in Danny's face at the most inopportune moments for the rest of his professional life. Danny thought of Sam, and Tyler, and concluded, *worth it.*

"Yeah," he said.

"You got it." Mayhew wasn't one to waste time when he didn't have to. "Some reason you're not taking this to your AIC?"

His agent in charge would be Crittenden. And no, Danny didn't feel like he could take this to him. Like Sanders, Crittenden would consider Sam and Tyler as not critical to the mission.

"I want them completely out of this," he said. "And I want them kept safe."

"Any way I can get in touch with you? I don't suppose you want me to call you back at this number."

"No."

"I'll set it up. Operation Romeo. You'll be hearing from me shortly."

Mayhew hung up before Danny could say thanks.

The name Mayhew had chosen for the operation, Romeo, registered as Danny removed the battery from the cell phone again, and wrung a wry smile from him as he considered it. One thing was for sure, it hadn't been chosen at random. Mayhew never did anything at random. Restoring the phone to its hiding place, reassembling the crutch, he thought back over what he had said. He'd given the associate deputy director only the briefest of thumbnail sketches of who Sam and Tyler were, so how Mayhew had divined his romantic interest in Sam he had no clue. Except the operation name told him that he had; it was Mayhew's way of taking a dig at him. The only explanation was that there must have been something in his tone as he'd talked about her. Plus, Mayhew knew him pretty well.

Whatever, just as soon as Mayhew got Sam and Tyler out of there, he'd sleep a whole lot better.

The clock was running down. The word on the street would be that Marco was going to be playing show-and-tell any day now, and the Zetas, with their wide-flung contacts, would have picked that up. By now the cartel would be getting desperate, and since the purpose of the assignment was for him to provide a decoy while the real Rick Marco gave chapter and verse to the government, the path that led to this safe house would be followable. It wouldn't be easy to find, but it would be there, because it was supposed to be there. All he had to do was stay one step ahead of Veith and/or any other cartel enforcers until Marco was done, and then Marco would go into witness protection and he, Danny, would be finished with one more assignment and free to live his life until the next one. In St. Louis, however, staying one step ahead of the hit squad on Marco's tail had not worked out so well, and the more Danny thought about it the more that bothered him. The key was for him to get out of this alive, and that almost hadn't happened. Either somebody had fucked up big time, or . . . or what? He didn't know. What he did know was that here, although the marshals had him under round-the-clock protection and Crittenden and his team were supposed to be set up somewhere nearby monitoring the house as well as keeping tabs on any suspicious movements on the part of any known cartel associates such as Veith, he was starting to feel uneasy.

He'd been doing this job long enough to know to trust his gut, and his gut was telling him that something wasn't right.

The first order of business had to be to get Sam and Tyler out of harm's way.

The second? Well, that would depend on what came up.

Tightening up the head of the crutch, Danny was pondering the possibilities when he heard a kind of strangled sounding cry. At first he had trouble placing it. Then he realized: Tyler.

Even as Danny shot to his feet and, balancing on one leg, grabbed for the nearest crutch, he remembered Tyler had nightmares and told himself to calm down.

A nightmare. That was all it was.

Still, he hurried to the boy's room just to make sure.

Just as he reached Tyler's doorway, the kid let loose with a shriek that made Danny wince. The room was dark, but not totally. He could see Tyler sitting bolt upright in the middle of the bed, his eyes closed, his arms stiff as boards at his sides, screaming like someone was cutting his throat with Sam nowhere in sight.

Jesus.

"Tyler." Danny swung over to the bed. *"Tyler."*

Then, because he didn't know what else to do, he sat down on the side of the bed. Tyler's eyes opened as he felt the mattress give, and for a moment he stared at Danny like he wasn't sure who he was.

"It's okay, Tyler, it's me," Danny said hastily, bracing himself for another of those eardrum-shattering screams.

"Trey." Tyler launched himself at him, throwing his arms around him, burying his face in his chest. Danny could feel his small body shaking. "The bad men were here, Trey. They were after me."

"I got you. It was just a bad dream." A little awkwardly, Danny patted his back; then as the kid snuggled closer, shuddering, he hugged him because it just felt like the thing to do. "You hear me, Tyler? It was only a bad dream. I'm here, and I've got you safe."

"Tyler!" Still in her jeans and tank, Sam flew through the door, then pulled up short when she saw Danny. For a moment she paused, seeming to practically vibrate on the balls of her feet, and then she came toward the bed, giving Danny an impossible to interpret look even as she sat down on the edge of the bed beside him. "Baby, I'm here."

"*Mom.*" Tyler let go of Danny to throw himself into his mother's outstretched arms. "I had another bad dream."

"I know," Sam said soothingly, rocking him a little. "I know."

"We used the monster spray. But it didn't matter, because I dreamed about the bad men."

"Oh, Tyler." Sam kissed the top of his head. "Everything's going to be okay."

Danny looked at the clean, elegant lines of her profile as her cheek rested against her son's tousled black hair. Her hair was still in that single braid, slightly messy, sexy as hell. Her body— well, he didn't need to be looking at her body.

Their eyes met.

Danny felt as if every solid thing around him was slipping away.

"Can you sleep in here, Mom?" Tyler asked. Sam's attention reverted instantly to her son.

"Sure, baby," she replied.

Danny picked up his crutch from where it had dropped to the carpet at his feet, and stood up.

Still rocking Tyler, Sam watched him as he got the crutch in place beneath his arm.

"Do you need me for anything?" he asked her quietly.

She shook her head.

"Just sing out if you do."

She nodded.

Danny swung out of the room. Glancing back as he reached the hall, he saw Sam gently easing her son back down onto his pillow.

The sight had a weird effect on his insides. They felt kind of tight and achy, almost like he'd just taken a sucker punch to the gut.

It took Danny a moment to figure out what was going on. Then he realized with a sense of dismay that what he was feeling was Sam and her kid starting to twine themselves around his heart.

CHAPTER TWENTY-ONE

Trey, Trey, Trey: that was all Sam had heard out of Tyler all day. Earlier, Tyler had looked on with fascination as "Trey" worked out in the backyard, starting with a series of pull-ups on a branch that showcased his brawny arms and shoulders, and that Sam, aside from a couple of sneak peeks, resolutely refused to watch. He followed that up with other exercises that she was surprised that, injured as he was, he was physically able to perform. She remembered him saying that he needed to get up to speed again ASAP, and supposed that this was his way of doing it. His overall level of fitness and the hard-muscled body it showcased were truly impressive: once again she thought, *the man is strong.* But what took the cake was that Tyler earnestly tried to imitate everything he did; it underlined to Sam how much her son wanted a father figure in his life, and how much he was missing out on by not having one. The sad thing was, as right as their growing interconnectedness with Marco might feel to her on some internal, cellular level, by any objective measurement Marco was absolutely the wrong guy, both for Tyler and for her, to develop any kind of connection to. In an attempt to disrupt it, she tried everything—calling Tyler in for a brownie, playing cars, reading to him, turning on the Disney Channel on TV—and still Tyler ended up wherever "Trey" was. What made it even sadder was that Marco was absolutely sweet to Tyler. Where many men—Tyler's own father included—might act like an endlessly inquisitive and talkative four-year-old was a pain in the rear, Marco did not. He treated Tyler like an interesting and valued companion. And Tyler basked in his attention. There was no future in it, which Sam knew perfectly well. But about the third time Tyler sneaked away from her to "see what Trey is doing," Sam gave it up.

Right now, at shortly after five o'clock, "Trey" and Tyler were once again out in the backyard, where a glance through the sliding glass door showed her that "Trey" was teaching Tyler the finer points of dribbling a basketball. Given that "Trey" was leaning on a crutch as he bounced the ball up and down, his efforts were surprisingly dexterous. The other crutch lay discarded in the grass just beyond the patio. Beside it, in a lawn chair looking bored out of his mind, sat Groves, who was on guard duty.

In a weird, parallel universe kind of way, given the truth of the situation, the day was unwinding in an almost normal-seeming, mundane fashion. Sam still felt edgy and anxious whenever she thought about practically anything beyond the confines of the town house's four walls, so she just refused to, because worrying about what she couldn't control or, alternatively, scaring herself senseless didn't do any good.

Instead, since she actually enjoyed cooking when she had the time, which she rarely did, and had the necessary ingredients, another rarity, she had nixed the supper suggestion of carry-out KFC and volunteered to make something. As she put the finishing touches on the lasagna she was getting ready to pop into the oven, Sam found herself watching the man and boy playing on the patio with resignation.

Keeping Tyler from growing attached to Marco under these conditions was pretty close to impossible, she decided. Last night had told the tale. She had been in the kitchen, getting a glass of milk in hopes of soothing her frazzled nerves in the wake of that sizzling encounter with Marco. The milk, plus the hot bath that was next on her agenda, should help her sleep, she had hoped. If it didn't, she had already made up her mind that she was just going to have to lie awake all night, because the alternative—climbing into bed with Marco, which was what she really wanted to do—wasn't going to happen. No matter how hot just thinking about it made her. But when Tyler had screamed, and she had gone running upstairs to find Marco sitting on the edge of the bed and Tyler clinging to him just like he would have clung to her if she'd been there, she'd been blindsided. Tyler wasn't a physically demonstrative child with anyone but her; he didn't throw hugs and kisses around, or cling indiscriminately. But watching him with Marco, she immediately saw that whatever Marco might be or might have done, Tyler had admitted him into the tiny, privileged circle of people he trusted. It was clear as glass that Tyler was getting attached to him. Just like, Sam feared, she was starting to get attached to the damned man, too.

Even if she wanted to stop it, to back away and drag Tyler with her, there was nothing she could do. For now, the three of them were stuck together in this prison of a town house. And she knew already that there was just no way it was going to end well.

So as she made lasagna and watched her son and the guy who was just about the last man in the world they should be playing happy families with bouncing a ball around outside, she felt an ache in her heart. If there was going to be a price to pay for Marco's intrusion into their lives—and one thing she had learned in a hard school was that everything always came with a price tag attached—she would worry about it later. Right now, Tyler was outside in the late afternoon sunshine laughing and unafraid despite the terrifying things he had been through, and that was all she was going to focus on, because that was the only good news around and there was nothing she could do about anything else.

While the lasagna cooked, she made a salad. Then, when the food was ready, feeling so much like June Cleaver that she made a snarky face at her reflection in the glass as she reached it, she opened the sliding door to call them in to eat.

And was just in time to watch her little boy heave the ball through the warm, late summer air and make a basket. It was a regulation height goal, so that was quite a feat. Certainly it was something that he had never accomplished before.

"Two points! Yes!" Tyler gave a fist pump that made Sam grin.

"Good job! Way to go, Tyler," Marco exulted. As Sam, clapping, stepped out onto the patio, he exchanged low fives with Tyler.

"Yay, Tyler!" Sam called, then added, *"Supper,"* to which only Groves responded by starting to rise from his chair.

"Hey," Marco said to Sam as their eyes met. Tyler, meanwhile, ran across the grass to retrieve the ball. Marco was grinning, eyes sparkling, hair mussed, a little sweaty, looking ridiculously carefree under the circumstances. He had shaved last night sometime after she had last seen him, and in the bright sunlight she saw that his jaw was lean and strong. His nose was almost all the way back to normal, his black eye was fading away, and while the bruises on his face were still there the swelling was gone. Apparently he had been telling the truth when he'd told her that he healed fast, because she was able to see now the clean, hard planes and angles of his face. Good looking was an understatement, she thought unwillingly. He was a gorgeous guy, and somebody like Kendra, for example, would be drooling over him.

Fortunately, Sam thought, she was made of sterner stuff than that: she might notice, but she absolutely did not drool.

"Hey, Mom!" Tyler yelled. The heads-up was followed by the basketball hurtling her way.

Sam caught it just in time to keep from getting whomped in the head, pivoted, made a neat two-pointer, and grinned at her son as he whooped.

"Whoa, *swoosh.*" Marco grinned at her, too, clapping just as she had done for Tyler. "What other unsuspected talents are you hiding, I wonder?"

A little proud of herself, she flicked a look at him, then found herself caught by something that she saw in his eyes. Suddenly she felt hot all over, and more than a little flustered.

Things were getting out of hand when just looking at him made her think about sex.

"Supper's ready," she said in a repressive tone, and with Tyler charging ahead of her went back inside the kitchen.

Groves was happy to eat with them. The conversation centered on sports, particularly basketball and the upcoming NBA championship game. Animosity sometimes darkened Groves's expression when he looked at Marco, but on the surface at least the atmosphere was friendly enough. Tyler listened intently to everything that was said, and finally piped up with, "My mom used to play on a basketball team when she was in high school, didn't you, Mom?"

Sam was saved from having to reply by the arrival of Abramowitz to relieve Groves. In the act of putting his plate into the dishwasher with the rest of them, Groves looked so guilty when Abramowitz caught him at it that Sam almost smiled.

If Groves was quietly hostile toward Marco while being perfectly friendly to her and Tyler, Abramowitz was evenhandedly terse with them all. After supper, since Tyler had claimed the couch and the TV remote, he set himself up in the den with a book. After Sam had done everything she could think of to keep busy—which, aside from a little laundry, wasn't much—she admitted to herself that she had cabin fever. Being cooped up was getting to her. Outside, twilight was deepening into full dark, and clouds were blowing in from the west, bringing with them the promise of rain. Not used to being cooped up, Sam longed to get out of the house—and by out of the house, she wasn't talking about stepping into the backyard. But remembering how nerve-racking just going to Walmart had been, which then segued into a too-vivid memory of Mrs. Menifee's fate and the criminals who were still hunting them, she gave up on any hope of even so much as going for a walk down to the end of the street and back. Instead, she headed back into the great room with the idea of joining Tyler in front of the TV. By now, he would be deep into *Escape to Witch Mountain*, which she had rented for him a few months before and which they had both loved, and which by happy coincidence had been playing on the Disney Channel. She wouldn't mind watching it again. But when she saw that Marco was sitting on the couch beside Tyler, Sam hesitated and almost turned around again. More happy-family interaction with Marco was something she just did not need.

But Tyler spotted her.

"Have you ever seen Bruce Lee, Mom?" Tyler asked excitedly over his shoulder. Sam's mouth about dropped open as she realized that the images on the screen weren't what she had been expecting to see at all. Some kind of martial arts bout was going on, and her gaze shifted to Marco accusingly. "He's awesome. You want to watch it with us?"

Marco responded to her look by raising both hands in the air and shaking his head, which she interpreted as *don't blame me,* which he immediately spoiled by grinning at her.

"What happened to *Witch Mountain*?" Determined not to overreact, Sam sat down beside Tyler and frowned at the TV.

"There were too many commercials. I found this. Trey told me it's Bruce Lee." Tyler sounded distracted, and Sam realized that it was because he was focusing so keenly on the action in front of him. On Tyler's other side, "Trey" was shaking his head at her and mouthing *I had nothing to do with this* when Tyler added, "Trey says that some of his nephews take karate. Do you think I could take karate, Mom?"

"Trey" dropped his head in shame.

"We'll see." A mom's stock response, which she followed up with a dirty look shot over Tyler's head at Marco.

Before Sam could decide whether watching men hack and kick each other into cowering bundles of submission was unsuitable enough for a four-year-old to be worth the howl of protest Tyler would undoubtedly send up if she turned it off, the movie ended. As the credits rolled, Tyler said, "I loved that!" and then leaned over to whisper something in her ear. As Sam nodded, he leaped up and ran from the room.

"He needed to go potty," Sam explained in response to Marco's questioning look. Then she gave him a dark look. "Bruce Lee?"

"It wasn't my fault, I swear. He was already watching it when I got in here."

She eyed him suspiciously. "And did he already know that your nephews take karate lessons?"

He looked a little sheepish. "I might have told him that."

"Yeah." Sam's response was dry.

Marco looked at her. "Jesus, Sam, he's a *boy*. He's going to like stuff like that. We're hardwired that way, all of us. Playing games like *Halo* and watching Bruce Lee—that's normal boy stuff. Ask his dad."

That was a sore point. "I couldn't even if I wanted to, which I don't," she said.

"Oh, yeah?" Marco raised his eyebrows at her, inviting a reply.

Sam sighed. She didn't talk about her circumstances very often, because it was personal and it felt like whining and because she'd learned from a young age that the only thing to do when something bad happened to you was suck it up and go on. But she suddenly found herself *wanting* Marco to know the truth.

"Like I said, he's out of the picture. I've seen him like twice since Tyler was born. I'm fairly certain he couldn't pick Tyler out of a lineup, and the only reason Tyler would recognize him is because I've got a picture of him in Tyler's baby book that Tyler likes to look at." Actually, every time she found Tyler looking at that picture it broke her heart a little, but she had thought it was important for the little boy to know he did have a father so she had put it in there and kept it in there.

"So what happened between you?"

Sam shrugged. "I was stupid, what can I say? I started seeing him when I was a senior in high school. He was in my class, popular, good-looking, big party guy. Well, I was into having fun then, too. I thought I loved him. I thought he loved me.

Then I found out I was pregnant. It was about a month and a half after I graduated from high school. To make a long story short, turned out he did not want to know. He still doesn't. As far as I'm concerned, if I never saw him again in my life it would be too soon, but I hate it for Tyler."

The look she gave him must have had more emotion in it than she knew, because his brows contracted and he reached over and picked up her hand.

"The guy's a jerk. And an idiot."

His fingers twined with hers. They were warm and strong and gorgeously masculine, she thought as she glanced down at their joined hands. With self-preservation in mind, maybe she should have pulled away, but she didn't. All he was doing was holding her hand, after all, but the comfort it gave her was enormous. The worst thing about it was, she had never, until right this very second, realized how much Tyler's father's abandonment of her and their son had hurt.

"Yeah, he is," she said over the sudden lump in her throat. "He's missing out on Tyler."

"And you." His fingers tightened on hers, and for a moment there she felt a terrifying prickling at the backs of her eyes. She *never* cried—another thing she'd learned early on was that all crying got you was a stopped-up nose—but all at once she feared she might as he continued with, "You're something special, you know."

At what she saw for her there in his eyes a hard little knot that she hadn't even realized existed inside her melted away, like a snowball in the sun. It had been a long time since a man had looked at her like that, she realized. Not with lust, but with—tenderness? With maybe a little respect mixed in? Whatever, it was intoxicating. Her breath caught. She was conscious of a warm glow starting to build in the region of her heart.

"Sam—" Marco's voice was deeper, and she thought that he was starting to lean toward her. Then the sound of a chair squeaking from the den made him shoot a look in that direction and stop. Sam heard it, too, and pulled her hand from his. The idea that Abramowitz, or any of the marshals for that matter, might see her holding hands with Marco struck her as not smart. Just why, she couldn't have said, but . . .

"So you played basketball in high school, huh? What high school?" Marco's tone had changed. It was lighter, faintly rueful. He was firmly unmoving now, back on his end of the couch, just as she was on hers.

"St. Clair County Alternative School." Not altogether sorry to put the intensity behind them, Sam made a face at him. "Just to be clear, there were only six girls who wanted to play basketball, so we all made the team. It was a last-resort high school for kids who had problems with the system, so it wasn't very big."

He was looking at her with interest. "What kind of problems?"

"I missed a lot of school. I was rebellious." She gave a small shrug. "By the time I graduated, I had lived in six different foster homes, all right? Going to school wasn't my top priority. Hey, I was a kid. What can I say?"

"Where were your parents?"

"My dad was kind of like Tyler's: he was never around. And

my mom—she remarried when I was in fourth grade. My new stepfather wasn't interested in having a daughter. She took off with him, moved to Florida. I lived with my grandma and my great-aunt for a while, until my grandma died and my great-aunt had a stroke. Then there was nobody left who wanted me, so I went into foster care. I was in eighth grade."

"That sucks." His tone was matter of fact, but his eyes had darkened.

Sam nodded. "Yeah, it did. I guess I kind of went off the deep end for a while after that, nothing too bad, just being a little wild and wanting to have fun and blowing off school. When I met Justin—Tyler's dad—I thought everything was going to change." She smiled wryly. "Which it did: I got Tyler." The glance she shot him as soon as the words were out of her mouth was fierce. "For the record, he's the best thing that ever happened to me."

He smiled at her. "He's a great kid."

"Yeah, he is. He totally turned me around, too. Once I had him, and I knew it was just the two of us, him and me against the world, I grew up fast." Feeling uncharacteristically shy suddenly from having revealed so much, she shot him another look. When she spoke again, her voice was slightly gruff. "So there you have it: the story of my life. If you've got any, I'll take questions now."

"I do have one." His eyes gleamed at her as he followed her lead into less emotional territory. "Who's Carl?

Whatever Sam had expected—maybe a request for a definition of what "a little wild" entailed—it wasn't that.

"Carl?" She gave him a puzzled look. "Carl works at A+ Collateral Recovery. How did you hear about Carl?"

"When Tyler called you and I answered, he asked if I was him."

"Oh." The smallest of pauses. "Carl's been calling me lately, trying to get me to go out with him." At the inquiring look Marco gave her, Sam shook her head. "Not going to happen. I'm careful about the men I bring into my life now that I have Tyler. In fact, I don't *bring* men into my life now that I have Tyler." Which, proving the previous conversation had not been a completely useless whine-fest, brought her to the point she'd been wanting to make to him: "As a matter of fact, I've been meaning to ask you if you would kind of cool it with him. He likes you a lot, and . . ."

The ninety-second warning beep of the alarm in the kitchen interrupted. Both Sam and Marco stiffened and looked toward the doorway. A heartbeat later, clearly drawn by the same thing, Abramowitz came out of the den. For a moment all three of them waited, looking toward the kitchen. Then the sound of the code being entered eased the tension. Footsteps could be heard crossing the kitchen, and then Sanders appeared in the doorway. He was dressed in the usual dark suit and tie, with the usual grumpy expression on his face. As the marshal in charge of the security detail, it wasn't out of the ordinary for him to appear at times other than the shift on which he stood guard, but there was a kind of tension in his demeanor that told Sam something was up.

What alarmed her was that he was looking at her.

"I got a call just a few minutes ago," Sanders said without preamble, stopping just over the threshold and folding his arms over his chest.

Uh-oh, Sam thought.

"About what?" Marco leaned forward to fix Sanders with an intent gaze.

"Her," Sanders said. Sam had known it. She felt her stomach tighten. "She's out of here. The kid, too. Tomorrow, eight a.m. Transferred to the custody of another team. Deputy Marshal John Romeo will take charge."

Sam couldn't help it. She immediately glanced at Marco, expecting him to say something along the lines of *no way in hell.* But he didn't. Instead he just looked at Sanders kind of thoughtfully.

"Wait a minute." If she had to stand up for herself, she could. After all, she'd been doing it practically all her life. "Don't I get a say in this?"

"No." Sanders's reply was blunt.

"To hell with that," Sam said hotly, shooting to her feet and glaring at Sanders. "I'm not going to—"

"Sam, hold up." Marco's quiet interruption had her glancing around at him. Still seated on the couch, he met her gaze. "This is a good thing. You and Tyler need to go."

"What?" Realizing how much she didn't want to leave him rattled her. "Aren't you the one who kept saying we were safer with you?"

Sanders snorted derisively at that, but Sam paid no attention to him. Her attention was all on Marco. Her hands were clenching into fists at her sides, and that would be, she realized, because she was in full combative mode. And also because she was scared. And, so deep inside that she could barely even acknowledge the emotion was there, maybe even a little hurt. No, more than a little. A whole hell of a lot hurt.

"That doesn't apply anymore." Marco looked at her steadily. "Veith found the safe house in St. Louis. The longer we stay here, the more likely it is that they'll find this one, too. Having you and Tyler here just isn't smart anymore."

"There you have it," Sanders seconded.

"So why don't we move on? As in, all of us?" Sam demanded accusingly of Sanders, who shrugged.

"Got no orders to move. But I do have orders to hand you off. And that's what I'm going to do. Eight a.m. sharp, so be ready." As if to forestall any further argument, Sanders turned and walked away, heading back the way he had come.

"No *way*—" Sam would have gone after him, but Marco grabbed her hand. This time his grip felt very different: he wasn't letting go.

"Wait. Listen. Sam, hear me out. This is for the best," Marco said as her furious gaze skewered him. "You remember how you called where I am ground zero? You were right. It is. They're after *me*. You and Tyler are better off somewhere else."

"You didn't think so before!" The beep of the code being entered into the security system again announced that Sanders was already on his way out the door and out of her reach. Desperate to confront him while she could, she tugged at her hand. Marco held fast.

"The situation has changed." Marco's expression was grim.

From the corner of her eye, Sam saw Abramowitz giving them a once over. Clearly he hadn't missed the fact that Marco was holding her hand. As if he realized that she was looking at him looking at them, Abramowitz cleared his throat noisily. Then as she transferred her glare to him he said, "Uh, you need any help with that?"

Sam realized that he was referring to Marco's determined possession of her hand, and that he was offering to step in to protect her if she needed it. It was a decent thing to do, and she would have appreciated it more if she hadn't been so damned mad.

"No," she snapped. With a shrug, Abramowitz retreated back into the den.

After he was out of sight, Marco continued in a soft and urgent voice, "Look, I know this John Romeo, okay? He's a good guy. You and Tyler will be safe with him."

"No." Sam shook her head. The thought of being separated from Marco was making her feel weird. Kind of panicky and— totally resistant to letting it happen. Unreal to think that she now associated being with him with being safe. "I'm not going. We're not going."

"I don't think no's an option." Marco's grip on her hand was warm and strong. It was also, she had little doubt, unbreakable unless and until he wanted to let her go. "Look, Sam—"

He broke off as Tyler called from upstairs, "Mom? Can you come here? I need help."

Sam kept her eyes fixed on Marco even as she raised her voice to respond to Tyler. "I'll be right there."

Marco said, "Everything will be okay, I promise. I need you to trust me on this."

Sam's eyes searched his. At what she saw in them, she felt cold all over. "So you really want us to go?"

"Yes."

"Fine," Sam said, and yanked her hand free from that not-so-unbreakable-after-all grip as Tyler called, *"Mom?"* again.

Without so much as a backward look, conscious of Marco's eyes on her until she was out of sight, she headed upstairs. She was furiously angry, she realized, and refused to even try to analyze why.

For the next couple of hours, she was busy. She got Tyler to bed without telling him what was getting ready to happen in the morning. That would be because she knew that he would be upset at the idea of leaving "Trey" and she didn't want to deal with what that might entail, which would almost certainly include but not be limited to his being unable to go to sleep, while her own emotions were in such turmoil. After Tyler was finally asleep, she set out the clothes that they would wear tomorrow, then packed their newly acquired belongings in a trash bag. Not that anybody had said she would be allowed to take said belongings with them, but it didn't matter; she was determined that she would. Then, finding herself totally wired with sleep the last thing she felt like doing, she went along to the second bathroom and took a long, hot bath. When she emerged from the bathroom, all rosy and still faintly damp and wrapped in her white bathrobe with her hair twisted into a loose knot on the top of her head, she cast a quick glance down the hall toward Marco's bedroom. His light, which had been on when she entered the bathroom, was now off.

He had gone to bed. Without even trying to talk to her, to clarify what she'd thought had been building between them, or even to say a private good-bye. Maybe he was hoping to make his good-byes brief and unemotional, and thus was saving them for the rush and confusion of the morning. But, she discovered, she needed more than that.

Sam felt furiously angry all over again. As she stood there in the shadowy hall, glaring at Marco's dark bedroom door, the reason she was so mad at him hit her.

Once she and Tyler left the town house, they were probably never going to see him again.

Her heart broke at the thought. And the jackass didn't even seem to care.

Sam couldn't stand it. No way was she leaving it like this. There was too much unsaid—un-everythinged—between them.

After tonight, she would never get another chance.

Tightening the belt around her waist, shaking her head so the knot of her hair came loose and spilled around her shoulders, she turned, padded down the shadowy hall, and walked through Marco's open bedroom door.

CHAPTER TWENTY-TWO

Marco was indeed in bed. It took Sam's eyes a second to adjust to the gloom, but when they did she had no trouble picking out the long, large mound under the covers that was him. If she'd heard snoring, she probably would have killed him there and then and been done with it, but luckily for him she did not. Looking around, she located the switch on the wall, snapped on the light, then blinked at the sudden brightness as a single bedside lamp came on. By its light, she could see him lying on his back with one arm curved beneath his head. He was bare to at least the waist, where the striped blanket that was the top layer of bedclothes ended. Above that, he was all broad shoulders and sinewy muscles and tanned skin against white sheets. Even as she absorbed how absolutely sexy he looked lying there like that she saw that his eyes were open. He was awake and looking at her. That was when the thought hit her that maybe coming into his bedroom like this had been a mistake—okay, coming into his bedroom like this definitely had been a mistake—but she was too mad to care.

"Something wrong?" Sitting up suddenly so that the covers puddled around his hips—he was wearing boxers, and, God, the guy looked good bare-chested!—he reached for the crutches propped beside the bed.

"Oh, yeah." Sam frowned right back at him. No, scowled was a better word. Then, mindful of Tyler and not wanting to wake him up, and remembering that Abramowitz was downstairs and might even be able to overhear, she closed the door. And locked it, because what she had to say was absolutely private. By the time she strode to the side of his bed, Marco had apparently divined that whatever she wanted did not require him to be up and on crutches, because he'd quit reaching for them and was leaning back against the headboard with his brawny arms folded over his hunky chest, watching her. Planting her fists on her hips, she gave him a ferocious glare and said, "Tomorrow morning, before we leave, you're going to get up and say good-bye to Tyler. You've gone out of your way to make him like you and he's going to be upset at the idea that we're leaving you. You're going to lie to him, do you hear? You're going to lie and tell him that you'll be in touch just as soon as all this is over."

For a moment Marco just looked at her without saying anything. Divining what he was thinking was impossible. She could not read a thing in his face.

"You really think lying to him is a good idea?" he asked mildly.

"Under the circumstances, yes." By that time Sam was the opposite of mild. She was tense, angry, practically vibrating with hostility. "He has no idea that he's probably never going to see you again. If he knew that, it would break his heart." To her horror, her voice wobbled a little on the last word.

"Sam." He reached out, caught her hand. "I'm doing my best for you and Tyler here, believe me."

She jerked her hand away like the warmth of his skin burned her. "You know what? I don't care. I just don't want you to hurt Tyler any more than can be helped." She gave him another of those fierce looks. "So you're going to lie to him, and later on when he asks about you I'm going to keep on coming up with excuses about why you haven't been in touch until eventually he forgets all about you. Which he absolutely will do, although it's going to be a little rough on him until then."

"I wasn't going to let you guys go without saying good-bye, you know. And I will be in touch, just as soon as I can." He was still being mild, and that mildness killed her. Caused her actual, physical pain in the region of her heart. Because, she realized, it meant that he didn't care that he wouldn't see them anymore. Not nearly as much as Tyler would. And not anywhere in the same universe as much as she did.

"What are we talking about, letters from prison? Or, that's right, Groves said you'd made a sweetheart deal with the government that'll probably put you in witness protection for the rest of your life. So are you saying the plan is to give us a shout-out from your new secret life? Get real: you won't." Afraid she might be revealing too much about the pain that she was so unexpectedly experiencing, Sam broke off and turned away, throwing the rest at him over her shoulder. "All you have to do is lie to Tyler tomorrow. I'll take care of the rest."

"Sam, wait. Come back here. Damn it." Lunging after her as she stalked toward the door, he grabbed the trailing skirt of her robe and yanked. Caught by surprise, Sam stumbled backward and sat down hard on the edge of the bed. Immediately his arm snaked around her waist, capturing her, hauling her back against him, holding her in place with her back against his chest. She was all too conscious of how nearly naked he was, and the knowledge made her pulse quicken. He felt warm and solid, muscular and overwhelmingly masculine. The scent of him—the faintest whiff of soap and toothpaste and man—was so familiar that it scared her. Her hands found his forearm, curled around it as if she would sink her nails into the firm, hair-roughened flesh in an effort to make him let go, but she didn't. Pride kept her stiffly resistant in his hold, but she made no attempt to get away.

"What?" She turned her head to glare at him, and found that his face was just inches from hers. His dark eyes were so close that she could see herself reflected in them. His broad shoulders curved around her, solid as a wall and breathtakingly sexy. She could see the smooth texture of his skin, and the slight yellowing of his bruises, and the tiny lines around his eyes and each individual whisker in the new stubble that darkened his jaw.

Bruises and all, he was so handsome that just looking at him made her pulse quicken. Their eyes held, and a sizzling tension seemed to shimmer in the air. Chemistry, she identified it instantly, but then she realized that the sexual attraction that blazed between them didn't tell the whole tale. In the brief time she'd known him he had become incredibly important to her, someone whom she'd come to feel that she could confide in and seek advice from and depend on. A friend.

More than a friend.

You should have known better, she told herself savagely even as the ache in her heart at the idea that she was never going to see him again intensified times about a thousand. *How many times do you have to get the rug pulled out from under you before you realize that the only person you can depend on is yourself?*

He was watching her. His eyes were dark and intent. His mouth—what was she doing looking at his mouth?—was way too close to her own.

"Have a little faith in me," he said as he had once before. His hand came up to slide along her jaw, a little abrasive, very warm, keeping her face turned to his. Then, even as she glared at him some more, he leaned forward and kissed her. Softly, tenderly, devastatingly. Her heart pounded. Her pulse raced. Her body started to tighten and throb. For a moment, a hard-won moment, she let him ply her lips with his but didn't respond, knowing that the smart thing to do would be to pull her mouth free of his, to jump up and leave the room and banish him permanently from her mind. But she didn't. She couldn't. She was, she discovered, weak where he was concerned. Her blood heated and her bones liquefied and she gave in to temptation, gave in to the hunger he roused in her and that she could no longer resist. Slowly, slowly, she closed her eyes and slid a hand behind his head and kissed him back. The instant she surrendered he deepened the kiss. Electricity shot through her, making her shiver, making her burn. It was then that she knew that this was why she had come marching into his bedroom. This was why she had shaken her hair loose, why she had locked his door, why she was naked beneath her robe. This was what she'd been seeking, what she wanted, what she craved.

I've fallen in love with him. The thought was terrifying. As soon as she had it, as soon as she knew, she would have pulled back if she could have. But it was too late, impossible to do, because she was already lost in the hot sweet elixir of his kisses, of his hands sliding beneath the edges of her robe, of her own passion.

When his hand found her bare breast, covering it, caressing it, hard and warm and yet exquisitely gentle, the bolt of excitement that shot through her made her dizzy.

Oh, no. Oh, no. Panic beat in her breast like the fluttery wings of a frightened bird. *You need to stop this* now, *because you're going to get badly hurt.* She knew it with an icy clarity that managed to surface even through the flash fire of arousal that was hotter than anything she had ever imagined. But the sad truth was, she wanted his hands on her too much. She wanted him too much.

She was going to go with it, and to hell with the consequences.

"You okay?" He must have sensed her agitation, because he gave her a chance, she had to give him that. He broke off the kiss, stilled his caressing hand on her breast, asked the question in a husky voice that, funnily enough, just ratcheted up the level of her desire. Because he asked, she opened her eyes and looked at him. So there the opportunity was: she still could have stopped, still could have stood up and walked away. But his eyes as she met them were hot and dark with passion, and his face was hard with wanting her, and she could feel the uneven rhythm of his breathing feathering across her lips. Instead of saying *forget this,* or shoving his hand off her breast, or even turning her face from his, she went all light-headed and shivery with longing and nodded her head *yes* in reply. And that was when she understood: she was going to do this because if she didn't she would regret not doing it every single moment for the rest of her life.

Because this was the only chance that he and she were ever going to get.

"Make love to me." The words spilled out of their own accord. But she wouldn't have called them back even if she could have.

"Sam." His eyes blazed at her, yet she sensed a kind of hesitation in him. She could feel his chest expand as he inhaled. Like he was struggling with something, like something was holding him back. She knew, *knew,* that he wanted to make love to her, with an absolute certainty that left no room for doubt.

"Don't you want to?"

"No condom." His voice was thick and rueful at the same time.

She appreciated that he would think of that, that it would make him hold off. In the heat of the moment most males, as she knew all too well, didn't consider such things.

"It's okay. I'm covered." After Tyler, she had vowed to take no more chances. She had chosen a long-lasting method that didn't require any kind of daily or on-the-spot usage. Not that she'd expected to need it, and not that she really had, but there it was, just in case.

"Oh, yeah?" She couldn't tell if he sounded relieved or not.

"Yeah." This time she didn't wait for him to take the lead. She closed her eyes and wrapped her arms around his neck and fitted her lips to his and licked into his mouth, kissing him as if she'd been waiting to kiss him for all of her life. She thought he said something like, *ah, hell,* against her lips but she couldn't be sure because her blood was drumming in her ears and her heart was thundering.

Kissing him felt so good. So *right.*

She loved the taste of his mouth, the feel of his lips on hers, the bold invasion of his tongue, the hot wetness of the inside of his mouth. She loved how broad his shoulders were, and how heavy with muscle they felt, and the warm smoothness of his skin beneath her hands. She loved the way he tilted her head back against the hard bulge of his upper arm and took control of the kiss. She loved the way he handled her, like a man who knew his way around women.

She loved the way her body caught fire.

When he slid an arm beneath her knees and lifted her across him to lay her down on the bed, then leaned over her and parted her robe and took a moment to just look at her, she went up in flames. When he found her breast with his mouth, pulling the hard little nub that her nipple had become into the wet heat and taking his time with it before moving on to her other breast, she trembled and arched up against him and buried her fingers in his thick black hair.

When his fingers slid between her legs, she moaned.

"You are the most beautiful thing I've ever seen in my life." He was kissing her throat, her breasts, sliding his fingers against the most sensitive part of her, making her legs part, making her pant, making her move for him. Her blood sizzled, her heart pounded, her body softened and quaked. His fingers were inside her, slipping in and out, teasing and touching until he had her mindless and clinging to him and begging, yes, begging, for more.

She, who had never in her life begged for anything.

When her eyes flickered open, just for an instant, she saw that he was looking down at her with a blazing intensity that made her melt inside. His hair was ruffled and his jaw was set and hard and his eyes seemed to scorch her everywhere they touched. Knowing that he was watching her reaction to what he was doing to her embarrassed her. It also brought with it its own fiery thrill.

"Please," she whispered, eyes closing again, moving against his hand, so turned on that she could feel herself starting to spiral out of control. She was asking him to do her, to come inside her and get on with it and get the job done before she expired from need, and although she was still too shy with him to be quite so explicit she knew that he knew what she wanted, what she meant. "Marco, please."

"Trey." His voice was low and rough.

"Trey," she repeated obediently, and then her heart gave a

great, shuddering leap when, instead of giving her what she was pleading for, he kissed his way down her body until, finally, he replaced his fingers with his mouth.

Her eyes opened wide when she felt his lips on her, felt his tongue on her, felt him kissing her there. Senses reeling, she looked down at her own slender body, at the full, pink-tipped slopes of her breasts that were still damp from his kisses, at the sleekness of her stomach, at her pale, slim thighs that were raised now over his broad shoulders and the dark masculinity of his head pressed between them. It was the most erotic thing she had ever seen in her life, and it ignited a wildfire inside her that was like nothing she had ever experienced. The intimacy of what he was doing to her, the heat of it, the sheer, mind-bending pleasure of it, was shocking and incredible and so intense that she came just like that, digging her fingers into the mattress and crying out.

After that, she was wild and wanton, willing to do whatever he wanted, to let him do whatever he wanted. When he thrust inside her at last, she was on fire for him. He was huge and hot and hard, and just what she had always wanted. Woozy with helpless pleasure, she kissed him and wrapped her legs around his waist and moved with him as he took her with a carnality that had her writhing and gasping and crying out at the sheer wonder of it.

When she came again, it was earth-shattering.

When he came, with his arms locked around her and his face buried in the curve between her shoulder and neck, he shuddered and called out her name.

For a long moment afterward he didn't move. Neither did she. She simply lay in his arms, boneless, mindless, totally spent in the aftermath of so much well-satisfied lust.

About the time that it occurred to her that besides feeling warm and solid and deliciously masculine against her he was also as heavy as a cartload of bricks, he shifted slightly, sliding onto his side just enough to take most of his weight off her and, she thought, his injured leg. At that point she opened her eyes. And realized several things.

The lamp had been on the entire time. The bed was bathed in a soft yellow glow that left absolutely nothing—like his big hand still wrapped around her breast, and his long, hard-muscled thigh that was still purple with bruises and adorned with a ridiculously small Band-Aid curved on top of hers—to the imagination. The covers had gone the way of her robe and his boxers, disappearing somewhere over the side of the bed so that they were both naked with no defenses. Her head was pillowed on the hard bulge of his upper arm, giving her a good view of most of his body. He looked even better out of his clothes than he did in them, all sculpted muscles with just the right amount of black body hair stretched over a tall, athletic build. His skin was tan all over except for his bathing suit area, and she thought it was supersexy that his small, tight butt—she could just see the uppermost curve of it—was a couple of degrees paler than everywhere else. And, oh yeah, even at half-mast as he was at the moment, the man was ridiculously well endowed. And when he wasn't at half-mast—well, even exhausted as she was, she felt herself starting to tingle just remembering.

He had just rocked her world.

The bad news was, it wasn't only the sex.

Impossible as it seemed, she had fallen head over heels, crazily in love. With a guy whom, after tonight, she was probably never going to see again.

To her dismay, at the realization Sam felt tears start to leak from her eyes.

"Sam?"

Oh, my God. His eyes were open and he was looking at her. She shut her eyes quickly, willing the tears to go away.

"Sam, open your eyes. Look at me."

She didn't want to, afraid of what he might read in them. The last thing she wanted was for him to guess how she felt. She didn't think she would be able to bear it if he did.

"Sam?"

Okay, he wasn't going away. Because the tears had stopped, because she was strong, because she could deal, she opened her eyes and met his gaze defiantly.

She was still on her back and he was lying on his side facing her. His arm and leg were still draped possessively over her. He'd snagged a pillow from somewhere and tucked it beneath his head. With her face turned toward his, she found herself looking directly into his eyes. At first they were heavy-lidded and slumberous, looking as sated with passion as she felt, but as they moved over her face she saw heat gathering at their backs and then they started to gleam. When they met hers a second time they were hot for her all over again.

"Great sex," she said, proud of how cool and casual and gee-that-was-fun-but-really-no-big-deal she sounded.

"What's the matter, baby doll?" He brushed a wayward strand of hair away from her face, smoothed the unruly mass that spilled over his arm.

It was the tenderness that did it. Nobody was ever tender with her. She was unprepared.

"Don't call me 'baby doll,'" she growled, and then shocked herself by bursting into tears.

"Sam." He sounded as surprised as she felt. He gathered her close, rocked her against him, smoothed her hair, patted her as she wrapped her arms around his neck and wept. "Don't cry, sweetheart. Talk to me."

But she had nothing to say. At least, nothing that she wanted to say. Bursting out with *I love you* and *please say this isn't the end* would be humiliating. Worse, it wouldn't change a thing. So she shook her head, and did her best to suck it up, and then when he got done kissing her damp cheeks and moved on to kissing her mouth she kissed him back.

This time, when he made love to her, it was slower, more deliberate, but no less thrilling.

When it was over, she fell asleep in his arms almost at once.

Only to wake up to the sound of Tyler calling for her. "Mom?"

Struggling out of the warm male embrace that had her trapped, she kicked aside the blanket that had found its way over them at some point and scrambled off the bed. The room was dark. Trey—God, calling him that felt funny—had obviously turned off the lamp after she had fallen asleep.

"Sam?" He stirred as she frantically searched the floor around the bed for her robe. "What's up?"

She couldn't help it. She had to turn on the lamp. Her robe was nowhere to be found. The sudden brightness made her blink. He propped himself up on an elbow, and despite everything that they had done together knowing that he was looking at her while she was just standing there naked made her self-conscious.

"Tyler," she said, as if that explained everything, which for her it did. She was slightly surprised Tyler hadn't called for her again. Had she imagined it? Because unless he had a nightmare, he didn't usually call for her in the night. But it didn't matter: she had needed to get up and get out of *Marco's* bed anyway. Their sexy little interlude was over. Time for reality to bite.

"Want me to check on him?" He was blinking at her a little owlishly, obviously still half asleep. With his black hair mussed and his broad shoulders and wide chest bare above the striped blanket, he looked good enough to eat. A thunderclap of knowledge—*this is probably the last time I'll ever see him like this*—caused a shaft of pain to pierce her heart.

No matter what, she wasn't going to cry. Not over him, not over any man, not ever again.

"No thanks, I'll handle it," she told him, giving up on the robe to yank on the first items she found—sweatpants and a T-shirt that had been laid out on the chair in the corner. His clothes for tomorrow? Probably. He could find more.

Dressed, tightening the drawstring on the pants so they wouldn't just drop to her ankles as they'd shown an alarming tendency to do, she took the few steps necessary to reach the lamp, and in the process found her robe, which had ended up almost under the bed. Too late, she thought, making a face at it as she clicked off the lamp. The last thing she wanted was a bright swath of light bursting out into the hall to pinpoint her location when she emerged from Marco's room.

"Hey." He caught her hand. A solid shape in the darkness, he was sitting up on the edge of the bed now. He drew her toward him, slid a hand in her hair, pulled her face down to his, and kissed her, a quick hard kiss that did screwy things to her insides.

"I have to go." Freeing her hand, she turned her back on him and headed for the door.

"Sam," he said as she opened it, and she shook her head before she realized that he probably couldn't see the gesture. So she said, "Shh," over her shoulder at him and "Good night," then walked out of his room with her head held high and her heart breaking, knowing that her first real, all-grown-up, God-I'm-crazy-about-him love affair had just officially ended.

She should have known better. She should have stayed more on guard. But, oh, God, she had forgotten just how very much falling in love with the wrong man could hurt.

The pain lasted until she walked into Tyler's room and saw that he wasn't there. Hurriedly she checked the second bathroom, and her bedroom and bathroom, calling him softly, turning the lights on in each room to make sure, then off again as she left so as not to draw Abramowitz to the second floor with a blaze of lights and commotion. Tyler wasn't in any of them. Had he gone downstairs?

Padding quickly down the once-again dark hall, Sam had almost made it to the top of the stairs when she saw her son. He was standing on the second step from the top, almost invisible in the gloom as he pressed himself flat against the wall on the far side of the staircase.

Frowning, she was just about to say *Tyler* when his demeanor stopped her. From that alone, her heart was already slamming in her chest when she reached the top and looked down the stairs. At what she saw at the bottom, she stopped breathing: Abramowitz lay sprawled on his stomach at the entrance to the great room. By the faint glow that seemed to be emanating from the kitchen, where the light was apparently still on, she was able to see that there was a great gaping wound in his neck and that the dark stain soaking into the carpet around him was blood.

CHAPTER TWENTY-THREE

Inside her head, Sam screamed like a steam whistle, but she didn't make so much as a sound out loud. Instead, as her son's wide eyes swung around to her, she pressed her finger to her lips in the age-old gesture of *hush*, reached out, and caught his hand.

His fingers were as cold as ice. They locked onto hers as if he were never going to let her go. Heart jackhammering, being as quiet as it was possible to be, she drew him back up the stairs toward her. As soon as he was off the stairs and in the hallway she whispered *"Shh"* in his ear and pulled him with her in a headlong run down the hall.

Thank God for the carpet! It muffled their footsteps as they fled as one toward Marco's room and burst through the doorway that she had left open just a few minutes before. His light was still off, but Sam could see him: he was on his feet by the closet. He'd gotten dressed while she'd been gone, in what, by the dark outline of his shape that was really all of him that she could make out through the shadows, looked like sweats and a T-shirt similar to what she was wearing. Clearly startled by their sudden eruption into the room, Marco swung around to face them.

"*Shh,*" Sam warned him in a barely audible but urgent whisper before he could say anything. She was so scared that she could feel goose bumps racing over her skin.

"They're here! The bad men," Tyler blurted, whispering, too, as he made a beeline for Marco.

"They killed Abramowitz! He's down there on the floor!" Sam only realized that she had rushed for Marco right along with Tyler when she found herself wrapping her arms around his chest while Tyler grabbed him somewhere around his hips. Marco was only using one crutch for support. Despite that he was apparently pretty steady on his feet because he didn't so much as stagger as they latched onto him. Instead his arm came around Sam to pull her close even as he peered at them through the darkness.

"Abramowitz is dead? How?" Marco's whisper was sharp. She thanked God that he was astute enough not to waste time on the whole *what?* and *are you sure?* thing but instead cut right to the chase.

"Just dead, okay?" She didn't want to get too graphic with Tyler listening. "He's lying at the bottom of the stairs. I think whoever killed him is in the house right now!" Striving for calm, Sam failed miserably. She was practically jumping out of her skin. At any second, she expected gunmen to come storming up to the second floor. At the thought, panic surged through her veins in an icy tide.

"Trey, hurry! We've got to get out of here!" Tyler's whisper sounded as terrified as Sam felt. He looked up at Sam with eyes the size of saucers. Still hanging onto Marco, he was jiggling from foot to foot in agitation. Sam wrapped an arm around him, which pretty much completed the circle for a big group hug.

"Don't worry, bud. I got this." From its tone, Marco's whisper was meant to be reassuring. Tyler obviously trusted him implicitly, because the reassurance seemed to calm him. Despite the fact that Sam had a way clearer idea about whom and what they were facing than her son, it calmed her a little, too. Even with everything she knew about Marco, her heart persisted in identifying him as someone she and Tyler could rely on in a tight spot. In a deadly spot. Like this.

"Tyler's right. We've got to go *now*." Fear, thick and cold and oily, rose up in her throat like bile. Swallowing hard, Sam remembered her little research project, the one where she'd checked out all possible exits from all possible areas of the house, and realized that she knew the perfect spot for their escape. "We can go out Tyler's bedroom window. Come *on*."

She tugged at Marco's arm.

"Hang on a minute." Instead of moving as both she and Tyler were now urging him to do, Marco let go of her and balanced on one leg while he did something with his crutch. Sam's mouth dropped open as he flipped it into the air, twisted it, and the thing came apart in his hands. Seconds later, he extracted a gun—a gun!—from inside it.

"Wow! I didn't know that was in there." The gun's appearance seemed to fascinate Tyler. He watched with awe as Marco snapped the slide back on the small black pistol and then thrust the gun into the waistband of his sweats. Marco then dumped something out of the crutch's shaft into his hand and thrust whatever it was into his pocket.

Sam goggled.

"You've had that this whole *time*?" She recovered the power of speech to hiss at him even as Marco grabbed his other, still-in-one-piece crutch and the three of them headed en masse for the door.

"*Shh.* You two stay back." Gun in hand now, Marco stepped into the hallway like a capable professional who knew his way around a dangerous situation. Sam remembered with a little spurt of thankfulness that not so long ago he had been a federal agent. A moment later, blocking them out from any threat that might emerge from the staircase with his body, he made a gesture for them to move out behind him and head for Tyler's bedroom. Clutching Tyler's hand, moving as quietly as possible, Sam ran down the hall with her son at her side. The whole second floor was dark except for the faint glow coming up the staircase. Now that she knew what lay down at the bottom of that staircase, just looking in that direction gave Sam the willies.

What was even scarier was the thought that they couldn't have much time. Whoever had killed Abramowitz had to be looking for Marco, and any minute now they would come up the stairs and . . .

She couldn't finish the thought.

As she and Tyler darted into Tyler's bedroom, Sam saw that

Marco was headed for the stairs. Her stomach turned upside down. She wanted to call after him, to beg him to come with them, but anything she could say that he might be able to hear would be too loud. And her first priority had to be getting Tyler to safety.

"Where's Trey?" Tyler whispered, looking around as Sam rushed toward the window. Instead of staying beside her, he pulled free. Out of the corner of her eye, as she raised the shade as quietly as possible and then reached for the cool brass window latch, she watched as he grabbed Ted from his bed and, in a gesture that brought a lump to her throat because she knew that it meant he was aware of how expensive shoes were to replace, stuck his feet into the slip-on sneakers she'd just bought him.

"*Come on, Tyler.*" She unlocked the window easily. The town house was new: nothing had as yet been painted shut. The window was triple-glazed and designed to crank out. Sam cranked with all her might, wincing at the very slight creaking sounds that resulted as it slowly opened. The night air was cooler than she had expected, midsixties maybe, and heavy with the promise of rain. The moon and stars were hidden beneath a dense cloud cover. As a result, it was very dark. But down below, in the yard, the kitchen light shone out through the sliding glass doors so she could see as far away as the tree.

At the thought that someone might be waiting for them down there, Sam shivered. Her heart pounded like a piston in her chest.

"Here, Mom." Tyler thrust her shoes and the bear mace at her as he rejoined her, and she took both with a quick spurt of surprise that he'd thought to gather them up and appreciation for the levelheadedness it indicated. She'd left her shoes under his bed when she'd read to him earlier, and the bear mace had found a permanent home in his nightstand because she had figured that if anyone broke into the house, the place where she was most likely to make a stand was at Tyler's bedside. Dropping the bear mace into her pocket, grabbing Ted from Tyler—"I'll hold him!"—and tucking him under her arm, she helped Tyler out onto the cedar shake overhang that ran along the back of the house and shaded the sliding glass door.

"Be careful," she warned, because the overhang, while not steep, had a definite slope to it. At the same time, she thrust her feet into her shoes, stuck Ted into her other pocket, and looked back over her shoulder one last time in hopes that she would see Marco coming toward her. She did not. The house was still and quiet. She couldn't even hear Marco, much less anything else. But she knew that the quiet was an illusion, knew the most terrible danger could engulf them at any second, and the knowledge made her stomach knot and her pulse race.

"Come on, Mom."

Sam was halfway out the window when Marco appeared in the doorway. Until she actually saw his tall dark shape swinging toward her, she hadn't realized how terrified she had been that something might have prevented him from rejoining them. Some of the anxiety that had been constricting her throat eased.

Oh, God, I'm crazy about him. There was absolutely no future in it, and she didn't have time to dwell on the implications of it, but there it was: a fact.

"I can't figure out why nobody's coming up here after us."
Reaching the window, thrusting his crutch and then his head
and shoulders through the opening, Marco said it as if he were
talking more to himself than to her.

"You wouldn't happen to have another gun in there, would
you?" Sam whispered, gesturing at the crutch.

"Fresh out," Marco whispered back.

Seeing her clinging to the shingles just outside the window
looking back at him, he added, "Go. Don't wait for me. Hurry."

If Marco was telling her to hurry, hurry was what she was
going to do. Icy little curls of fear spiraled through Sam's stomach as she scrambled carefully along the overhang. One thing
she didn't need to worry about was Tyler's climbing ability, she
saw with relief. He was clinging to the layered gray shingles like
a monkey, moving in the direction she had indicated, toward
the edge of the overhang nearest to the gate in the fence that
surrounded the backyard, through which they would ultimately
escape the property. Despite having both hands and feet planted
flat against the shingles, she wasn't quite as good at negotiating
the shingles as Tyler seemed to be. The surface was uneven and
slippery with moss in places, with no convenient handholds.
Her boots were having trouble finding purchase, too. Twice
she slid almost all the way down to the gutter, but she kept going. Between his bad leg and the need to hang onto his crutch,
Marco seemed to be having some difficulty as well. Sam kept
casting anxious glances back at him as he moved awkwardly in
her wake, but there was nothing she could do to help him. All
she could do was keep going.

Tyler reached the edge of the roof, crouched, peered over. Sam felt her heart stutter as she watched his small body teeter in midnight-black silhouette against the charcoal black of the sky. Out in the open air as they were, with no way of telling if anyone was below them in the yard, or anywhere else within earshot, Sam was afraid to call out to him to wait for her, to warn him not to try to jump. But—smart boy!—he stayed where he was anyway, looking back at her.

Reaching him, Sam clung precariously to the shingles and looked down, too. The drop wasn't that far—maybe twelve feet. Far enough to hurt them? Maybe. Maybe not, if they were careful. What scared her more was wondering what might be waiting for them below. Although they had tried their best to cross the roof as silently as possible, inevitably there had been slithering footsteps and the slight dragging sound made by Marco's crutch as he hauled it along with him. Had they been heard? Was Abramowitz's killer tracking their progress across the roof even now? It was a chance Sam knew they were going to have to take. As far as she could tell, this corner of the yard was deserted. It was also thick with shadows; unless someone knew exactly where they were, they should be able to drop down unseen. The gate was nearby. Once they were off the roof, it would only take a couple of minutes to get through it. Then what? If Abramowitz was dead, what about the others? Realizing that she had absolutely no idea what was waiting for them sent a shiver racing down her spine.

Marco had caught up to them. Tyler scooted close to him as Sam looked around at him wide-eyed.

"Should we just jump?" Tyler's whisper, directed at Marco, was full of fear.

"Hang tight a minute." Marco looked at Sam. "I'm going to lower you down." His instructions were low and rapid. "Then I'll hand Tyler down to you. Then the two of you run like hell. Don't wait for me."

"You're coming with us, right?"

He nodded. "Count on it."

"Are we going to the other town house? Or—"

Shaking his head, he broke in before she could finish. "I'd like to hook up with Sanders if we could. We may need the firepower. But we're going to get away from here and see what's what before we decide." Passing Tyler the crutch to hold, Marco stretched out on his stomach on the shingles and looked over the edge, then a moment later beckoned to Sam to come closer. "When you get through the gate, run around the outside of the fence toward the street behind us. In case somebody's watching from out front." The prospect made Sam's blood run cold. She nodded wordlessly, and he held out his hands to her. Scooting into position, she put her hands into his. "Okay, go."

Sam slid over the edge. Briefly she dangled in space, suspended from Marco's strong hands. When he let go, she dropped the few remaining feet to the ground, landing softly on the balls of her feet. Nobody attacked her. Nothing bad happened. Glancing fearfully all around, she saw nothing beyond the rectangle of fuzzy light thrown by the sliding glass window, and the tree and the basketball goal and the chairs and the grill, along with the ghoulish shadows they cast. Everything looked

absolutely as it should, everything was absolutely still. And
something about *that* made the hair stand up on the back of her
neck.

The killer could be anywhere.

"Mom."

Looking up, she caught Tyler as Marco lowered him down
to her. He weighed practically nothing at all, and she gave him
a quick hug as she set him on the ground. Then she grabbed his
hand and together they ran for the gate, staying low, hugging
the shadows near the fence as they went. A slight thump made
her look back: the crutch lay on the ground. Marco had dropped
it. Out of the corner of her eye, as she fumbled with the latch,
she watched Marco swing over the side. Landing lightly on his
good leg, he hopped once or twice before he got his balance.
Then he grabbed his crutch and came after them.

Finally the latch opened. She and Tyler made it through the
gate and around the corner and were running through the even
more absolute darkness of the strip of empty land on the other
side of the fence when she glanced back to make sure Marco was
following.

He was. Her gaze had just found him, coming around the
corner of the fence, moving fast for a man using a crutch, when
the town house exploded behind them with a sound like a sonic
boom.

CHAPTER TWENTY-FOUR

The force of the blast slammed Sam face first into the ground. Debris flew past her, pelting the grass around her like some hellish rain. Behind her, the night was suddenly as bright as day as flames engulfed the town house with a roar. The acrid scent of the fire reached her nostrils on a whoosh of blistering air. Stunned, she lay there for a moment, ears ringing, cheek pressed into the thick grass, and then she thought *Tyler*, and lifted her head.

He was a few feet in front of her, lying flat in the grass, facedown just like she was. Even as Sam's heart skipped a beat he rolled into a sitting position and looked back at her, and then past her, at the blazing town house. Blinking dazedly, he watched the conflagration shooting through the roof. The fire painted his small face, and indeed everything around them, a flickering red. Sam looked back, too, and saw Marco sprawled on the ground behind them. He was unmoving; if he were hurt, she couldn't tell. Beyond him, she watched flames reaching like bright orange fingers toward the sky. The roar of the fire had a fierce crackling quality to it now, and she could feel its intense heat.

If the explosion had occurred only a few minutes earlier, they would have been dead now. The certainty made her insides clench.

"Tyler, are you hurt?" Her voice was high-pitched, wobbly.

"No—" He broke off, his head turning sharply to the left. *"Mom, look out."* Fear infused his voice.

In the process of pushing herself into a sitting position, Sam jerked a glance in the direction in which he was looking just in time to see someone racing at her from the shadows. Her heart leaped into her throat. Every instinct she possessed screamed *danger.*

"Run, Tyler!" she shrieked, and with her heart in her throat watched him scramble to his feet and bolt even as she shot to her feet and started to run herself. The bear mace in her pocket: remembering it, she grabbed for it, fumbled to pull it out. But the man—it was a man, stocky and strong—caught her too soon, grabbing a handful of her shirt even as she tried to get her finger on the nozzle, tried to whirl and spray him. He knocked it from her hand before she could get it into position, then yanked her back against him. Going into instant, instinctive self-defense mode, Sam slammed an elbow back into his rib cage—*"Ummph!"* he said—and directed a potentially knee-cap-shattering kick backward. Before it could land her assailant dodged, then wrapped an arm around her throat in a chokehold that abruptly cut off the scream that had been tearing out of her lungs. Clawing at the arm around her neck, still kicking and fighting despite the pressure on her windpipe that felt like it would crush it and that had her choking and coughing and gasping for air, she watched with burgeoning terror as a white paneled van with some kind of writing on the side barreled over the grass toward her.

It screeched to a stop just feet away at the same time as she felt the cold barrel of a gun jam hard against her temple.

Her captor yelled, "Stay back!" Then, to her, he growled, "Make another move, and I'll blow your fucking head off."

She was no fool: the gun at her head meant instant compliance. She immediately stopped fighting and stood perfectly still in his hold. She could barely breathe, and she couldn't talk; the arm around her neck was too tight.

"I said, *stay back!*"

The warning was directed at Marco. Sam's terrified gaze slewed around to find him on his feet aiming his pistol at the man holding her. He was maybe fifteen feet away now, two-handing his gun, only slightly favoring his bad leg as the crutch lay forgotten at his feet. He'd clearly been rushing her assailant, and had just as clearly stopped when the gun had made contact with her head. Now, despite the weapon in his hand, he was as helpless to help her as she was to help herself. As she realized that, her blood turned to ice. Her heart thundered. Her pulse raced.

"Let her go!" Marco never faltered. His eyes stayed fixed on the man holding her. But Sam knew, and she very much feared her captor knew, that he would never fire as long as that gun was at her head.

Sam's attention was jerked away by the sound of the van doors opening. *White's Irrigation*—that's what the lettering on the side said, in big dark letters. Camouflage for the van's real purpose, Sam thought with a sickening certainty as a man jumped out of the passenger seat and another came around the front of the van. A loud rattle—the sliding door in the van's side being opened—made her glance that way again. The passenger seat guy had done the honors; the van's black interior yawned like a hungry mouth.

"Drop your weapon, Marco. You're outgunned." That voice—it belonged to the guy who'd come around the front of the van. Sam recognized it instantly. A thrill of horror ran down her spine. The man in her house—the one who had stepped into view in her kitchen as poor Mrs. Menifee's life had drained away—the one who had called her by name—it was him. She would never forget his voice for as long as she lived. Average height, average weight, completely ordinary looking, and to her, now, totally unmistakable. Cold sweat washed over her in a wave. He had a gun in his hand. It was aimed at Marco. The passenger seat guy had a gun pointed at Marco, too. Behind them, the van doors were open and the engine was running, although the van itself appeared to be empty. There was a reason, and the only reason Sam could come up with—she was about to be forced into the van—was horrifying. Terror chilled her blood. Her stomach churned. The orange glow of the raging fire gave everything a hellish aspect, elongating shadows, distorting faces. The roar of it blocked out any sounds from farther away. Hot flakes of ash floated earthward like a flurry of black snow.

"You want to take me on, Veith? Even if I only got one shot off, I'd make sure it drilled right through your skull. You want to live, let the girl go." Marco's voice was hard. His weapon was aimed at Veith now.

"You fire a shot, and she's dead. And you know it." Veith gave a jerk of his head, which, from the tightening of the arm around her throat, Sam deduced was a signal to the man holding her. Clinging to his arm, she fought to suck in air. In the distance, the barely audible wail of a siren gave her a flicker of hope. They were in an empty lot at the very end of the street, blocked off from seeing much of anything except the raging fire by the fence and the van, which also kept them from being seen. But people had to be spilling out of the neighboring houses. With the explosion and fire, help in the form of police and firefighters had to be on the way. And Sanders and Groves and O'Brien—where were they? God, were they even alive? Casting desperate glances in every direction, Sam searched for help: nothing. She searched for Tyler. He was nowhere to be seen.

Thank God he got away.

Veith said, "Here's how this is going to go down, Marco. Either you drop your weapon and come with us like a good boy, or we'll leave you here and just take the girl. And the next time anybody sees her, she'll be chopped up into so many pieces she'll look like fish bait."

"Back up, bitch." The low voice in her ear was accompanied by the grinding pressure of the gun barrel against her temple.

Sam's heart slammed against her rib cage as the man holding her started to pull her backward. She tried to resist, but with his arm crushing her windpipe and a gun to her head there wasn't a whole lot she could do other than be clumsy and drag her feet, which earned her a quick, vicious tightening of the arm around her neck. She choked, gasping for air. Her eyes fastened despairingly on Marco. His expression was impossible to read, but his stance hadn't changed, and his weapon remained fixed on Veith.

"Let her go and I'll come with you," Marco said. Dread twisted Sam's insides into knots as she recognized the desperation that underlay the offer. It was the sound of fear, of defeat, of knowing that they had him and he couldn't win. Hearing it beneath the studied calm of Marco's voice rammed the almost unthinkable truth home for her: on this terrible night, both of them were probably going to die.

"No." Dragging her heels, Sam managed to gasp the word out even as she was forced right up to the side of the van, right up to the open sliding door.

It was an instinctive protest, made because she loved him. She couldn't bear the idea that he would sacrifice himself for her. For Tyler's sake, if it came right down to it maybe she would have let him, but she knew, and she was sure Marco knew, too, that the bargain he was trying to make just wasn't going to happen. They weren't going to let her go no matter what he did, so the best thing he could do was stay out of their reach and save himself.

"Goddamn it, Veith, let her go!" Marco's gun tracked Veith. "You want me, not her."

"I want you both," Veith said, confirming what Sam already knew. "But I'll just take her if I have to."

"Get in," said the voice in her ear, and when she wouldn't, when she refused to climb into the van, the gun jabbed harder into her temple and the arm around her neck tightened so viciously that she choked and gagged and went instantly light-headed. Then, without ever removing the gun from her head, he stepped up into the van and she had perforce to step up behind him or be strangled to death. Out of the corner of her eye she saw that the van was configured with two front seats, a small, empty cargo area in the middle where she and her captor were positioned, and four bucket seats in the rear. The floor was carpeted, and there were three doors, all of them open.

Veith made a gesture. Then he and the other man started backing away from Marco, keeping their weapons trained on him but moving toward the van.

"You coming, Marco?" Veith asked.

In a semicrouched position just inside the big open doorway, her captor's arm still around her throat and the gun still at her head, Sam saw Marco's focus slip from Veith, whom he'd been tracking like a predator, to her. For a split second their eyes met. Then she watched in horror as Marco abruptly raised both hands in the air in the age-old gesture of surrender.

"I'm coming," he said. "Just let me get my crutch." Still keeping the gun up where they could see it, he bent down to get his crutch, then wedged it into place beneath his arm and started moving toward the van.

"Get his gun." Veith ordered the other man as they converged on Marco. Sam was shoved into the back, forced into a seat. Seconds later, Marco threw his crutch into the van, stepped in himself, then had his hands secured behind his back. Heart in her throat, Sam realized that she was witnessing the man she loved putting his life on the line for her.

He could have saved himself, could have left her. But here he was.

Their eyes connected. His were hard and dark and absolutely unreadable. Hers, she felt, probably had her heart in them.

Then Veith, who had entered behind him, clouted him over the head with his gun. The thud was so loud Sam felt it like a physical blow. Marco dropped like a stone.

Sam cried out, started to rise. She was roughly forced back into her seat.

"Good to see you again, Samantha Jones." Veith smiled at her as the thug who'd been holding the gun on her secured her hands behind her with a zip tie, then locked her in place with a seat belt. It was an absolutely evil, terrifying smile. Her pulse rate soared. Her mouth went dry. "Pity we couldn't bring the little boy along, isn't it?"

She hated him then, hated him with such magnitude that for a moment the force of it almost wiped out her fear. An angry reply surged to her lips. But then she looked into his eyes, and realized that a reply was what he was hoping to provoke her into. He was going to hurt her; that was a foregone conclusion. But hurting her while she was defying him? That would just add to his fun.

So she clamped her lips together and said nothing.

The door rattled shut as the third man closed it from the

outside. Seconds later he was behind the wheel and the van took off.

As it bounced across the grass and then sped away down the street, Sam caught a glimpse through the windows of the milling crowd that was starting to accumulate in front of the blazing town house. She wanted to bang on the van windows; she wanted to scream for help. The first one she couldn't do; the second one she knew better than to attempt. But she looked out at the huge, shooting flames stretching toward the sky, and willed someone to notice the fleeing van, then scanned the crowd hopefully to see if anyone did. The fire made the area around the front yard almost as bright as day. Among the crowd—*yes, that was Groves.* His blond buzz cut was unmistakable. With Groves was Sanders, who was crouching while he talked to— Tyler. Oh, what a relief! That brief sighting of her son's small, slender frame and black hair imprinted itself on her heart. Why? Because it just that moment hit her that she might never see him again. Even as her heart shattered into a million pieces at the thought, Sam felt a surge of thankfulness that he was *out there* rather than *in here.*

He's safe. Tyler's safe.

But the hard truth was that she and Marco were not. As the van, carefully observing the speed limit now, drove past onrushing fire trucks and police cars, Sam looked down at Marco, still sprawled unconscious on the floor, and at the thug in the seat across from her, and at Veith, sitting with a smug smile on his face and his gun pointed at Marco's head, and tried not to think about what these criminals had done to Mrs. Menifee.

But she couldn't help it. The image of the woman's severed fingertip, and the blood running across her kitchen floor, became lodged in her head. By the time the van stopped some fifteen minutes later, she was sick with terror.

She didn't pray much, because she had figured out a long time ago that if God really was up there, as her grandma had sworn he was, and if he really was in the answering-prayers business, which her grandma had sworn was true, the only answer she was going to get from him was no.

But now she prayed so hard that if God didn't hear her he had to be deaf.

Please, God. Please. I just want to see Tyler again.

CHAPTER TWENTY-FIVE

Fear was not something Danny experienced often. Handling dangerous situations was what he did for a living. He had been in so many life-or-death spots that they were pretty much par for the course for him, just another day at the office, so to speak.

But he was afraid now. And the reason he was afraid had nothing to do with the distinct chance that he wouldn't live through the next hour. What it had to do with was the silky-skinned, smart-mouthed, tender-hearted, gorgeous girl whom he'd just fucked into next week.

If Veith had been willing to blow up the town house to kill them, with all the attention that was sure to attract, he wanted them dead *now*. No more torture time, no more questions about money. Just dead. As in, a bullet to the head as soon as they were in a suitable place.

Danny would have told Veith the truth about his identity, and to hell with the assignment, if he had thought it would do any good. But the terrible fact of the matter was, as undercover

FBI Special Agent Daniel Panterro, he had no value to Veith or the Zetas at all. With no reason to keep him alive, Veith would kill him instantly. And Sam, too.

Telling the truth would be tantamount to signing his own, and Sam's, death warrant.

The thought made his gut clench. Cold sweat beaded his brow. His mind kept wrestling this thing around and around, which wasn't good. He kept getting the feeling that he was missing something, but he couldn't for the life of him figure out what, and wasting time worrying about it wasn't what he needed to be doing. What was important at the moment was to stay coldly focused, but he was having trouble getting there.

Because of Sam.

If he hadn't stepped up, Veith would have taken Sam, and he would have killed her. Danny had no doubt about that whatsoever. The bastard would have done exactly what he had threatened, and enjoyed himself doing it. He would have tortured her, done God knows what to her, and in the end he would have cut her up just like he had said he was going to, and left the remains somewhere where they would be found. That was how Veith operated.

Just thinking about Sam with Veith made Danny want to kill the bastard. It was his newest, most pressing ambition. He only hoped that he would be afforded the chance. If not, well, he was going to save Sam. Or die trying.

At this point he was perfectly willing to give his own life if that was what it took to protect Sam, and Tyler, too. They meant something to him, something personal. Something special. In giving up his weapon and turning himself over to Veith, Danny had done what he had to do, following the devil into hell in hopes of maybe being able to bring Sam out again.

Not that success was looking likely.

When the van stopped, every muscle in Danny's body tensed. Adrenaline flooded his system. His instincts went on red alert. This might very well be it.

The van door opened. Hands reached in to haul him out.

In the rear seats, the thug guarding Sam stood up, unsnapped her seat belt, wrapped his arm around her throat, and stuck a gun to her head.

Even in the dark, he could tell her eyes were on him. They looked wide and scared.

It killed him that there was nothing he could do or say to reassure her. But any attention he paid her just gave Veith more reason to think that he could use Sam to get to him.

"Let's go," Veith said, shoving Danny with his foot.

Danny groaned, and let himself be hauled out of the van. The object was to pretend to be still groggy from the blow, and a lot more hampered by his leg wound than he was. If he had to put up a fight, the element of surprise was always good. Having free hands was even better, and he couldn't use a crutch with bound hands. The crutch was the key: he really needed to keep the crutch with him. He was out the gun—Veith had taken it—but the phone Crittenden had provided was still inside the crutch. The phone could be tracked, and by now Crittenden should be tracking it. Rescue was what Danny was hoping for, either by Sanders and company or by Crittenden, although he figured that the chances that it was going to happen were dicey.

During the van ride, while he was mostly feigning unconsciousness, he had hit on a workable plan to keep at least Crittenden on their trail: Danny was a big guy, and if he couldn't walk, somebody was going to have to help him get from place to place, maybe even carry him. The phone was why he had stopped to pick up his crutch before getting into the van with Sam. He hoped the memory of him needing that crutch enough to stop for it would resonate with Veith now. With only two men and himself, Veith didn't have the manpower to spare for hauling Danny around, not and keep a gun on him and deal with Sam at the same time. Easiest thing to do would be to free his hands and let him walk with the crutch to wherever Veith was taking them.

If he were taking them anywhere. Danny had a bad feeling that whatever was getting ready to go down would go down now.

But no, as it turned out Veith apparently had a different killing field in mind.

Which was the good news.

The bad news was that, hands bound behind her, Sam was being hurried along ahead of him at gunpoint, the better to keep him docile, he knew. Still, Veith was taking no chances: Danny had a gun pointed at him, too, every step of the way.

The other good news was, Danny was hobbling to wherever they were going on his crutch.

The other bad news was, he had no idea where that might

be, although he had a pretty good idea about what was going to happen when they got there.

The long, low, white building that the van was parked beside looked like an airplane hangar, Danny saw as he and Sam were hustled past it. A faded sign on the side of the building confirmed that. It said Hayfield Airport, but if this was an airport it was a long-abandoned one. The place was deserted. Because of the cloud cover, the night was dark as pitch. The only light to be seen was a yellow bug light beside the hangar's garage-type door. That made it hard to be sure, but aside from the hangar, and a paved parking area surrounding it, he got the impression that there was farmland all around. The smell of crops and fertilizer blew past him on the breeze.

Just beyond the hangar, sitting on a turf runway carved out of what looked to be a wheat field, sat a Cherokee Six. Danny knew from planes, and he recognized it instantly just from its shape. This one was a little beauty: a six-seat, single-engine, fixed-landing-gear light aircraft with a range of around eight hundred miles. Which just went to prove that crime paid way better than law enforcement.

As his eyes ran over it, Danny slowed down. Wherever this sweet little bird was taking them, he didn't want to go. Plus, the chance of rescue went way down if they were flown, say, eight hundred miles away.

Making a stand here and now, out in the open, occurred to him, but the odds didn't look good. Veith and company had at least three guns to his zero (and if he knew Veith, they probably also had ammo out the wazoo) and he had a bum leg to hamper him in a fight, plus Sam to worry about. Avoiding getting killed himself was doable; keeping her from getting hurt or killed might be harder.

Because they would use her to control him.

Veith was a fast learner, and he had already learned how well that worked.

Until he had Sam where he could protect her, he was better off waiting, Danny concluded. If Veith had been going to kill them immediately, the showdown would already have occurred. Apparently he had something else in mind, something that required a plane ride. Which meant that they still had some time.

As Sam reached the Cherokee, its lights came on, the engine started to rumble, and the propeller started to turn with a fast *whap-whap*. A pilot must already be on board. The plane was vibrating, readying for takeoff as soon as they climbed inside; the steps were already down. Veith meant to waste no time, clearly. He must be concerned about a rescue party, too.

Where the hell are you, Crittenden?

Sam boarded at gunpoint, and a few minutes later, Danny did, too, blinking at the brightness of the cabin after the almost pitch darkness outside. The interior was tiny; he had to bend almost double. The seats were configured two by two by two. Sam was already strapped into a middle seat, with her hands bound in front of her this time because the seats were so small there was no room to put them behind her back and still allow her to sit properly. He saw at a glance that Veith retained his fondness for zip ties. The thug who had Sam in charge ostentatiously aimed his gun at her head as Danny hobbled down the narrow aisle. Silently, Danny promised him a world of hurt when the time came.

Then he found himself praying that he could deliver.

Sam's eyes met his as he got close to her. If he had expected to see panic in her face, he'd been wrong. She looked surprisingly composed. There were shadows underneath her eyes, and maybe some tension around her mouth, but although he knew how terrified she must be—he well remembered how fierce her determination to survive for Tyler's sake was—she didn't show it.

Jesus, she was pretty. No, not just pretty, but mind-blowingly beautiful. Even the plane's harsh light couldn't blunt the impact of her delicate features, or the thick-lashed blue of her eyes, or the creamy perfection of her skin. Her glorious mane of hair hung loose, waving over her shoulders, black as soot. His too-big white T-shirt didn't cling, but since he knew that she wasn't wearing a bra he had no trouble at all visualizing the firm round breasts beneath, or the pert nipples that he actually could see nudging the cloth. Not an hour before, she'd been lying naked in his arms, and they'd been having some of the best sex he'd ever had in his life. Now the effect she had on him was so intense that he could almost feel the air between them catching fire as he looked at her.

He still couldn't quite figure out why, after all that red-hot sex, she had cried in his arms.

But remembering that she *had* cried affected Danny like a punch to the stomach.

He didn't think his expression changed—under conditions like these, he had a hell of a poker face—but it must have, because she smiled at him.

It was just a small smile, but under the circumstances it was so brave and unexpected that it pierced his heart.

I'm not letting this woman go, was the thought that popped fully formed into his head, even as, with the gun-holding thug watching him, he didn't smile back. He didn't want to direct any more of their attention to Sam than he could help, although that was probably a lost cause. At some point, he knew full well he was going to be engaged in a fight to the death with them in an attempt to get her out of this alive.

Pushed into the seat opposite Sam by Veith, Danny had his hands strapped together in front of him as well, with another zip tie. The crutch got handed off, and tucked away behind the backseats.

The door closed and the plane started bumping down the runway while Veith was still strapping in. He sat in the seat in front of Sam. Danny could see the pilot in the tiny cockpit. The third gunman had gone forward to sit in the copilot's seat, leaving only four of them in the cabin.

Danny stayed face forward, but he kept a careful watch on Sam out of the corner of his eye. She had her eyes closed now, and he once again would have thought that she was perfectly composed if her hands hadn't been clenched into two hard fists in her lap.

He knew her well enough now to guess that she was thinking of Tyler. Thank God the kid had managed to get away!

Like Sam, he was smart and resourceful, and he would be all right even if he and Sam didn't make it back. Although Danny meant to do everything in his power to make sure that Sam at least did.

They picked up speed, and then the plane didn't so much lift off as leap into the air. Because of the air currents associated with the coming rain, the ascent was rough, and they were bobbing up and down one minute and rocking from side to side the next. Looking out the small oval window by his seat, Danny checked hopefully for headlights traveling toward the airport. The only lights that he could see were on a road several miles away, and they were going the wrong way.

Then the plane entered the clouds, and Danny couldn't see the road anymore.

When he glanced away from the window, he found Veith looking at him.

The other man's eyes were blue, Danny noticed for the first time. Not the beautiful deep blue of Sam's, but a pale watery blue with a menacing cast to them.

"You lied to me about Santos having the money," Veith said. "I don't like it when people lie to me."

His tone was so unemotional that only someone who knew what Veith was would know to be afraid. But Danny did know, and his gut churned. And that would be on Sam's behalf, because Veith gave Sam a significant look as he said that last part, then smiled at Danny. For now, the plane's turbulence would keep Veith in his seat. But not forever.

"What makes you think I lied?" Danny parried. The implied

threat to Sam had his adrenaline pumping, had him doing a discreet but thorough analysis of the plane as a battleground. The confined quarters might actually work in his favor, but there were significant obstacles to be overcome. One huge plus was that only a fool would fire a gun in a plane while it was actually in the air. Of course, underestimating the stupidity of Veith's thugs might be a fatal error.

"I asked him. He never laid a finger on Mr. Calderon's nine million dollars. Never even heard of it. Pity I didn't believe him until he was all chopped up. Of course, it was too late then."

Danny made a conscious effort not to look at Sam. Even so, he couldn't help but see the sudden tension in her face, her widening eyes.

"That money belonged to Mr. Calderon?" Danny asked carefully. José Calderon was head of the Zeta cartel, and stealing money from him was about as suicidal an act as he could think of right off the top of his head. It ranked right up there with letting Veith know that he'd had no idea the money existed until Veith had started trying to torture its whereabouts out of him. And that was ranked only slightly behind letting Veith in on his true identity.

"Don't get cute with me, Marco. You took the payment for that shipment of blow. You never delivered the payment to Mr. Calderon. He wants his cash. Which is why I'm taking you to talk to him personally. Although thanks to Miss Samantha here, I'm betting you'll have told me where it is long before we get there."

Veith pulled a wire cutter out of his pocket and held it up for them to see. As much as Sam tried to stay expressionless, her face paled. Danny felt a rush of deadly anger, and did his best to channel it productively. But he made the same internal promise to Veith that he'd made earlier to the guy who'd held a gun to Sam's head: *I'm coming for you.*

His major problem was going to be that as soon as a fight started, one of them was going to grab Sam, Danny reflected. Somehow he was going to have to get between her and them, and stay between her and them, while he took them out.

The plane bobbled a little, then swooped left, and Danny found himself thanking God for the turbulence.

"Nine million dollars is a lot of cash to try to hide." Danny was still feeling his way with that. What had happened there? Had Marco really kept the cash? If so, that painted Marco's sweetheart deal with the government in a whole new light. It was something that ought to be looked into, although if he didn't survive the night nobody was going to know about it. Too bad he wasn't wearing a wire; it would have solved a host of problems. "I'm guessing that's why you didn't believe me when I told you it was in my sock drawer. So where do you think I stashed it?"

"For my money, it's still in the eighteen-wheeler it came to you in. And you *are* going to tell me where you hid it. I'm guessing you don't want to see your pretty little lady over there get her fingers and toes snipped off, one by one." He snapped the wire cutters in Sam's direction suggestively. Her lashes flickered, and he thought he saw a tiny muscle jump beneath her eye. Otherwise, she managed to remain impassive.

"No, I don't," Danny agreed, having hit on a solution that probably wasn't going to work to hold Veith off, but that he felt needed to be given a shot. At the very least, it would get Veith's attention off Sam. From the corner of his eye, he could see that she was keeping very still. Her expression was almost grim now, and he guessed that was because she was determined not to show fear.

Danny continued, "I give up, okay? I didn't know that money belonged to Mr. Calderon. Now that I do, how about I just tell you where that eighteen-wheeler is?"

Veith's mouth tightened. His eyes hardened. His hand went to his seat belt. Danny tensed and thought *here we go.*

Then the plane—bless it!—shook like a wet dog. Veith let go of his seat belt. A deep red flush crept up his neck to steal over his face. He glanced meaningfully at Sam. "It's a shame your boyfriend here is such a smartass, don't you think?" Then he switched his attention back to Danny. "When Mr. Calderon is done having his conversation with you, he's going to let me have you. Then you and I are really going to have some fun together. And not just because I like you, either. You know that bomb you planted in your town house tonight? It killed one of my best men."

It took a second for that to compute, but when it did a thrill of alarm snaked down Danny's spine. Before he could finish working the whole thing through, or come up with a reply for Veith, or do anything much except internally freak out because *Veith did not plant that bomb,* there was a loud boom, and the plane bucked like a rodeo bull and then began an ominous roll to the left.

Not good, was Danny's instant verdict. He heard Sam suck in air.

The plane rolled right. Its yawing brought with it a whole different kind of fear.

Sam's eyes shot his way. Their gazes caught and held. Once again, he knew from planes. What was happening with this one wasn't promising. He didn't have a whole lot of reassurance to offer her. She seemed to be able to read his assessment of the situation in his eyes, because her face tightened, and she wet her lips.

"What the hell . . . ?" Veith grabbed his armrests.

"Mr. Veith, I'm declaring an emergency." The pilot's voice came over the loudspeaker. It sounded calm but strained. Danny could see the dark outline of his back in the cockpit as he frantically worked the yoke and pedals. The plane continued to yaw drunkenly from side to side. Its nose seemed a little pitchy, too. Looking at Sam, he saw that she had gone utterly white. Her hands were clasped tightly together in her lap. "We've been hit by something and lost part of our tail. I'm going to try to take us back to the airfield. Please keep your seat belts fastened and—" The pilot broke off.

A sudden glimmer of moonlight caused Danny to glance out the window. The Cherokee had just burst through the thick cloud cover into a clear, starry night sky. The moon was a silvery crescent floating high overhead.

"*Oh, my God!*" the pilot screamed. "*Pull up! Pull up!*"

That's when Danny saw it: looming directly in front of them was a mountain.

"Brace!" he yelled at Sam, but didn't even have time to follow through on his own instructions before they hit.

CHAPTER TWENTY-SIX

She'd survived a plane crash. That was Sam's first dazed thought as she picked herself up out of the snow and started brushing the icy crystals from her skin and clothes. Just how it had happened she didn't know. After Marco had screamed at her, she'd barely had time to jackknife into position—head on knees, hands on top of head—before she'd heard a loud banging on the fuselage and the plane had started shaking like a paint mixer. She'd caught glimpses of branches flying past outside the window and known they were going down, skimming through treetops on their way to the ground. *Bam, bam, bam, bam, bam:* the sound of branches hitting the metal fuselage had come as fast and loud as machine-gun fire. Then the cabin had started breaking up and she'd screamed as she'd felt herself falling. She didn't even remember hitting the ground, but the next thing she knew she lay sprawled in about a foot of snow.

A major part of the fuselage was directly in front of her,

lying in a large clearing that sloped downward, down the mountain, which seemed vast. Most of the passenger cabin, she realized. It was ripped open like a tin can, jagged edges exposing the twisted interior of the cabin. From where she stood, the wreckage and the path it had gouged as it landed looked like a terrible gash in a sparkling layer of snow. A searching look around found broken trees and fallen branches that marked the plane's descent through the forest.

Marco. Sam's heart lodged in her throat. Was he inside the fuselage still? Stumbling toward the wreckage, surprised to find her body working and seemingly unhurt, and then in the next breath realizing, too, that the tie that had bound her hands was gone, she called his name. "Marco!"

"Sam!" His voice came from behind her. Turning, she saw that he was walking toward her from the woods, the edge of which formed a stockade of tall pines that ended only a few yards behind her. Now that she thought about it, she could smell a heavy scent of pine in the air, along with a gasoline-y smell that she guessed must be airplane fuel. Marco was moving pretty well, fast actually, using—she had to squint to make it out—a sturdy piece of branch as a cane. She registered then that somehow he'd managed to get his hands free, too.

The sight of him made her feel warm all over, even though, as she was just starting to realize, where they were the night was cold. A few fat flakes of snow were falling, floating down around them like swan's down.

"Are you hurt?" His eyes were busy checking her out even before he reached her.

"No, I don't think so." Feeling like they were where she belonged, she walked right into his arms. "What about you?"

"I'm good." He wrapped her up in a warm embrace, and she said, "I'm so glad to see you," because it was true, and hugged him back and lifted her head. He kissed her, a quick hard kiss that did a lot to erase the fog that still gripped her.

"Come on," he said, and let her go. "I want to see if I can find a gun and then we need to get the hell out of here."

That's when the fear returned: she and Marco weren't the only ones on this bleakly beautiful mountainside. Somewhere—somewhere nearby—Veith and his thugs were probably regrouping, too.

Her heart started to pound. Casting scared glances around, she hurried toward the wreckage at Marco's side.

Even before they got there, he stopped to scoop something up out of the snow with a sound of satisfaction. It was a pistol, and as he straightened and snapped the slide into place and checked the magazine he said to her, "That's better. We're in some business now."

Sam was all for turning tail and leaving then, but he spotted another gun in the snow even nearer the wreckage and went to retrieve that one, too, which he checked and then passed to her with the admonition, "Just don't shoot me," which she found vaguely insulting and so she frowned at him.

He wasn't looking at her. Gun at the ready, surprisingly agile with only his makeshift cane for support, he was already moving toward the torn fuselage. A moment later he had his head and shoulders in the largest gap, looking around inside.

Keeping a careful eye out all around—the night was beautiful and still, no sign of any of the others—she joined him.

"You don't want to come in here," he pulled back to tell her. From that she deduced that he was going inside, which he did. Taking him at his word, she stayed outside by the gash, keeping nervous watch.

The thought that Veith might very well be out there somewhere scared her to her back teeth.

When Marco reappeared, she saw that he had a whole arsenal of pistols and some ammunition, too, which he was busy stowing around his waistband and in his pockets. That made her feel a little better. Against all odds, she found that she was still trusting him to get her out of this alive. And forget the whole *if he could* thing.

"Anybody still in there?" she asked as he stepped through the gap. He had his crutch back, she saw as he handed something to her—a blanket, one of the small, thin airplane variety.

"Pilot and the guy in the copilot's seat. They're both dead." He said it matter-of-factly, no grief there. Well, she wasn't feeling any, either. "Veith and the other guy are missing. At a guess, I'd say they fell out like we did."

That was all she needed to hear. She shivered. "Let's get out of here."

He nodded, and she started walking away, down the slope because that seemed the logical thing to do, keeping a firm grip on the pistol and wrapping the blanket around her shoulders as she moved because the night, while not freezing, was way too cold for just bare arms. Realizing as she got it settled that there was only one, and that he was wearing an identical T-shirt that left his arms bare, too, she indicated the blanket and asked, "What about you?"

"Worried about me, baby doll?" He smiled at her, the first smile she'd had out of him since she'd left his bed what seemed like a lifetime ago, and she realized that one thing hadn't changed: it still did funny things to her insides. "Don't be. I don't feel the cold."

"Think somebody will be sending a rescue team? Does anybody even know that the plane went down?"

"The plane should have a transponder," he said. "Which means somebody should be coming after us sooner or later. In the meantime, we probably want to see if we can't walk down to a lower elevation, where we'll have a better chance of running into people. Climbers, hikers, campers, somebody should be on this mountain. Especially once it's daylight."

Sam was just thinking that something seemed different about him, an air or an attitude that she hadn't quite picked up on before, when she heard the moan. It was a low, drawn-out sound that raised the hairs on the back of her neck. It seemed to be coming from behind a large outcropping of snow-dusted rock just down the slope on their left. A glance at Marco told her that he heard it, too.

By consensus they moved toward the sound.

"Stay behind me," he whispered as they reached the outcropping, which was taller than he was and twice as long. Sam had no problem with that, hanging back as, gun at the ready, Marco stepped around the rock.

Sam couldn't see what he saw, but she could see his reaction to it. She watched his broad back as at first he froze, pointing his pistol purposefully at whatever was on the ground. Then a weak voice said, "Help me," and Sam recognized it as belonging to Veith even as she followed Marco the rest of the way around the rock.

Veith lay on his back in the snow, visible from about midchest up, trapped in a good-size chunk of wreckage that was jagged and torn and heavy enough to keep him pinned to the ground. Sharp-looking tendrils of metal wrapped around his upper torso like barbed wire. Around him, the snow was dark. Sam realized that it was from his blood.

"Watch my back," Marco said in a low voice to Sam, then moved to crouch near Veith's head. To Veith he said, almost conversationally, "Looks like you're in a bad way."

"Get me out of this," Veith replied. His voice was weak. He looked first at Marco, then at Sam. Standing close behind Marco, listening for any stray footfalls, she watched for signs of danger. Unwillingly, she registered how white Veith's face was and how shrunken and dark his eyes looked. Despite everything, she felt a twinge of pity for him. Not for him, precisely, but for a living creature who was obviously hurting.

Sam didn't hear Marco's reply, but something, either his expression or a gesture that Sam missed, must have told Veith he wasn't feeling a Good Samaritan vibe.

"I can help you out." Veith sounded desperate. "You need somebody like me on your side."

"I'll think about it. And while I'm thinking about it, suppose you tell me what happened tonight at the town house."

Veith grimaced. "What's to tell? We showed up, damned place blew up."

"You didn't blow it up?"

"Why would I do that? Calderon wants his fucking money back. Kill you before I know where the money is, and my ass is in a sling." Veith moved uncomfortably. "You think you could move some of this crap off me now?"

Marco gave a negative shake of his head. "Keep talking. If you were there, why didn't you get blown up with the house?"

"Something seemed screwy about that whole deal, so I sent a guy in to case the place while the rest of us cruised around in the van. He was supposed to text us, let us know if you were in there, before we tried hitting it. He sent a text saying he was in, and the next thing we know the whole place goes sky-high." He took a labored breath. "You didn't do that, then you got more troubles than me."

"Maybe." Marco seemed to be thinking. "What do you mean, something seemed screwy?"

"We got tipped off that's where you were. One of our usual informants. But it was too easy. It just didn't feel right." He wet his lips. "You stay in the business long enough, you develop a nose for things like that."

"The guy you sent in? He say anything about offing the marshal standing guard?"

Veith shook his head. "No time. He didn't have no time to off nobody. What happened was, he walked in, the place blew. At a guess, I'd say it was rigged to explode a couple of minutes after someone opened a door. It'd take a real pro to do that, but it wasn't me."

"Yeah." The affirmative was terse. Marco stood up and looked down at Veith almost meditatively.

"Hey." Veith sounded alarmed. "You're not leaving, right? You get this stuff off me, and I'll tell you something else."

"You tell me something else, and I'll see about getting this stuff off you."

"All right. All right." Veith made a gesture toward a piece of wreckage. "You see that piece there? That's part of the tail. I'm an old military man, served my fair share in war, and I know the signs. I've been lying here just looking at that. See those scorch marks? See that jagged edge? We didn't just hit something up there. We got shot down."

"Don't get within his reach," Marco turned to say softly to Sam, then went over to the piece of wreckage Veith had indicated and examined it.

Sam was left looking at Veith. His eyes gleamed up at her through the dark.

"I'm sorry I threatened you," Veith said humbly. "Nothing personal, you understand. I was just doing my job."

Sam thought of Mrs. Menifee, thought of Marco as she had first seen him, thought of the unknown number of others whom Veith had undoubtedly killed, and didn't even bother to reply. A moment later, Marco had rejoined them and also stood looking down at Veith.

"See? Was I right?" Veith asked.

"Looks like it." At Marco's terse confirmation, Sam looked at him with a frown. They were *shot down*? By whom? But Veith had started talking again, so she saved her questions for later.

"See, you got more enemies than me. Maybe I can help you out with that. Maybe that even puts us on the same side in this. The enemy of my enemy is my friend and all that, right? Right?"

Marco was looking down at Veith thoughtfully. Then he shook his head. "Nah. The enemy of my enemy is still my enemy," he said, then glanced at Sam. "Head on down the slope, would you? I'll catch up in a minute."

For a moment Sam just looked at him. Then she turned and did as he said.

A few minutes later she heard it: a single sharp *bang*. She knew what it was: kill shot. Bad as it might be of her, she couldn't even feel a smidgen of sorrow. As long as Veith was alive and on this planet, she never would have felt safe for herself or for Tyler for the rest of her life.

Or for Marco, either.

She stopped, waiting for him, and when he rejoined her she asked: "What about the other guy?" in reference to the last remaining unaccounted-for thug. It was a tacit acknowledgment that she knew what he'd done.

"Without Veith, he won't bother us. If he's alive, he'll slink away with his tail between his legs."

After that, they walked down the snowy slope in silence for a while. Neither of them mentioned Veith. Finally the silence got old, so she glanced at him and said, "Marco?"

Instead of the reply she had been expecting, he looked at her, sighed, and said, "About that . . ."

CHAPTER TWENTY-SEVEN

"About that?" Sam repeated, frowning at him questioningly.

Marco caught her arm, stopped walking, and turned to face her. They were a good distance from the plane now, with a wall of woods to one side and the mountain stretching up to its towering peak behind them. It was cold, but not bitter, and at this elevation the darkness was alleviated by the moon and twinkling stars. The snow underfoot was just deep enough to cover the ground. A light flurry of flakes floated in the air.

Marco's expression was rueful as he looked down at her. He was tall and broad shouldered enough to block her view of the woods behind him, dark and tough and handsome, a man to depend on even if, she realized with a little catch in her heart, tonight was probably all they were ever going to have.

"Do you love me?" he asked.

Sam's eyes widened. She searched his face as her pulse started to pound. "Yes," she said, because she did.

He blinked. "You do?"

Not the response she had been hoping for. Her brows snapped together. "Are you telling me that that was a rhetorical question?" Her tone was acerbic. His hand tightened on her arm when she would have pulled away.

"No," he said hastily. Then a smile just touched his mouth. "Maybe. But guess what, baby doll? I love you, too."

Her heart lurched. She felt vulnerable suddenly. Exposed. She didn't like it. She couldn't deal. Unless—he was telling the truth.

"Really?" She searched his eyes suspiciously. Maybe there was a hint of insecurity in that look somewhere. If so, maybe it was because she was feeling slightly insecure.

"Yes, really." He slid a hand along her cheek, unsmiling now. Then he bent his head and kissed her. It was a sexy kiss, hard and hungry, and she closed her eyes and kissed him back for all she was worth. Her arms were still around his neck when he lifted his head to nuzzle her cheek, then straightened to look down at her. Opening her eyes, she smiled at him.

"I love you, Sam. This whole fiasco has been a nightmare from hell, except for the fact that I found you."

After the *I love you* part, she barely registered a word he said. She was standing there smiling up at him, stupidly, with flowers blooming in her heart and stars blazing from her eyes, when he sighed and added, "Keep that in mind, would you? Because there's something I need to tell you."

That did not sound promising, but she was too dazzled even to frown. "What?"

"Let's walk and talk, shall we?"

Not even worried about whatever horrible deed he was about to confess to—she knew the worst about him, right, and loved him madly anyway—she withdrew her arms from around his neck and fell in beside him as they resumed their trek down the slope.

"So tell me," she said.

He sighed again and said, "I am not Rick Marco. My name is Daniel Panterro. Danny."

"*What?*" Sam heard that with a sense of shock. Her eyes flew to his face. She would have stopped walking, except he caught her arm and urged her on.

"I'm an FBI agent. This has been an undercover operation. I've been pretending I'm Marco—there really is a Marco, and he really did do all the bad things you've been accusing me of—while he spills the beans on all the Zeta cartel's secrets, including its distribution channels and the corrupt law-enforcement agents who work for them."

He told her the whole story.

"Oh, my God," she said when he had finished. As he had talked, it had started to occur to her that if he were not Rick Marco, then he would not be going to prison or to witness protection or wherever. She would *not* never see him again. Unless . . . "It's all been a big lie?"

He took one look at her face and shook his head. "Not all of it. Not you and me. Not Tyler, either. Everything between us was real."

Sam frowned suddenly, remembering. "You made me cry. I never cry. But I thought I was never going to see you again."

"I know." At least he had the grace to look slightly sorry. "I never meant for that to happen. I was dying to take you to bed, but I was going to hold off until this was over and I could tell you the truth about who I was. But you came on to me last night, and I lost my head. You were way too sexy to resist."

She was indignant. "I came on to you?"

"Oh, yeah." He grinned at her. "You made me hotter than I can just about ever remember being, too."

"The way I remember it, *you* were coming on to *me*. This whole time."

"Well," he said. "There's that."

Sam frowned at him, he grinned at her, and all of a sudden she realized she could have him if she wanted him. A real relationship. With nothing to take him away.

The very idea made her wary; she had learned a long time ago not to believe in happy endings.

"So what now?" she asked, a little gruffly. By this time they'd walked a long way, and the first pink fingers of dawn were stealing over the eastern horizon.

"First things first: we get off this mountain."

She made a face at him. "After that. You know what I mean."

"Well, let's see. Probably you want to go grab Tyler, and then—" He broke off abruptly as a low pulsing sound filled the air. They both looked around. Sam was excited to see a helicopter soaring over the woods toward them. It was big and black and official looking, and she grabbed Marco's—no, Danny's; that was going to take some getting used to—arm excitedly.

"We're rescued," she said happily.

"Yeah, so you'd think." He sounded grim suddenly. "I want you to walk away from me straight into the woods. Go right now."

"What?" She looked at him in bewilderment.

"Sam," he said. "Just do what I say. Please."

After one look at his face, she did. She turned and left him and walked into the woods as the helicopter soared above the clearing she'd just left.

As he watched the helicopter land, Danny was resigned. He'd hoped against hope that he was wrong, but he'd known he wasn't. Ever since Veith had said he hadn't blown up the town house, Danny had known who his real enemy had to be.

He'd made his plans. Back there when he'd taken Veith out of their lives for good, he'd set them into motion.

When the helicopter was on the ground and Crittenden stepped out, Danny waved and walked toward him like he was expecting to be rescued.

Crittenden was regulation FBI today: dark suit, white shirt, dark tie. His salt-and-pepper hair was blowing a little in the breeze cast up by the rotors.

"Where's the girl?" Crittenden greeted him. He sounded tense.

Danny jerked his head at the woods behind him. "She had to take a tinkle."

"We need to get her back."

"She'll just be a minute."

Looking past Crittenden at the man who'd descended from

the chopper on its other side, Danny got a surprise. Crittenden had Rick Marco with him. Danny had seen his picture, read his file, knew who he was instantly. In fact, the man felt like an old friend.

The kind you love to hate.

Both men drew on him at the same time. Bottom line, as far as Crittenden was concerned it was clearly game over; he wasn't even going to bother to pretend anymore.

Danny didn't even reach for a gun.

"Nine million dollars worth it, Crittenden?" he asked his boss.

"Four and a half million," Crittenden corrected with barely a pause. "Marco and I are splitting it. How'd you find out?"

"A little bird told me." Danny looked at the man he'd worked for for the last four years with a mixture of sadness and anger. "You sent Army Veith after me for real. You blew up the town house I was staying in. You shot down the damned plane I was in last night."

"It wasn't anything personal." Crittenden sounded almost apologetic. "You just happened to be the best stand-in for Marco. When I busted him for being a crooked agent, and he told me about the money, it just seemed like too good an opportunity to pass up. Nine million dollars in cash! You just don't get that coming your way every day. I knew that the only way we were going to be able to keep it was if the Zetas thought Marco had hidden it someplace where they couldn't find it and then he was killed. So I hid him, and the money, and got you on board. I had to use you because you were one of mine, and since this wasn't going to be a real operation nobody else in the chain of command could know anything about it. I needed somebody who reported to me, and no one else. The reason I chose you instead of one of the other members of the team isn't because I don't like you, you know. It's just that you look something like him"—he nodded at Marco, who was standing silently with his gun trained on Danny, Crittenden's perfect henchman—"which made it easier. So I got you into witness protection, put the word out on the street that Marco was going to sing his little insides out about the inner workings of the cartel, and waited for them to kill him. Uh, you. Only they kept screwing up."

"Sorry about your luck," Danny said.

"You always were a lucky son of a bitch." Crittenden regarded him almost with affection. "So how did you figure out it was me?"

"When the town house blew up I knew something was wrong. Veith didn't want to kill me until after I told him where the money was. Blowing up the town house wasn't something he'd do."

"I thought blowing up the town house might be a little strong," Crittenden admitted. "But I started getting antsy about Veith. Once he started talking to you about the money, he worried me. So I thought, why not tip him off about your whereabouts, then wait until he came to kill you and kill you both in one fell swoop? Plus, I started thinking that it would be better if your body weren't so recognizable, if you know what I mean."

"Yeah, I got that." Danny's voice was dry. "But it was shooting down the plane that did it. I remember your military record:

you did that in Afghanistan all day and all night. You should have known I'd catch on after that."

"I had to do it. That damned Veith was taking you to José Calderon. He'd know you weren't Marco the minute he set eyes on you. Anyway, you were supposed to be dead."

"Again, sorry about your luck."

Crittenden glanced toward the woods. "Where the hell is that girl? How long does it take her to pee?"

"I think I see her coming right now," Danny said, and lifted an arm in a big wave.

Almost immediately, an army of FBI agents in black covert attire came out of the trees, their weapons trained on Crittenden and Marco. Directing them was Mayhew.

"Drop your weapons!" came the roar. "Hands in the air!"

"Surprise," Danny said gently as the agents advanced.

Crittenden and Marco dropped their weapons and put their hands in the air.

"How the hell did you get them here?" Crittenden growled.

Danny put his hand into his pocket and pulled out the cell phone Crittenden had provided him with.

"I made a call," he said.

CHAPTER TWENTY-EIGHT

A few days later, Tyler was practically hanging out the window of Kendra's second-floor apartment. Watching him, Sam felt a wave of thankfulness so strong that it almost brought tears to her eyes. When she had been brought down off that mountain—Danny had stayed behind to do whatever it was FBI agents did—she'd had the agents escorting her take her straight to Tyler. He'd been with Sanders and Groves and O'Brien in a back room in the FBI office in Pocatello. When she had walked in, he'd yelled, "Mom!" and rushed into her arms. Hugging him like she was never going to let him go, Sam thought about how close she had come to never seeing him again and sent a profound *thanks* winging skyward.

Sometimes, apparently, prayers were answered after all.

"We looked out for him," Sanders told her, and she smiled at him as she finally let Tyler go. "He's a smart kid. He came right to us, told us what had happened. Otherwise we probably all would have died trying to pull you guys out of the damned fire."

"I'm sorry about Abramowitz," she said, and he nodded in acknowledgment.

"He was a good man." He glanced around, lowered his voice. "Goddamn FBI. Glad this mess is their screw-up and not ours, though."

"You know that you weren't guarding the real Rick Marco, right? His name is Danny Panterro. He's an FBI agent."

"We just got filled in." Sanders's tone was sour. "Not saying I'm happy with your boyfriend, mind you. I don't like that we were duped one bit. But at least he's a cut above the real dirtbag."

"Is Trey your boyfriend now, Mom?" Tyler piped up, looking at her with interest and hope and a whole host of other things in his eyes. Sam was once again reminded of how true the saying was about little pitchers and big ears.

She sighed, admitted to it, and told him who Danny really was, along with a highly edited version of what he had been up to since he'd entered their lives.

When Danny joined them, in a guarded hotel suite hours later, Tyler had walked into Danny's arms right along with Sam.

"I brought you something, buddy," Danny had said when he let them go, and reached into his pocket to pull something out: Tyler's teddy bear. It had been in her pocket, Sam remembered, and realized that she'd lost it in the crash. Danny must have found it up there on the mountain and brought it back for her son.

"Ted!" Tyler grabbed the bear and hugged it, beaming at Danny. Sam smiled at him. Bringing the bear back was a small gesture, but it told her that he knew what it meant to Tyler—and cared.

"I love you." She mouthed the words at him over Tyler's head.

"I love you, too," he responded, and didn't bother to mouth the words.

Later, when Tyler and Sam had arrived back in East St. Louis to find that their duplex was still a crime scene, Kendra had invited them to stay with her. Which had worked for Sam: no way was she going to be able to face living in that place for even one more night, she had discovered as soon as she saw it again. The memories were still too fresh, and still too horrific. Anyway, they had other interesting options, and she had decided to explore them.

Because you only live once, right?

So here it was, 6:00 p.m. on a Saturday, and Tyler was expecting someone special. Sam was, too, and she had dressed accordingly: in a deep blue silk dress she had borrowed from Kendra. They were the same size, same height, same age. The only difference was that Kendra had hazel eyes and blond hair that she wore straight to her shoulders. But as for swapping clothes, well, they did that all the time.

When the car pulled up at the curb across the street, Tyler, still hanging out the window, let out a yell.

"Trey!" he shrieked, waving wildly.

Sam and Kendra, both of whom had also been waiting, although they hoped not as obviously as Tyler, looked out the window, too.

Dressed in a dark suit and tie because they were going to dinner in some fancy place he'd booked across the river in the big-time St. Louis, looking so handsome he took Sam's breath, Danny was crossing the street. He was waving at Tyler, and as he saw Sam and Kendra looking out at him he grinned.

"Oh, my," Kendra said, impressed.

"Told ya," Sam said smugly.

Tyler was already tearing out of the apartment. Really, the dignified thing to do would be to wait, but Sam found she couldn't. She headed for the door, too, and ran down the stairs in Tyler's wake.

Danny already had an arm around Tyler as she met him at the downstairs entrance. As she approached them he gave her a classic male once-over, and grinned.

"You look gorgeous."

He held out his other arm to her, and when she walked into it pulled her close for a kiss. The quick kiss hello she'd meant it to be was turning into something a whole lot hotter when she recollected Tyler, and Kendra, and broke it off.

But from the way Danny grinned down at her, she knew her cheeks were pink.

"So you guys all packed?" Danny asked as he escorted them inside.

See, they were moving to the D.C. area next week. To live with him. Because he said he loved them both, and because they loved him, and because Tyler was over the moon at the prospect, and Sam wanted to give it a try. She was going to sell Big Red, and use the money to finish up her EMT classes fast. That, plus a scholarship Danny's friend Mayhew had hooked her up with as, in his words, a *thank you* for her service to the FBI, meant she didn't have to be financially dependent on Danny, and he didn't have to feel responsible for Tyler and her.

She had been excited and a little scared when she had realized that the only thing that was left to bind them together was love. He'd asked her to marry him, and she was thinking about it.

Maybe she would, one of these days.

Because hard as it was to get her head around, maybe she was starting to believe in happy endings after all.

KAREN ROBARDS

The Last Victim

Dr Charlotte Stone sees what others do not.

An expert in criminal pathology, Charlie regularly sits face-to-face with madmen. She's been obsessed with learning what makes human monsters commit terrible crimes since she was sixteen, when a man butchered the family of her best friend Holly, then left the girl's body on a seaside boardwalk one week later.

Charlie kept quiet about her eerie postmortem visions of Holly and her mother. And even years later, knowing it might undermine her credibility as a psychological expert, she tells no one about the visits she gets from the spirit world.

Now all-too-handsome FBI agent Tony Bartoli suspects the Boardwalk Killer is back. A teenage girl is missing, her family slaughtered. With time running short for the innocent girl, Bartoli turns to the only person who could stop this vicious murderer.

But Dr Charlotte Stone sees what others do not. And she sees the Boardwalk Killer coming for her.

The Last Victim is the first in a red-hot new paranormal romantic thriller series by *New York Times* bestselling author Karen Robards.

HODDER

KAREN ROBARDS

Sleepwalker

When rookie cop Micayla Lange arrests a man she discovers breaking into her old family friend Nicco Marino's mansion, her troubles have only just begun.

Because, as she pulls a gun on professional thief Jason Davis, he drops the bag he's stolen – and it spills open to reveal photographs of Micayla's genial 'uncle' Nicco handing money to a number of Detroit's most powerful politicians and law-makers.

No one was meant to see those photos, least of all a police officer. And – with close circuit cameras capturing every moment of Micayla's realisation that Uncle Nicco is seriously involved with the mob – she may now be in mortal danger.

But Jason has a suggestion. Perhaps if they team up – then maybe there'll a chance they'll both get out alive . . . He's her only hope. But can she trust him with her life?

HODDER

KAREN ROBARDS

Justice

She's changed her identity . . . but she's still being hunted.

Jessica Ford was the only witness to the First Lady of the United States being killed in suspicious circumstances, and has been in hiding almost ever since.

With a new name and new image, so far she's successfully kept a low profile. But when her job at a Washington's most powerful law firm puts her back in the public eye, she comes under threat again.

There's only one man who can help her – and he's the person she hates most in the world. But she may have no other option than to turn to Mark Ryan. Because there's someone out there killing women.

And unless they can stop him, Jess could be next . . .

HODDER

KAREN ROBARDS

Pursuit

The car crash that leaves the First Lady dead and Jessica Ford badly injured is just the beginning of a nightmare.

Jess is thrilled when her law firm's senior partner asks her to meet the President's wife in a Washington hotel late one Saturday night. But the lawyer who drew her into the disaster commits suicide, his secretary is killed in yet another car accident, and the Secret Service agent on the case, Mark Ryan, believes that Jess, the only survivor, is hiding something.

As her world falls apart around her, Jess realizes that everyone who knew what the First Lady was doing that Saturday night is dead – except her. And if she remembers, she'll be dead too.

Terrified, certain that the car crash was no accident, Jess will have to put her trust in Mark Ryan. Or suffer the consequences.

H

HODDER

KAREN ROBARDS

Shattered

Nearly thirty years ago, a woman and her entire family went missing. Dead? No one knew. But they never came back . . .

When Lisa Grant is sent by her disagreeable boss Scott to help organize the courthouse basement, she finds a cold case file. And she is horrified by what she sees.

Because the woman in the picture – who went missing thirty years before – looks just like she does now.

Lisa is determined to find out if there's a link between them, and enlists Scott's help to do so. But before they can learn anything more, a series of catastrophes strike close to home.

And, as they race to find out the truth about what really happened to the missing family, it becomes clear that there's someone out there who will go to shocking lengths to make sure certain secrets stay completely buried . . .

HODDER

KAREN ROBARDS

Guilty

One cold November night when Kate White was fifteen years old, her friends held up a store. One of them killed an off-duty cop. They got away with it.

Thirteen years later, Kate has built a new life for herself. Now a single mother with a nine-year-old son, she is a prosecutor in the Philadelphia district attorney's office.

But when the boy who shot that cop so many years ago reappears and tries to blackmail Kate, it threatens to disrupt her whole life. But then he is found dead in Kate's house, with Kate's fingerprints on the pistol, and suddenly she's the prime suspect.

Homicide detective Tom Braga shows up to investigate the murder and things get worse: she and Tom have clashed since their first meeting. And he knows she's lying about something. And he's determined to find out what.

HODDER

In the best books, the ending often comes as a shock.
Not just because of that one last twist in the tale,
but because you have been so absorbed in their world,
that coming back to the harsh light of reality is a jolt.

If that describes you now, then perhaps you should track down
some new leads, and find new suspense in other worlds.

Join us at www.hodder.co.uk, or follow us on
Twitter @hodderbooks, and you can tap in to a
community of fellow thrill-seekers.

Whether you want to find out more about this book,
or a particular author, watch trailers and interviews, have
the chance to win early limited editions, or simply browse
our expert readers' selection of the very best books,
we think you'll find what you're looking for.

And if you don't, that's the place to tell us what's missing.

We love what we do, and we'd love you to be part of it.

www.hodder.co.uk

@hodderbooks

HodderBooks

HodderBooks